CONTENTS

To the generations who came before
To the next, who explore new shores,
And to Nancy, my beautiful work of art,
A tough immigrant lady, such a tender heart

AUTHOR'S NOTE

Giovanni was my immigrant great-grandfather. I was born five years after his 1939 passing, both events taking place in South Brooklyn. My mother, Vina, related precious snippets of her beloved grandfather Giovanni's (mis)adventures, habits, sayings, and quirks. I should have paid more attention—such a sad, common, refrain.

But Giovanni and I have now interacted: I frame-shifted his life at least thirty years, to 1969. I have benefited from his wisdom and resonated with his doubts. He is surprisingly deep, yet a fun guy.

I know nothing of Giovanni's parents. Three generations and an ocean came between us. *All accounts herein of my great-great-grandparents are complete fiction.*

Five hundred years of voluntary and forced immigration form the fabric of an American weave boxed in a Native American weaving frame constructed over millennia. Giovanni's thread goes back to Naples, Italy, around the turn of the twentieth century. His story is historical fiction which behooved me to make that history an accurate backdrop for Giovanni's family story. While most family escapades and experiences herein are real, several have been transposed to different generations. Last names have been changed and new family members introduced, mainly to portray relations among immigrant groups.

In places I use Neapolitan dialect, and always in context—the goal being to add color, not to confuse. In standard Italian, *nonno/nonna* are grandfather/grandmother, and *zio/zia* are uncle/aunt. In Neapolitan American households, we addressed Grandpa and Grandma as *'o nonn* (ooh-NŌNo) and *a nonn* (ah-NŌNa). Uncle/aunt were *'o zi* (ooh-TSEE)/*a zi* (ahh-TSEE). Pronouncing them stimulates my Neapolitan taste buds.

In any language, Giovanni dealt with racism, foreign wars, a flu pandemic, the Great Depression, Mussolini's long arm, internment, a polio epidemic, civil rights/anti-war movements, the American justice system, and the American mob. The accent is Neapolitan, the story American.

May you find your own interwoven immigrant thread.

Family Tree of Giovanni and Filomena Ragnuno

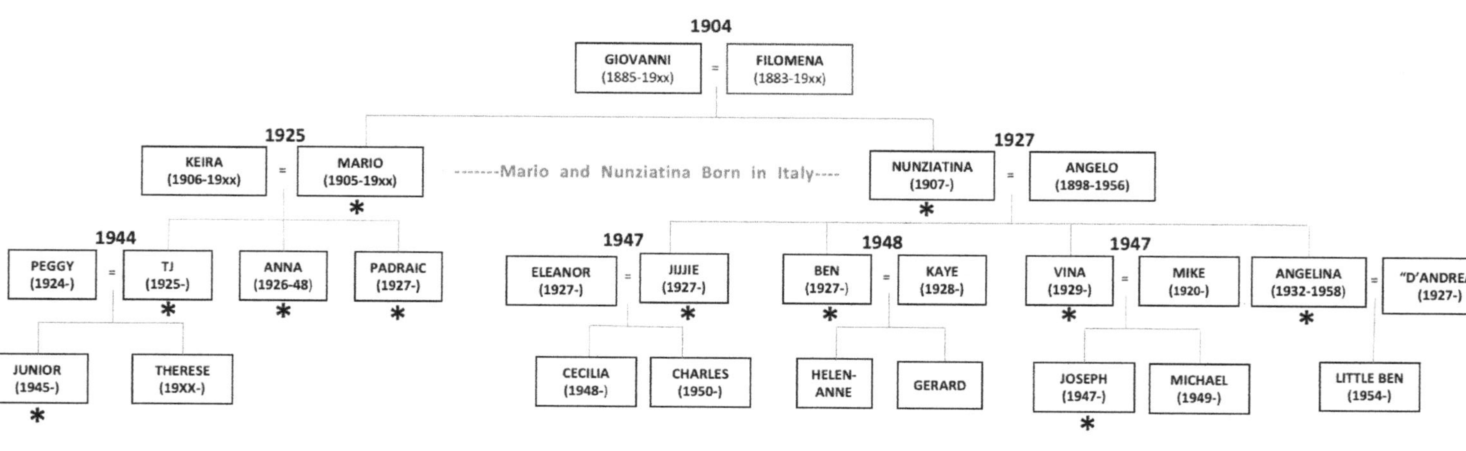

*Blood descendants of Giovanni and Filomena who played a major role in the family story

1

VILLA VALERIA (1898–1899)

At the end of a long, tortuous flight
Scruffy fledgling on a bough did alight
He perched next to an untested young bird
Whose touch the traveler's heart bestirred

"Good afternoon, young man!" In my urchin's rags and best Tuscan dialect, I greeted the rich boy silently enclosed in his villa. Looking down to show respect, I fixed my eyes on his polished brown fine leather shoes contrasting with my bare feet. The villa was a green, glowing gem of abundance and order. But its real lure was this mute boy of about ten within the villa's stone and cast-iron enclosure. Immaculately dressed—crisply ironed linen shirt tucked into woolen pants held up by blue suspenders—he was oblivious to the activities of the young people playing in his midst. He was much more aware of me, on the other side of the cast-iron barrier.

On my first visit we had made fleeting eye contact. On later visits his penetrating hazel eyes locked my gaze, even at the distance separating us across the fence. That distance decreased as he furtively approached closer over time, with the alert guards always close at hand. He ignored those steely-eyed sentries in black berets and shirts, brown Cossack pants, and tall black boots. The guards, each bearing a shoulder-holstered carbine, contrasted with the bucolic charm of the villa's vineyards, orchards, vegetable gardens, and the more distant wheat fields. Blue tiles over the heavy wooden door of the main house read "Villa Valeria."

One day the boy put his hand through the grating. He wordlessly touched my shoulder, then immediately retreated.

"Calogero!" yelled a guard, running to the fence. "Scugnizzo, we will bar you from the barrier if you try to harm Calogero," the guard shouted at me as he slowly drew back while facing me. I did not so much fear the guards. I was more deeply touched by the boy's silently reaching out. From that encounter I tried to make daily visits to the villa. I needed to win the confidence of the guards, but my real goal was to pull back the layers that hid the boy's inner being. Was it calling for help? To be discovered?

Still, silence followed my daily question, "What's your name? *Come si chiama?*" I started to doubt the boy's ability to speak or understand any language. "*Come si chiama?*" Several weeks after the touch, he answered with a whispered "Calogero."

Ahh, a nibble, but not yet time to set the hook; time rather to play my lure. "*Io mi chiamo Giovanni*" was my immediate answer, but spoken softly and without haste. Of course, he had to know my name was Giovanni. With time, Calogero greeted me without prodding, at first in a whisper, but then with an increasingly spirited "*Ciao, Giovanni.*" Was I the fisherman or the fish?

We chatted clumsily at first, then in increasingly long conversations. We had very little in common. I was a thirteen-year-old refugee from the streets of Naples. So, conversation with this indulged villa boy of about ten would have been difficult even under the best circumstances.

"*Buongiorno, Calogero.*" I started using the familiar form and even lapsed into dialect at times. "*Comme staje oggi?*"

"I am fine, thanks."

Young Calogero showed some fine manners. When he finally spoke, he spoke very well, intimidating me, really. For he showed he was educated, well-educated in manners but also educated, *istruitito*, in much of modern Italian history. That history was painful to me because my family had suffered under the central government in Rome.

"Giovanni, the tutors said Italy was unified in 1861 after many years of struggle."

" I don't know much history, but I know the streets of Naples of our modern Italy. I hope that we all can live as well as you in this villa." It was almost as if I were hearing someone else talking. I was thankful that my irony did not seem to register with Calogero. Or was he withdrawing defensively?

"And our history will get better," Calogero said. "We were founded by heroes. I can name the eleven prime ministers since unification!" Eyes wide, he proudly named them—in the proper sequence, I guessed. Yet his feat of memory did little to whet my appetite for the history of our modern Italy. Calogero, in turn, was very curious about the history of my own life. "Tell me, Giovanni, about your family. Where do you live?"

I was not ready to reveal details of my vagabond life in the country, and certainly not the current life of my family, my mother and two sisters, still in Naples. I contrived a temporary escape.

"I must return to Naples to visit my family, but I promise to return to this spot when I am back in Campania."

I turned to leave as Calogero dropped his head and slowly returned to the villa house, looking back at me a few times. But I did not go to Naples. I stayed in the vicinity of the villa, planning to reappear at the fence after a few days.

Setting out to perform chores for farmers in the area—cleaning out stables, weeding, and looking after sheep—my goal was to call upon nearby and goodly Don Giovanni Santa Croce. He was getting on in years. His children had escaped the farm for the city and America, but he held on stubbornly. I was happy to help him for any kind of payment in lodging and food. He probably appreciated my company more than my labor.

I treaded a weed-infested stone path off a side road to reach Don Giovanni's house. The dilapidated yellow brick farmhouse and its wooden door showed their age, as did farmer Don Giovanni himself. I made a few gentle knocks on the fragile door. "*Chi è?*" came from inside, "Who is it?"

As the rustling got closer, I shouted an answer, "Giovanni from Naples!" The door slowly swung open as squeaky hinges sang a greeting of annoyance. But Don Giovanni's face lit up upon seeing me. "Ahh, *mio onomino*!" He loved that we both had the same first name—we were each other's onomino. We were namesakes.

"Come in, youngster! What brings such a beautiful *guagliò* to the humble, degraded home of this forgotten old man?" He asked that question every time he saw me, and he knew the answer: *la miseria*, the hunger that was too well-known in Naples and all of the surrounding region of Campania.

"I have come asking if I may help on the farm with the animals, with any chore you might need."

He scratched his huge nose with its very prominent brown mole halfway up the left side. "*Bene*, but you know I cannot pay you much except for a place to sleep in the stalls, a few pieces of bread and cheese, maybe an egg and some olives that have fallen off my trees."

"Whatever you can provide, Don Giovanni," I said with both open hands in front of me, palms pointing to the heavens, my eyes on his.

He touched the side of that huge nose with his right index finger and winked.

So, the agreement was reached. I fed the chickens, collected eggs, cleaned out the stalls of the donkey and Don Giovanni's sole cow. In

Naples I was one of many *scugnizzi* of the streets—one of many street urchins. And there was one scugnizzo of the stalls that I had trouble casting off—the diligent dung beetle. I relocated them and much of their quarry to the roadsides, out of sight. The holy scarabs were more sanitary and industrious than many of the wretched, luckless *disgràziati* of the maze of fetid alleys and dead ends that was my Naples. The beetles rolled balls of dung to secluded spots and laid eggs in them, providing nourishment for their young grubs.

Don Giovanni caught me providing succor to the dung beetles. He understood. "The industrious among us, especially the most wretched and insignificant, receive God's blessing. You are a good guagliò, Giovanni." He mentioned the Greek fable in which a beetle wreaked revenge on Zeus's exalted eagle by pushing eggs out of her nest, set ever higher.

That evening, when I was half asleep, Don Giovanni came into the stall and put an old blanket over me. And on the day of my departure, he had collected, in a threadbare towel on his wobbly old table, hard savory *taralli* twists, eggs, olives, bread crusts, dried figs, and a wonderful surprise: *scamorza*, cheese from the faithful cow. Overcome by his kindness and generosity, I gave him a tearful kiss on each leathery cheek, negotiating around his nose. Words did not seem sufficient.

"I don't know when I will see you again, Giovannuzzo, mio onomino, but you are always welcome here," Don Giovanni said haltingly, retreating from the table to the back of his home. I knotted the towel around a stick and made my way back to Calogero's villa.

Calogero must have seen me approach. He ran to our spot along the fence, jumping up and down before I got there. My ploy seemed to have worked, because he was not so intent on learning of my family's living situation in urban Naples. I did my best to occupy him with other topics.

"Calogero, tell me what the tutors are teaching you."

Calogero's happiness erupted into speech. "We learned of the destruction of Pompeii and Herculaneum by Vesuvius in AD 79."

I didn't think he appreciated irony, so I didn't playfully deride him for rejoicing in the destruction of two beautiful towns. "Bravo, Calogero!" was all I could muster in the face of Calogero's overflowing spirit.

"Ash and poisonous air covered the city. Many people died, and the ash that buried them hardened over the centuries. Today archeologists pour plaster into the empty spaces that were the bodies of the buried victims."

"Bravo, Calogero!"

"They said something like the plaster replicates the bodies that had, er, putrefied, inside the hardened ash." His explanation momentarily put him back in his own shell.

"Bravo, so well explained!" I took advantage of my opening. "Do you know that in Naples I go to the garbage pile behind the Archaeological Museum to retrieve incomplete casts of the Pompeii victims?"

I got the same intense stare of the first day of our encounter across the same villa fence. I went on. "But you know, I am able to pick up only the failures that the archeologists threw out. Yet even those incomplete casts can have value. You just have to convince the buyer of the value. There are many reasons why people buy, sometimes just out of pity."

I got the stare, his hazel eyes beacons of curiosity.

"Here in Campania, I try to be honest and not make enemies. I bring items from Naples to sell, like those partial casts I picked up from the museum garbage piles."

Calogero blurted out, "I will tell *Babbo* of your Pompeian treasures!"

"I think I can be more useful to your father by helping in the villa."

Calogero knitted his eyebrows quizzically—my cue to carry on.

"Here in Campania I have been cleaning out stables, feeding farm animals. Sometimes I help in the harvest of lemons, oranges, figs, persimmons, and other fruit."

"Babbo has people who do those things."

"I can see that. You are so lucky to have time for learning. Your babbo is very wise."

It was clear to me that Calogero's father was the master of the villa. I was extra careful to treat Calogero with respect and to speak well of his father. In return, I hoped that Calogero would speak well of me to his father. I suspected that any form of conversation by Calogero would be appreciated by his father.

The guards had long stopped shooing me away, but they still kept a watchful eye at a distance from Calogero slightly longer than his distance from me. Maybe I was fooling myself, but our interactions seemed to meet the guards' approval. My scugnizzo days had taught me to show the guards proper deference and respect.

"You are always in the company of guards," I said to Calogero.

"Well, that is true when I speak with you, but I think they like you. I can see some smile when you appear at the fence."

Just then one of the guards, shorter and darker than the others, approached Calogero. I started to jump back, but he just put his hand through the fence and offered it in friendship. I took it gladly, though I would have preferred a bag of fruit or pistachios.

"*Bonasera, signore.*" My dialect slipped out as I wished him a pleasant afternoon.

The guard said nothing. He looked directly at me and made an exaggerated wink.

This expression of approval, though perhaps not shared by all the guards, was not lost on Calogero. "Carlo is my favorite guard, and he's also the favorite of *Zia* Bettina, my aunt."

I had no idea about Aunt Bettina, but at least I knew the name of one of the guards. More important to me, Calogero looked forward to my almost daily visits. On a few occasions, his father was present, and he seemed most intent on our conversations. He said little, but sometimes he nodded. I thought he was pleased with the interaction of his son with this wayward scugnizzo.

I would have loved to continue visiting the villa fence, but it was time to return to my family in Naples, and this time for real.

"Calogero," I said. "I have told you of my life here in Campania and something of my activities in Naples, but there is more about me that you, and your babbo as well, should know. First, I need to return to Naples to visit with my mother and my two young sisters."

"But you just left!" screamed Calogero, with such force that he shocked me.

"I apologize deeply. I did not leave the countryside; I just had to get away from the villa for a few days to decide the next steps in my vagabond life."

"Don't go, Giovanni!" bawled Calogero. I pulled my sleeve out of his grip across the fence. The guards were on alert.

"I will return, I promise. But I want you to know about my life in Naples and why I go back there to help my mother and two younger sisters."

Calogero went silent, tears streaming down his face, but his expression was one of attention, matched by that of the guards.

"Before we met," I said, "I spent about a year and a half trying to live in the streets of Naples. It was a dangerous and dirty life. There was dirt all around, yes, but I felt like I was becoming dirty inside. I decided to return to the country, where I was born, not too far from here."

"You were very young to live on your own, and in the streets!" said Calogero, showing emotion, but now better controlled. "Where did you sleep?"

"Well, wherever I could find shelter—a hallway, sometimes a church, under boats stored at the waterfront, wherever."

"And before the streets, you lived on a farm?"

"I lived on a farm closer to Benevento with my mother, father, and sisters. When I was very young, we all fled our farm and went to Naples. We had no choice, we lost the farm—poor harvests, high taxes, and then…." I did not want to tell this young man about how we were forced out by La Camorra and its absentee landlords. I harbored doubts—maybe his father owned other properties beyond Villa Valeria, properties that once belonged to poor, displaced families.

"And then what?" Calogero asked, actually raising his voice. I loved his enthusiasm and curiosity, but I would have preferred another topic. Surely his dad being an absentee landlord was a concept Calogero would not understand. "So, our whole family—my father and mother, my sisters, and I—went to Naples. We moved into a hole, in the *bassi*."

"Hole? In the bassi?"

I appealed to Calogero's love of history. "We can thank the ancient Greeks for the bassi. The Greeks created the holes by quarrying, digging up the soft tufa stone for their buildings. Today the bassi are terrible because people are forced to live in them. The area is called the underground chambers. *I quartieri bassi* are fit only for rats. My mamma and two sisters still live in the same hole. No plumbing, cholera all around, and the rats are always stealing our food or nibbling on our toes and fingers at night."

Calogero's eyes widened. He visibly paled. He had a strong aversion to rats.

"Our chamber was damp and very cold in the winter nights." I commented on the street noises but for Calogero's sake stayed away from the scuffling and squeals of the nighttime rats. "And on summer days we baked under the sun." I tugged on my ragged collar for emphasis. "And then my father started to drink a lot. I suppose he felt disgraced for losing the farm. His disgrace turned to anger, and he took his anger out on us when he was around. Finally he left for good." I wondered if I should go into all this detail. I wanted to win Calogero's confidence—I hoped his father would provide me some kind of work. But I did not want to attract too much negative gossip. Pity was good, but bringing a luckless wretch, un disgràziato, into the villa could bring bad luck along with him. "So I went out to the streets, leaving my mother and sisters in the bassi. I became a scugnizzo. Have you heard that word?"

He shook his head.

"I became a street urchin, one of many in Naples. I was only a year or so older than you. Other scugnizzi were my age, but they had years of experience. Still, I survived."

Calogero went back to his almost expressionless stare, then muttered, "But how?" I was describing a life so different from his. He was captive in his world of plenty, while I had almost complete freedom in my miseria, in my abject poverty.

"I learned how to survive, but I could never be comfortable with how violent and dishonest many scugnizzi were. I did not want to be like them. That's what I mean by being dirty inside. Still, I had to eat and to provide for my mamma and sisters. I had to survive so they could survive."

Calogero leaned his head to one side. His raised eyebrows were a signal for me to continue. And I would have continued had not Calogero's father shown up, probably alerted by Calogero's emotional shouting at the prospect of my leaving for Naples.

The respect that the uniformed men paid to Calogero's father, his dear babbo, told me he was the lord of the villa, *'o donno 'e villa.* The guards addressed him as Don Giuseppe, and the attention that Don Giuseppe paid to me was a further signal for the forbearance of the guards. I never received that kind of respect, and I tried to overcome my awe of Don Giuseppe by imagining him as an older but darker version of Calogero. Like his son, he had hazel eyes, which now fixed my attention—a family trait, apparently. I dared not avoid the scrutiny of his eyes, but once engaged I showed humility by dropping my gaze to my bare feet. I tried to show both respect and inner strength. The streets of Naples had prepared me for this important encounter.

"*Un piacere conoscerla, Don Giuseppe*"—a pleasure to know you—I stammered in my best Tuscan, picked up from the few Northerners who still thought Naples worth a visit to see the museum, the Castle of Virgil's Egg, and other sights. Don Giuseppe offered his hand through the grating and uttered a simple "*Un piacere per me.*" He did not give me his title or convey his importance. "A pleasure for me" was disarming enough. He showed no hesitation in taking the hand that had been involved in unknowable urchin activities.

He turned toward the house. To me, his intent was to leave Calogero and me to chat. The guards, however, remained vigilant, at their judicious distance.

"So, Calogero, how do you feel about my going to Naples to check up on my mother and sisters? *Va bene?* Is it OK with you?"

My purpose was not to receive permission from Calogero but to make him feel our special relationship. He played his part perfectly. In the rich manual and oral dialect of Campania, he answered, "*Mèza, mèza*" while holding his hands out, palms up, alternately raising each one, and shaking his head side to side. "Hey, ups and downs, whether you stay or go."

Don Giuseppe's face lit up with an indulgent smile as he turned to go back to the main house of the villa. While Don Giuseppe and Calogero could always retreat to the villa house, my duty was to return to my family in Naples, offering whatever support I could provide.

2

STREETS OF NAPLES (1899)

In filthy, ill-formed plumage unpreened
The nestless fledgling hardly weaned
Pecks at a mirror seeking a friend
And sees, instead, a darkened dead end

My country accent and phrases ingratiated me with the farmers who were my transportation back to Naples. I resisted reverting to scugnizzo in language and attitude. My cause was further aided in that I had helped some of these chauffeurs by performing menial chores on their farms, even spending a night or two in their stables. My services included being an extra male in the cart as a deterrent to highway robbers. There was room in the cart for my own fruit, hard taralli bread, and other items that were part of my pay for helping the humble farmers. I thought of Don Giovanni and wondered if I would ever see him again.

I offered other services to my chauffeurs, such as lightly spiced narratives of my city adventures. The drivers, in turn, could not resist telling stories of the tumultuous history of Naples, from the ancient to the not so ancient. The tales were always filled with modern-day caution. One friendly old man, whom I knew only as Pasquale, reined in his donkey and faced me. A conspiratorial smile lit up his wrinkled face as he winked one already half-closed eye.

"*Ascota, guagliò*, listen up, young man, life in Napoli is dangerous. While avoiding your fellow scugnizzi, don't put your back to the *zoccoli*, our famous rats of the waterfront." He looked at me with the one and a half eyes. "And the evil eye is everywhere."

I agreeably took in this advice; no need to antagonize my coachman. The advice was colored with typical Neapolitan symbolism. A zòccola was not only a rat but also a woman of the night, and the ever-present evil eye, *'o maluocchio*, was only warded off by eternal vigilance. The maluocchio could be like an old loaded Beretta handgun, accidentally discharged by its carrier in a moment of hateful envy.

If Naples had taught me anything, it was that in negotiations I must always be deferential and gracious to business partners. In this case, my partners were the cart drivers carrying me back to Naples.

"Don Pasquale, so many thanks for your advice and counsel. I hope to have one day lived a long and successful life such as yours."

We both knew I was being a typical *scugnizzo-ruffiano*, but my two-faced urchin praise was a combination of good manners and good business. At the least, people found me entertainingly transparent. At best, I was perhaps charming. Whatever my manner, it helped secure the most direct routes to my squalid destination.

I was not as two-faced as most other scugnizzi, whose second face usually harbored the devil's evil eye. My goal was not only transport back to Naples, but sustenance. Sincere or otherwise, my conversation with the farmers was often rewarded with a swig of homemade red wine and a bite to eat: a couple of dried figs, a few pickled broad *lupini* beans, a piece of horse cheese—*caciocavallo*. On good days, I was treated with a *muzzarella in carruzzèlla*—a mozzarella sandwich heated in a mold in the form of a small carriage, or carruzzèlla, which sometimes also contained passengers of cured ham, *prosciutto*. I used to watch Mamma prepare the carruzzèlla over the fireplace when farm life was better. I made sure to save most of my cheese treasures as a gift to my mamma and sisters.

On the last leg of my return to Naples, I was usually faced with a difficult question by my carriage man. "Where can I drop you off, young man?"

"Signore, I recall where I lived in Naples, and I can fix the location by landmarks like Vesuvius and the bay."

"I am not in a great rush. Where exactly is your family?"

I did not want to steer the farmer to the quartieri bassi, first because of the horror he would feel at where I lived, but also because in that area he would be in danger of being assaulted. "Signore, just leave me off by the waterfront docks."

"*Va bene*," he answered, lifting an eyebrow as if catching on that I wanted to go home but also that my home was in a neighborhood not so welcoming.

And so I was let off by the docks. "*Bona furtuna*, guagliò," my chauffeur said, wishing me luck. I deeply thanked him.

Before making my way to the bassi, I took advantage of being close to Don Toddo's restaurant, *Trattoria da Toddo*, on the corner at the top of a steep street that bled out to the scurrying life of the waterfront. Don Toddo was one of my Neapolitan guardian angels. I regularly visited his humble eatery, never as a customer but rather to glean scraps of bread or edible plate scrapings to present to my mamma and sisters. I usually gained Toddo's attention by way of the back door, the best front-door service this scugnizzo could expect. But this time I loitered at the front window.

"So, still a scugnizzo," I muttered to no one except my unimpressive image in the foggy side window of the trattoria. The window reflected my practiced appeals to visitors and fellow citizens. I scowled at my reflected face, making it look even worse.

"Hey, Giovanni, don't stare so much through the window, you're scaring my diners. They're trying to eat!"

Roused from communing with my reflection, I heard myself greet Don Toddo, who had come out the front door, chatty as usual and with a fatherly smile. Don Toddo was one of the few rotund citizens of Naples. His small black vest paid humble homage to his ample girth.

I turned away from the foggy glass to face him. "So sorry, Don Toddo." I was so glad to see him, but I just followed with "I was trying to see if my face was clean enough not to scare people away."

"So good to see your beautiful face back in Naples, even if it's only through my front window!"

I could only smile and put my head down.

"Even with such a beautiful face—*faccia cchiù bella*—staring at the window gives my diners *àgita*, and Naples gives us all enough acid indigestion!" Don Toddo pinched my cheek. "You're making my few miserable flowers wilt in their hanging baskets."

I covered my bowed head with my hands, not knowing if I wanted to laugh or cry.

"Giovannuzzo, I hope you are doing well in the countryside. Your mamma and sisters are doing their best. I drop in when I can, or I send Pietro on the bicycle."

I felt emotion welling up, but in the middle of a fatherly belly laugh, Don Toddo exhaled and said, "Go around back. I have two-day bread I can't use." My ears pricked up, but before I could express adequate thanks, Toddo cut me off. "And I have enough breadcrumbs to feed all the pigeons in the piazza of the University of Naples!"

I used to be one of those Neapolitan pigeons, I thought. *I made a life in its streets and alleys and on its rooftops before I went back to the country.*

Toddo interrupted my musings as he turned to enter his place. "The bread's yours if you want it. Better for you than the birds."

He stepped into his trattoria, peering at me over his shoulder. I ran two buildings down, over broken street tiles and shards of glass, then down an alley littered with trash, garbage cans, and more broken glass. I was sure Toddo had little idea of my route. I jumped a fence, avoiding an open sewer trench, and reached the trattoria back door just as Don Toddo opened it. He had learned not to express surprise at the speed and cunning of this scugnizzo. He handed over the loaf.

The bread was not so hard as to resist the squeeze of my grip. "But Don Toddo, you can still use this bread for paying customers."

Don Toddo didn't just tell me not to think about it, he sang it operatically: "*Nun c' pensà, bello!*"

I put my head down, and Don Toddo lifted it with a gentle fist under my chin. "Caro, just be careful and honest. Try to stay clear of the ugliest of your ex-comrades, your so-called friends." As I tried to hold back tears, Don Toddo had me laughing again. "Some of them are so ugly and perfidious, they scare the rats. I am surprised they have any friends!"

"A thousand thanks, Don Toddo!" I said before taking off to see Mamma and my sisters.

Don Toddo well knew that not all urchins were alike, and most would have preferred money or valuables over food. I always tried to avoid too many interactions with the worst of the urchin guild. Most city dwellers and visitors did not make such distinctions. My last name was Ragnuno, but to them it might as well have been Scugnizzo. When I roamed the streets, they rarely let me forget my status, spitting, avoiding my gaze, shielding their children from me. I did not blame them—at the dawn of the twentieth century, few of us *napulitani* could count on security, sanitation, and daily bread.

Loaf under my arm, I turned a corner, looking for a place to enjoy this repast. The streets of Naples had eyes—I would have to make myself and my prize invisible. Then a tinge of guilt: *I have to present this to my mother and sisters*. The image of *mia Mamma* was always vivid, and I thought of her magically turning the bread into something more appealing and nourishing for our family of four—Mamma, my sisters, and me. She had mastered the harvest of edible weeds growing in nearby fields or popping up between sidewalk tiles in front of decaying and abandoned buildings, and with my bread, she could work wonders over a street fire of driftwood and garbage. *Now, if I can grab a fish head and bones from a fisherman filleting his catch …*

But *mannaggia*! Dammit! I paid more attention to satisfying my immediate hunger than to the ever-present danger all around me—this scugnizzo was getting soft in the countryside! I walked almost straight into Nunzio, one of the scugnizzi ruling class. I tried to wipe any expression of fear from my face and posture.

"*Ciao*, Don Giovanni!" Nunzio further exaggerated his greeting, doffing the pea cap I had seen him lift from a dockworker. I shared guilt in that crime by having pointed the pursuer in the direction opposite Nunzio's flight. Nunzio's doffed cap was accompanied by a bow, his curly head almost butting against mine. His new leather shoes further accentuated the difference in our heights, especially with me in bare feet. His shallow gray eyes met mine as he lifted his head. Nunzio was always on the edge of threatening, but this time he exuded more respect than normal.

"Haven't seen you in a long while. There are rumors you're trying to live in the countryside," he said, returning his hat to his head. Something was up.

I shrugged and raised the coned fingers of each hand to my scowling face, as though to say, "And who told you such a story?" I hoped this was good enough for Nunzio.

"I bet that bread is from Toddo's place. I have fresh figs for your stale bread," said Nunzio, smirking and confident, as if he harbored a secret.

I met Nunzio's predatory eyes. His look, and the uneven trade offer, raised the small hairs on the back of my neck. Not only was Nunzio five or six years older than my thirteen, he was at least five street years more experienced.

"*Ciao, Nunzio, come sta Lei?*" I used the polite greeting of respect, but I also asked to see inside his bag. Being submissive is not a strategy for survival on the streets. Nunzio complied all too quickly, and *Ave Maria*, the figs were beautiful and ripe. Their aroma weakened my resolve to resist or to ask what he wanted in return. My grip on the fig bag tightened.

He must have lifted the figs from the market, and he's just trying to get me to take off with his haul. I bet there's a couple of carabinieri *on his tail.*

Or he wants my services.

I chose to satisfy my hunger—after all, it was none of my business how he had gotten the figs. I made the trade, handing the bread to Nunzio. "Don Nunzio, these are superb figs, at the peak of ripeness."

As I sank my teeth into one, Nunzio said, "I need a getaway guy."

I had a reputation as the *aucelluzzo*, "the little bird," for my jumping from rooftop to rooftop. I was agile, fast, with no fear of heights. But I wanted no part of Nunzio's offer. I had left Naples to live a less dangerous life, and a more honest one.

Honesty had its own dangers when it led to turning down collaborations with others of my guild. Nunzio was no ordinary scugnizzo. He was independent, strong as a bull, fearless, and remorseless. It was no secret on the streets that he was being groomed by La Camorra to join their underworld brotherhood.

Better to fool the devil than the innocents. "I would love to help you, Don Nunzio, but the last time I helped you guys, I thought I'd never get away from the guards and the carabinieri."

Nunzio laughed out loud. "Don't worry, Giovannuzzo aucelluzzo."

He mocked me by fluttering the fingers of each hand. "Little Bird Giovanni, if you cross your brothers, you will have a lot more to fear than the police."

"Cross you, Don Nunzio? I just don't want to fail you."

Nunzio's generous nostrils flared a little. I lowered my head to accentuate further the difference in our heights, and putting my right hand to my heart, I turned very sincere. "It is an honor to be asked to be of service, but I do not want to mess up your operation. I am learning at my own pace. I hope someday to be a valuable *compare*—a confederate, not just a friend."

Nunzio's face broke out in an expression of confusion. He knitted his thick eyebrows and almost puckered his lips.

If only he could have sensed how this little bird's thirteen-year-old heart was racing.

Just then Vincenzo appeared out of thin air—maybe my instincts were not so sharpened after all. Short, stocky, and dark, Vincenzo was Nunzio's frequent companion. His charmless eyes were black and cold, under heavy eyebrows that met over his huge chiseled, hooked nose.

Now there were two pairs of eyes. Vincenzo and Nunzio both looked at me as if I were a condemned man. Nunzio turned to address Vincenzo, but I knew he was talking to me. "Vincenzo, this guagliò is turning down a deal. All he has to do is take a handoff of loot and head the other way from the poor sap victim and our scattering 'friends.'"

Being called a guagliò, a kid, was a not-so-subtle insult. Vincenzo kept staring at me as Nunzio went on. "With all the confusion, the little sewer rat can outrun and confuse anyone trying to follow the loot."

Then Vincenzo showed a poetic side. "Even if they saw him, try jumping from rooftop to rooftop when the rat turns into a little bird and flies away!" Vincenzo's narrow forehead wrinkled over his arched eyebrows. His smile revealed missing and broken teeth.

I dared to interrupt. "Those Northerners and their ass-kissers think they can push us around. They act as if we're worse than rats, sneaky, filthy *chiaveconi* sleaze, but not very smart. Let them not worry about me, and then someday we can really make a hit right under their noses."

I was sure my meaning did not come through to them. Nunzio

and Vincenzo were not the kind of businessmen to make long-range plans. So, I offered my right hand to each—my left was soiled with fig innards—and bid a farewell, an insincere *addio*. Nunzio turned to Vincenzo, and I did not have to hear all his words. Under his raised chin, he was waving his right hand, formed into a cone of four fingers around his thumb: "*Cchiù strano chisto guagliò!*"

Yes, what a strange kid. But this strange guagliò still had a few figs to present to Mamma and my sisters. Farther ahead, I saw Nunzio break up Toddo's bread and broadcast it on the street. I resisted the temptation to compete with the pigeons for the larger pieces.

When the coast was clear, I retrieved my countryside loot from its hiding place at the docks. I had to get back to my mamma and sisters! Seeing them again would flush out the bad taste of Nunzio and Vincenzo—I hoped. Life could not be good for my family. I had promised my mother I would rescue her and my sisters when I found my fortune in the streets. Well, that had not worked out so well, but at least we all had survived.

Ahh, my precious sisters. Calogero's tutors had told him that the elder's name, Elena, was from the Greeks—the Hellenic founders of Naples. She was indeed a "shining light." Giorgietta was born when our family still lived on the farm, and her name aptly meant "girl from a farm." Each sister was a *contadina*—a country girl trapped in the fetid urban labyrinth of Naples.

I was eager to present them my prize from Campania, but I dreaded seeing the conditions they were in. I knocked on the half door leading into their half-submerged chamber. Mamma approached, carefully and then ran straight at me, almost screaming. "Giovanni! Belluzzo!"

"Mamma!" I could not hold back my emotion. I tried to go into my practiced pitch, that I was doing well and that I had come bearing food and gifts.

She looked into my eyes. Her face seemed older, with strands of gray in her dark hair. What would become of her if evil befell me in the countryside?

"Mamma, where are Giorgietta and Elena?"

She cast her eyes to the dirt floor and almost whispered, "They are outside, trying to earn a few coins."

"What?!"

"Giovanni, they are growing up, and what is there for them to do all day in this dungeon? They try to read the pieces of newspaper we pick up from the streets, but they have to get out. A kindly tourist gave them a tambourine, and they dance in the streets. People love to see the *tarantella* danced well. I have a pair of dull scissors and a few sewing needles from our farm, and I use thread and material from old clothing to make peasant dresses."

I could only think of the zòccole of the waterfront. Mamma read my mind. "They are good girls, and a neighbor's sons protect them."

"You don't worry?"

"Of course I worry! But I have to trust people. Don Toddo and his assistant Pietro have been angels. I can offer you some *biscotti* to dip in a cup of wine to celebrate your return, thanks to that wonderful man."

How different my life would have been if Mamma married someone like Toddo!

Just then, the girls returned. Elena yelled, "Mamma, we have a few coins!" She stopped in her tracks upon seeing me, but shrieked as if seeing the dead.

We four engaged in a communal hug, feeding off each other's emotions. I stepped back and saw girls on the verge of becoming young women, especially almost-thirteen-year-old Elena. My mind instantaneously flashed farmer Pasquale's admonition about the zòccole, ladies of the Neapolitan night.

No! I will rescue my family first!

The chamber's straw pile was arranged to seat four. I was full of stories about the countryside, which made Mamma wistfully recall our happier days as a farm family.

"Oh, Giovannuzzo, we were poor, and we struggled, but the land was ours, and we worked it."

"I still can't believe we wound up here in the filthy bassi."

"Well, here we are. We cannot give up hope. I do not worry about me, but I have three beautiful gems of children. You deserve so much more than this."

"I met a young man at a villa near Benevento," I said. "He's the only child of 'o donno 'e villa. He has everything except true happiness."

"Ahh, give us everything we need, and we will find ways to be happy!" Mamma burst out. Her face lit up with a wry smile, her eyes now twinkling.

Elena and Giorgietta giggled. Elena asked the boy's age, and when I responded, "Almost as old as you," she raised her eyebrows. *Yes indeed, Elena is on the verge of womanhood.*

"Mamma, at least I am not living the dirty life on the streets." Why had I said this? Was it to suggest that my sisters might be getting close to the life? Mamma raised her eyebrows too, her head bobbing up and down.

"I remember once when I came down here with a few coins and some bread, cheese, and olives. Do you remember what you said?" I asked.

Mamma stared back a no.

"You looked at me like I was a ghost and asked, 'Are we eating the misfortune of others? When will this life kill you?' You emphasized the 'you' as if I were already killing others."

"You're a good boy, Giovannuzzo. Your heart is too big to make a living on the streets. I knew you did not victimize people, and I'm so sorry I said that."

"When we lived on the farm, people used to say, 'See Naples and then die.' Well, we have seen Naples. We came here, but not to die. We will find a way out. Our salvation is in the countryside that we fled."

"Be careful, Giovannuzzo. You will help us escape, but don't try to be a hero."

I found myself in another embrace with the three beautiful women of my family. They were sobbing, while I tried to be strong.

I stayed no more than a few days in Naples. The danger of a chance encounter with Nunzio, Vincenzo, and other scugnizzi impelled my departure. I was also repelled by the mire and pestilence of the bassi. Guilt gnawed at me for leaving my family in such a situation, amid garbage, filth, open sewers, stench, and cholera. The dung beetles of the country barnyards were fastidious in their habits in comparison to the humans dwelling in the bassi.

I escaped, drawn to the countryside, to the Villa Valeria, and to young Calogero. By this time I knew which farmers to implore for rides out of Naples.

3

THE VILLA FAMILY (1899–1900)

The fledgling took off from city street
Hopeful heart and wings in unison beat
He flew back to the fields of his birth
His goal to prosper and prove his worth

Back in Campania, I returned to hiring out as a field hand at places near the Villa Valeria, gladly accepting lodging in barns and stalls. They were much safer than the alleys, doorways, and bassi of Naples, and much cleaner. I visited mio onomino Don Giovanni again. I always thought each visit would be the last, but he was well, and happy to see me as always.

At the villa fence my conversations with Calogero were increasingly animated. We stoked each other's fire of curiosity. To provoke his, I left out details or introduced inconsistencies in my stories.

My own questions were more direct. "Calogero, tell me what you are learning from your tutors."

He usually responded with a detailed sermon on Italian history and law. Those subjects captured his imagination more than mathematics, and much more than the study of insects.

"Why, you are receiving a treasure of knowledge and wisdom!" I would say.

Calogero would just nod, perhaps embarrassed by his outburst on the wonders of history and law. The more I asked, the more he seemed to appreciate his tutoring sessions. He put more effort into preparing for them, even mathematics.

One afternoon, Calogero met me with a smile, almost dancing. "Guess what I learned today?"

"Well, how would I ever know? Your smile tells me that you enjoyed the lesson."

"Did you know that *la campana* was named after Campania? Bronze for the bell has been mined here for centuries."

"Calogero, that is perfect! You are like a campana, a bell that absorbs the impacts of your lessons and then rings them back to me."

"I think the word is *resonate*," said Calogero earnestly, his head slightly tilted to one side.

"Yes, you resonate the history of Campania, a history we can be proud of."

Of course, I did not express my other thoughts: *What can we be proud of in modern Naples? Seen from the villa, Naples is beautiful to this privileged guagliò. I hope my dress, manners, and stories don't make Calogero think otherwise.*

Calogero became increasingly "resonant" with Neapolitan history, from ancient through Roman times to our modern Italy, unified between 1860 and 1871, not even forty years before. He was a sponge for Italy's historic events and dates, and he needed minimal encouragement to recite them. I knew, from Mamma, that Naples's three- to four-thousand-year history went back to before the seafaring Greeks, and Calogero filled in much detail.

I avoided the villa in the mornings, when Calogero was inside with the tutors. The lessons took place in the two-story "school building" behind the chapel in back of the villa main house. My own mornings were devoted to my odd jobs in the country, and also to peddling my meager wares. Calogero's recounting his morning lessons to me in the afternoon helped him master concepts, though he needed no help to memorize historical details. My reading skills were rudimentary, and Calogero's briefings sharpened my desire to read better. I learned to bring a fragment of a discarded newspaper, usually recovered from a barn or roadside, to learn new words and eventually connect old history with current events. We were each other's best tutor.

My investment in Calogero's lessons seemed genuine to Don Giuseppe: he would reward me with old tracts and fresh newspapers. I loved that he usually gave me the materials by way of Calogero, who, in turn, dutifully passed them through the fence. It was like a ritual strengthening of the ties connecting we three. Calogero, on his own, imparted new words and historical facts to me, often looking back at his babbo for confirmation.

Before greeting me one afternoon, Calogero exploded with "Giovanni, Antonio Starabba is no longer our prime minister!"

"Oh?" was all I could say before Calogero continued, showing me a copy of a recent newspaper, dated 1899.

"He was from Sicily, but Babbo told me he was a man of culture. Our tutors say he was a great ally of Giuseppe Garibaldi. He was a hero of the new Italy, but he lost the Battle of Adowa in Abyssinia." Calogero suddenly clammed up, looking downward, embarrassed by his passionate outburst.

"Thank you so much for this information, Calogero! I have to admit, though, that Roman Pompeii is much more interesting to me than what my own eyes show me of modern Italy and Naples."

Did I put his recent history in too negative a light? I could not understand why the central government would ignore Naples and go to war in far-off Abyssinia.

"You have a good head for government and history," I said as I reached through the fence to place a hand on his shoulder. He neither offered it nor pulled away. The guards did not move, but their eyes bored into me with an intensity I could almost feel.

The forbearance of the guards indicated to me that Calogero's father was intrigued by his son's scugnizzo friend. I tried to turn that intrigue into charm when I addressed Don Giuseppe one spring morning across the fence. Calogero was with the tutors in the classroom building behind the chapel and so was out of earshot. A look at guard Carlo and a nod to the villa house had brought Don Giuseppe to the fence. I kept my hands off the fence to show deference to Don Giuseppe's domain.

"*E poi?*" Don Giuseppe asked.

"Well, most respected Don Giuseppe, I have come to know Calogero better, and I am very happy that he finds me good company."

The word *Calogero* riveted Don Giuseppe's attention. His intense stare was almost unnerving.

"I would be most indebted if I could spend more time with Calogero on the same side of the fence. I believe we both would benefit from such an arrangement."

This was a prepared and practiced speech. Even now, at this distance of space and time, I can almost hear Don Giuseppe's inner voice, in his great diction, saying, "*Cosa straodinaria questo guaglione*, what an extraordinary lad! He has a sharp wit and no shortage of charm."

My family would chide me for being so self-congratulatory in my interpretation of Don Giuseppe's thoughts, but I did get through to Calogero's babbo.

Don Giuseppe finally spoke to me across the fence. "Giovanni, *giovane.*" Yes, he purposely apposed *GiovANNI* with *GIOVane*, or youngster, to make it clear that this young kid was asking to be a working member of the Villa Valeria community. "I can offer you employment in the stables."

Maybe my odor tells him I have experience in animal care.

"Or perhaps in the vineyard or pruning olive or lemon trees. Those activities require training and experience before you gain confidence and skill."

I bit my tongue so I could respond after a decent interval. I spied Carlo the guard, but his face was stone-silent, expressionless, and seemingly distracted.

"I accept any work you may offer, esteemed, *Egregio* Don Giuseppe, though I be young, untested, and perhaps unworthy. I know my training will require your patience before I become of any value to you. And before that may come to pass, I ask with the deepest humility that I be paid by being allowed to accompany Calogero when he is with his tutors."

I thought I spied a smirk creeping onto Carlo's face. Don Giuseppe's face was more expressive in response to my practiced appeal. I thought I could see that he was moved by my eloquence. However, he kept his cards close to the vest, until I had doubts about the power of my so-called eloquence.

"Well, this is an unusual request. I admire your desire to improve yourself and to acquire skills that separate gentlemen from rabble. But first, I want to consider your request and then speak with the tutors."

To me his avowed hesitation was to show this giovane that Don Giuseppe was in charge, that he was a businessman, *uomo d'affari*, a man of respect. I thought I knew this, but sharp pebbles of doubt impeded my walk away from the villa.

"*Arrivederci*, Don Giuseppe."

"Until then, Giovanni."

I stayed away from the villa the whole of the following day, trying to keep to my routine in the country. When I returned to my spot by the fence the next day, there was no Calogero. Don Giuseppe came out to greet me, and he was well beyond the earshot of workers, guards, and children, who all maintained their distance.

"Giovanni, I approached Calogero yesterday, and I mentioned that you might be living on his side of the fence."

"Living on his side of the fence" made me realize the radical change of our lives that I was requesting. The lives of Calogero, Don Giuseppe, and this miserable scugnizzo would never be the same. Or, I thought fearfully, they might never be the same because no agreement had been made.

"Don Giuseppe, if my presence in your domain in any way disturbs Calogero, I want no part of it." I banged on the fence with a fist without even noticing my actions. I soon realized that in my heart were intertwined two desires, one for my own betterment and another for that of Calogero.

"Babbo!" came a cry from near the vineyard. Don Giuseppe went to Calogero and brought him by the hand to his normal spot inside the fence, where he could face me.

"Calogero wants to tell you something." Don Giuseppe's voice reinforced the look in his eyes, which were directed straight at me.

Calogero's head was bowed and he seemed to find something of great interest in his polished brown shoes.

Please don't dwell on my bare feet was all I could think.

Finally, looking directly up at me, Calogero recited, "Welcome to our home, Giovanni."

I had trouble keeping my composure; my training as a street urchin was failing me. My tears welled up.

"Thank you so much, Calogero, a thousand thousand thanks. I will be a most respectful guest, and I will work my hardest to bring favor and prosperity on your home."

Don Giuseppe walked toward the main gate, accompanied by Calogero. He signaled me to follow along on my side of the stone and iron barrier. Don Giuseppe took it upon himself to open the gate. A slight upward movement of head and eyes were signals enough to his guards to back away, but Calogero stayed close.

I felt as if I were passing through St. Peter's gate, making me even more aware of my appearance, filthy and shoeless, with baggy pants and a shirt that lacked half its buttons. Don Giuseppe bid me follow him and Calogero to the main villa house. We entered the magnificent hall and made a sharp turn to the kitchen, where I finally met Donna Bettina, chief cook and head of the indoor staff of the Villa Valeria.

Her large kitchen had two fireplaces and an oven for baking bread. Cauldrons and frying pans were hung from rafters over a large middle table with a chopping top.

She rose from a smaller table. "Ahh, so this is the scugnizzo that I see almost every day at the fence!" She was so welcoming, especially her greeting in dialect: "*Viene ccà, figliemo.*" "Come here my child." She looked at me as if at a wounded bird. "We will get you some clean new clothes, but only after you have washed yourself."

I gave her a quizzical look, to which she responded, "With your beautiful face, I want to give you a hug and a kiss, but first you have to clean up, because I am *'na signora*, you know."

Yes, I understood that a real lady hugs only the cleanest of young men.

Bettina reminded me a little of Don Toddo. She could have been his wife. I soon learned that she was as generous of character as her physical appearance first suggested. Her white blouse and large, loose purple dress covered a generous bosom and an expansive belly. All I could think was *abbunnànza*, the abundance that was still obvious under her beautiful white apron embroidered with flowers and grapevines. She had a proud nose over full lips. Heavy lashes lined her black eyes under arched, seemingly woven eyebrows that gave her a look of constant surprise and amusement. Her black hair, with streaks of gray, was tied on top in a bun, adding to her air of authority, and she exercised it. She pointed to the next room, which held a bath.

"Throw your clothes outside the door. I am going to bury them in the vineyard. They will fertilize a beautiful vintage!"

I could not help myself. I had to laugh, and Donna Bettina joined in.

"Ahh, a generous soul is never beaten down by poverty and bad luck! You will do well here, Giovannuzzo. Just make sure that you are good to my Calogero, whom I love very much."

"Signora, Calogero has been angelic with me. I will be his faithful friend, confessor, and defender."

"Ave Maria, you have the makings of a poet. Go take that bath so that your body can be as pure as your soul."

In my undeserving life there have been many moments of pleasure and happiness, but that hot bath had to be one of the best. I was thinking of the bathing scenes in the Pompeian frescoes at the Archaeological Museum. I was also thinking of how fortunate I was and that I would have daily work, both to learn and to live up to the bestowed blessings of Don Giuseppe.

Towel around my waist, I was shown to a small room. It had a cot and a modest wardrobe of clothes that were hand-me-downs from some of the other children of the villa. Some later reminded me that I was wearing their cast-offs, but it did not bother me at all. I had presentable clothes for the sessions with the tutors.

In the mornings, I received instruction. I was an enthusiastic student. Moreover, the tutors loved that young Calogero, instead of being distracted by my presence, was more absorbed in the lessons.

Indeed, I eventually helped Calogero with some concepts of mathematics, geometry, and natural science. Calogero's confidence grew, and he became more of a leader among his young friends and relatives at the villa. My wardrobe was improved, thanks to the generosity of Don Giuseppe and Donna Bettina. If Calogero became more sociable, my own self-esteem and my stature in the eyes of my peers greatly improved as well.

In the afternoons, I worked in the vineyards, among the fig trees, or wherever I was needed. But visions of Mamma, Elena, and Giorgietta haunted me. They were still in the teeming, filthy bassi, where even the foul air was poisonous. Yet even worse for them was that they did not know anything of my fate, nor I of theirs. I was haunted by my being driven so relentlessly to fix my own lot that my sisters and mother suffered as a consequence. How could I be so selfish?

Elena would soon be fourteen, an age at which some country girls married. I knew there were some in Naples who would try to force her into servitude as a zòccola. It hurt me just to think that word. My own happy, well-fed situation was in sharp contrast. I felt too indebted to Don Giuseppe to prevail upon him to look in on my mother and sisters, or maybe I feared undermining my own status. Was my fear of jeopardizing my position at the villa greater than my desire to help my family?

I settled on asking Donna Bettina for help.

One afternoon, as I brought tomatoes and eggplants into the villa kitchen, Donna Bettina was alone except for Carlo, the friendly sentry, sitting at the kitchen preparation table. He was finishing off a bowl of minestrone. Donna Bettina was extremely kind to him, and he seemed to enjoy her attention, though at the villa fence he acted like a disciplined, stern guard—except for that one time he greeted me through the fence. He put his beret back on and grabbed his carbine. He gave Donna Bettina a peck on the cheek, winked at me, and was on his way to his post.

I realized that Donna Bettina and I were alone. "*Scusa*, Zia, can I speak with you?"

"But of course, *piccirillo*!"

I did not mind being her "little boy." "Cara Zia, I am so happy to be here getting an education with the tutors and getting an education helping in the garden, the vineyard, and the olive and lemon groves."

Donna Bettina's eyes said she was expecting the down note. "Poi?"

"I am also well fed. But—you know, I left my family in Naples to go back to Campania."

"*Ma, sì, bello!* But yes, my beautiful boy, thanks to you, Calogero talks like a clucking hen! So how could I not know about your family? I have made sure that Don Giuseppe knows."

I instinctively embraced my dear Zia. I could barely get my arms around her generous body.

"Go do your chores, and that includes keeping your room neat. I know Don Giuseppe will not leave the beautiful ladies of your family to be prey to the evil that walks the streets of Naples."

"But Zia—"

"*Nun stà anziúso*," she said. "Don't worry. I know the women in your family are strong. I can see it in the strength and goodness of your character."

Some days later, after an afternoon work shift, I was making my way to my room in the workers' quarters. Carlo intercepted me.

"Guagliò, Il Capo wants to talk with you."

He pointed me to the villa main house, accompanying me through the ornate anteroom to the entrance to Don Giuseppe's waiting room. The double doors were open. Don Giuseppe was sitting in a large leather easy chair.

"Guagliò, go in. Don Giuseppe is expecting you."

Carlo retreated. I entered the waiting room, trying not to be distracted by the wood-carved ceiling and family portraits. The Don sharpened my focus. He did not mince words.

"Sit down, Giovanni." He pointed to a facing wooden chair. "I have enquired about your family. The stories you told Calogero and Donna Bettina helped our friends locate them. Your mother is doing as well as she can mending others' clothes. She has a pair of old scissors, a few needles and whatever material and thread she can find in rag piles.

I was shocked by this unexpected news but kept my silence and listened avidly, though curiosity and concern forced the obvious question out of me. "What of my sisters?"

"Your sisters and mother are still living together in that single chamber in the subterranean bassi. Worrying to me is that your sisters have been seen dancing on the streets for handouts. My people approached your mother. She was very suspicious at first, but when they mentioned your name, she was all ears and tried to contain her panic."

Ahh, Mamma mia, what have I done to you and my family!

I was sure Don Giuseppe could read these thoughts in my eyes and countenance.

"She now knows that her only son is well, earning a living and becoming a well-rounded man. She was grateful for the news."

Don Giuseppe observed the emotions of surprise, shame, and gratitude competing to dominate my facial expressions. "Your sisters dancing in the streets is like a dagger to her heart, though she would never say so. Elena and Giorgietta bring in a few coins, but they are exposed to the evil side of Naples."

I was impressed that he knew their names. There was a long pause. The changing expressions on Don Giuseppe's face gave me no indication of his thoughts or true feelings, but his eyes, always fixed on me, seemed to soften.

Finally he declared, almost stoically, "In Naples, I have friends of friends who will take on your mother as a housekeeper and cook. She is an honorable and honest woman. She does not deserve the constant torment of poverty and of her daughters in the streets."

I thought again about my own happy situation compared to theirs. *How could I be so selfish!*

Don Giuseppe broke into my thoughts. "The three will live under the same roof, well away from the bassi, and will be associated with a respectable family."

The news washed over me, and then I overflowed, breaking out in sobbing for the wonderful turn of events. But I also sobbed out of guilt for not having returned to Naples sooner to seek out and rescue my fatherless family. I may have been self-reliant, but caring people such as Don Toddo, Donna Bettina, and Don Giuseppe had saved my family.

I was able to collect myself enough to call on my best tearful oratory. "Don Giuseppe, I can never repay you. You have given me something that has no price. The value of a man is not measured in fig trees, horses, or land, but in the goodness of his heart and in the loyalty and protection he offers his associates. I am not even of your blood, but you would do this for me! This is the greatest lesson I have learned under your care."

I did not know the source of my oratory—perhaps the distillation of my pent-up feelings—but it seemed to affect the composure of Don Giuseppe, who waved me off with an all-too-cavalier swipe of his hand, as if at an imaginary gnat. He was not such a stoic after all.

After a length of time uncomfortable for both of us, Don Giuseppe slowly said, "If I have helped your family, Giovanni, you have greatly helped mine."

To me, Giuseppe Gentile embodied "patrician," a word I had learned from the tutors. He was an accomplished man, well and fit in his early forties, and a noble father in manner and action. Don Giuseppe adjusted his posture and looked straight at me. He was more in control now.

"Calogero was always a distant boy, hardly acknowledging those around him. If he were not my son, I am afraid he would have been cruelly ridiculed. Perhaps he harbors guilt that his mother did not survive his birth. To him, his mother lives only in the name 'Villa Valeria' and in that portrait on the mantel."

I looked up at that forever young beautiful woman. Don Giuseppe paused before saying, "You have awakened the human spirit in him. He admires you." My patron pulled himself up and continued, "Dare I say, he loves you."

Again a pause, and an uncomfortable one for Don Giuseppe, but I was too taken with my own emotions to take full notice at the time.

"And that love now imbues his interactions with others. He is rescued and I have you to thank." His direct look spoke of a noble humility. "I would like for you to stay near Calogero."

My emotions were riding breaking waves. I had been so absorbed in getting Calogero out of his shell and improving my lot in the process, that I had almost forgotten my beautiful family back in Naples. *Giovanni Scugnizzo, the excuse that your wayward father might return to your family was always a complete fiction. Scugnizzo, did you inherit too much of your father's nature, or were you molded by the Neapolitan streets?*

"Don Giuseppe, I vow that I will be a loyal friend to Calogero. And from now on, I will be a loyal son and brother to the beautiful women of my family."

Don Giuseppe rose and offered his hand and then a strong embrace before suddenly turning away. He turned back to me, his eyes glistening, "Giovanni, you are more than Calogero's friend. You have made him part of your family, as you are of ours."

Outside Don Giuseppe's study, I found Calogero waiting. Wordlessly we walked toward the main door of the villa.

Calogero, on the stairs to his room, turned to me as I made my way outside to my quarters. He called out in a confident voice, "*A domani*, Giovanni."

"See you tomorrow, Calogero, my brother."

From that day, Calogero was more like my little brother, *mio fràtemo piccirillo* in our lovely dialect. I told him about my mother and sisters and how he would meet them someday and that my sisters would embrace him like a second brother. Such talk about interactions with a family he didn't know made Calogero uncomfortable. His lowered eyes told me so. I felt a little guilty putting such discomfort on him when I was in reality trying to atone for being the prodigal son to my Neapolitan family.

Much easier for both of us were my discourses on the wildlife in the orchards and vineyards. I was especially fond of the insect and bird life attracted to specific plants and trees. Tutors taught me about pollination, how bees, birds, and even bats often aided in fertilization of flowers that would later bear fruit. Upon leaving the classroom, Calogero and I often took tours of the garden.

I learned that male flowers did not have just one simple use. After the male flowers of the zucchina squash finished their service to the female flowers, Calogero and I would carry male flowers to the villa kitchen so the cooks could fill them with cheese, dip them in batter, and deep-fry them into delicious flower fritters—*frittelle di fiori di zucchina*.

Donna Bettina, who oversaw the creation of these treats, was a distant aunt of Calogero's and now firmly my adopted zia, my aunt Bettina. She seemed to hold me in a special place in her affection. "Johnny Boy, what treasure do you bring me today?" She almost sang it operatically as she wiped her hands on her apron of abundance: "*Giovannuzzo! E che tesoro me porta ogge?*" She was careful to include Calogero in her praise. We would proudly display the treasure of our harvest, always being sure to show up in time to feast on our prize.

At the kitchen table, Zia Bettina nourished my body and soul. While we munched our fritelle, she would share news about my family back in Naples and how well they were faring. Calogero nurtured me too, on the history of Italy, especially that of Naples and its laws and traditions from pre-Roman times to the late nineteenth-century times of our youth.

Calogero and I prospered in our mutually reinforcing relationship. We nestlings in Zia Bettina's kitchen became *cucini*, perhaps even more than cousins, maybe even brothers, but certainly more than friends. We helped each other to fly without fear, but more importantly, with firm destinations in mind.

What could come between us?

4

FILOMENA (1900–1904)

Fierce iron fence, yet radiantly flowered
The Eros of my soul it empowered
For it attracted a perfumed uccellina
Songbird *sublime, a gift most* divina

I can see and sense her flowery youth even at this distance. She appeared at the villa on the first and third Saturday of each month to barter for what was in season in the groves—grapes, figs, lemons, chestnuts—as well as herbs and produce from the garden, like tomatoes, eggplants, peppers, *zucchina* squash, *broccoli friarielli*—bitter greens—and *cucuzzo*, or calabash. I learned her name from Calogero, who gave me a suspicious look as he rasped out, "Filomena."

More than a beautiful flower, she was a precious fruit—the only child of her widower father. Benedetto Minicello was a landowner from a respected family, and his daughter was his trusted representative. I got this information from Donna Bettina, who relayed it with twinkling eyes and a tug on my earlobes.

Filomena showed up at Don Giuseppe's with cheeses and dried, cured meats to offer in trade for fresh produce. She had a large four-wheeled barrow, and even when it was filled to the brim with produce, she skillfully navigated it over the kilometer of dirt road back to her father's farm home.

How could I, a virile and worldly fifteen-year-old, not notice Filomena? Her languid, almost willowy form contrasted with her country girl's wiry strength. She was tall for Campania, black hair down to her waist in a wide, thick single braid, pulled back from a large, light-skinned forehead and overly abundant black eyebrows. They shaded beautiful eyes that evoked the Moorish, *Mudejar*, pointed arches that I had admired in the history tutorials. Like all napulitani, I resented the extended Spanish rule in Naples, but it left a lingering admiration for Iberian architecture. Filomena's long, dark eyelashes beat Flamenco flashes of restrained rage.

Her soft mouth betrayed her, and through full, smiling lips shone her perfect white teeth. Filomena was tall and slim, yes, but had entered into full womanhood. There was a supple nature to her angular frame, and her white blouse with lace borders did not fully hide her breasts. Her apparent softness was belied by how her chest flexed as she maneuvered the wheelbarrow.

"*Buongiorno*, Signorina Minicello," was my initial good-day greeting, but after a few encounters, we were on a first-name basis. I was mesmerized by her "Buongiorno, Giovanni." Yes, she was beautiful and moved with grace, strength, and confidence. Being addressed so sweetly by her felt like an undeserved blessing.

One memorable day in the fruit groves, I had two treats for Filomena in separate muslin bags. "I harvested some very nice figs, and these are for you and your father, Filomena."

As she bent slightly to peer into the first bag, undoubtedly pleasantly assailed by the figs' aroma, I added, "And, surprise, some pistachios!"

Filomena looked up and lifted my gaze into her eyes. She ignored the bag of pistachios. I feared my eagerness to please her was tipping my hand. Then she looked straight over and smiled at Calogero, as if we three were just good buddies. She eased my embarrassment but not my guilt that I had made Calogero feel peripheral.

I led Filomena and Calogero to two pistachio-laden trees, reemphasizing that my gift was not only for Filomena but for her babbo as well. In our threesome Calogero patiently listened to what we had learned from the tutors—that pistachio culture was concentrated in Sicily.

I gingerly opened the subject of the sex life of the pistachio. "Don Giuseppe has several trees, but only two are fruit-bearing females." The implication was that one or more nearby male trees had admirably played a role in pollination. Filomena's look made me stammer, and I quickly ended my biological discourse.

During the uncomfortable lull, Calogero added some history. "The Romans and the Arabs brought the pistachio to Italy." It was then his turn to lower his eyes, surprised and embarrassed by his own outburst.

Ahh, but Filomena came to his rescue. "Bravo, Calogero!" was her immediate response.

She tried to embrace him, but he reflexively pulled away. However, Calogero stayed in our company in the garden—one might even think as a chaperone designated by his father, though that was far from the truth. Filomena and I both knew that Calogero normally preferred the solitude and comfort of his well-appointed room/study in the villa main house. But to him I was a resource that had to be defended against the advances of Filomena who, in turn, did all she could to make Calogero feel welcome in our group.

Not only I but Don Giuseppe looked forward to Filomena's visits. Of course, Don Giuseppe had known Filomena far longer than I had, and I think her relationship with me added a new dimension to her relationship with Don Giuseppe Gentile.

One day, Don Giuseppe was the first to greet Filomena. I overheard some of their conversation as I was about to prune grapevines.

"*Ciao*, Filomena, what treasures do you bring us today?" he asked as he kissed her on each cheek.

"Well, Signor Gentile, I have some nice aged prosciutto. And Babbo is very proud that his latest batch of mozzarella is *di bufala*. There is a small buffalo herd not far from our villa."

In the midst of my thoughts that I had to visit that mozzarella operation, Filomena continued. "There is also ricotta and some pecorino cheese."

"Ahh, I will carry these treasures to Donna Bettina."

I put off pruning and made sure to be extra quiet. Then I heard Filomena comment *sotto voce*, "Your new helper is an interesting lad."

"He sure is, and Calogero really seems to love him. Calogero is a different person when he's with Giovanni."

"Calogero is more open with me now as well."

There was some silence. I tried to stay still.

Filomena said, "Signor Gentile, if you pardon my saying so, sometimes I think that Calogero is a little jealous of Giovanni showing friendship with me."

"Filomena, *cara*, friendship is not something that is divided into ever smaller pieces. If you and Calogero become good friends with Giovanni, Calogero will love you even more." The word *love* seemed a little strong to me, but there are all kinds of love, and I chose to accept friendship as a form of love.

I nonchalantly turned to the next row of grapes and feigned accidentally happening on Filomena. Don Giuseppe, who had already started returning to the villa main house with some of

Filomena's bounty, saw me first. I nodded to him and then turned to Filomena. "*Ciao*, Filomena! So good to see you again!" I hoped that Filomena did not see the blush that I felt on my face.

I usually tried to offer Filomena items of interest and quality. On one visit, I presented her with succulent persimmons from the *legnas-anta*, the holy tree.

"Oh, Giovanni. They are beautiful and juicy," she proclaimed as she bit into one, while leaning over so as not to stain her blouse.

Yes, they were beautiful fruit, and Filomena's expression and contortions of pleasure were a gift to me as well. She caught my gaze but redirected me with a question. "Do you know how the fruit got its name?"

Not composed enough to venture a verbal answer, I shook my head no. She definitely noticed my wandering eyes. Filomena then insisted that I call Calogero to join us to explain the name. Filomena had something to separate her ears, *per spartere 'e rrecchje*, as Donna Bettina liked to say. Filomena was smart as well as beautiful.

I ran off to call on Calogero in his study. I did not want to leave Filomena but was thankful to be able to change my focus for a while. As usual, Calogero was in his study, head buried in a book. Sensing my presence, he looked up with the blank face he had shown on our first encounters.

"Calogero, Filomena is here and wants you to join us in the grove."

He seemed perturbed but brightened a little when I followed that she wanted to ask him a question about a subject he knew. He rose slowly and we both ambled to the grove, where Filomena showed no sign that she had dispatched the persimmon. Her smile was as white as her blouse.

She musically asked, "Caro Calogero, why is the *legnasanta* tree so holy?"

Calogero's face lit up. Suddenly he was bursting with eagerness to explain. "If you cut an unripe fruit in half from the top to the bottom, you will see a white form that is similar to Christ on the cross."

"Bravo, Calogero!" and this time Calogero did not resist Filomena's embrace.

"Well, Filomena," I said plaintively, "I harvested the fruit," at which she turned and gave me a hug. This contadina was not stupid. I did a rapid inventory of Filomena's cargo and offered to help load her barrow for the return trip.

Filomena bade farewell to Calogero and me, but not before she gave Calogero a sweet kiss on his cheek. If her purpose was to gain Calogero's approval and to stoke my jealousy, she was successful on both counts.

One day, Filomena's cargo was larger than she could easily navigate to her home. With Don Giuseppe's blessing, I volunteered to help her along the journey. We set off, taking turns pushing the cart and riding on an agreeable donkey.

This arrangement became a twice-monthly ritual. When days grew shorter, I was faced with a return trip in the darkness, so Filomena's father granted permission for me to spend the night. A farmhand mounted on my donkey would relay the news to Don Giuseppe in the early evening. Naturally, Don Benedetto Minicello treasured his only child, and his servants made sure that I was both comfortable and at a comfortable distance from Filomena when I was obliged to spend the night under the Minicello roof.

Filomena had lost her mother at an early age. I often thought of the irony. She had grown up in a home of plenty, and though I was assailed by poverty and misery, I was not separated from my dear mother, except for the distance from the villa to Naples.

On our trips between the villas of Don Giuseppe and Don

Benedetto, Filomena and I were never in any special hurry. We chatted the whole time. I was so very eager to relay what I was learning about history, math, grammar, and syntax. I did not delve too deeply into the beautiful nature occurring in the gardens and orchards. The insect life, especially, seemed almost repulsive to Filomena, so I tried to play down this fascination of mine. Of course, I realized that most of the garden's bounty was the result of lovemaking among the plants, whose courtship was facilitated by insect and bird intermediaries. I was intent on displaying only a portion of this knowledge while learning as much as I could about Filomena.

"Filomena, I have lost many opportunities to gain an education, but Calogero, Don Giuseppe, the tutors, and the wonderful people of the villa have provided me a means to learn of the world around me."

"You are so fortunate," she said. "Young ladies are not considered worthy of too much education. My father looks so much to having grandsons."

"Yes, I understand." She gave me an almost threatening look, so I quickly added, "But you are very intelligent, and you could provide your father's grandchildren with much wisdom and knowledge." I said it, and I believed it.

"You're very kind, Giovanni. I bet that as a father, you would share with your wife the responsibility of educating your children."

"Yes, I would, and our experiences are so different ..." I stopped, embarrassed that I was already making the jump to our being married and having children.

"Giovanni, you are so charming." Still holding the barrow she turned her head to me. "I can see why you did not starve as a scugnizzo in Naples."

She let the barrow down and faced me, grabbing my hands in hers. Those Moorish eyes stared deeply. Her eyelashes seemed to pulsate. We were embracing, and then I was experiencing those generous lips on mine. The buzzing in my ears resonated with my own physical yearning.

We continued walking. The donkey was just a companion, a very discreet one, especially when tall grasses provided us a roadside refuge for another of nature's tutorials.

While I looked forward to Filomena's visits, Calogero was not so sure. He started to feel like an outsider again, almost ignored in Filomena's presence. To her credit, Filomena recognized his disquiet. Perhaps she also felt that to win my favor, she had to gain Calogero's. Indeed, he had to be an ally, and making him an ally also made one of Don Giuseppe—Filomena was not blind.

Filomena, as were all we Southerners, was skilled in Byzantine relationships and intrigue. Yet I was surprised the day she asked me, "Cannot Calogero help us in the harvest? He can be dedicated to a task, and he loves to recount his knowledge of history and government. He will feel useful and we will all learn from his lectures."

I hoped my look was not open-mouthed.

"And you will have a much more receptive ear for your discoveries in the world of plants and insects." I looked at her with newfound understanding but played stupid for a few seconds.

"A wonderful idea!" I said. "We can even test each other on our lessons as we work." I also knew there would be less privacy between Filomena and me in the harvest, though she henceforth managed to be much clumsier, often tripping while grabbing on to me for support.

Filomena praised my insight, and before too long, I accepted Calogero's participation as my own idea. Of course, this arrangement was forged under the approval of Don Giuseppe. I knew better than to ruin a developing relationship by going behind my patron's back. This tangle of willful deception and self-deception is civilization practiced to a fine art. Neapolitans know when to fool and when to allow themselves to be fooled.

We are all in the guild of the scugnizzi.

Calogero was easily drawn into conversation during the harvest and loading of produce, especially on topics of history and law. I was more a student of nature than of history, but I found intriguing horticultural connections between the histories of America and Campania.

I loved to tell Calogero, "History does not happen if a civilization cannot feed itself." While this was not very profound and probably not even true, it was a great lead-in to what I really wanted to say. "Did you know that the *pomodoro*, the golden apple that is now red, came from the New World? We Italians have adopted it and improved it, and it is now an important part of Zia Bettina's kitchen. Can you imagine Sunday dinner without a *ragú* sauce?"

Indeed, Calogero could not, and the eloquent silence of his direct gaze indicated so.

Filomena won Calogero's favor by promising to show him how to prepare ragú from the ripe plum tomatoes of our garden. On this mission, she could count on the forbearance of Zia Bettina, who allowed Filomena in her kitchen. Bettina understood cooking and the spells conjured by properly blended tomatoes and herbs. She certainly knew of the love life of the male and female flowers of the zucchine.

Calogero was even more intrigued when informed by Babbo Giuseppe that he had become a partner in an export business, shipping canned peeled tomato preserves to America. The cans said "*pomodori pelati*" on one side and "peeled tomato preserves" on the other.

The neighboring region of San Marzano sul Sarno, whose soil was enriched by the volcanic offerings of Mount Vesuvius, gave its name to this rich, meaty, pear-shaped fruit, and San Marzano became increasingly known in the growing Italian neighborhoods of the Americas. Of course, we napulitani called the tomato *pummarola* —a name enhancing its flavor.

Babbo told his son on more than one occasion, "Calogero, America is like a part of Italy now. Maybe someday you will choose to live there."

Calogero's expression reinforced what I already knew: that he could not even think of leaving the villa, especially if that meant leaving his babbo and his friends Filomena and Giovanni.

So, the Calogero-Filomena-Giovanni triumvirate was cross-linked on multiple levels. But one of the strongest links was my growing romance with Filomena. In 1902 she was a nineteen-year-old beauty, two years my senior. While Italian unity under King Vittorio Emmanuele III was buffeted by the poverty and unrest of the South, Filomena and I enjoyed the stability of our own and ever-stronger relationship. It appeared not only that Filomena's *papà* approved of me, but that Don Giuseppe also facilitated the liaison. They both strove to make Calogero feel as if a brother-in-law.

The Italy around us was disintegrating in many ways, but our own society in the *regione di Campania,* near Benevento, was thriving and blissful. These were beautiful times, abundance on the farm and happiness in the hearts of Filomena and Giovanni—and Calogero.

In 1904, I was a strapping nineteen-year-old and felt like I could conquer the world. I knew that the two landowners, Don Giuseppe and Don Benedetto, had been discussing my relationship with Filomena for a while—they had eyes and ears all over Campania. So naturally I was nervous when I faced Filomena's father in his ornate drawing room. He had seen it coming, and I still wonder what Don Benedetto thought when this guagliò asked him for the hand of his twenty-one-year-old Filomena.

"I stand in front of you, Don Benedetto, in all humility, and you can be assured that I will do whatever is in my power to protect Filomena and to provide for her." My head was slightly bowed as I tried not to tower over the shorter but stockier Don Benedetto.

"Giovanni, you know I have much affection for you, and I admire how you have always succeeded in bettering yourself," Don Benedetto told me firmly.

I dared not interrupt.

"You are young, but you are much older in experience and struggle. You value an education, and you value my precious Filomena—that is easy to see."

"Thank you so much, Don Benedetto. You can—"

Don Benedetto raised his right hand, and I quickly gave him all my attention. "Just understand, young man, that Filomena is not the prize at the end of the contest. If you become her husband, you will be under sacred obligation to continue to honor and serve her. Any transgression against her I will take as an assault on my house and an insult to me and to my late wife."

I wasn't sure if this was a veiled threat. *Is Don Benedetto connected with La Camorra?* I quickly rejected that thought.

"Egregio Signor Minicello, for me the blessing of being Filomena's husband carries with it my solemn obligation to honor and cherish her, just as I do her family." It was certain that in Campania, a young man does not so much marry his love, his *nnammuràta*, as he marries her family. Benedetto Minicello gave me a bear hug, and then with his hands on my shoulders, a kiss on my lips. This *bacio* was sacred. It meant that I was in. However, it also meant that there was no honorable way out. It wasn't lost on me that Filomena and I had embraced and kissed for the first time not so far from her home, the home where I was now dealing with her father.

I also was reminded that family included not only those of Don

Benedetto and Don Giuseppe, but also my own immediate family. My beautiful mother and sisters were now living in a more stable situation in Naples, thanks to Don Giuseppe's intervention on my behalf. I had a lot to prove as a trusted and respected family member.

The news of the impending wedding spread rapidly. I believe my mother and sisters knew well before I could inform them, which was not surprising since their employer was a family friend of my future father-in-law.

Calogero and I discussed the wedding in the privacy of the groves and vineyard of the villa. My love for Filomena did not detract from the affection that Calogero and I shared for each other. Indeed, there was no love triangle. Rather, we three formed a strong foundation, a self-reinforcing trinity of love.

"Giovanni," he said, "I hope you and Filomena have many children, more than my father or Filomena's father could have."

"Don't saddle me with a football team. You know what your father likes to say, 'Slow and steady wins the race.'"

"Yea, Babbo loves his sayings. I have heard '*Chi va piano arriva lontano e sano*' many times. He must be descended from Aesop." Calogero smiled. "I just wish you a happy and *fruitful* marriage."

Calogero was well prepared to accept the idea of making our three-way relationship more permanent. He knew Filomena from well before my arrival, and our marriage would intensify the kinship that I felt with Calogero, now a much more confident lad of fifteen. Ever-wise Filomena kept Calogero involved in the wedding plans. She also made sure he played an important role in the ceremony, and she backed up my suggestion that he be my best man, though a young one.

I became the pampered son of two families. Both Don Giuseppe and Don Benedetto seemed to spoil me with attention and praise.

Each time I showed up at Don Benedetto's home, he guided me to the drawing room where I had asked for Filomena's hand. Usually he offered me a sampling of *strega*. "Giovannuzzo, this is our local product. It celebrates the witches of Benevento. We are descended from the Samnites, a proud people that gave Rome all it could handle. Perhaps our witches were a source of our resolve."

To me the strega was indeed a witch's brew, a powerful concoction of elderberries and many other unknown ingredients. "Thank you, Don Benedetto. I drink to your health and that of beautiful Filomena, the greatest gift you could bestow on me." On one particular day, Filomena was present, seated on a settee. I looked over at her and mightily suppressed a giggle, which would have been a fatal show of disrespect. Her eyes, under pincer eyebrows, induced me to recall her playful suggestion that strega was also prepared with bat wings and lizard eyes—a true witch's brew.

On that day, Filomena's maid of honor, Emilia, was also present. She was the red-haired daughter of Alice Molinelli, chief domestic servant and stand-in mother for Filomena. Emilia and Filomena had grown up together and were almost sisters, though their social statuses were so different, akin to the differences between Calogero and me. I was always a little awkward interacting with Emilia because I had no idea how much Filomena had confided in her about our relationship. Emilia, for her part, had a country girl's sense of humor, and her uninhibited laughter always put me at ease. Emilia showed me much affection, as if she were a sister, and Alice was like the mother-in-law I could not inherit.

Emilia toasted me, though she was not drinking. "Giovannuzzo, *a salut' vost*, a drink to your good health, and may the strega keep away the maluocchio of the jealous women in your villa. Filomena has stolen their golden boy."

Filomena chided Emilia, but she loved the compliment. "Oh, Emilia, please!" Filomena's blush belied her annoyance. She darted a look at her father, who beamed, warmed by the strega and the young people around him.

"Filomena, you know how evil a jealous woman can be. If she can't have Giovanni, she would prefer to ruin him for anyone else," said Emilia as she pinched my cheek. She raised her hand overhead with a meaningful "Ehhh!" Her skirts rustled as her jutting hip emphasized her gesture. From another room her mother, Alice, beckoned Don Benedetto to discuss something of importance, leaving we three young people in the drawing room. At last we all could sit down.

Emilia was good for both Filomena and me. If I was a rough-hewn scugnizzo who needed some smoothing, Filomena also had hard edges that needed softening. Emilia did her best to train Filomena to show her feminine charm at the ceremony, for instance, not to grab the bouquet like a bunch of weeds plucked out of the garden.

Arriving a few days before the ceremony, my mother and sisters were special wedding guests of Don Giuseppe. They were lodged in the main house of Villa Valeria and were made to feel like the family they rightfully were. Much more than providing the groom, they were very much involved in this family event. Mamma and maid of honor Emilia helped Filomena's aunt arrange the gown. Young Giorgietta was instructed to be a flower girl. Elena and Giorgietta fawned over Calogero, as if making up for the long absence of big brother Giovanni. By the night before the wedding, the plans were set and there was nothing left to do but wait, perhaps the toughest task of all.

Finally, the wedding day! The entrance to the villa chapel, behind the main house, was decked out with garlands of fall-blooming flowers—dahlias, chrysanthemums, and veronicas and a few pruned grape canes. I passed a fitful night and had no problem meeting early with Calogero and Father Vittorio at the chapel. The good father made the rounds of several churches in the area. I did not have close male relatives or friends to usher wedding guests to their seats in the chapel of the villa, so this chore was done by more distant male cousins of Filomena, some of whom I met for the first time as they arrived at the chapel entrance.

Guests arrived, and after some confusion, all were seated. I was so disoriented and nervous that I really needed Don Giuseppe's intervention. I took my seat at the front alongside Mamma, Elena, and Giorgietta. We awaited the arrival of Filomena. I had not seen her since the night before. The anticipation of Filomena's entrance had my nerves on high alert.

And then she appeared in her satin wedding gown as she was escorted down the aisle by her father. In her mother's gown she was the personification of the beautiful fruit of Campania that Calogero later invoked. Though over two decades old, the gown was well kept and its satin still lustrous. It had required only a few alterations and a new train—this I learned from Emilia. Filomena took after her mother in height and bearing. She had her mother's slim waist, and from it the gown flared up her back to her strong shoulders that were covered by lace. The lace went over the bodice, extending down to her waist. Her neck was graced by her mother's golden pendant that now was inlaid with tourmaline, honoring her mother's birth month and the October birth of our marriage. The gown hugged her hips and reached down snugly to the abundant train at her feet. Filomena was radiant and happy, crowned by black curls under a modest tiara, behind which trailed more gossamer fabric.

The ceremony had to be especially heartrending for Don Benedetto. He was giving away his only daughter in a gown that inspired the memory of his long-lost wife. After his wife passed, he had had trouble looking at the gown—its satin seemed to have lost its luster. But on Filomena, the gown was like a rejuvenated spring lily.

Filomena's shifting her bouquet from one hand to a more delicate two was very endearing. She was a woman of strength and delicacy at the same time. I felt both protected and a protector.

Father Vittorio welcomed the gathering to this most holy and joyous occasion. "Dearly beloved, we are here to witness the holy matrimony of Filomena Minicello and Giovanni Ragnuno."

He looked at us, beaming, then directed his eyes to Calogero, who was seated in the first pew. "But before we proceed, the best man, *il testimone* Calogero Gentile, has requested permission to recite a few words in honor of the holy betrothed."

Calogero rose and pulled a paper from his vest pocket. He turned to face the assembled and addressed them with his original poetry on the glories of Neapolis, Naples, and Campania, and how Filomena and Giovanni were two beautiful fruits of its rich history, culture, and soil. Two of his stanzas stood out for me. Of course, Calogero later wrote them out for me on special parchment. They were especially beautiful in our beloved dialect, and came to occupy a special place in our wedding photo album:

Our beautiful, fertile, and productive Campania
Spawning civilizations from the Hellenes to the Romans
Eden of wine and olive, fruit of God's beautiful bounty
Whose citizens, oft assailed and downtrodden,
Have blest its conquerors with science, art, and poetry

May two of its beautiful muses, Filomena and Giovanni,
Extend our traditions and civilization
And help bear the fruit of Campania's future.
As they have opened me to its all-encompassing beauty,
A beauty of nature and of friendship—of caring and love.

. . .

After the reading, Calogero wiped an eye, then took his place as best man by my side. I loved the Italian word *testimone.* More than best man, testimone implied "witness," something that reinforced the memory and solemnity of my marriage to Filomena.

Calogero's reading of his own poetry heightened my emotions. When I first met Calogero, I would never have imagined him baring his feelings to an assembly of people, and all seemed to be in emotional harmony. I spied Zia Bettina in the pews, handkerchief in hand, dabbing at her eyes. Next to her was Carlo the sentry, for this occasion in his finest suit and bow tie. He grabbed Zia Bettina's free hand and gently kissed it.

There was love all around. I hoped I was worthy enough to justify the gifts of love from Filomena and her father, Don Benedetto.

5

MATING BIRDS UNITE THEIR FLOCKS (1904)

Two young fledglings formed a strong pair
Uniting three families in one combined prayer
For their safety, wealth, and enduring love
And strength embodied in the Mourning Dove

Calogero's poem evoked images of the intertwining vines of Filomena and Calogero, reinforcing our love. And fittingly, the post-wedding celebrations were in the main flower garden of the villa, between the main house and the chapel behind it. In the cooler evening the wedding party moved to the lower level of the chapel. The space was spare, but well-appointed with paintings and local sculptures. Though in the basement of a holy place, a generous bar served "holy" wines of the region, and even liquors such as the ubiquitous, if not iniquitous, strega. The offerings were rounded out by cheeses, salami, fruit, sesame cookies, and flaky *sfogliatelle* pastries.

Giorgietta and Elena attracted the attention of more than one young man. I was proud to see it, but I had to fight a feeling of protectiveness. The feeling made me especially grateful for Don Benedetto's accepting me into his family, accepting me as the son he never had.

My sisters' former lives as street performers made them facile in the tarantella and other dances. Elena barely had a chance to sit down, as most of the young men wanted a turn on the floor with her. Local musicians played the traditional mandolin and tambourine. Others played the Neapolitan bagpipes and oboe, the *zampogna* and the *ciaramella*. Those instruments grew up together over centuries playing many beautiful ballads from the regione. Their music was yet another wedding gift. Since we were married in the fall, the occasion was a good rehearsal for the Christmas music that would later grace our villas and streets.

Very surprising to all, Calogero asked my sister Giorgietta to dance, with my blessing, of course. I tried to hide the joy I felt seeing Calogero become so genuinely involved in the celebration of this most important day of my life. Ahh, the music, poetry, and beauty that could be Naples—a Naples not assailed by poverty, La Camorra, cholera, Vesuvius, or invaders, nor by Rome.

When neither of us had a dancing partner, I was able to chat a little with Calogero. We found two empty chairs beyond the dance floor. It was obvious that he was gaining in confidence, and his love of history was now growing into an appreciation of the law, or the absence of it in much of the *Mezzogiorno*, as he liked to call Italy south of Rome. I think Calogero liked the sound of Mezzogiorno because it was one of the few poetic references Northerners made about us.

Calogero—poet, historian, budding lawyer—also had a nose for business. "Babbo's tomato business is amazing," he said.

"How so?"

"Well, we accept that tomatoes grow well here, but it's easy to forget that in much of the world, tomatoes were almost foreign, almost like forbidden fruit."

"Eh?" was my articulate response.

"We embraced the tomato, made it ours—an indispensable part of our cuisine."

I looked at him, questioning.

"Well, we always speak of the uccelli, the birds that flew off to America, but to Babbo, their absence does not mean the loss of their business," said Calogero, now more excited.

"Ahh, yes, you mean export to America!"

"Yes!" And Calogero became poetic yet again: "In their New World nests, the *aucielli* still need the offerings of the parental culture of the homeland. They still need sauce for Sunday family dinners, so they still need tomatoes. Babbo can provide it, and I can help."

I loved that Calogero used the Neapolitan *aucielli* for *uccelli*, but in any dialect, many of us napulitani were migratory birds, and soon our calls would be in English or Spanish or Portuguese in the Americas of the New World.

Calogero admitted feeling a little guilty, thinking of business on this most happy and important event in the life of his adopted brother. But he was genuinely fascinated by his babbo's expanding business in exporting San Marzano tomatoes, and Babbo Don Giuseppe made sure to employ tutors who knew something of import-export licensing.

"Enough talk of business! Giovanni, this is our wedding celebration." Filomena gently lifted me by an earlobe and directed Calogero to find a young lady dance partner.

After the second day of celebration, Mamma and my sisters made ready to retire to their quarters in the villa main house. I went to wish them goodnight and a good night's sleep before their trip back to Naples. But there was something on my mind, no big thing, really, but it was clear that Carlo the sentry was often in the company of

Donna Bettina. I was in no way jealous, because Zia Bettina had an abundance of love for all her nephews.

"Mamma, why are they so often together? And why was Carlo one of the few sentries at the wedding ceremony?"

"Ahh, figlemo. You are observant and industrious, but there are things that a woman's heart is best at deciphering."

"Well, I did not know there was a mystery to decipher."

"You just expressed that mystery, the closeness of Carlo and Donna Bettina."

Paternosto! Oh God, how blind I am! "Bettina and Carlo resemble each other! He is small, and the difference in their ages …"

"Yes, Carlo is her son. His father was a brigand in Naples, fighting against the Northern troops sent down to Campania to enforce unification. Young Bettina provided the brigands food and shelter. Bettina and Carlo's father fell in love. Many here considered Rome a pillager, and the Northern troops its agents," Mamma said, casting her now saddened eyes downward.

"Mamma, I'm not the only villa scugnizzo! I can see why Donna Bettina took me in so willingly."

"O mio Giovannuzzo, love conquers many sins, and blessed be Don Giuseppe Gentile for allowing Bettina to show her love and caring. Don Giuseppe's last name is so appropriate to his nature."

I approached Mamma to kiss her goodnight. She appeared to be torn by contrasting emotions, more than the news of Donna Bettina and Carlo could provoke. I sensed she was not sure she wanted to go back to urban Naples. She smiled radiantly, but her eyes, glistening and at times downcast, told of darker secrets.

"Giovanni, caro, *mio tesoro, mio tesoro.*" I knew I was her treasure, but repeating it revealed a deep pain. She looked determinedly into my eyes. "Caro Giovanni, you cannot appreciate the joy in my heart that you are well, married, and associated with a beautiful and well-to-do family."

Awaiting the rest of her declaration, I took stock of dark, wiry and, still beautiful Donna Nunziata. Her flowing curls increasingly showing locks of gray was no surprise to me, for I knew the difficult life she led. I had inherited her high cheekbones, her noble chin.

"Mamma, I am crazy with joy that you are here on the happiest day of my life, and I know that Elena and Giorgietta will marry well and be a great support for you."

She took a deep breath, then blurted out, "We are here without your father, and you have not asked about him, though his absence must weigh on you."

I dreaded what might be coming next. I had trouble looking into my mother's eyes. Elena and Giorgietta looked only at each other, avoiding me altogether.

"Before we return to Naples," Mamma said, "I must tell you that your father met a violent end on the docks of Naples. It amazes me that you survived the life of a scugnizzo while your father, a street person in his own way, did not."

This volley of news appeared rehearsed. Once it was blasted out, Mamma gained control of her emotions and pinned me with her gaze.

I had both dreaded and expected this news. It saddened me, yes, but it also stirred guilty feelings—for I found it hard to work up genuine and deep sympathy for a father who even in the best of times was a distant disciplinarian with hard, cruel hands. My mother had felt those punishing hands too many times.

"Mamma, my father was not part of my life, even when we lived under the same roof." Mamma put her fingers to my lips, but I continued. "He was a man to avoid. I did not know how to escape his anger and violence. I could not stand how he treated the three of you."

"Oh, you could not fully understand the pain in my heart, Giovanni, when I saw how your father treated you and your sisters."

"We should not bring up such memories."

"I want you not to judge him so harshly. He fathered three wonderful children."

"And the stray dogs outside the farm also sire large litters." I was immediately ashamed of my outburst. If my father was a stray dog, did it speak well of my mother and the three youngsters of her brood?

"Please, Giovanni! Your father was a good man, even gentle, but poverty shamed him and made him bitter. He was confused and reacted the only way he knew how—by turning to crime and then to drink."

"I will be the man that you wanted my father to be," I said. "Don Giuseppe is almost like a father to me, and my new father-in-law has shown me love and respect. I will never disappoint them or you."

I could not hold in my emotions as I embraced my mother. *This is no way for a man to behave on his wedding day.* I was also thinking, *Please, dear God, don't let me be an uncaring father, as was my own.*

Blessed Filomena. When I returned to our wedding suite soon after and she saw the obvious signs of the eruption of my emotions, she put her hands on my cheeks, and then, through an embrace, she said softly in my ear, "You convince me every moment that I have married the right man."

That night I learned a good woman provides not only physical love and passion but also a salve for a wounded soul.

Mamma returned to Naples early the next morning. Don Giuseppe arranged the carriage and rose early to wish Mamma and my sisters a good trip.

"*Buon viaggio*, Donna Nunziata." He held her at arms' length, a hand on each shoulder—"*Fatti viva.*" Mamma took those words to heart. She made herself much more alive to the villa. On her frequent visits she often stayed with us instead of in the villa house. Filomena and I had extra room in our quarters, a small stone farmhouse adjacent to our parcel on the outer edge of Don Giuseppe's holdings.

Over the years, Filomena and I became specialists in the production of cheeses and dried, cured meats, and our products were in increasing demand in the area. Don Benedetto's family had many generations of artisans in the production and curing of *soppressata*, prosciutto, pancetta, and other pork products. He generously shared his knowledge and business, much as Don Giuseppe shared his land with us.

On our own, Filomena and I produced two children over the next three years—rambunctious Mario and stout, pretty Nunziatina, my mother's namesake. Both loved their uncle Calogero and aunts Elena and Giorgietta. Mamma was delirious over her two grandchildren. She came around even more frequently, as much as her obligations and economic situation would allow. She always came for *Capodanno*, our New Year's celebration. It was a humble affair, with Mamma, my sisters, babies Nunziatina and Mario, and my father-in-law, Don Benedetto Minicello, joining Filomena and me around the table. We always partook of lentil stew to assure a good year. Blessed we were to be able to fortify the lentils with our own pork sausage, *cotechino*. Wine was offered, properly diluted for our two *bambini*. Ahh, those were such beautiful memories.

But we Neapolitans cannot long endure happiness.

6

FRACTURED UNITY (1910–1911)

Migratory birds attempting to take off
From a troubled land, were finally aloft
Fearing the long dark dangerous night
They flew at last from the cavern into light

By 1910 Mario and Nunziatina were five and three years old. My family was growing and growing stronger. My love for Filomena deepened, and we both resonated in our love for our children. But outside our door the family that was Italy was becoming ever more unstable and unhappy, and the poor South, our miserable Mezzogiorno, was almost a forgotten stepchild. To me and to my companions and countrymen—my *compari*—the government in Rome was a distant parent. It was as foreign as the Ottomans in Turkey, the unified, resurgent Germany, and Austria-Hungary under the Hapsburgs, who had ruled us not so long before.

Calogero! Ma perché? Why do you have to give me a daily lesson on current events?

The powers around us were engaged in intrigue and shifting alliances, and we poor Southerners looked on helplessly. While the Mezzogiorno—Naples and Campania, Calabria, Pùglia, Sicily, and even Sardinia—was treated as a colony, the rulers in Rome, Tuscany, and Lombardia aspired to establish real colonies beyond Italy. They initiated a senseless war of colonial pride against the Ottomans to "defend" Italian interests in Libya. All they accomplished was to embolden the rebellious Balkans, making the Adriatic shores of Pùglia even more treacherous. I didn't want to know how much Rome had already invested in their southern adventures in Somaliland and Eritrea on the Horn of Africa. And right under Rome's nose, our own Italian South, our Mezzogiorno, was also being colonized, by absentee landlords, usually the *capi*, the bosses of secret societies. The existence of La Camorra, the loose alliance of those secret societies, was not so very secret.

In the face of a creeping threat, the unwise and unwary may distract themselves with their mundane daily activities. Filomena was not unwise, and she engaged me in an almost nightly ritual when the children were finally fed and asleep.

"Caro, we make a decent living here, but our customers are poor and getting poorer."

Filomena intervened as I was trying to read the November 11, 1910 issue of *Il Mattino* at the dining table in our kitchen, warmed by the embers in the stove. Though the morning newspaper was getting stale, it had to wait.

I tried to cut off the floodwaters of her argument. "*Abbastà*, Filomena! Enough, please! I know where this is going."

It was if I had said nothing. She was into her polemic yet again. Repetition had polished the eloquence of her argument, whose logic also seemed to get stronger over time. "Giovanni, will our children find schools as good as Don Giuseppe's tutors? And our customers tell me of the local bosses of the secret societies." She hissed, "They are so secret! They charge the few businessmen a fee for protection from other bosses. Soon they will knock on our door, *Santissimo Gennaro.*"

They would be surprised if San Gennaro answered, I thought, but Naples's patron saint dealt with much larger interventions. I tried to concentrate on my paper, but I knew the sermon well and knew where it was heading. Filomena held the reins of her galloping argument.

"I keep on telling you about customers and neighbors who have gone to America, Argentina, and Brazil. You know they are prospering because they find ways to send a lot of money home, and some of that money pays for our cheeses and salamis. Many have returned with stories of success and the good life on the other side of the ocean. They buy land and build houses here or they take their families over the ocean to live in America for good."

I think she exhaled all that in one breath. She paused for a second, like a great prima donna, and continued: "We should cross the ocean ourselves. What will become of us if Don Giuseppe no longer shelters us or becomes a victim of one of the societies' soldiers? My father loves you like the son he never had, but he is not well."

Was she going to tell me even more bad news?

"Giovanni, that newspaper will not help you out of our predicament. Listen to me!"

I folded the paper, already almost a day old, and placed it on the table next to my wine bottle and saucer of thick-skinned pickled lupini beans. Maybe it was an omen? The paper had a feature on three automobile factories that had opened in Northern Italy over the previous eleven years—Fiat, Lancia, and ALFA—while we were still using donkeys in the South.

I tried to look straight into Filomena's eyes. They still had that flash, and extra so on this night. Mannaggia, Calogero's history lessons had rubbed off on her, and he was now curled up with a book on history while I faced the opera *Le Fiamme della Filomena,* and the flames of Filomena were making me uncomfortably hot, temperature-wise.

She took advantage of her opening. "I know this is your beloved land and your own family is not far away. My own father and your protector Don Giuseppe are even closer. Both love you like a son. Our Mario and little Nunziatina, thank heavens, are growing up healthy, but Mario speaks only our dialect and his little sister already knows our expressions."

"Well, Neapolitan is a beautiful language, and it is ours," I said.

My words vaporized, unnoticed. "And what will be their future? We can leave the nest."

I tried to look her into silence, but she added, "And migrate to more fertile wintering grounds and then return. We can be part of the flock of the birds of passage, *gli uccelli di passo*."

I thought that she was not only an historian, but also a poet—probably descended from the Greeks. She even expressed "birds of passage" in Tuscan dialect. She stabbed me with leaving Italy, but also injected the hope of our triumphant return.

"This prime minister, this Giovanni Giolitti." Filomena sneered, and it seemed to me that she emphasized too heavily his first name, Giovanni. "He promises a lot, but people here are living in miseria and they're *mortifame*."

Well, she was right about the poverty and the hunger killing our neighbors. But she didn't stop there.

"Our business dealings show us that most are still illiterate." It seemed as if her voice then rose an octave. "That Giolitti is in the pocket of the Piedmontese and their local bosses!"

Just then Nunziatina cried out, almost shrieking. I ran off to her, feeling guilty that I was more intent on escaping Filomena's wrath than attending to Nunziatina's panic.

Nunziatina was on her knees in bed. "*Mia dolcetta*, why are you crying so?"

Nunziatina loved being called "my sweetness." She calmed

down, but her chest was still heaving, and tears dripped onto her white night apron, sewn especially for her by Great-Aunt Zia Bettina.

"Mamma hollers about birds every night!"

I hugged Nunziatina to my chest. She eventually put her head on the pillow after kissing me sweetly on my cheek. I covered her and walked meekly back to the kitchen.

"Filomena, please try to keep your voice down. Nunziatina can read anger, and if Mario wakes up, we have a real problem."

I raised my hand as if asking for prisoner of war status, hoping my hand would be a combined request for pause, peace, and patience. No luck. She looked my hand down and continued her argument from where she had left it, but at least at a lower volume.

"Mannaggia, Giolitti was born in the Piedmont, just like Cavour and Mazzini. Don't forget Mazzini's *genovesi* gave Corsica to the French not so long ago. Garibaldi's birthplace, Niza, is now Nice, a part of that same *la belle France*. Giovanni, we are foreigners in our own land!"

My wife has a nice French accent. No, no way on earth she is having a liaison romantique *with a Frenchman. At least there aren't any in our corner of Campania.*

"Yes, cara," I said, "if I didn't want to sell prosciutto, I would kick the arrogant, prideful Northerners and Romans out of our business. Their *superbia* kills me."

Filomena saw an opening. She went in for the kill, to impale my spirit on her sharpening diatribe. "They may kill you for real! The Northerners forget that Naples was flourishing way before Imperial Rome was founded. Back then the Romans came here to enjoy our beaches, our beauty, art, architecture. They knew Greek culture flourished here, even before their own compari were in loincloths, and Romulus and Remus were suckling at the teats of that she-wolf —*La Lupa Capitolina*!"

She is a poet! "But cara, if the Northerners think us animals, what will the Americans think of us? Only twenty years ago they hanged eleven of our countrymen in New Orleans, and that is supposed to be a more European city." *And French.* I kept that last thought to myself while Filomena lashed out with her fatal blow, almost in a whisper.

"And how many of us in Campania will be sacrificed to the colonial ambitions of our Northern masters?"

We shared a glance, each reading "Mario the recruit" in the other's eyes. I was impressed with Filomena's mastery of Roman mythology, her eloquence, and her logic. Indeed, Rome and the North were enriching themselves at Naples's expense. The words *birds of passage* stuck in my mind. They had been nesting there for some time.

I was also reminded, while Filomena railed, that she had added some weight to her strong frame, *better for nourishment over the long flight to the New World.*

"Yes, Filomena, I realize that we can be lulled into staying in our nest, while bad weather and birds of prey encircle us. Believe me, I have thought much of our future and the fortunes of Mario and Nunziatina."

"E poi?" Filomena repeated it in her best English. "And so?"

"Filomena, cara, help-a me spread the wings." I said it in English, a language I would need to learn much better. I repeated it in dialect, which wasn't necessary because Filomena read the resignation in my eyes. We would be taking flight.

Spreading our wings was an important step, but we also had to loosen our tether to the Campania nest: at the very least, to prepare loved ones, and ourselves, for the news of our intent to fly off to America. Mamma, Elena, and Giorgietta made frequent visits to our family. Our impending takeoff was never a central point of conversation. Perhaps we softened its impact by reinforcing how our families formed a supportive flock, one that could easily extend to the New World.

My mother was happy that Mario was named after her own father and not after her late husband, my father, the normal custom for firstborn sons. Even Don Giuseppe was named after his grandfather and Calogero after Don Giuseppe's father. Nunziatina was named after my mamma, Nunziata.

Mamma thanked Filomena for not objecting to Mario's name. After all, Filomena's father, Don Benedetto, had every right to expect his only grandson to be named after him. We made a solemn promise that a great-grandson of his would be a Benedetto.

Eventually, my mother and sisters became reconciled to our leaving for America. We were far from pioneers. After all, many uccelli came back, so Mamma held on to the prospect of seeing us again, and in Campania.

When it became apparent to all that we were America-bound, Calogero started retreating inside himself. He avoided me, in stark contrast to times not so long before when he would seek out his worldly friend, Giovanni 'O Scugnizzo.

One afternoon I found Calogero in the vineyard, showing unusually focused interest in a cluster of young grapes. I felt as if we had reverted to one of our earlier meetings. I positioned myself so that Calogero would have to include his old friend in the same field of vision.

"Calogero, you look so withdrawn and sad, caro."

Looking up and almost through me, Calogero forced out a "Ciao, Giovanni."

Time for my prepared speech: "Calogero, you know that Filomena, Mario, Nunziatina, and I will take a ship to New York, America. I wanted to be the first to tell you, but you know how fast gossip flies."

Calogero still seemed to find great fascination in the grapes.

"You will always be in my heart," I said. "I want us to stay friends—brothers, really. If it were not for you and your babbo, I would never have improved my life and met Filomena. You are the uncle to Mario and Nunziatina in my beautiful family."

Calogero finally looked into my eyes. His fixed stare was almost unnerving, but his eyes eventually softened, signaling both understanding and sadness. He sighed. "And if not for you, I would still be isolated and scorned by the rest of the villa."

"Calogero, fràtemo, my brother, I found your company so charming, while your mannerisms were such a mystery. You were the opposite of the person I had to be to survive in Naples and then in Campania. At first you were a challenge, but with time, we helped each other become more human."

I continued because I sensed the glowing of Calogero's spirit, the same signals I had received some fourteen years before, when the iron fence of the villa separated us. "You always impressed me with your command of the history of Naples. That history is now even more complicated and, yes, more tragic, since we were forced into a marriage with the Piedmontese in 1861."

I felt myself warming up to a speech. Filomena was having an influence on me. "You are very much needed in Naples, as Rome taxes us even as it ridicules us. Naples is pressed in a vise between the rulers in Rome and our own Camorra."

"And so?" replied Calogero with little hesitation.

"Your babbo's great dream is for you to study law at the University of Naples. Yes, the haughty, *i superbi* of Ferrara, Milano, and Florence can say what they will about us. They can beat their chests with the wonders of the Renaissance, with their language of Dante, Petrarca, and Boccaccio, but we Neapolitans have a history that goes back to the Greeks. We produced poets such as Tasso, who was driven from Sorrento by the Spanish. The oldest Church-established university in the world is right here in Naples."

I congratulated myself for remembering these facts—put to

memory for this very soliloquy. I felt that I should have expressed inaccuracies to induce Calogero to correct me. But I got his attention in any case. His intense eyes emboldened me to go on. "Since the Roman Empire, we have been raped by the barbarians, Saracens, Turks, Normans, French, and Spanish, and the Camorra. I do not need to recount historical details to you, of all people. Just follow Babbo's counsel. Learn our law and protect our rights and traditions."

Calogero had not a word in response. His eyes, still fixed on me, watered as his chest heaved. When we embraced, I realized I had not sobbed like this since learning of Don Giuseppe's rescue of my mother and sisters. This time I sobbed because I could repay, in small part, my hero and champion, Don Giuseppe.

Ahh, Mamma, Giorgietta, and Elena. Would I ever see them again? My own family of four would be challenged enough to reestablish in strange new America, as hospitable and prosperous as I hoped it might be. How could Giovanni 'O Scugnizzo, a young man of twenty-six, with only a little knowledge of English and a family to support, even think of uprooting and dragging along his mother and sisters? They were now somewhat established, living with a supportive family just beyond Naples in a lovely hamlet that appeared to have escaped much of the depredation that affected Napoli and the Campania countryside. Besides, Elena was now engaged, and our mother was still beautiful and was being courted by a man of means, an artisan who worked in leather and who employed two apprentices in his shop.

It wasn't as if we were moving to a different planet. Don Benedetto had been sending some of his cheeses and pork products to Mott Street in Little Italy, New York. The same store, a pork and dairy Salumeria & Latticini Freschi, carried the Sul Sarno brand of San Marzano canned tomatoes from Don Giuseppe's operation.

I tried to explain to Mamma and to Calogero that if we could not return to Italy right away, we would always be in touch. I would write weekly, and we would encourage little Mario and Nunziatina to do the same, as their education progressed in America.

How could we forget our Neapolitan families? They would forever be in our hearts.

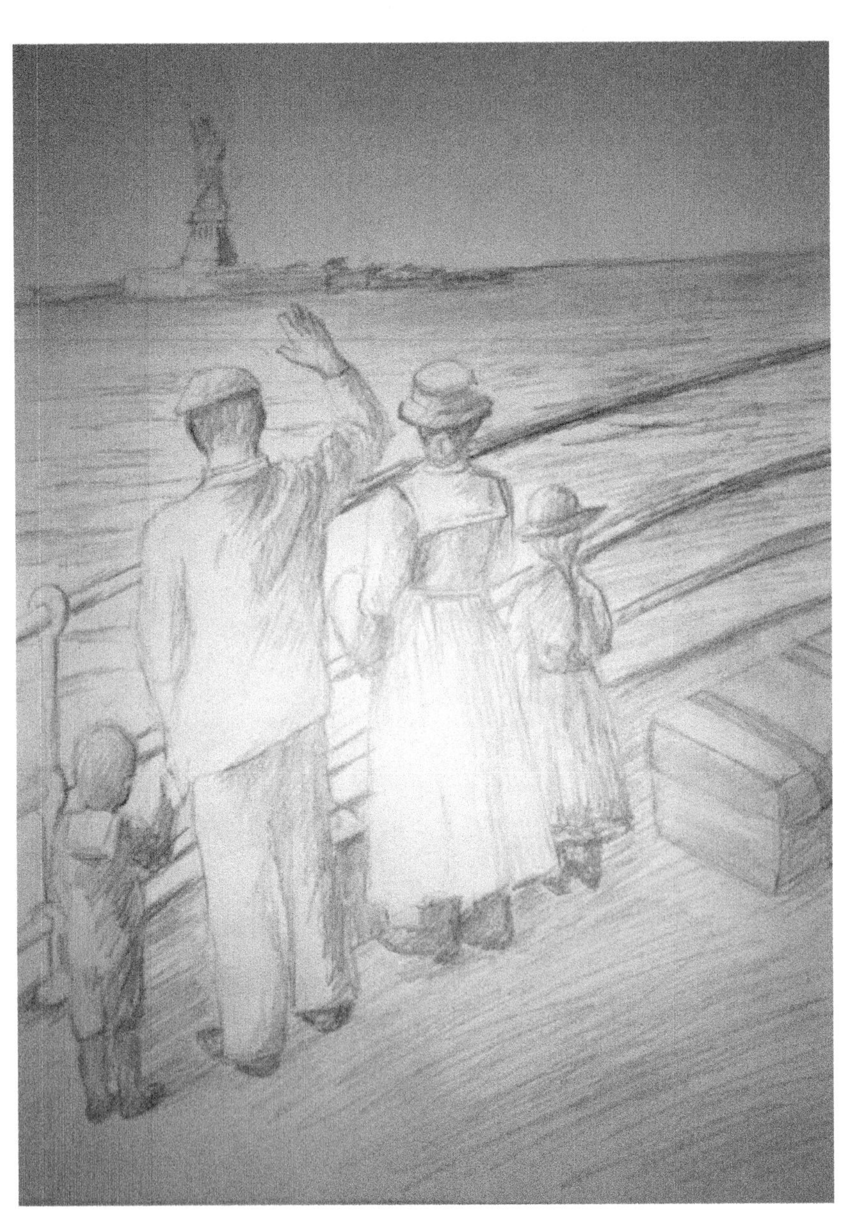

7

UCCELLI DI PASSO, BIRDS OF PASSAGE (1911–1918)

Vultures over Naples circled and swarmed
In their wake sulfurous ash forewarned
That the city descends into dark desolation
Take flight, Ragnuno, *find a new nation!*

All signs pointed to leaving Italy. Vesuvius had erupted in 1906, devastating much of Naples. It was a perverse fireworks display, celebrating Rome's winning bid to host the 1908 Olympics. Rome, to its credit, gave up the games, diverting Olympic funds to the rescue and rebuilding of Naples.

But cholera was ever-present before and after the 1906 eruption. It had ravaged Naples in the nineteenth century. Cholera returned in 1910 and 1911, and this time Rome did little to come to Naples's aid to confront the pestilence. It even went so far as a cover-up. But the folks in the streets, especially in the bassi, knew better. Yes, there was a *malattia*, a disease among them.

If the street people knew of the malattia, learned Neapolitans appreciated the advances that the British doctor John Snow and the German doctor Robert Koch had made in dealing with infectious cholera in the nineteenth century. I didn't need to go to Calogero for this information, but he was only too happy to tell me in any case. He sat back in his study, and now, with confidence and aplomb, fixed me with his stare.

Dammit, we brought him back too far, I thought, only half jesting with myself.

"Yes, Giovanni, those English and German good doctors were descendants of Rome's far-flung colonies, while many of Rome's current rulers still claim that cholera is the result of tainted air, *il miasmo*."

"Hey, my brother, I'm not one of the ignorant. Filomena and I boil all our family's water, just as Zia Bettina does in the main kitchen."

I think my comment registered with Calogero. His head drooped perceptibly, but he recovered and once again looked me directly in the eye. I knew this twenty-two-year-old was ready to jump to the university. "You know, Giovannuzzo, Dr. Snow's London really did deserve to host the 1908 Olympics."

Calogero's oratory was now gushing. "An eloquent symbol of Italy's failed potential is Dorando Pietri, so-called winner of the marathon. You know the marathon is the last Olympic event, the modern connection to the ancient Greek games. And what poetic justice for an Italian to win it!"

"I love that you use the word *poetic* in your poetic commentary."

He went on, finishing a story whose end I knew well. "Pietri was the first competitor to enter the stadium—but he ran the wrong way around the track. He eventually fainted and was disqualified for being helped to the finish line."

I knew this, but I enjoyed the narrative, especially Calogero's closing coda: "Even our defeats are operatic."

My foreboding thoughts about Naples hastened preparations for our family's 1911 migratory flight. Calogero unintentionally added to our haste: *Calogero, you make me think of history all the time, and most of its lessons are not good for we napulitani.* But when our departure date was fixed, late September 1911, Calogero increasingly tried to diminish the lure of America. He gave me a gift of Jacob Riis's 1890 book, *How the Other Half Lives*, about our destination, the Lower East Side of Manhattan.

"Giovanni, I know you are busy and have lots to keep you preoccupied, but if nothing else, read chapter five." Calogero had that look of distracted intensity. There were now two internal forces fighting for his soul—the desires to wish us a safe journey and to keep us in Italy.

I looked at chapter five's title, "The Italians in New York," then straight back at Calogero.

"Giovanni, he painted us Italians as desirable tenants, respectful but a little too gullible."

"Hey, mio fratello, I was a scugnizzo. Maybe I should call you fràtemo in our beloved dialect, my brother. I survived on Naples's streets and in the Campania countryside. There is no way I'm too gullible."

Calogero looked into my eyes as if reliving the first few moments of our friendship.

I did get around to chapter five, but more fascinating to me was Riis, the author. He was a solitary Danish immigrant who lifted himself from la miseria, abject poverty, to fame as a journalist. He did not have the aid of rich sponsors, not even distant cousins, in the old country. Filomena and I had a much better start than Riis, and our path was better paved. We had small loans from Dons Giuseppe and Benedetto, as well as some savings, and we worked long shifts and were able to save more. I was certain that we would not have to become pickers of rags and rotten fruit like the immigrants in Riis's chapter 5.

Wednesday, September 27, 1911, we boarded a ship out of the port of Naples for New York, New World. We avoided the floats that passengers of fewer means had to endure. They were quarantined on harbor floats for several days before boarding.

Mario and Nunziatina were wide-eyed and brave, and in some ways made their parents stronger. But I still felt the weight, the full weight, of being the protector and champion of our family. Before boarding we were screened by medical personnel. This was more comforting to Filomena than to me. "At least we are more certain that cholera is not a fellow passenger," she said.

I agreed by silently meeting her eyes but without expressing the discomfort I felt that our family had one of the better berths, though one far from luxurious. Yes, our second-class quarters minimized contact with poorer emigrants confined to steerage, emigrants who could be carriers of cholera. Was it only the fear of cholera and disease that made me want to avoid the poorer passengers, or was I a scugnizzo with superbia?

The ship was a converted German freighter. The *Berlin* carried American cotton and agricultural products to Europe, and desperately poor Italians to America on its return trip. Most of this human cargo was confined to steerage. They did not see blue sky until they arrived in New York Harbor, where they were transported on barges to Ellis Island for processing. Our family could associate with other first- and second-class passengers—*la bella gente*, the beautiful people. I found it difficult to separate "class of berths" from "classes of birth."

We sailed on the eve of the 1911 Turko-Italian War, yet another stupid war, yet another cause for worry as we traversed the Mediterranean.

On deck, I looked over at Filomena. "If I see an Ottoman Fleet warship, I do not know what I will do," I said, making sure that the children were out of earshot.

"Well, wave your American flag. I'm sure the Turks are not interested in eliminating fleeing Italians."

Amazing to me how calm Filomena could be under stress. However, we eventually passed the Straits of Gibraltar without incident and were Atlantic-borne to the New World. I carried with me letters of introduction to friends and relatives of both Don Giuseppe and father-in-law Benedetto Minicello.

How could I be so fortunate? I was sure that the spirit of Vesuvius had a perfectly evil fate in store for me. *That black spirit is probably gurgling in Vesuvio's bowels at the moment.* I kept pondering my incredibly good fortune and blessings in the unspoken belief that gratefully recounting them would forestall a counterblow. Then again, was pondering my good fortune a form of gloating, setting me up for that counterblow? Was Vesuvius's crater a glowing evil eye?

While many of my fellow travelers knew only worsening miseria, I had been taken under the wing of a rare landowner, one who maintained his land, who lived on it and managed it well. Therefore, he could count on the loyalty of his workers. It was serfdom in a way, though I did not like to use that word. I hoped Fortune's counterblow would not be so devastating.

The *Berlin* embarked from Naples, but it drew passengers from many points in the Mezzogiorno. Filomena and I dealt with the accents, dialects, and unique expressions of Campania, Basilicata, and Calabria and even those from Abruzzo and Pùglia on the Adriatic. Regional differences, jealousies, and suspicions were set aside. We were all Italians seeking shelter and sustenance in America. *We have to leave Italy to achieve unification*, I thought. Filomena expressed not quite the same sentiment in our semiprivate quarters.

"Sure, we get along now, but blood is thicker than water. Best we associate with our own kind."

According to Filomena, the history of our peninsula was too rife with jealousies, competition, invasions, and plots.

"Giovanni, we trust those who have earned our trust and who truly need us. You earned the trust of Don Giuseppe and my father. You earned it by hard work and by showing you were a man of honor."

"Just because a refugee speaks our dialect doesn't mean he is more trustworthy than one who doesn't."

Filomena responded with a raised eyebrow and a short, eloquent "*Dai*. Come on. Just you wait."

I was madly in love with Filomena, and I relied on her strength. But I was more inclined to follow my own judgment when dealing with others. Then again, I would probably choose to live near Neapolitans. At least I could understand their dialect and curses. As a scugnizzo I had learned not to give in to blind trust.

On board, it was even more obvious that our family was fortunate. We traveled together, we could go on deck, and importantly, we were educated. Most of our fellow passengers were illiterate men who already longed for their wretched homeland. They were driven to America to send money back to their families. Those *miserabili* were forced to mix together down in the crowded and dark steerage,.

We rarely saw them, and we would not have seen them at all if we hadn't "invited" several up to the deck. Here Mario helped me, and I am thankful he was not caught. I was proud of my little Mario —a guagliò with scugnizzo in his soul. He was only six but found ways to avoid the crew and sneak residents from the steerage netherworld to the light of day on the deck.

Mario was of a male lineage in which his grandfather was killed on the Neapolitan docks and his father survived as a scugnizzo. Was Mario's life in the New World preordained? Would he become an underworld figure, an eel always sliding out from the grip of American justice?

In America, I will keep my eye on this boy.

"Mario, I'm happy that you help these people make it up to the deck. They enjoy the air, wind, and sunlight and the smell of the ocean."

"Papà, I always try to be good. I just do what you want—help people not as lucky as us."

"You are a good boy, but I also want you to be a good citizen in America."

What kind of lesson was I conveying? *Do we just wink at minor transgressions for the greater good? Who decides the greater good? What kind of example am I for this guagliò?*

Life in America would be enough of a challenge. I would have to be resourceful but also respectful of the laws of our new country. Could I recognize the boundary between resourceful and bending the law? I resolved to be the best example I could be for my Mario and Nunziatina, for example by how I interacted with the miserabili.

Before sunrise one morning, Mario helped a middle-aged man escape to temporary liberty on deck. I thought middle-aged, but I am sure the people in steerage went through accelerated aging. He was stooped over but seemed to revive as the rays of the rising sun swept across him.

"*S'a benediggu.*"

I knew immediately he was Sicilian. I could answer only in my own dialect: "*Comme staje, signore?*"

He understood, haltingly replying that he was well and looking forward to America.

"I am Giovanni, father of this guagliò." I patted Mario on the head. "We come from Campania, outside of Napoli and not far from Benevento."

"A pleasure, and my deepest thanks to your son for helping me escape that purgatory down below." He bowed as he said this. His skin was deeply burnished, permanently so, as if it were of cured leather. "You can call me Stefano."

"Where are you from, Stefano? Your accent tells me you're Sicilian."

"Yes, from near Catania."

"Ahh, so we both live in the shadow of a volcano. I faced Vesuvius every day, and you Mount Etna."

"So true, signore, er Don Giovanni. And my wife and children still confront Etna."

"We all have enough problems in the South, and just in case we get complacent, the volcanoes remind us that life can get suddenly worse."

He nodded that resigned, wry smile, so common among us Southerners. "I hope to make enough to bring my family to America, and I'll do all I can to keep them out of steerage." Stefano stuck the knuckle of his straight forefinger under his nose. Just his gesture gave me a whiff of steerage.

"I pray you can do it," I said, carefully placing a thumbnail against my cheek, pinky pointing out—my meaning was that he would find a way. Luckily, he did not misread my gesture.

"I'm a bricklayer. May there be a need for my skills."

"America is growing and building. There should be work for masons and bricklayers," I said, more in hope than in certain knowledge. Filomena stoically took a step back.

Stefano seemed to look beyond me, to his new life. Was my optimism justified?

"I am glad we can help you steal a few moments of sunlight and ocean air, Stefano."

A ship official suddenly came into view. My eyes widened at Mario as my index finger, pressed to my chest, signaled downward for Mario to return Stefano to steerage. Mario guided Stefano, who turned to me, face full of gratitude, as if this small taste of salt air, sunshine, friendship, and freedom was a sign of good things in life yet to come.

I hoped that I provided a good example for Mario by helping people from other paesi and regions. *After all, America is full of people from different countries.*

We Italians drew class and regional distinctions, but the crossing did much to blur or even erase those differences. I thought of our ship almost as a mobile village. But I also accepted that in America we would join different social clubs, each drawing members from the same Old World village, or *paese*. Stefano would find comrades in a club of *catanesi*, and I in one of napulitani.

Shelter was more secure with those of the same village. They were the more trusted comrades or countrymen, i compari. I would soon learn that smirking Americans liked to pronounce *compare* or *compari* as "goombah" or "goombahs." We appropriated that ignorant American pronunciation, even calling the Irish and German Catholics our goombahs.

When the *Berlin* docked in New York Harbor, I turned to Filomena. "Look at the human cargo in steerage being transferred on a barge to Ellis Island."

Filomena silently watched. I thought she was too emotional to face me.

"Filomena, they look more like surprised maggots writhing in the light than people."

"We are also immigrants and can't afford the luxury of pity."

"See how they try to move along with dignity, carrying all manner of decrepit baggage?"

Filomena made no response and looked away. I could not make out Stefano in the procession, now moving along as if a single organism with many feet. In my history lessons I had learned how America received the human cargo of slave ships in the last century. Those Africans indeed moved as one, united by chains. In this new twentieth century, how much better off were my countrymen, my *paisani*, in those lower quarters? Much better, I concluded, or hoped. At least the paisani could look forward to freedom and opportunity. The Statue of Liberty told us so.

I did not voice this lecture to Filomena.

Look forward to freedom and opportunity? I asked myself. To Filomena, the answer was yes, but just before we left Naples, Calogero had felt obliged to tell me of the Triangle Waist Company factory fire, not far from Little Italy in Lower Manhattan. Factory owners had locked the building's doors so the seamstresses could not sneak out for a break. Close to one hundred and fifty underpaid Italian and Jewish immigrants, mostly women, died when they were trapped in a horrible fire. This occurred in March and we docked late the same year. Yes, freedom and opportunity—the freedom to fight for opportunity. Most of the goombahs we left behind did not have a fighting chance to better themselves.

While we were witnessing the docking from the deck, two young men appeared seemingly out of nowhere. They must have been stowaways, because I had no recollection of them. They jumped overboard, made a safe landing in the cold, oily waters, and swam to shore. Our fellow travelers tried not to cheer, so as not to notify authorities. The stowaways were last seen running to a waiting car and then to who knows where.

I almost whispered to Filomena, "Those two young men remind me of my scugnizzo days, but they're real urchins, urchins of the sea, like barnacles on the hull of the boat."

"Giovanni, stop trying to be a poet and think of our next steps in this new country. Don't praise those two miserabili in front of our kids."

"*Sì, amore.*" *Maybe I will come across them in this crazy new land*, I thought. *And why did they bypass immigration? Are they criminal elements?* I again thanked my good fortune at being rescued in the old country by Calogero, Don Giuseppe, Filomena, and her father. Could my own Mario and Nunziatina develop the survival skills shown by those two young stowaways? *I hope my children do not have to be tested like those two* guaglioni. *Who knows what awaits us in this new land?*

As second-class passengers, we did not have to go through processing at Ellis Island. Instead, officials came on board to examine and question us, but it was still a confusing blur. Behind a long table, a bored official with "Bureau of Immigration and Naturalization" on his shirt confronted me, barely making eye contact. "Last name?"

"Ragnuno, sir."

"Spell it," he said, his voice flat as if he heard unpronounceable names all day.

"R-A-G-N-U-N-O." I had practiced spelling my name in English letters.

"That is not *Ron-yuno* but *Rag-nuno*. Let us change your name so it is not so confusing, so it sounds more American. How about Runyon, R-U-N-Y-O-N?"

"Signore, my name-a is Ragnuno—the name-a of my mother, the name-a of … *sóreme*, my-a sisters!"

The wise-guy agent gave me a sneer. My English was not good enough to express that my name was my most precious possession. Filomena nudged me to go easy, for fear I would be taking the boat for an involuntary return trip. But I seemed to win this battle. The official recorded "Ragnuno" on our papers.

My winning streak was short-lived. The same official listed my hometown as Cercemaggiore in Benevento. This was impossible. Benevento is a province in the region of Campania, not far from Don Giuseppe's villa. Cercemaggiore is in the province of Campobasso in the region of Molise on the other side of the border with Campania. I decided to go along, since keeping my surname was already the bigger victory. Besides, my home was now America, and my paisani knew I was *napulitano* to my core.

Better to let this American feel the pride of this small victory. This I had learned from my scugnizzo days.

As we moved through the complicated processing, I told Filomena my opinion of the *stunad*, the dummy official who did not know the difference between Benevento and Cercemaggiore. Out of earshot of the official and of Mario and Nunziatina, I confided to Filomena, *"Cchist'americano nun capisce niente."* I expressed "This American doesn't understand anything" in dialect just in case we were overheard. Also crudely and on purpose, I mispronounced *cchist'americano* as "*cchista mmerda di cane*"—this piece of dog shit. Filomena's flaming eyes shot me stiletto darts. If I had not known her better, I would have thought she escaped from a *pazzaria.* Well, she did escape—from the madhouse that is Naples—'a pazzaria napulitana.

"Giovanni, don't let stupid pride keep us out of America! You can tell people back home that by insulting an official we lost entry to America."

"Sì, amore."

So, I tried to be on my best behavior. I could not even imagine returning to Naples with our family. The rest of the registration process went more smoothly. We even came across officials who spoke some Italian, and one or two actually knew my real paese near the province of Benevento, region of Campania. Our family finally made it through. Mario and Nunziatina behaved like heroes.

Since we bypassed Ellis Island, we escaped the *Berlin* directly to Manhattan's crazy streets. We escaped, but I knew that some of my paisani in steerage were already being processed for the return trip from Ellis Island back to Naples. These were the so-called mentally inadequate or diseased. Sure, who could not appear either infirm or mentally deficient after being kept in steerage like swine. For them, those poor disgràziati, Ellis was the Isle of Tears—*l'isola delle lacrime.* I prayed that Stefano made it through. Talk about a pazzaria of rejected immigrants on that ship headed back to Italy!

Going by the written directions of our sponsors, we hired a horse cart to Little Italy, to an address on Mulberry Street, where the napulitani were concentrated. The street was a pazzaria of pushcarts, people haggling with vendors, and many American scugnizzi running madly about. The driver found the right address. We struggled our luggage up four flights through a stairwell mix of stale aromas that Zia Bettina would never tolerate in her kitchen.

We knocked on door 4D. It was opened by a youngish man dressed much better than his surroundings.

"Pietro!" screamed Filomena. They embraced in the hallway before I could say anything.

"Giovanni, Pietro Donato is a second cousin of my father," said Filomena as Pietro grabbed my hand and directed us inside 4D.

"Ciao, Don Pietro. I have heard a lot about you. May I present our letters of reference?"

He dropped my hand, took my envelopes, and threw them on a table strewn with dishes, pots, and coffee cups. We were in a very cramped kitchen with an icebox, a coal-fired stove in front of a sooty wall, that one table, and a single window that looked out on spider webs of clothes lines that did not filter out the street noise.

There was no sink in sight.

"Welcome to America, Giovanni, Filomena, and bambini. You made it here, which says a lot about you. Letters are just words on a paper!"

Pietro had a beautiful handlebar mustache, a natty checkered vest that sported a watch chain, and a stiff collar and bow tie that made me feel uncomfortably warm.

I mentioned that the apartment was hot.

"Ahh, you have arrived in fall. You don't want to be here in midsummer."

Just then, a lean, dark woman with haunting azure eyes came out of a second room, holding a baby.

"*Mia moglie Celeste*," Pietro announced. His wife Celeste greeted us shyly and found a seat.

"Piacere, Donna Celeste." I bowed. She turned her attention to the baby.

I learned that the second room was a combined bedroom and

living room. There were no other rooms. A common bathroom serviced several apartments. The building had indoor plumbing. Other buildings, we later learned, were not so well-endowed.

It was comforting to be with family and to speak our beloved dialect. Nunziatina and Mario, four and six years old, did not seem surprised to be in an Italian-speaking country after such a long trip. They took the living conditions in stride.

Pietro was a prince. He found lodging for us that was palatial by the standards of the Lower East Side. Our family of four shared an apartment with three other immigrant families. There was a common kitchen and bathroom and a small all-purpose room for each family. We were all thankful that the plumbing provided water, though it was as cold as a witch's heart.

Through Pietro we found menial work at the Salumeria & Latticini Freschi store that received some products from Don Benedetto's villa. Mario and Nunziatina often accompanied us at work. Since we knew the business, we were entrusted with more responsibilities over time.

Mulberry Street was not Don Giuseppe's villa, but neither was it the bassi of the Naples waterfront. In the late nineteenth century, Mulberry Street could have been worse than the bassi, "the foul core of the New York slums," as journalist Jacob Riis described it. But to me, Mulberry Street in 1911 was Neapolitan slums with hope.

We were in America to stay. Even little Mario attended a few classes in the basement of the nearby Most Precious Blood Church. The church was established by the Franciscans, who were able to receive a relic of the blood of martyred San Gennaro, patron saint of Naples. America was a new and strange land, but Little Italy, with its Most Precious Blood Parish and Mulberry Street craziness, made it feel less foreign. And little Mario helped us pick up some

English. Nunziatina was a soldier and Filomena my napulitana Statue of Liberty.

Filomena and I worked hard, and we saved, but not for the return flight. My scugnizzo days and Don Giuseppe's guidance had made me appreciate the importance of timing in business deals. Don Giuseppe liked to say, "Discarded lottery tickets are worthless. To win tomorrow, buy a ticket today." Of course, Don Giuseppe favored less risky investments.

So, instead of longing to return to our Neapolitan nest, I pored over the pages of *Il Progresso Italo-Americano* and became aware of nesting sites much closer to Little Italy than to Campania. The Italian-language daily reported that many Italians were moving to Brooklyn, some even straight from Italy. Land prices were much lower in the natural wilds of South Brooklyn's marshland than in the urban wilds of South Manhattan's Little Italy.

What really caught my eye was that plans were finalized for the construction of the final link of an elevated train line along Stillwell Avenue in South Brooklyn's Gravesend neighborhood. The line was to link Coney Island, Brooklyn, and the middle of Manhattan. That Brooklyn train could only increase the value of properties along the line while also providing a means of transporting merchandise and customers.

The time to act was now, and businessmen Giuseppe Gentile and Benedetto Minicello back in Campania agreed. They reversed the normal flow of funds, extending a loan so that we could invest in a small one-story brick building just off Stillwell Avenue on (Gravesend) Bay Forty-Seventh Street. There, we eventually opened our own store. We lived in the back and stored olives, salamis, and canned goods in the basement.

The West End train running along Stillwell Avenue would eventually offer access to Coney Island, two stops away. In the other direction, it navigated through Brooklyn and into Manhattan up to Fifty-Seventh Street at the southern end of Central Park, a block from Columbus Circle. The whole trip cost five cents and offered a beautiful view from the new Manhattan Bridge as the West End train made its way over the bridge into Manhattan.

Business was good. We quickly repaid the loan in US dollars. The Bank of Italy was an ally. No, not a bank in the old country, but the Bank of Italy that was founded in San Francisco, California, in 1904. By 1912 it had branches in New York City and facilitated the loan from Naples.

Calogero lived our adventures vicariously, and he loved the connections to the Bank of Italy, connections I explained in our correspondence. First, the Bank of Italy was a leader in the reconstruction of San Francisco after the earthquake of 1906, the same year that Napoli was yet again devastated by Vesuvius. Second, its founder was the Italian American Amadeo Giannini. Il Signore Giannini was the product of a marriage between a Genovese and a Sardinian—a beautiful example of fruitful Italian unification. I loved the "Italian American" designation since it made no distinction as to regione or paese in the old country. We were all *americani* even if we were just Dagos to the real Americans, who usually did not distinguish the North from the South.

I could sense the excitement in Calogero's letter maintaining that the double-entry bookkeeping technique was invented in Genoa in the year 1340. He said it was natural for a son of Genoa to be a banking pioneer in America.

The loan currency was in American dollars, which were much more solid than the Italian lire. Our two creditors, the two Dons, Giovanni and Benedetto, kept their cherished dollars in a most secure and trusted place. I avoided referring to Giovanni and Benedetto as "Don" to my American acquaintances. I knew most of them immediately thought *mafioso* upon hearing the honorific.

I often made the West End trip into Manhattan and tried not to read too much symbolism into meeting up with the statue of

Columbus in the circle that carried his name. I could imagine the great navigator welcoming me, his humble paisan, Giovanni Ragnuno, who arrived over the same course of discovery. Not to worry that Columbus was a Northerner, a Genovese. We were all Italians. Why else would we put up with so much to unite into one country? Cristoforo Colombo and his Genovese descendant, Amadeo Giannini, were pioneering navigators, the first in seafaring and the second in banking. I kept these thoughts to myself because Filomena was not a good audience for such vocalized mental excursions. Besides, when I was in Columbus Circle, I was not "minding the store," so I had to be on my best behavior with Filomena.

Eventually the Ragnuno family made another investment, a down payment on a simple two-floor wood-frame house on Bay Fiftieth Street, three blocks from the store. The street was closer to Coney and less developed than Bay Forty-Seventh. We immediately set out to make the basement livable and to replace some of the siding with brick. Little Mario tried to help, but neighbors who had been artisans in the old country did the brunt of the labor. By 1915, ten-year-old Mario and eight-year-old Nunziatina slept downstairs, while Filomena and I occupied the upstairs. We loved the privacy but were always aware when our children were playing or arguing or both.

The neighborhood provided not only help in home renovation but also a large market. It resembled a mix of urban Naples and rural Campania and, yes, there were Sicilians as well. Business was so good that we added a second floor to the store on Bay Forty-Seventh.

In our Bay Fiftieth Street upstairs living room, I was sipping an after-dinner *amaro* and looked across at Filomena just returning from the kitchen. "*Poi, cara.*" I got her attention. "Well, dear, that meal could have been made in Campania. We are truly blessed."

"*Boh*, the greens don't taste-a the same. The friarielli are never as good and spicy as in Campania."

Would she say the same about the children we are rearing in Brooklyn? Let Filomena think Brooklyn is different from Naples. Maybe it is, only better.

"Filomena, you may not like the greens, but they are ours, and I think they are beautiful. And we grow our own, in our own way."

Her five-fingered cone bobbed near her mouth accompanying an elongated "*Magari*, if only!"

I stupidly persisted. "And those we don't grow we can harvest from the empty lots. Americans call our *cicoria* wild dandelion greens. I'm sure when they see us bent over pulling up weeds, they think being a peasant is in our blood."

Filomena did a wonderful pantomime of uninterest, drying her hands on the dish towel.

"And we can get *cardune* for free in the same lots."

"Hmph."

"You know something? Some American customers call it gardoon. Or even burdock, talk about a name destroying the desire to eat."

I had lost Filomena. She retreated into the kitchen. The amaro and Filomena's cooking made me a little sleepy.

Yes, we old-timers harvest cicoria and cardune and cook them according to the regional recipes in the neighborhood kitchens. Probably our children and grandchildren think we're strange, maybe even crazy to eat the wild mushrooms we harvest from our secret spots.

But this neighborhood is a thing of beauty. Pigeon coops on rooftops provide meat for our tables and fertilizer for our gardens. Chickens and goats still walk the neighborhood streets.

Our street language is a beautiful minestrone—an assortment of Southern dialects. And it is flavored with English, Yiddish, Irish brogue, and who knows what else?

"Giovanni, are you going to get out of that easy chair? Leave the amaro alone!"

"Sorry, Filomena. I was just-a counting our blessings. You know, when I think about it, our stores, gardens, and dialects tell me we could be back in Italy, but at the same time, in prosperous America."

"Yeah, and die from the cold, living behind shut, shaded windows like hibernating animals."

"But we have seasons, and every year spring is like a reawakening."

"If you don't lift your *motz* out of that chair, you'll need a real reawakening for sure." Filomena again disappeared into the kitchen.

My stake in the easy chair became stronger. As my body became more immobile, my mind went into higher gear. *Our salumeria produces mozzarella, ricotta, and provolone. We convert cuts of pork to prosciutto, guanciale, capocollo, soppressata, salami, fresh salsiccia, and other delicacies. We are satisfying the demand of the uccelli who haven't yet flown back to their Old World nests and who long for the milk of their mother's love.*

"Giovanni! Get up and help me in the kitchen!"

"Sì, amore."

Filomena threw a towel at me as I ambled into the kitchen. I dried dishes and tried to paint our American paradise to her. *Maybe we need a new set of china with American flag designs*, I thought. *Nah, we would have a lot of breakage.*

"Filomena, we owe so much to your family in Italy and Little Italy who taught us cheese- and sausage-making, at least beyond what I learned at Don Giuseppe's villa. The demand for our products is good, and growing, and the customers pay cash."

Filomena kept scrubbing and handing me dishes, her head down toward the sink.

"Cara, you have to admit, Sunday dinners in the neighborhood are family feasts of abundance. We celebrate the abbunnànza of America, and maybe we eat too much to forget the miseria of the old country. Every Sunday is Thanksgiving, and for the American holiday, we have antipasto and lasagna, and only then comes the turkey."

Silence. I looked over at Filomena. Her tears were falling in the dishwater.

The business grew, as did our responsibilities, but Filomena, Mario, Nunziatina, and I still found time to take the trolley to Coney Island or the West End line to Central Park in Manhattan. Getting off at Fifty-Seventh Street and Broadway, on the way to the park we'd pay homage to Cristoforo Colombo in his circle of honor. Filomena would give my head a sharp knuckle if I got too symbolic or carried away. That sharp knuckle to the head was just another way we napulitani expressed affection. It also reminded me that we went to the park to enjoy the zoo, the lake, the greenery. More importantly, Filomena and I could enjoy each other's company while Mario and Nunziatina frolicked in the playgrounds or in Sheep Meadow. We could sit on a bench and actually snuggle a little, sneak a kiss—ahh, a bacio while the bambini played, practicing their English with other kids. The whole scene helped me learn the English word *bucolic*, which was similar to burdock but much more poetic. Even we napulitani say bucolico, but never *burdocko*.

But Brooklyn was our home. As a pioneer of the neighborhood and a nephew of Benevento, I joined with some paisani to start a social club. The front proudly bore its name in two languages: "The Benevento Mutual Aid Society" and "*Società di Mutuo Soccorso di Benevento*." The Benevento club tied our Brooklyn neighborhood to the old country. We presented a plain storefront under a yellow, white, and red sign bearing the name and the colors of the province. At first, all members were men. Inside, we had an espresso machine, card tables, a small bar, and flags and pictures of the old Benevento, Campania, and Naples. The Pasticceria Testaverde pastry shop, three doors down on Stillwell Avenue, provided pastries and ices, which we enjoyed outside in front of the club when the weather was good. Sensitive business was always taken inside.

The club made a major investment in a Victrola record player. Filomena and I danced often to "Core 'ngrato," by the great napulitano tenor Enrico Caruso. The song had great meaning to us and to the paisani at the club. Enrico was one of us, and the song was sung in our dialect, written in 1911 by two immigrant songwriters from Napoli. Of course, just like Naples, the song was both beautiful and sad, a plea to a now-distant lover with an "ungrateful heart."

War broke out in Europe, and storm clouds collected over our Brooklyn piece of Campania. War eventually engulfed all of Europe, including Italy, and it came to be called the Great War. Italy was a US ally, so the loyalty of us greenhorns was not questioned. The Germans torpedoed and sank the British ocean liner *Lusitania* in May 1915. Over one thousand perished, and many were Americans. Still, America waited almost two years to declare war on Germany. And when it did, April 1917, President Woodrow Wilson called for patriotic Americans to enlist.

Filomena was dead set against my enlisting. She cornered me in the store. "We struggled so much to migrate to America and to make a life here. We have two young children, and now you want to go back to a Europe that is at war?"

"Ahh, cara, our president is calling for able-bodied men to enlist. Italy is an ally, and Italians here should answer the call."

"I don't see your fellow Americans running to enlist, the real Americans, the ones who were born here." Filomena accentuated the "real" with her right index finger describing a rising vortex, and her face getting closer to mine.

"But Filomena, America and Italy now have common enemies, and Italian Americans should be at the forefront defending our common goals."

"Don't be stupid! You are over thirty. There are plenty of

younger men who can enlist, American men." She hissed the "American."

"Oh, so I'm too old and not American enough? America took us in, and we should show our gratitude."

"Sometimes I think you're really stupid, and this is one of those times. You'll make a great stupid soldier, jumping at enemy lines without even thinking the consequences."

"Filomena ..."

"And gratitude! Write a letter of thanks to our great Wilson. And sign it 'Giovanni *'O Pazzo*,' your crazy, loyal son."

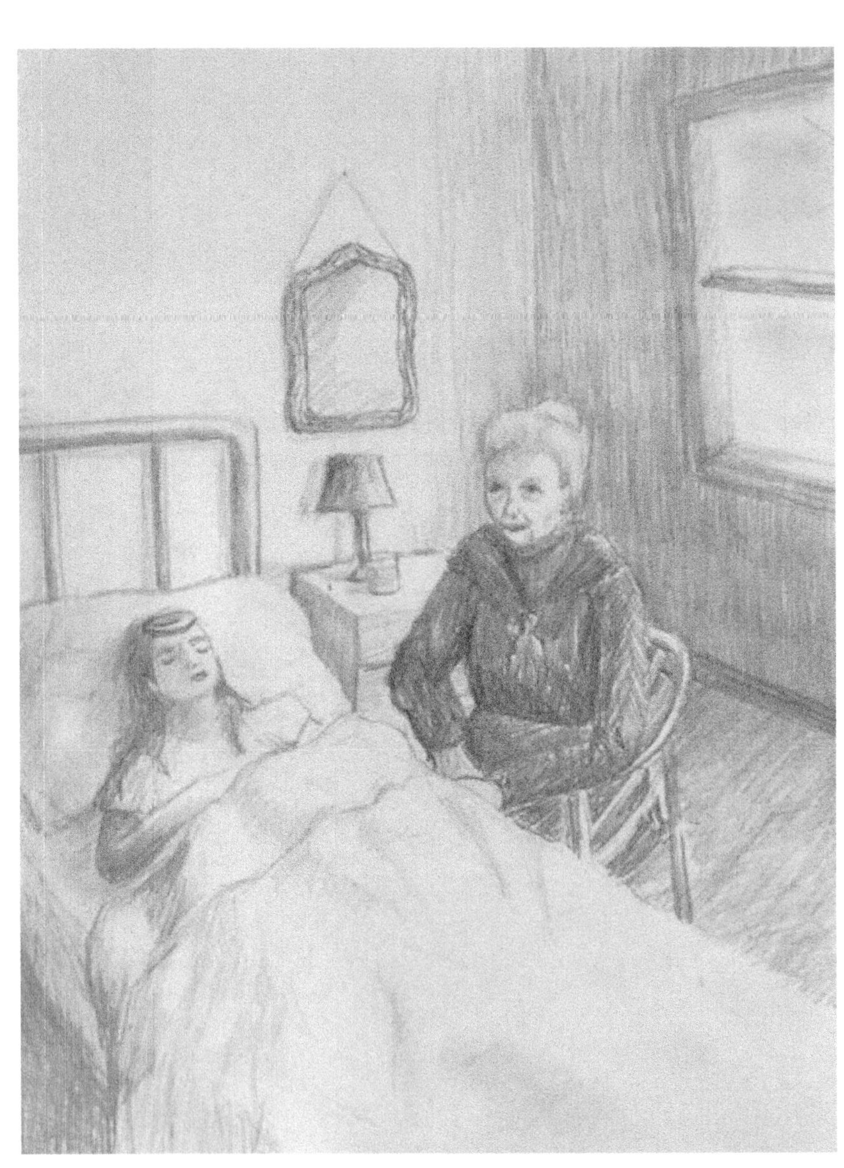

8

REFUGE BETWEEN WARS (1920-1923)

The mirror stared back, with its evil intent
Cruel in response to my wartime descent
Willow-the-wisp, *its evil bird's eyes*
Punished me with my loved ones' cries

I enlisted to fight for America in the Great War. Maybe I was stupid. Maybe if Filomena had encouraged me to enlist, I would have stayed in Brooklyn. Many Americans did not enlist. Most of our fighting force was drafted instead.

I saw action in the muck of St. Mihiel, France, in September 1918. Everything happened so fast, my basic training experience was a blur. Once facing enemy lines, I was just concerned with staying alive—yes, I confess.

The war was over soon after, November 11, 1918, Armistice Day. When I returned from the "war to end all wars," I was not keen to tell war stories. I really did not need to be a storyteller, because Filomena filled my head with news from the Brooklyn front

—Nunziatina had lost most of her hearing after a bout with meningitis. To Filomena meningitis was English for the maluocchio, the evil eye.

At home, the evil eye was the focus of conversation too often repeated. On one particular evening she cornered me in my favorite easy chair after dinner. I got her version of the eye, again.

"Giovanni, you know how bitter and resentful those war widows are. They live every day knowing their husbands will never return."

"Yes, a real tragedy that we read daily on their faces, *le poverine*." I was talking about both the Italian and American widows, poor things. Grief knew no nationality.

"You came back, but when you were away, you left our family more exposed to the widows' *maloik*!"

"Filomena!" I shouted reflexively, then regretted how vehemently I had expressed her name. It was not as if I had not heard her accusation before, but this time she was especially blunt. Mannaggia, she had me taking *Effervescente Brioschi* almost daily for my àgita. I could not believe how she kept on assailing me with this guilty verdict for leaving my family to wage war in Europe—leaving my daughter susceptible to the evil eye. She used the neighborhood expression for the eye—the "maloik." Even non-Italians used it, and feared it.

"But yes!" Filomena was not deterred. "Those widows, wretched disgràziate, can't even be *uccelli femminili*. What would female birds fly back to—the nest in the Mezzogiorno? Ha! No married woman in the old country would welcome a widowed desperate donna in her midst, especially a worldly one, and rich."

"Filomena! Please! You're composing an opera!" *She could write a great libretto.*

"Oh, I'm making an opera?" She repeated the question in dialect, "*Sto' facceno un'obra?*" and then she let me know that this opera was based on the "facts" of the old country. "The widows know they would be constant targets of the evil eye in Italy. So, they stay in Brooklyn and practice the maloik on others."

Well, for an opera, not a bad plot. They don black dresses of mourning for the rest of their lives. Instead of birds of passage, they become homebound corvi *—the black crows of the neighborhood—casting the eye on more fortunate survivors. Imagine the arias!*

Filomena snapped me out of bird land. "Giovanni, if you were around, we could have caught the signs sooner. We could have warded them off." Filomena did not tell me, at least not right away, how she determined that the maloik had in fact assailed our Nunziatina, nor how it was eventually exorcized. I learned details of Filomena's dealings with the maloik from Mario and from neighborhood gossip.

I got the lowdown from Mario when we were finally alone in the store. "Mario, why does your mamma blame Nunziatina's sickness on the eye?"

"Because of Donna Lucrezia."

Donna Lucrezia Lucia was still in her twenties but was one of the wisest women of the neighborhood. She had lost her husband in the Battle of the Argonne Forest in 1918, the last battle of the war. She didn't remarry, though she was attractive in her trim black dress of mourning. Married women shunned Donna Lucrezia, and even men were afraid to get too close. The word was that she knew the dark arts and no one, especially men, could keep a secret from her.

"Tell me more, Mario. It's OK, I won't tell your mamma you spilled the beans."

Mario gave me a quizzical look.

"I learned that from the other doughboys," I said. "It means to reveal a secret you were trusted to keep."

Mario's face was a mixture of relief and guilt. He let out a sigh. "It was a Sunday afternoon. You were in Europe and the store was closed. We had our big meal, and then there's a knock on the door. So, I open it, and there's Donna Lucrezia. Before I could even welcome her, she marched straight in. She only stopped to ask where sick Nunziatina, la *malata*, was."

"Ahh, too many strong women in the neighborhood," I said.

"By this time, Mamma is up and escorts Donna Lucrezia to Nunziatina lying face up in her bed. Donna Lucrezia asked Mamma to join her in an old prayer in dialect. They took opposite sides of the bed. Then Donna Lucrezia turned to Mamma and yelled, 'Give me a saucer, a glass of water, and a bottle of olive oil.'

"Pops, I never saw Mamma wait on you like that. She ran into the kitchen." Mario's eyes widened. "So, Donna Lucrezia places a saucer of olive oil on Nunziatina's forehead. Then she adds a little water to the oil."

I was spellbound, my silence compelling Mario to continue: "I looked from a distance, and the water broke up into separate droplets. She screams, '*Tene uocchio!* She has-a de eye!' She repeated that a few times."

"Ahh, women talk to each other like they talk to us men."

I could tell Mario was afraid to smile. "So, they flushed the mixture and repeated the oil and water test. Finally, on the third try, the water did not break up, and Donna Lucrezia said that Nunziatina was free of the maloik."

I never believed in the maloik, and I thought, *All that flushed olive oil imbued with the spell of the maloik probably was responsible for Naples's horrible plumbing and sewers, maybe even cholera.*

Though Nunziatina eventually recovered from her illness, her hearing was not fully restored, and I never dared tell Filomena that the exorcism was not complete.

Over time, instead of discussing the cure, I relied on consoling Filomena by words and deeds. I felt almost as much for her as for poor Nunziatina. I made a big sacrifice for Filomena—I bought the golden *cornetto* horn on Mulberry Street and wore it around my neck. The horn, which always looked to me like a hot pepper, had legendary power to ward off the maloik, but to me it also labeled me "greaseball."

No sacrifice is too great for Filomena. Who knows? It might work.

The first day I wore the cornetto, nothing was said by either of us. After dinner I helped Filomena in the kitchen, but not so much as to arouse suspicion. I was wearing the cornetto now outside my shirt.

"Cara, amore, Nunziatina is OK now, and we will work with her so she can overcome her handicap." My words were especially believable with the cornetto hanging in plain view, at least I hoped so.

"We will work together?" was Filomena's quick response, her eyes focused only on mine.

"But of course! Nunziatina is as strong as a bull, pretty, and very independent. She will be fine, especially if we work together. I see a lot of intelligence behind those charming eyes, and she acts as if she has no problem at all."

I looked straight into Filomena's eyes. *They are still beautiful, even more so than Nunziatina's.* I know that Filomena read my love for her in my own eyes.

I could not resist adding, and I hoped that Filomena did not hear cynicism in my tone, "Filomena, bad luck to the miserable witch who tried to put a curse on our sweet Nunziatina!" For effect, I repeated the malediction in dialect: "*Mala furtuna â streca desgràziata!*" A bear hug and a fervent kiss told me that I was believed. The kiss also told me I had better follow through on joining with Filomena in taking care of Nunziatina.

Mario helped me meet my obligation of care. Together we trained Nunziatina to enunciate, using feathers and mirrors as monitors of the breath and breadth of Italian and English words exiting her mouth. Nunziatina was so endearing as she tried to express in words the yearning look of her dark eyes.

Disease was all around us. It appeared to follow us from Europe. In 1918, people in our neighborhood had been getting sick from the Spanish influenza. No, I do not blame the Spanish. They just happened to be more honest about reporting their own cases. The Spanish called it the Naples Soldier, of all things. For all I knew, the influenza could have started in America, my America. Could we have exported it, with winged doughboys as the carriers?

Pandemic—how could such a beautiful word describe something so horrible? Perversely, older people were usually spared, but their children, young parents, fell prey and many passed away. And their children, the next generation of uccelli, were orphaned. Relatives adopted neighborhood orphans, and some relatives emigrated from Italy to do so. The flu spared Filomena and me. Maybe that cornetto did have some value. Maybe I was vaccinated in Europe. At least no one accused me of bringing the flu to the neighborhood.

My discharge papers stated "Battle of St Mihiel, France Sept 12-16, 1918 (8 battles, 4 minor operations, 1 engagement)." During my absence while fighting the Great War, and while Filomena was totally engaged in the battle with Nunziatina's sickness, our son Mario became very useful in the store—sometimes too useful. He engaged in yet another battlefront.

My young son seemed worldly beyond his fourteen years. Many of the Americans in the neighborhood called our store "the Italian deli." To Mario, they could call it what they wanted as long as they dropped in to shop and as long as they did not run up too big a tab. Mario tended to the customers with absolutely no accent, though he could speak napulitano when called upon.

Nunziatina helped in the store when her health improved, though her hearing loss often impeded interaction, especially with English-only speakers. While Nunziatina needed special intervention, it became obvious that Mario was no longer a fledgling.

While I was in Europe and Filomena was dealing with the maloik and the family, Mario spread his wings beyond the store. He learned new skills. And they had to do with oil. One skill was counterfeiting olive oil. The streets talk.

German U-boats and wartime disruption made it almost impossible, and very expensive, to import olive oil from Europe, and very little was produced in America, in far-off California. Argentina was even farther away, and its olive oil was even more expensive than the extra virgin Italian stuff. But counterfeiting wasn't too difficult. American cottonseed, peanut, and corn oil were available, and with the right herbs, the aroma and color of olive oil were reproduced. For authenticity, the mixture was topped off with about one-tenth volume of genuine olive oil. The ten percent that anointed the concoction was as if it were holy water—not only an ingredient but also a balm to the conscience of the oil alchemists, at least those who had a conscience.

I'm being too kind to the oil alchemists. Most were bootleggers with no conscience. They were making fake olive oil even before the war. If they were adulterating olive oil, what they did to Mario's character was even worse. And, mannaggia, Mario appeared to admire those guys while I was back in the Old World in service to our new country. These thoughts tormented me.

Came the morning of encounter. I was positioned on the elevated flooring behind the counter, looking down on Mario as he walked into the store. The high ground made my case more effective. "Mario, I know about your fake olive oil."

His facial features dropped, and then he bowed his head, making him look genuinely chastened. "Poppa, I'm so sorry. We never had oil to sell to our customers, and then Jimmie Taps and his buddy told me they could get some for us. I knew it wasn't real, but it got customers into the store."

I stared down, suppressing any inclination for a smirk of paternal pride. Scugnizzi needed no reinforcement.

"I promise not to deal with Taps and his buddies."

It was now easier to import olive oil, so access to the real stuff probably had a lot to do with the conviction of Mario's promise. "Mario, it's-a wrong to fool people. When you fool them, you insult them. You tell them you have no respect for them or for you-self."

"Pop, I'm sorry, I really am. They told me that nobody sells pure 100 percent extra virgin oil."

"So, you go along? Not only do you put our customers in danger, 'cause nobody knowsa what's inna the oil, but you get yourself in trouble, and also our whole family."

"Pops, I told you I'm sorry, and I won't do it again."

"Even when I was living on the streets of Napoli, I did not want to be dishonest with people," I said. "You know what *fraud* means? It means you make a living being dishonest, playing people for *chooches*."

Mario kept his head down, waiting for the storm to pass.

"You know a chooch is a jack-assa. I'd rather lose fair and square than be played like a fool."

Another look from Mario, but this time I detected more shame than anger in his eyes.

"They'll get back at you." I did not want to add "with the maloik" because I did not want to saddle him with guilt over Nunziatina's condition.

It did not take long to be confronted by uniformed personnel of the New York Police Department. An officer of the NYPD, accompanied by a federal agent, presented me with a subpoena to appear in downtown Brooklyn federal court for foisting fraudulent extra virgin olive oil on our customers. I was dwarfed by the FBI guy. He resembled many of the New York Irish I served with, and I expected to hear "greaseball" and "Dago" leave his mouth, but he was very civil and official.

They set up a court date and left. Filomena was beside herself. "You escaped a life of crime in Naples, and with the grace of God and wonderful sponsors like my father, you made it to a prosperous and respectable life in America."

She was working up to her crescendo. She covered her ears with her open palms, as if what she was about to say was too much even for her to hear. Then those open hands reached out to me. "You risked your life for your new country! Now you wind up again a scourge of the law!" Filomena used earthy dialect. I was either a turd or a jackass, and that was just for starters.

Amazing how Filomena could summarize my life in a couple of sentences and make it all seem so futile. But her rage was not directed solely at me. She made sure that young Mario was in earshot, and her look brought on the full power of the old country maluocchio.

I watched Mario and thought I detected a certain unexpressed pride in his being resourceful and independent, just as his old man was during his scugnizzo days.

I also thought, *The real test of the oil is that it can detect when the maloik has been exorcized.*

I had been through too many scrapes to despair. "My love, do not worry." I repeated it in dialect for greater effect: "*Ma, cara mia, nun stà anziúsa*, we live in a country of law and of lawyers. Young Mario was misled. I met a young man in the army from a good family in Brooklyn. His brother is a lawyer. I am sure he can help us."

That's what I said, but I thought, *Do I have scugnizzo in my blood? If so, who can blame Mario?*

My war buddy's big brother was young counselor Myron Pollack. He had an office just off the West End elevated line on Eighty-Sixth Street, between the Bay Parkway and Twenty-Fifth Avenue stations. It was a short walk to his upstairs office that emanated the odor of new plywood and fresh paint. *Did he just move in? This youngster better be good. I hope he's not training at my expense.*

Myron Pollack himself opened the door to my knock. He was maybe thirty years old, already mostly bald, a shiny bare top with a fringe of thick, curly brown hair embracing the sides and back of his head. Thick eyebrows over hazel eyes were separated by a surprisingly small pug nose. His lips were thick, but women might say shapely. He immediately took my hand and welcomed me in.

"Hello, Mr. Ragnuno, it's such a pleasure and an honor to meet the army buddy of my kid brother Mitchell."

I nodded, and Myron continued, "He speaks very well of you."

Myron showed me to a seat in front of his desk. On the wall behind his swivel chair hung a framed certificate from Brooklyn Law School.

He wasted no time. "Shall we get down to the specifics of this case? Between you and me, everybody adulterates olive oil, but some so-called manufacturers can be very unscrupulous, and then there is the matter of health endangerment to your customers, with the liability falling on you."

"Mr. Pollack, Myron, I don't wanna trouble with my new government. I served it in Europe, and now this."

"Your military service will be an important plus in your case, especially since in your absence you could not assert strict control over your inventory."

Mario's name was never mentioned, but it was drumming loudly between my ears. And I thought that "assert strict control over your inventory" was something only a lawyer could invent.

"We need to address the 1906 Pure Food and Drug Act," he said. "It's a federal law and was passed by Congress because people were dying from improperly mixed and prepared drugs and foods."

"Whatever you canna do; I just wanna get back to my bizhiness and my family."

"I think we have a good case, Mr. Ragnuno. May I call you Giovanni?"

Came my day in court. All that marble and those majestic columns were intimidating—Americans do a good job mimicking ancient Rome. We climbed many stairs and inside were confronted with more columns and statuary. Myron found our chamber. We walked through a heavy carved wooden door and were greeted by an empty courtroom—no one in the spectator seats and certainly no jury in the section to the left of the judge. He was alone in his very ornate room except for a clerk and a guard at the door, with the seals of the United States and New York State behind him. He was seated on a pedestal, expressionless, so different from my first impression of the Statue of Miss Liberty standing on hers. He was black-draped and had a generous upside-down horseshoe mustache that made him seem permanently scowling.

The clerk announced the case. We approached the judge. He looked at me and then at Myron, who described the service I had bravely carried out for my new country, my hardworking family, and my contributions to the immigrant community. He also emphasized that the community longed for the fruit of its beloved country of origin, Italy, "which is an ally of America, as Your Honor well knows."

The judge gave me a quick glance, then turned his attention back to Myron, who continued. "So, Your Honor, Ragnuno Salumeria & Latticini Freschi provides sustenance for the very loyal Italian American community."

He was just warming up.

"And olive oil, Your Honor, is more than a cooking ingredient. It is an emollient from an ancient and respected culture. It is a bond to that culture and is a unifying ingredient among this noble community."

This got the judge's attention. He looked Myron in the eye, and Myron took the cue. "There was no intent to mislead the customers, Your Honor; the label says 'Contains 100% Virgin Olive Oil' and the product does indeed precisely contain 100 percent virgin olive oil. It is a *component* of a mixture lovingly prepared to satisfy the discerning palates of this exacting community."

The judge looked down at his docket—at least that's what Myron told me later. I wanted to think he was also considering my wartime service to my new country. He looked up and stared at me, unblinking.

"Charges of fraud and violating food purity regulations are hereby waived. The plaintiffs don't appear to be vengeful, but I am afraid that your appearance here will go into the court record, and it may be used against you in the future. So, Mr. Ragnuno, now that you are better able to manage your business and are unfettered by wartime complications of commerce, I seriously urge you to oversee your family and family business, provide only the finest products, and strive for absolute honesty and openness in dealings with your clients and paisani."

I was surprised to hear "paisani" leaving the lips of Judge William Feurstenauer. Then again, this was America, a minestrone, a vegetable soup of people, languages, and religions.

I took minestrone to heart. Filomena and Nunziatina, going by President Wilson's edict, had developed one of the most productive Victory Gardens of the neighborhood while I was in Europe. Mamma Filomena, later aided by Mario and me, used our Old World know-how to produce an abundance of tomatoes, squash, peas, and eggplant. They fed us and a lot of the neighborhood as well. The Victory Gardens eased America's burden in providing food aid to the starving of Europe. So, if we birds did not passage back to the nest, by feeding ourselves we effectively sent much sustenance in our place.

Hey, we even produced figs from trees that had to be pruned and cloaked in tar paper and burlap to survive Brooklyn winters. Those ghostly trees seemed harbingers of death in January, only to come alive in spring and summer, providing figs in the fall for year-end holiday meals.

The community garden efforts also provided a sort of penance for Mario, who did not reveal that he was involved in other schemes during my absence. I learned on the street that he was pilfering motor oil from the Fort Hamilton army base between Bensonhurst and Bay Ridge. What was not used for our rickety company delivery truck, one of the first in the neighborhood, had good resale value on the streets. But slick activities, from olive to motor oil, were halted when I returned. Mario followed his father's commands and, I hoped, his good example.

Besides, the postwar prosperity made it unnecessary to work underground for dishonorable gains. America was well positioned to provide goods and commodities to Europe. Did Americans fully appreciate their good fortune that no battle of the Great War took place in their homeland? I meant our homeland. We Italian Americans were eating in the style of the rich of the old country, and Ragnuno Salumeria & Latticini Freschi could provide Italian specialties.

I drove the company truck to deliver large orders. Nunziatina, barely twelve years old, took the subway to deliver smaller orders to far-off neighborhoods not reliably or economically reached by truck. She used her eyes, poise, and intelligence to navigate by train. The number, color, and arrangement of the lights over the conductor in the first car indicated the line and the route. Most travelers were blind to these signs—Nunziatina proudly explained them to me.

She delivered provisions mostly to homes but also filled small emergency orders to Italian restaurants, which were gaining in popularity among non-Italians. Nunziatina also delivered lamb heads for Easter dinner. Customers were charmed by her presentation of those heads as she expressed "*i capozelli d'agnelli*" in her Neapolitan accent.

Mario became the main worker inside the salumeria, though just a guagliò of eighteen, in 1923. I changed the name from Ragnuno Salumeria & Latticini Freschi to Ragnuno e Figli Salumeria & Latticini Freschi for the roles he and Nunziatina, my children—*'a mia figliulanza*—played. After all, Mario was no longer doing business on the street, and giving him some standing in a legitimate business I'm sure helped his self-esteem. Mario dealt with customers and suppliers alike. In the back, he became the prima donna in the fabrication of cheeses, ravioli, and meat products, and he counted on Nunziatina's help as much as mine.

At the salumeria counter, he made sure to serve regular customer Keira O'Donnell, whom Mario liked to call "Cara Keira"—"Key-ra" in their language. Keira came from a small Irish area on the other side of the West End el, and she frequently stopped to chat with Mario, even if her visit did not result in a purchase.

Filomena told me more than once, "But Giovanni, for an Irish girl, she really loves-a Italian food."

"Well, the girl has good taste, and I think she's learning a lot about our food from Mario."

"Don't be a stunad, Giovanni! She uses the food to get close to Mario. He's-a the cannolo she wants!"

I ignored her allusion to the cannon-shaped pastry. "She seems like a nice girl, well behaved and educated."

"Eh, sure, she wantsa be educated about Mario."

I waved in protest. To Filomena, it was a signal to play on. Call me Toscanini. Filomena was Caruso.

"She never orders food with potatoes in it, no *gnocchi*, no potato *crocchette*. We Italians do a better job with potatoes than the Irish. Let them try to match our dishes!"

"But cara, when Mario is with Keira, I'm sure he's not thinking so much about new rackets and scams. Besides, she has police in her family."

I got a closed fist and bent elbow, but Filomena did not escalate to the more obscene open hand on the shoulder of the bent arm. "Ahh, IRISH cops!" She went off in dialect, but her message was clear. "Remember how they call us greaseballs and worse. They came over before us, and they speak English, and they're whiter, so they think they're the original Americans."

I was thankful she did not get off on the Irish monsignor at the neighborhood Most Precious Blood Parish on Bay Forty-Sixth. I said nothing to inflame her further.

Filomena was right, of course. There was something between Mario and Keira, and it was about more than food.

9

LETTER FROM CALOGERO (1921)

I perceive the twittering of uccelli left behind
Messages to which I am now fully resigned:
That the nests I did so willingly escape
Will always be part of my new landscape

The letter arrived at the store. Calogero knew the address well from his business dealings with our salumeria. Before opening the envelope, I imagined the honeyed fragrance of the almond blossoms of the villa.

Villa Valeria, Campania, 20 November 1921

Caro Giovanni:

Come stai, mio fratello? Doesn't the Italian—OK, Tuscan—sound so much more affectionate than "How are you, my brother?" I write in English so you can share this letter with your American friends and family. Just don't laugh too much at my new language that I have been trying to learn to aid my research. I trust you to be discreet with some of the personal items.

We see your mamma and sisters frequently. It is so beautiful that they all survived the war! Living outside of Naples helped. It is amazing how much Elena's and Giorgietta's children love their Nonno Giuseppe. Babbo actually wants to be called Nonno. I love seeing him so happy with children. I deprived him of that joy and happiness when I was young, before I met you, before you rescued me. I am so glad that someone is providing him the joy of dealing with grandchildren.

It is so fitting that our families are increasingly linked and your Mario and Nunziatina are part of it. It is hard to believe how grown up they are! What are they, seventeen and fifteen? They are much older than we were when we first met across our villa fence. I am so glad that you are back in America from the Great War. Filomena and family need you at home, though we Allies needed you in Europe when a certain Giovanni Ragnuno served.

We have witnessed, lived through, and survived yet another war on our Italian soil, not to mention our troops that served elsewhere in Europe. The history of the Italian Peninsula is so full of jealousies, suspicions, treachery, plots, coups, battles, rebellions, invasions, forced migrations, pogroms, vendettas, blockades, fratricide, and massacres. I would say we Italians—and I put us all in the same boat—are particularly cunning, savage, and warlike compared to the rest of Europe. I <u>would</u> say that, if history did not tell me that such an assertion is <u>untrue</u>. At times I despair that we humans in general are not fit to live in peaceful cooperation, but I am not writing to depress you.

I write to catch you up, to ask how you are, and to send a transatlantic kiss—un bacio grande. I hear that American men don't like to kiss each other. Ahh, if a kiss were the worst affront we made to each other! My affection comes through much better in our beloved dialect: Comme staje, guagliò? Nu granne vaso. Here I am full of expressive feeling, and I think how difficult it used to be for me even to make eye contact with another human being or exchange words in any language! But I carry on.

Yes, your mamma and sisters and our villa survived the war. I repeat it as if pinching myself to make sure I am not dreaming. Fortunately, ha! there was not that much action on the soil of Campania. It appeared that Rome was eager to fight our former northern masters, the Austrians. Many sons of Campania were sent north to train and then to face the Austrians.

The Austrians, in turn, aided by their German brothers, appeared to try to punish us for breaking the yoke of their dominance and then aligning against them. We Neapolitans can complain, and we do, about the actions of Rome and the North of Italy, but at least we are united—yes, a fractious, quarreling family, but it is our family.

Some of our local problems were from La Camorra, but Babbo's sentries were loyal and fierce, even keeping intruders away from Filomena's villa next door, to the great relief of Don Benedetto. Aunt Bettina's Carlo was a lion. I say no more.

Italy has another claim to fame: In losing the Battle of Caporetto, we lost more soldiers than any country has ever lost in a mountain campaign in any war. That tragedy was in the North, not that far from Venice. I have not seen the official tally of soldiers from the South who paid the ultimate price. But Italy overall paid a steep price in blood. That has to mean something to the leaders in Rome. We Italians, Northern and Southern, handled ourselves with valor and eventually came out on the war's winning side. Of course, we must always ask at what cost. Was this so-called victory worth the price?

I have finally enrolled in the university. There was my own initial reluctance to step beyond the villa, and then there was the war—your President Wilson's "war to end all wars." But I'm still young, and many of my classmates are as old as, or older, than my thirty-three years. I find the study and practice of the law fascinating. The complex history and legal traditions of Naples are special joys for me. I will keep on sending you articles of interest and newspaper reports, especially about relations between Italy and America. Our library at the university is a great source of current information. Some of it shows that Americans are reacting against the large numbers of Italians in the New World. I know it is not because of your actions—just kidding, my brother. The Roman-Germanic clashes and the Austrian-Italian battles from Garibaldi's time through the Great War are perhaps being replayed in America itself.

Be careful and seek allies among fellow immigrants, Italian and otherwise. Of course, befriend all Americans, as challenging as that may be. You survived from the bassi of Naples to your new life in the villa. I know you will continue to thrive in America. And as a scugnizzo and an immigrant, you don't need my advice on how to survive

Babbo Giuseppe is doing well. He is such a driven businessman. I think his interactions with the Milanese and Florentines showed the Northerners, some of them at least, that we are not all tribal, undisciplined peasants and mobsters down here. During the war, we napulitani did OK at home, not just on the battlefronts. The war provided jobs, for our women mainly, in Naples's productive munitions factories.

Overall we showed good business sense and that we were good citizens. Have you heard that the ALFA motor company became Alfa-Romeo in 1915? That year it was taken over by the napulitano engineer Nicola Romeo. Il Signor Romeo's manufacturing company in Turin helped the war effort, and last year his factory produced the first Alfa-Romeo car. Maybe you will see them in America. If you don't already know, Romeo was educated in Naples. I wonder if the patricians in Torino still laugh at his Neapolitan accent. I know you love how we napulitani can turn the tables at times, something I should not even mention to you, 'o scugnizzo di Napoli.

I also wonder, if a napulitano can find success in advancing a Northern industry, why cannot the South be fertile soil for industrialization? Sure, we have shipbuilding, but look at our harbor and beautiful bay, mio fratello. If we in the Mezzogiorno don't trust each other, how can the Northerners trust us?

I am fearful of the direction Italy is now taking. Yes, we "won" the war, but wars just lead to other wars. The losers suffer resentment, yes. But there is also dissatisfaction felt by the so-called winners. I see winners and losers within our own country. I am afraid there is much strife in Naples and in Italy in general. I know you have read about Benito Mussolini. He transformed himself from a socialist to a Fascist and now fancies himself a new Roman emperor. His dream is to expand Italy to the borders of Italia Irredenta: Ticino, Nice, the islands of Malta, Corsica, Corfu, and the Dalmation coast of the Adriatic—for now at least, because those are only Italy proper. He has perverted the ideas of Plato, who advocated a strong state of warrior citizens. But Plato did not advocate conquest, just a country with a strong defense.

Mussolini wants to see expansion of Italy into its vital space. And while moving into this *spazio vitale, all'inferno* with the people who currently live in those vital spaces—the French, Slavs, Arabs, whoever. A vital space can easily become an inferno—one does not have to be a poet or historian to envision it.

In our Naples Benito Mussolini's henchmen are making life difficult, especially for labor unions. Forgive me, Giovanni, for my crude talk, but Mussolini's supporters act like thugs. They terrorize people. In spite of this, or maybe because of it, the fascisti are growing in numbers. People and government officials are afraid to oppose them.

Last month, in a speech in Sardinia, Mussolini proclaimed, "We should not be afraid of new victims. The Italian border should run across the Brenner Pass, Monte Nevoso, and the Dinaric Alps. I would say we can easily sacrifice 500,000 barbaric Slavs for 50,000 Italians."

Giovanni, Mussolini is trying to subjugate, on racial grounds, the European cousins of Americans who consider you a member of an inferior race. Anglo-Saxons and Nordic peoples are embracing this so-called field of eugenics, this genetic justification for immigration restriction in America. Strong forces in America seek to keep out Italians (and Jews and Slavs), and now they can spout their openly racist reasons in the guise of the new science of eugenics. Forgive me, mio fratello, for bringing up such ugly business, but I have been following news coming out of America.

I fear Il Duce, our leader, may come to power, and if successful he will stay in power. Well, he will stay in power until Italy collapses or he meets his end. Nothing is permanent. The history of warring imperial families in Naples has taught us that.

Yes, I am getting carried away. I'm glad you don't see the pages I crumpled and threw in my wastebasket.

Don Benedetto sends his love and kisses, but his health has been failing since the end of the war. Babbo sends you a big embrace. And one, of course, from Donna Bettina, un forte abbraccio. She swooned looking at the pictures of your Mario and Nunziatina. She misses them, and she told me to tell you that Filomena is a very lucky lady.

Cu ammore,

Calogero

I read parts of the letter to my family and to my compari at the social club. The letter took a while to make its way from Campania to Brooklyn. A few months after the letter arrived, Mussolini and his black shirts marched on Rome. He was declared prime minister in 1922. Such is the orderly change of government in our democratic Italy.

Mussolini, the brutish strongman who caused a whole government to cower, was named after the diminutive Mexican indigenous hero Benito Juarez. "Don Benito" is so ironic. *Benito* means "Little Ben." But Piccolo Benedetto Mussolini became prime minister with no experience in any executive office.

I held out hope that the responsibilities of office would make Benito more mature and responsible. Hope is often the refuge of blind fools.

I wanted to say these things in my letter of response to Calogero, but who knew if the authorities in Italy were reading mail?

10

FEATHERED NESTS OF BROOKLYN (1923–1927)

We preen our young, warbling our affection
In nests set up for shelter and protection
While raptors perched on nearby limbs
Ever spy and plot with intent most grim

Ours was a family of migratory birds—uccelli di passo. In America we came across other varieties of birds. Keira was from a different flock. No matter. It was no secret that Mario and Keira were head over heels for each other. She became almost a daily fixture in the store. She was so respectful to me, I didn't care if I was being cultivated as part of the courting ritual. I was completely charmed.

Mario was in the back of the store filling an order for delivery, leaving Keira in front to chat with me. Those greenish eyes alerted me to her question. "Signore Ragnuno, how do you and Mario know so much about preparing the delicacies of the old country?"

I loved the way she pronounced *signore* in her slight Irish brogue —"seenyaireh."

"Well, I would not call them delicacies, more like survival food. They are the cheeses and salamis that our ancestors made to preserve milk and meat. The old folks didn't have refrigerators. 'Preserve or die of hunger.'"

"But you are so resourceful, and your survival food, as you call it, is *sew* delicious."

I ate up the praise, and when she went silento, I went on, bordering on bragging. "There were chickens, sheep, and goats, and a few lucky folks had a cow or two. Pigs were easier. They foraged and ate kitchen leftovers, even garbage not even we would eat. They almost fed themselves. Then we slaughtered the pigs to feed ourselves."

I gave her a look and raised an eyebrow, adding, "So sorry for being so, how you say, so graphic. And those pigs gave us soppressata, capocollo, prosciutto, and all those beautiful salamis including blood sausage."

I came out from behind the counter because I felt like I was giving a sermon. Keira put a gentle hand on my shoulder, confiding in me. "I think your people are like mine. You came from a poor background. You struggled, but you produced food, music, poetry, and art."

I was too polite to compare corned beef and cabbage to lasagna and *osso bucco*, but this colleen had a point. And both our peoples struggled as though colonies of either Rome or London—Calogero loved making those parallels in his letters.

"Keira, I don't have to tell-a you that the Irish did produce music, poetry, and art." *And*, I thought, *not to mention fine whiskey, beer, and ale, and they still do, during this insane Prohibition.* "Your people appreciated beauty even when faced with war, poverty, and famine."

"Thank you, Mr. Ragnuno. And we have more in common. Your people and mine are children of the holy Church, in Rome."

O che bella! Keira is so beautiful! So charming! And conniving!

Finally, Mario came from the back with his parcels. "Keira, would you like to join me? I don't have far to go. I only got a few deliveries."

"Why, sure, Mario. I probably know most of your customers anyway. Be good to see them where they live."

Off they went, and I resisted saying, "Behave, now." I could not help thinking that back in Campania, we did not trust Italians from neighboring villages and hamlets. But here in America we could form alliances with the Irish. Well, at least Mario and I were falling for Roman Catholic Keira.

It was not too difficult to figure out what the next step would be. Days later I noticed a ring on Keira's right hand, a ring with a lovely greenish stone that almost glowed. Keira made no effort to hide the ring. In fact, she seemed to favor her ringed right hand when all of a sudden gesturing like an Italian.

I tried not to show curiosity or even that I had noticed the ring.

Filomena, Nunziatina, and I ate almost in silence that night. I could hold it in no longer. After dinner, Nunziatina went to her room. I helped Filomena dry the dishes instead of retreating to my easy chair with *Il Progresso* and the *Brooklyn Eagle*. Filomena looked at me quizzically, and it wasn't because she thought I might break a dish.

I blurted it out. "I think Mario bought a ring for Keira. She wears it on her right hand."

"Oh, Giovannuzzo, I wasn't so sure I liked this girl, but a *bellezza* she is, and very sweet, and she seems to love Mario."

Filomena's eyes watered, and her chin trembled a little—the way I had seen it tremble during our encounters in Campania. I myself was barely able to squeeze out the question "Why is she wearing the ring on her right hand?"

"Who knows! Maybe it's an Irish custom. Maybe she's shy about coming out to you that they're engaged." Filomena's sentimentality hardened, as those dark, Moorish eyes bore in on me. "This is America—a land that has no traditions."

That evening Mario had not come upstairs to eat with us. We went downstairs and confronted him in his quarters, which were now all his since Nunziatina had moved back upstairs. Mario looked up from his phone conversation. He blushed, and then a fast "Keira, I'll call back" as he placed the phone receiver on his bed.

"Mario, figlio mio, Keira has a beautiful ring, and she's-a happy to show it off."

"Pops, I was meaning to tell you and Mamma."

How could my confident and streetwise son look so sheepish?

Mario composed himself and sat upright on his bed. "I guess you can say we're engaged. I mentioned marriage, and right away she says she wants an engagement ring to show my commitment."

"Well, I know you can be committed to a crazy house, but you mamma and I can see that you are crazy over that Irish girl."

Filomena put a bony finger in my ribs, but that awkward smile from Mario was beautiful.

"How much-a you pay for the ring, Mario?" she asked.

Leave it to Filomena to spoil a beautiful moment.

"Mamma, I got it from Pappalardo. I got a good price and I have a whole year to pay it off. I can do it."

"Thassa the engagement, and then the wedding band, and then you really gotta expenses!"

"Mamma, she helps a little in the store. She's a smart girl and can get work as a secretary anywhere. She's talking about night school to learn accounting."

Filomena sat on the bed. I remained standing. After all, we were in Mario's space, and he did not offer us a seat—I couldn't blame him.

"The ring has a Connemara stone," he said. "It's marble from west Ireland, where Keira's people are from. The stone is beautiful, no? I thought marble came only from Italy."

"Yeah, we Micks and Dagos have more in common than meets the eye." I got another rib stab from Filomena, though she had to reach up from the bed to hit her target.

Filomena rose, and so did Mario. They embraced, both sobbing. Sonuvagun, so was I. I hoped that Keira had hung up on her end.

So, just like that, Keira was becoming part of our family. She was such a lovely, charming young lady. And she was a good influence on Mario. I'm sure she kept him from any scugnizzo tendencies—most, anyway.

There was no official engagement party. The word spread fast, though. Keira spent a lot more time in the store. She waited on customers and even learned some expressions in dialect. I loved to hear her explain to Americans the differences between cheeses. As their names exited her mouth—mozzarella, pecorino romano, Parmigiano-Reggiano, scamorza—the cheeses sounded more sophisticated, even as her accent improved.

In the fall of 1923, she and Mario made the official announcement at the Festa di San Gennaro celebration at the Benevento Social Club on Stillwell Avenue. Her mom and pop shared a table with Filomena and me. Tom O'Donnell was such a jovial guy, and for an Irishman he sure could put away Italian food. Since the club was private, we could discreetly go against the edicts of Prohibition. After all, what is Italian food without wine and an after-dinner *liquore?*

Tom and his wife, Maggie, even got up to dance a tarantella or two. I knew he was on disability, but on the dance floor he was not on the DL—dancing limited. The evening over, I said goodbye to

Tom at the front door. "Tom, so nice to meet you! Just think, our kids have to fall in love for us to know each other."

Tom, big and red-faced, with a mane of white hair, gave me a bear hug. I tried to breathe, thinking, *I'd much rather be loved than hated by this guy, but what's the difference?* We were going to be *consuoceri*, co-fathers-in-law—linked through our children in holy matrimony. Mr. O'Donnell was injured on his job as a boilermaker, and it was amazing to me that he was deemed fit only for less demanding part-time work.

"Gee-o-vanni, so great to know you. You like to fish? We have to go crabbing together in Gravesend Bay!"

"Sheepshead Bay is-a better."

"Sure, and *begorrah*, you're right! And great speakeasies in Sheepshead! Doesn't hurt to befriend some Irish politicos," Tom said with a wink.

"You'll love Filomena's crabs *fra diavolo*."

"Well, if they're spicy, they'll make the beer go down easier."

After more embraces all around, Tom and Maggie walked under the el, crossing the street to their enclave.

Back home, in the darkness of our bedroom, Filomena told me that Mario was too young to marry as a twenty-year-old.

"Cara, back in Campania you married a certain nineteen-year-old Giovanni, two years younger than you."

"Bahh, love makes fools of all of us. Here you are, going on fishing trips with an Irishman." She half giggled as she rolled over to kiss me goodnight.

Mario was pushing twenty when he announced his early 1924 wedding to this freckled, green-eyed colleen.

"Mario, whassa the rush?" We were behind the counter in the store, and he could not easily escape.

"Well, it's easier to reserve the church, and the caterers have lower winter rates."

I let him off easy. *Hey, love goes well with practicality, and Mario does know a lot about catering.*

"You know, Pops?" said my almost twenty-year-old sage, "Keira always thought about marrying a dark Italian because her Irish name means 'dark.' Then her dark baby eyes turned green, she got freckles, and now her hair is that beautiful auburn."

"Where you learn-a that word? *Auburn* is pretty. But I like *castano dorato*."

"Hey, they both mean golden brown. See, I been learning more than how to fill ravioli."

"Va bene, so Keira is marrying Mario to live up to her name."

The wedding, oh, the wedding! It so reminded me of my own marriage to Filomena in far-off Villa Valeria. Keira was so beautiful, I wanted to faint. Her eyes were radiant emeralds. Her gown was just as beautiful as Filomena's, but it revealed a lot more of her shoulders, and neckline, than Filomena's gown had revealed some twenty years before.

From the back of St. Bernadette's, I looked over the seated wedding guests. One side of the aisle was populated by dark-haired people and the other side mostly by blonds and redheads. Filomena and I took our seats in front, on the darker side. I resisted turning around, but as Tom O'Donnell walked his daughter down the aisle, I just had to look back. Weddings stir emotions, and many guests were in tears no matter their hair color. Tom's slight limp was hardly noticeable as he escorted Keira, and I knew he'd be dancing that night at the reception.

I felt honored that Mario and his family were deemed worthy

enough for Keira's parents to cover most of the costs of their daughter's marriage to Mario, son of Campania. Filomena made sure I contributed in spite of the custom of the bride's family paying expenses. I think her generosity was provoked by fear of her in-laws' culinary inclinations. "Giovanni, you wanna have boxes of donuts and chocolates for your son's wedding party?"

I held up an open palm for peace, then placed it on my *pancia*, signifying that our stomachs would be happy. She smiled, and I was only too glad to spring for the wedding cake and reception pastries from Pasticceria Testaverde on Stillwell Avenue near the Bay Fiftieth Street station. Only a soulless person would turn up a nose at sfogliatelle, *zeppole*, *rum babà*, and *zabaglione*. Testaverde made the best cannoli—just the right amount of chocolate bits and candied fruit in the ricotta filling, and the shells were crisp the whole evening. I'm making myself hungry.

We also contracted an Irish-Italian band, making sure they could play Neapolitan as well as Irish favorites. A very talented musician, Dino Dellaviaria, played both the Irish and Neapolitan bagpipes—the union and the zampogna. I loved the name of his band—Sons of the Old Country—'cause it described almost everybody on Bay Fiftieth.

We sent an invitation to Calogero, but I did not expect him to make the trip. On the phone he told me that responsibilities at the villa and in the law faculty kept him pinned down. I think, also, he feared a transatlantic voyage.

In a letter he warned me not to brag about the Italian name of the Knights of Columbus Hall that was to host the reception in Dyker Heights: "The Knights were named after Columbus, but they were founded by one Michael J. McGivney. We Neapolitans don't like to acknowledge that Columbus sailed in the name of Spain, for too long our masters."

I silently thanked Calogero for his lessons of history and humility.

At the reception, spirits were available in spite of Prohibition, which was now almost openly ignored. Discretion was the word. No one wanted to expose the Church to negative publicity. Much alcohol was danced off. There were Irish jigs and some tarantella, and most people danced the same steps to both kinds of music.

The ballads! I *loved* the ballads. I never told this to my goombahs at the social club, but I always considered "Oh Danny Boy" one of the most beautiful songs in the world. And right up there, "Come Back to Sorrento." It sounded much better sung in dialect. Listening to "Torna a Surriento" that night, I clearly saw the moon rising over the Bay of Naples. Each side brought their heavy hitter vocalists. Tom O'Donnell's cousin Eddie stood in for the old sod. Mr. Dellaviaria's Irish-Italian son, Danny, a tenor, represented our side. Young Dellaviaria was a singing waiter at Scarola Restaurant in Bensonhurst. I think he eventually made a living in the opera business.

"Well, Mr. O'Donnell, *cchisto*, this has-a been some day" were my parting words to Tom as I shook his hand in the parking lot of the hall. Too much wine put more dialect and accent in my English.

Tom's happy face was flushed as he embraced me. "Well, Jaysus, Gee-ovani! I love having you and Mario as part of our family. God bless you, Gee-ovani."

"Ahh, please call me John. I hope I can call you Tom."

"Yes, John, call me Tom, please. You are now part of an Irish family. Just be warned that sometimes our love breaks out in fights." He raised an eyebrow, and I saw just a hint of threat in his humor.

"*Madonna*, sounds like Sicily and Napoli. Take care-a you-self, *mio consuocero*."

Tom's eyebrow arc accentuated, so I followed with "And don't hit me, not yet, anyway. It just-a means we fathers-in-law of the same married couple."

He smiled, and I said, "When they married, they also married me to you, and my Filomena to your Maggie."

Tom's eyebrows dropped a little.

That night, I exited our bathroom in my pajamas, parading my Irish jig moves to Filomena. Sometimes that woman has no sense of humor, but I think I saw a smile trying to sneak out. We tried to be quiet 'cause the newlyweds had moved in downstairs. The Atlantic City honeymoon was some time in the future.

In 1925, late in the first year of their marriage, Keira bore Mario a son, Tommaso John—Tommaso for Grandfather Tom, and John for me, Nonno Giovanni. He went by TJ. He had dark eyes and black hair, but his facial features favored Keira.

The neighborhood ladies in the black dresses of mourning—crows who hovered near the nest—counted the months on their talons to make sure the *novena*, the proper nine, had transpired between holy matrimony and the blessed birth. All was well. And my first grandchild, TJ, was beautiful!

Over the next two years, Keira presented Mario with daughter Anna and son Padraic—three babies in three years, and all were perfect. Mario and Keira won full respect from the corvi, who cawed and cackled praise in and out of earshot. To the delight of Filomena and Nunziatina and of my Irish in-laws, Anna developed beautiful red curly locks that crowned her freckled face. Her eyes were a lovely hazel. Padraic, in spite of his Irish name, after St. Patrick, was more a throwback to his grandfather, Nonno Giovanni. No matter, Mario and Keira's kids were loved by all. And all I had to do was go downstairs to visit them. The three were a *trinità di bellezza*, a trinity of beauty in any language, and they were well behaved, at least when I was looking.

Speaking of trinity, Mario was now in the triple family knot. His own with Keira's was intertwined with me and with his sister Nunziatina. Nunziatina was a rock. She had no fear of the New York subway system on deliveries. In the store she helped manage inventory, but American agents of law and order were a different story. They made a trinity of visitations to the store, occasions that I never forgot. Nunziatina was present for the first two and was frightened to the edge of panic each time.

The first visit was brought on by the counterfeit olive oil gambit. That one was partially resolved, but there was still a mark on my record that Myron Pollack said would be addressed. Filomena always reminded me with a question and an answer, "*Ma quando? Mai.*" But when? Never.

More serious was the second visit, brought on by my apparent connection with Benito Mussolini. Paramilitary Fascist Mussolini received a cold reception in Naples in 1922. He never really liked the South, but days later he marched on Rome and became Italian prime minister. Calogero had warned me the year before of the takeover of the Italian government by Mussolini. By 1924 Mussolini was almost a dictator, but many Americans, including my paisani, looked upon him with admiration for his strong and unifying leadership. I was not so charmed by *Il Duce*, as "The Leader" became known.

I held out hope that Mussolini and America could form a strong bond. Instead of migrating back to Naples as an uccello di passo, I tried to build a two-way bridge between America and Italy. The bridge was the Italian American Culture Center on the second floor over Ragnuno e Figli Salumeria & Latticini Freschi. The mortgage on the building was more than half paid—all the more reason to feel secure in expanding the building's use. The center featured a portrait of Il Duce paired with US President Calvin Coolidge over crossed Italian and American flags. I should have had more of a *premonizione* because this Coolidge was the same president who signed the vile postwar immigration restriction act. But my scugnizzo sixth sense was dulled by my comfortable Brooklyn life.

In early 1925, Nunziatina was a beautiful young lady of seventeen. She was usually fearless, though she had trouble expressing herself, especially to strangers. When those strangers were huge federal agents entering the store, she almost gave in to panic. The two officials—blond, tall, and imposing—inspired near hysteria. They wore suits and ties and were very much American, and they towered over Nunziatina. To Nunziatina they might as well have been dressed in the uniform of a foreign army. Each one grabbing an arm, they guided me to exit the store's front door. I felt extremely short between them and especially helpless looking over at Nunziatina's now openly crying face. It was a cry more of abject fear than remorse.

They did not handcuff me as I was led through the door to the black sedan parked in front. The neighborhood was alerted, and news of the visit got back to Filomena, three blocks away in our Bay Fiftieth home. Maybe the corvi were old and arthritic, but their gossip flew like raptors.

As I was being escorted out, Filomena, in her housedress, rushed in and past the agents, showing them anything but a Christian face. She mumbled incantations in ancient dialect, thankfully incomprehensible to the agents. I knew that those curses were directed mostly at me. She made a beeline to our poor Nunziatina, whom she hugged and kissed. Keira, bless her heart, acted as if part of the family—which she was. She competed with Filomena to embrace Nunziatina. Keira was slightly impeded, though, because, as her people would say, she was noticeably "in the family way" with TJ, her first.

"Don't worry, dear Nunziatina, Babbo will be back home soon," Keira said, caressing Nunziatina's cheek.

According to Keira's later account, Mario came out from the back and tried to look strong, but he knew better than to compete with two women for access to Nunziatina. He just told his sister "Nun stà anziúsa," clearly mouthing the words that she should not be worried, as he looked into her eyes. Before being carted off, I glanced back at poor Nunziatina, now fully wrapped in the arms of Keira and Filomena, and winked. She did not smile but stopped crying.

I eventually came home, unescorted by the law. And just like in the olive oil caper, no formal charges were made, though I was thoroughly interrogated, and there was some kind of record of the encounter. Counselor Myron Pollack, my Brooklyn Calogero, came to my rescue yet again. He even drove me home.

During the interrogation, a young hawk agent named Jackson seemed to give me the "eye." "Mr. Ragnuno, you realize, do you not, that in 1922, barely three years ago, Mussolini seized power in Italy, your birthplace and former country?"

"Yes, sir, I do. I am not saying that he is my leader, but I think we need to show friendship and understanding." *This kid is probably twenty-five years old, and he is showing me no respect.*

Jackson fixed me with an expressionless stare.

"And, Mr. Jackson, my country is now America."

Myron interrupted. "Mr. Ragnuno is simply trying to preserve Italian culture as it is understood and practiced in America. The center over Mr. Ragnuno's store is not political but cultural. Mr. Mussolini is just a personification of the current leadership in Italy, a country whose culture goes back thousands of years."

Mr. Jackson looked solemn, alternating his gaze between Myron and me. "Well, Mussolini seems to be putting Italy into good order, and he has many admirers in this country," he said. "But I want to make sure you understand that relations between our American president and leaders of other countries are established in a formal manner. We questioned why a foreign leader's portrait was on the same poster with our own president's."

I tried to look dumb and just shrugged, not wanting to say

anything that would detract from Myron's beautiful distinction between culture and government.

Jackson went silent. Finally he told me I could leave, which I could not do fast enough. Myron gave me a lift. On the way he invited me up to his Bensonhurst office near the West End line. To my surprise, he had a *machinetta*, a beautiful imported model for making espresso. He prepared two cups. There were no sfogliatelle, and I had no idea if that flaky pastry was against kosher regulations.

Myron advised me, "as a client and a friend," that the mood in America was getting less friendly to Italians and to immigrants in general. He looked at me across his desk. "Need I remind you of the Immigration Act passed just last year, and what led up to it?"

"Myron, I'm not blind. I like to think-a that we all Americans, but—"

Myron, out of character, interrupted. "Giovanni, you and your Italian relatives, and we Jews, are not as welcome here as we once were. We have to be on our best behavior."

I did not need this reminder, and I did not like to think we were like children being observed by our elders. Myron broke into my thoughts. "America actually likes Mussolini as long as he keeps order over there, on the other side," he said, pointing east. "A prosperous Italy keeps its children at home."

I thought that Myron was also saying that we should stick together and that Italians should not fall prey to anti-Semitism. I eventually felt the double threat emanating from Mussolini's Italy and from my own adopted America—an America I served in the blood and muck of St. Mihiel in the Great War. Myron's brother and I were fellow doughboys in the war. Myron and I had different backgrounds, but in America we had so much in common. His son was a good boy who loved to come by the store to stock up on goods. His mom kept a kosher household, but Myron Pollack Jr. had *goy* buddies who often invited him over. The thought of anti-Semitism taking root in my family was repulsive.

An America that should have been grateful for the military service of its new immigrants instead enacted that vile 1924 Immigration Act, an extension of the restrictive 1921 act. I followed this closely in *Il Progresso.* It was the subject of much correspondence with Calogero, my brilliant brother who understood both history and the law.

The act lowered immigration from Italy and eastern Europe almost to zero, and immigration from China was shut off. The Lower East Side—Little Italy, Delancey Street, and Chinatown—was made of immigrants from those three places. America knew this, and so did Congress and President Calvin Coolidge, who signed the bill.

An America that seemed to admire Mussolini's Italy did not see that much use for Italy's "escaped" Italians. I saw quotes from congressional representatives and senators saying that immigrants from southern and eastern Europe were a danger to the health of Americans already here. Of course, everyone on Bay Fiftieth Street knew what *health* really meant. And it was easy to understand in light of a new term I learned: *eugenics*, or breeding people as if they were racehorses or farm animals, and worse, preventing undesirable stock from breeding.

We Italians were part of the inferior stock.

Calogero had sent me parts of a 1924 speech by US Senator Ellison DuRant Smith. I think Americans would use the word *ironic* that I learned from someone across the world about what was going on in my own Congress. But there was even more irony. The senator's speech wasn't given in a tavern or a pool hall but in the senate chambers of the United States Capitol Building—designed according to ancient Greek and—ha!—Roman architecture.

The speech was recorded for all future generations, in all countries. Calogero underlined some parts for my benefit.

> I think we now have sufficient population in our country for us to shut the door and to breed up a pure, unadulterated American citizenship.... Who is an American? Is he an immigrant from Italy? Is he an immigrant from Germany? If you were to go abroad and someone were to meet you and say, "I met a typical American," what would flash into your mind as a typical American? ... Would it be the son of an Italian immigrant, the son of a German immigrant, the son of any of the breeds from the Orient, the son of the denizens of Africa? It is the breed of the dog in which I am interested. Thank God, we have in America perhaps the largest percentage of any country in the world of the pure, unadulterated Anglo-Saxon stock...

As I read these lines, I could see more stowaways jumping from ships in America's harbors. Those "huddled masses" now being denied entry were the forge that steeled America for the Great War. There were other ways of describing the Lower East Side of Manhattan, but I preferred the more poetic.

Calogero and I both saw the irony of a Mussolini in Italy extolling the superiority of the "Roman people," while at the same time, many Americans wanted to keep out us "Romans" to preserve their superior northern European stock.

Coolidge and Mussolini, I realized, did indeed have a lot in common, and not just their sharing the welcome over the entrance to my Italian American Culture Center.

11

FEATHERED HATS IN NEW YORK AND CALIFORNIA (1927–1932)

Beyond sustenance and the parental touch
Migrants induce a yearning in their clutch
Yet a father flew off leaving his nest
Before his young learned to meet their test

On the phone, Calogero told me what he could of what he knew. "Babbo not only survived the war, but came through with an even stronger business spirit."

"Don't I know it, Calogero. I made contact with wineries in upstate New York to ship rootstocks to your babbo."

"You're a great contact. Prohibition may have hurt the winemakers, but it didn't kill the grapevines."

"Well, caro, the winemakers are not yet dead either. Some sell table grapes, some make sacramental wine for the Church, and others, well, others make wine for their family's personal consumption. And some people have very large families."

He chortled. "Ahh, mio Giovanni, America and Italy are not that different."

"We come to the same conclusion every time we chat. Kisses to Don Giuseppe, Donna Bettina, and la mia mamma and sisters."

"Ciao, fràtemo, my brother."

As I put the receiver down, I pondered that Don Giuseppe first helped to "export" me to America. And about twenty years later he commissioned me to ship American grapevine rootstocks to Italy to be grafted to Italian vines. Some of those vines were still falling to diseases that had been ravaging European vineyards. I thought of the irony. "Native" Americans railed against Italian immigration, and Europeans looked down on American wine grapes. Now, Italians and Europeans were dependent on American rootstocks to save a crop known to the Romans. We Americans introduced the fancy disease *Phylloxera*, and just like the mob, we sold protection, in the form of rootstocks. Through all of this, the 1920 Prohibition Act in America was losing importance and was "clinically dead" by 1932. It made my head spin, even without my sipping wine.

My conversation with Calogero reminded me that I had a thing in common with those emigrating American grape rootstocks. We traveled in different directions, but the final product had value on both sides of the Atlantic. I too was a graft—an Italian rootstock anchored in New World soil, and my growing family was the American scion. My family in the Mezzogiorno, though rooted there, was receiving nourishment from the New World.

In 1927, who could have predicted that we were on our way to an economic depression? And that in five years Nunziatina would face the Depression as a single mother of four? She was twenty in 1927 when a dashing milliner, napulitano americano Angelo Charles Piccolini, came into her life. They met in the Garment District, in the Manhattan shop where Nunziatina assembled fine gloves for fine ladies and Angelo made hats of his own designs.

Angelo was often called upon to interact with Nunziatina in catering to ladies who demanded tastefully matched gloves and hats. Angelo and Nunziatina worked together, which led to their sharing lunch breaks. Yes, Angelo was sampling some of the best offerings of our salumeria, and eventually that included Nunziatina. I would never express this so coarsely to Filomena.

The lunch breaks and collaborations were going on for a while. Nunziatina became chatty at our dinner table when it came to Angelo.

"Mamma, Angelo works with me. He's beautiful and he does beautiful work. He makes hats, and I make gloves."

"Oh yeah, and together you make whoopee," said Filomena. I wasn't sure she knew the meaning, but Nunziatina sure did. Her dark cheeks seemed to glow and pulsate.

Filomena took advantage of her opening. "Well, if he's so beautiful, why doesn't he come around to show us his beauty?"

This ended the conversation. Angelo's name was not mentioned for the next few days. And then weeks later we learned, only days in advance, that Angelo and Nunziatina were to marry in a semiprivate ceremony in Little Italy!

Nunziatina's courage far outweighed her good judgment. She cornered us just before dinner. "Mamma and Papà, Angelo and I are in love, and we're getting married."

Filomena did not shriek or try to rip the heart from her own chest. She had seen it coming, I had no doubt. Her calm demeanor scared me, as though she were a capo directing a mob hit. "Disgràziata. Thanks for letting us know. And this Angelo from heaven doesn't have the courage to fly down to say hello, to know us, and to ask for your hand?"

Nunziatina, now in tears, ran into her bedroom. We saw nothing of her until breakfast. She sat in her spot, and Filomena calmly filled her coffee cup, asking, with no introduction, "When, where, and who's invited?"

"Mamma, we're getting married soon. You don't have to worry about the arrangements. And we don't need a reception."

Filomena looked a double maluocchio at her daughter. "Well, not sure we can make it if you get married during a bocce tournament or when we're expecting a large order of pork butt."

I would rather have seen Filomena become violent. Her cold words were much crueler. Head down, Nunziatina ran out to catch the train to Manhattan and to her Angelo.

The couple arranged to be married in St. Patrick's Church. Yes, it was named for the patron saint of Ireland, but the church wasn't the cathedral on Fifth Avenue. This one is still in the heart of Little Italy, on Mulberry Street. We all knew it as La Chiesa di San Patrizio—New York's oldest cathedral—Cattedrale Antica, as it said on the marriage certificate. The bride and groom handled the arrangements, though I am sure Angelo played the larger role. They lined up two witnesses from the shop, Vincent Rossi and Elvira Margiotta. There were a few friends present, including two sets of parents. Our greetings to Angelo's parents were, as the Americans say, stiff.

The marriage certificate was in Italian, and the priest, the Reverend Pasquarelli, was Italian. But the marriage license was in English, of course, and was signed by clerk Donald Leahey, so it was an Italian wedding in an Italian church dedicated to an Irish saint, and made official by an Irishman. We were assimilating fast. What bothered me most, though, was that Nunziatina had stepped way out of the bounds of tradition.

At first the couple lived under our roof. We had to accommodate them upstairs with us. Filomena had that sourpuss look almost from the start. Yes, she was more than a little put off by Angelo. Once, while we were waiting our turn to use the bathroom, Filomena turned to me and, with little regard that her voice would penetrate the door, loudly hissed: "*Chisto Princepe mi fa andare in freva!*" Filomena went up an octave to her operatic best. I could see the libretto: "This prince really annoys me!"

I put my index finger to her lips, which just seemed to goad her. She continued without even bothering to slap my hand away. "The prince walks around like he's God's gift to women."

I heard this expression many times, but it especially hurt when we were talking about a family member, the father of my grandchildren-to-be.

The next verse flowed smoothly and musically: "And he never helps Nunziatina around the house."

As if on cue, Angelo left the steamy bathroom that now reeked of his cologne. His black hair was combed straight back, and it was obvious he had shaved sharper margins around his generous sideburns. He looked at each of us, and with a curt "Buongiorno," he hastily moved to the bedroom he shared with Nunziatina.

Happily, for us at least, the newlyweds soon moved out to Broome Street in Little Italy. Their place was just a short ride on the Seventh Avenue line to their shop on Thirty-Eighth Street near Eighth Avenue in the Manhattan Garment District—the shop where they first met. Two years later, in 1929, they were parents of three children—fraternal twins Benedetto (Ben) and Giovanni (Johnny, or Jijjie), followed by younger sister Vincenza. Later in the year came the stock market crash, then the Depression.

Firstborn Ben was named after Filomena's father, Don Benedetto, as Filomena and I had promised. Don Benedetto was not well, and we were glad he was alive to learn of the baptism of his namesake. Jijjie was named after Angelo's father, who was a Giovanni like me. Vincenza, or "conquering," was named by Angelo. Filomena was not impressed. "Eh, sure, he sees a woman and all he thinks of is-a conquest!"

Nunziatina and I did not like the full name of Vincenza. She became Vina on all official papers. We were not conquerors but children grateful to be adopted by America. Compared to us, Angelo had come over from Naples very young, as a three-year-old. So, he was much more at home than we were in America—his hunting grounds. He spoke good English with only a slight accent, but I know he accentuated that accent when speaking to the pretty ladies. I am sure they thought him more "continental" than the typical Southern Italian peasants, *cafoni*—or gavoons, as Filomena often said, with derisive emphasis on the "oon."

Angelo was no gavoon. He dressed well and knew how to appeal to the ladies. They ate up his tasteful praise as they posed in his creations. Word spread, and many of his *clientela* came from Broadway and the fancy society of upper Manhattan. Even some Hollywood people sought his services when they were in town.

Dinner was over. No grandkids—a tranquil evening, just Filomena and I at the table. I thought back to our quiet evenings in Villa Valeria, when young Nunziatina and Mario were put to bed. But this tranquility was deceiving. It was more like a pregnant lull. I could see the approaching storm in Filomena's direct stare. In the old days I would read passion in those pulsating eyes, but I knew there was a different kind of storm on the horizon.

"Angelo is-a no angel. He has eyes that wander."

It was easy to tell that Angelo was a bird of prey, but I didn't want to add fuel to Filomena's fire. She pressed on. "When they lived with us, we was-a crowded, but at least Angelo couldn't take-a the ladies to the house. He would never do that because he was-a more afraid of his mother-in-law than the maloik."

I got up to grab the bottle of Fernet Branco and offered Filomena a glass of amaro. She ignored my offer of the bitter *digestivo*. Indigestion was guaranteed in any case. I poured my own glass and begged, "Please, Filomena. He works hard and makes a good living. With children, he will be very responsible, I am sure."

She read the lie on my face.

"Ha!" was her single-word answer. It hit me deep because I knew she was right, but then she had to make it worse by playing her advantage. "Just-a like Mussolini is learning to act civilized with his neighbors."

The amaro tasted extra bitter—my digestion was not helped at all that evening.

Later, in bed, I tried to allow sleep to take over my mind, but thoughts of Nunziatina prevailed. She was a spirited, stocky young lady, but having children so rapidly in succession had taken its toll on her figure. Or, as Keira would say, being so much in the family way sapped some of Nunziatina's vivacity. Her hearing impairment meant that her English was heavily accented—gavoonish, I am sure Angelo thought. I could sense his embarrassment when they were out in public. So, maybe Angelo made negative comparisons between his good wife and his fashionable female clientele.

Wall Street crashed in October 1929, and an economic depression was inevitable. I feared for the nests of my fledglings, all of them, not just Nunziatina's three young ones. I did not know what was ahead for us. I was in danger of losing my properties, and I was still a suspect at the FBI. The Italian American Culture Center had succumbed to the harassment by federal agents. The mortgage was not fully paid on the building that housed it, so it was getting difficult to hold on to the store. My customers didn't come around as much. When they did, they spent less. Or they came around to complain about the economy, borrow money, or buy groceries on a growing tab. But no matter the storm clouds, Brooklyn was my home.

Brooklyn may have been my home, but it was no longer to be

Angelo's. By late 1932 the Depression reigned, and Angelo announced he was moving out. He was going west to Los Angeles with an aspiring starlet by his side. She was a young lady, and I used the term *la ragazza* to emphasize the *young* more than the *lady*. But under the *chapeaus* of Angelo's feathered design, she was *molto elegante e bella*—the elegant and beautiful bird of paradise who was to accompany Angelo on his westward migratory flight.

Little Angelina Piccolini, Angelo's fourth child, had arrived in 1931. She was named after her no-good father while he was probably planning his escape to California. To Nunziatina, Angelo was a piece of carrion, a real scum of the earth, but *sfaccím* in our dialect captured that in one word—vulture food at best. Nunziatina loved little Angelina with all her heart, though she referred to Angelina's father operatically as sfa-CHEEM! Her hearing deficiency tended to move her operatic renditions far higher than what Americans would consider genteel volume.

Then, shortly before Angelo made his great escape, Nunziatina learned that she was carrying the sfaccím's fifth child.

Years later, she explained to her kids that she had all she could manage to raise four. A fifth meant that five would starve. So, she made a "strategic" decision, not very different from a mother cat eating her kittens to survive a real threat, to live another day, to raise more kittens. Through connections in Brooklyn and Little Italy, an abortion of unborn child number five was arranged. She confided in me, but not in Filomena, though I am sure my wife found out through neighborhood gossip and the channels through which the evil eye is cast.

Nunziatina let Angelo know this consequence of deserting his family. She also made a point of dropping off baby Angelina with a supply of diapers at Angelo's shop. Angelo's shop was more than a workplace, of course. It was also his studio. The French say *atelier*, the place where Angelo's genius, great taste, and skill were converted into such divine crowning chapeaus, odes to the beauty of their wearers. A crying baby and dirty, smelly diapers were not conducive to elegant fashion and high culture. Angelo's face was one of torment, as if in purgatory before being elevated to his California heaven.

"Papà, he wanted to die when he saw me and Angelina. I know this hefty peasant girl he married was so different from his shapely and elegant clients."

We were in her living room in a three-story walk-up on Avenue T, near the Ss. Simon and Jude Parish.

"Ahh, Nunziatina" was all I could say, munching on a taralle dipped in espresso.

"I made sure that I showed up in a housedress. Maybe when his beautiful clients saw me, they lost some of their admiration for Angelo."

"I bet you pushed him to leave for California sooner than he planned."

Of course, Nunziatina pushed Angelo extra hard by making sure her mouth was as coarse as her dress. "Let's see you deal with your daughter while you are dealing with the whores that you love to serve."

Nunziatina recited this line to me like an actress in a Greek tragedy. She used the Neapolitan *puttane* for "whores"—definitely a stronger word, and one more easily accompanying the maloik.

I was sure that those encounters hastened Angelo's move west. Certainly, Angelo also feared being too close to me and especially to Filomena. My wife was a firm believer in evil spells, and Angelo probably felt that staying too close to his mother-in-law would invite a curse. Oh, sure, he was modern and continental, and he could talk issues and art with his lovely clientela and with their sugar daddy patrons. But I also know that the Old World tugged on his soul and that witchcraft was like a menacing moon rising over a dark horizon.

I suspected that Angelo thought not only of escape but also of the tough times ahead for Nunziatina. How could a man with any residue of decency not think of the consequences of his actions? I bet he suppressed those thoughts by rationalizing: *Yes, these are tough times, and tougher ahead. But after all, Nunziatina has her father, her Papà Giovanni.*

Tante grazie, Angelo, figlio di puttana. I gave a diabolical thanks to the SOB throughout this whole episode, but I have a stained soul for impugning the character of his mother, second grandmother of Nunziatina's kids.

Nunziatina found a dress shop near Avenue T. She also did piecework at home, once again making fine gloves for ladies at a salary clearly inferior to those paid to the men in her shop. She had to take the subway to lower Manhattan every week to deliver the gloves to the shop near Delancey Street and receive her fee.

During America's Great Depression, the movies coming out of Angelo's new Hollywood home were part of Brooklyn's escape from the unrelenting hard times. Brooklyn and the rest of America could get lost in those party scenes projected on the screen, at least before the lights went back on in the theater. I wanted to believe Nunziatina's small comfort in the Hollywood glow somehow got back to Angelo's conscience. But for years, Nunziatina received nothing from Angelo, no money, no news, *niente*. But indirectly, Hollywood helped Nunziatina, especially on Wednesday nights. Local theaters offered a free piece of chinaware on those special nights. Years later, Vina inherited a full set of Hollywood china from Mamma Nunziatina.

Wednesday was movie china night, and on Thursday Nunziatina religiously confessed her one mortal sin at the Ss. Simon and Jude Church. She lived with that lost child daily, and daily there were bills to pay and mouths to feed. Nunziatina felt that she was in no state of grace to be able to put Old World curses, spells, incantations, or evil eyes on Angelo. Besides, none of that would put food on the table. She took in two boarders and was once again thankful she lived closer to me and to Mario. Her brother Mario tried to help as much as the responsibilities of his own growing family allowed. Nunziatina also hired out to clean apartments and homes. She had heard stories of how her paternal grandmother—yes, another Nunziata—once lived in the vermin-infested filth of the low quarters of Naples. She wondered aloud to me if she had materially improved her own lot.

Jijjie, Ben, and young sis Vina became fixtures in the store, where I had to keep an eye peeled to shoo the numbers runners away from the adolescent twins. But I had to confess that I wanted to see those runners myself when a special number was due. Big ones were the day and month of a grandchild's birthday. Another was 246 for St. John's Day, June 24. I counted on the Americans mistakenly putting the month first so that 624 entrants were eliminated, leaving fewer winners to "split the pot," as the Americans say. My habits were always reminders that I had the traits of a scugnizzo in my blood and, that without a doubt, I had passed them along to son Mario and to Nunziatina's twin boys, Ben and Jijjie.

The more practical and logical side of me emphasized the value of an education and, more importantly, a business plan. You can't always count on providence. After the presidential election of November 1932, times were tough, but our family pulled together. We usually got the gang over for Sunday dinner—Nunziatina, Mario, Keira, and a bunch of grandkids. We made food go a long way. Our table was often blessed with cicoria, cardune, and mushrooms from our secret gardens, and the store got food wholesale.

"People have to eat," I loved to pronounce while we were eating. "If we live frugally, we will live much better than 'a miseria in the Mezzogiorno."

"Giovannuzzo, get off it!" Filomena jumped at me. "Live better than 'a miseria we left? People here don't know what will kill them first, 'a miseria, our own government, or the fat, rich crooks who run Wall Street."

"Ahh, Filomena. Not all rich guys are crooks. Our new president, Franklin Roosevelt, understands that putting money in people's pockets puts money in the businesses that sell to them."

"Dream on, Giovanni. Let's see what adventures Mr. Roosevelt has in store for us."

Well, Brooklyn, America did indeed provide a nest, but not always of the most sheltering kind. And the Italian nest I left behind was breeding birds of prey, raptors that threatened America.

UNITED STATES
POSTAGE
3 CENTS
NEW YORK
WORLD'S FAIR
1939

12

AMERICANI DAVVERO, TRULY AMERICANS (1932–1940)

Sunlight filtered through Balbo's metallic flock
His birds of war, each a gaudy fighting cock
This pompous visitor tears my fretting heart
And betrays my land of beauty, music, and art

We Americans were dealing with the early years of the Depression. These were not the best of times, but our Brooklyn family was a flock united against predators and bad fortune. I was at the top of the pecking order. Instead of acting like Mussolini in Rome, I increasingly emulated Don Giuseppe of Campania.

Don Giuseppe turned seventy-five in 1932. Son Calogero was a successful forty-three-year-old lawyer, a rising star really, despite his age. It had taken him some time to make his way out of the villa to his legal training. I hate to think that my flight to America may have further impeded his move to the university. Now he was not just a lawyer but a teacher. He gave lectures on Italian and Neapolitan legal history at the University of Naples Fredrick II. To me, were it not for Calogero's delayed start, he could have reached these noteworthy accomplishments ten years earlier, at age thirty-three—the age of *ordination* and the age of Christ at crucifixion. On Calogero's forty-third birthday I could not ignore the double impact of my relationship with my brother.

Mail was too slow, unreliable, and impersonal to wish Calogero a long and fruitful life on this, or any, birthday. But we were able to talk on the phone, which at times seemed just as slow. American operators had to deal with my accented English, and the connections were not always clear. But a call went through to Calogero at his university office. Calogero, ever modest, would never boast that he had helped his father hold on to his land—in the process withstanding the rapacious hand of La Camorra. He succeeded. Calogero knew the law and was friends with those who enforced it or who knew how to recruit the law to their side. This was tricky business in Mussolini's Italy.

"Calogero, please pass my love and birthday greetings to Babbo Don Giuseppe."

Calogero chuckled at my placing in sequence "Babbo" and the honorific "Don."

I went on: "I know you don't like to brag. But I also know that without you, your father would have lost his land—his precious villa named after your mother."

"Please, Giovannuzzo, no one is above the law, not even the bandits of La Camorra."

"You're too modest, my brother. You never liked to talk when I first met you, and you still don't like to talk about yourself."

"Ahh, I wish you could see me wink with my index finger drilling into my cheek. Law is a strong moral force, but it pays to have allies who can enforce it with strength. Babbo made many friends, including the families of his workers and guards. I think they helped keep the evil at bay."

"*Madonna mia*, you truly are a child of the Mezzogiorno, and a lawyer at the same time. May this tricky business succeed in Mussolini's Italy."

There was silence from the other end. I thought we had lost our connection. Then he said, "Pray for all of us in Mussolini's Italy." Calogero expressed it with unusual passion, as if cunning, politics, good business, and legal maneuvering might not be enough to sustain Italy's children.

"Amen, from your Brooklyn brother, fràtemo. A hug for your, our, dear father."

Don Giuseppe's great business sense came to the aid of both father and son. I did what I could from the other shore. Trade, in San Marzano tomatoes exported to America and American grapevine rootstocks exported to Italy, complemented the now smaller income of the villa. Nevertheless, it survived in a Campania lashed by cholera, political instability, and worldwide depression. I tapped connections in the neighborhood to help. It did not bother me that my Brooklyn competitors also offered cans of San Marzano Pomodori Pelati, the tomatoes that went into the aromatic Sunday sauce all up and down Bay Fiftieth Street.

The import-export business was complicated, and American offshoots of the mob were at the ready to get their cut. Legal advice from the neighborhood law firm of Pollack and Pollack greatly helped. Myron Pollack, Senior and Junior, both spoke highly of Calogero. My Brooklyn family, a cutting from Campania, was spreading its roots and growing strong vines. We were vigilant against the parasites of the crime families, and the Pollacks were important allies.

In the summer of 1933, my Mario, a twenty-eight-year-old family man, was with his Keira and their three kids on Coney Island Beach. While they were wading in the surf, the fleet of General Balbo passed overhead. They recognized it immediately, since the papers had announced the first-ever transatlantic flight by a military squadron. *Il Progresso Italo-Americano* had the most prominent headline, flashing a special pride in the fleet of twenty-five seaplanes.

That evening Mario carried on at our dinner table. "Can you believe, Pops, those planes were made in Italy, and they took off from Italy! Me, you, Mom, and Nunziatina got here on a slow boat made in Germany."

I raised a hand to quiet Mario down, but he went through my stop sign.

"And they went to Chicago first." I forgave Mario's excitement —he had seen the squadron firsthand. "Chicago fell all over itself honoring the general." Mario could barely get the words out of his mouth, otherwise full of Filomena's clams and linguine.

I secretly hoped that Mario and Keira's children were not similarly awestruck. I looked over at Keira, who gave me her best poker face. To me Balbo's feat was a sure sign of the wrong emphasis Italy was putting on its military. And we Americans encouraged Italy, mannaggia! In New York a ticker-tape parade along Broadway was planned, and later, lunch at the White House with President Franklin Roosevelt.

I thought that our great leader, no, not Roosevelt but Il Duce Benito Mussolini, must have loved that Balbo's first name was *Italo*.

"Of course I'm proud," I said. "We show the world that Italy is an advanced industrial country." But I also thought to myself, *Warplanes are tools designed to kill people, and the owners will find a reason to use those tools.*

"Pops, you shoulda been there," exclaimed Mario as his three kids went on with their own chatter while mimicking fighting planes with their little hands.

If only Italo, Benito, and the other fascisti could have foreseen the effects of military adventurism on the home country and culture —on its own people, for crying out loud! Italy seemed to be advancing on those military fronts, but for the wrong reasons and in the wrong directions. In my darkest moments I saw it doing the devil's work.

Time flew like a hawk after its prey. In 1941, eight years after Balbo's flight, Mario and Keira's Padraic, TJ, and Anna could take the West End to Coney Island as unaccompanied teenagers, but they spent most of their outdoor time in the neighborhood. Padraic was going on fifteen—strong as a bull but gentle as a young calf. He was the most "Italian" of Mario and Keira's three, my face on a longer and agile body. He also differed from me in one important way—he seemed not that drawn to girls. Well, he was always shy. I hated the way he was bullied by some of the stunad kids in the neighborhood. I knew he could have defended himself physically, but he was too gentle to inflict damage on his tormentors unless pushed into a corner.

His strategy to get the kids off his back was to go in for—what's the expression—bodybuilding. But he didn't lift weights. He hung around the neighborhood Hi-Bar. He impressed the guys with his feats, almost intimidating them. A few stunad kids did push him too far, and it wasn't pretty for them. Word got around fast: don't mess with Padraic.

The Hi-Bar club was on an empty lot on Bay Forty-Ninth Street. The neighborhood kids put the bar up with help from older guys who worked in construction. The bar was a thick iron pipe mounted in two concrete uprights. The kids usually just hung around and under the bar, mostly talking about the Yankees, the Dodgers, and girls. After all, you can't swing on the bar all day and night.

Padraic was a natural and became a neighborhood champion.

He held the records for kips and giants. He had to explain to me what they were—this boy did not need wings to fly. I bet he could have outflown me in my scugnizzo days. Padraic's records were painted on the Hi-Bar uprights, date and all. He had shoulders of steel, and grabbing the bar made his hands like stone. Guys still talked about him liking boys more than girls, but always behind his V-shaped muscular back.

Mannaggia, the Hi-Bar—that was a great tradition. You could tell which kids were in Hi-Bar clubs just by looking at their physiques. For some kids, pinball and small-time gambling were unhealthy distractions. You had to pay to play pinball, and Mayor LaGuardia was dead set against the machines. Gambling? The mob ran "the house."

I made a point of visiting the Hi-Bar lot in the warm months, when Padraic was there. I harvested a few mushrooms and wild cardune and cicoria while checking over my shoulder on the goings-on around the bar. Padraic's mother, Keira, could not bear to watch him doing giants, swinging in full circles like a propeller, holding the bar with two hands, sometimes one. He'd finish the routine by dismounting in full swing, landing on his feet, sometimes somersaulting in midair. He was "pumped up" after dismounting, and his fair skin took on a rosy complexion. I know the girls found him attractive. He was very polite but did not encourage their fawning over him.

I liked to tease the boys. "Hey, guaglioni, if you eat more cardune and cicoria, you can be Hi-Bar champs like Padraic." Cross-eyed stares were the usual response. Once, Padraic joined the fun by flexing, Popeye the Sailor–style, while holding a cardune in his mouth like a pipe.

Padraic and older brother TJ and sister Anna were such true Americans that they hardly understood Italian, well, except for food names and curse words. Filomena got frustrated trying to tell them napulitano proverbs. TJ played stickball in the street and loved the Dodgers. There were always fights with Yankees fans. Dodgers and Yankees fans formed stickball teams against each other, and I loved how the kids took the identity of their favorite players. Irish-Italian TJ became All-Star second baseman Tony Cuccinello, until Brooklyn traded him to Boston before the '36 season.

Speaking of fans, Anna became a big one of Frank Sinatra and other crooners. But she didn't just mope around for some Frankie Boy's attention. That ragazza sure could jitterbug, and then she caught on to the Lindy Hop. There was a jukebox in front of Shimmy's candy store a block down from Most Precious Blood on Bay Forty-Sixth, and the neighborhood kids would dance until Filomena came out to haul Anna home. The boys begged Filomena to let Anna stay out a little longer. Padraic's feats on the Hi-Bar and Anna's on the dance floor/sidewalk convinced me I was no longer a young uccello, as if I had doubts.

Mario and Keira's kids had two good parents. Sure, they struggled. But their vine was well rooted and strong, and it yielded sufficient fruit—this in spite of our American soil losing some of its fertility. And also, sure, the Depression made America not so nurturing. But to me, most of the blame for the loss of American soil quality went to Il Duce Mussolini. Benito did not make life much easier for at least two immigrant groups in America—Jewish and Italian Americans.

The glow was off America's romance with Il Duce when he invaded Abyssinia in 1935 and perpetrated two years of barbarism against a brave and proud people. Mussolini's aggression in Abyssinia aimed to coalesce Italy's African colonial sphere. Many thousands—Italians, but mostly Ethiopians—died for his vain dream.

I was glad I had had the "foresight" to shut down the Italian

American Culture Center in 1930, though my hand was forced by the Depression and by the downtown federal agents. As far as I could tell, the greatest crime of our center was to field not very good soccer and baseball teams in local youth leagues.

No matter that I kept my hands clean—I was still being investigated by the Feds. They wouldn't leave me alone, but this time the charge was more serious—recruiting for Mussolini among our neighborhood Italian American youth, our beloved guaglioni. By 1937 the US government was investigating me for being one of Mussolini's local henchmen.

I had heard stories of Italian agents recruiting our young people to return to Italy for the glorious restoration of Imperial Rome. These youngsters were not uccelli di passo. They were lured to be Mussolini's birds of prey. Sons of some of my social club paisani were recruited to attend meetings run by Mussolini's representatives.

I got it from the horse's mouth, from Girolamo (Jimmy) De Ramone, who had attended one of the meetings. Jimmy was a muscular young man who helped stack the shelves and hang cheeses in our store. In my fifties, I needed Jimmy's help. I couldn't always count on Mario or my grandkids.

"Jimmy, be careful, that provolone must weigh fifty pounds at least."

Jimmy grabbed it around its waist with one arm and climbed the step stool as if he were Romeo carrying a bouquet of flowers for his waiting *innamorata*, Giulietta.

The giant bullet of provolone was safely hanging but swaying like a pendulum. My mind went back to Mussolini. I looked over at Jimmy and tried to play stupid. "Jimmy, have you heard of Italy recruiting young people from the neighborhood?"

Jimmy knew that I knew more than I was letting on. He looked defensive, actually lowering his head. "Mr. Ragnuno, I went to one meeting and it scared me." He raised his beautiful head full of black curls. His dark eyes showed strength. *What a good guaglione*, I thought.

"It started off OK," he said. "The only reason I was there was because some of the guys convinced me to go."

"Don't worry, Jimmy, I tell no one. To me, you was never there, and I don't wanna know who else was there. I'm just curious about the meeting."

Jimmy, wiping his hands on his "Ragnuno and Sons" apron, got into his story. "They told us how Mussolini was doing great things and showed us a film of how Italy was now so modern. They played a lot of marching music, and then military people came out with black shirts and fancy hats. Before I knew it, guys all around me were singing, then shouting and saluting."

I laced the fingers of my two hands and held them over my head, Mezzogiorno for anguish. "That is so scary."

"Yeah, well, I was really scared. You're hearing it from me. I was there. I finally get up the nerve to leave. I head for the door, and a big gorilla type tries to stop me. Finally I get by him."

"Oh, Madonna mia!"

"Yeah, I was praying too. He grabbed my arm and told me to keep quiet about the meeting, but here I am a week later telling you."

"I heard of kids who went over. Some were older brothers of Ben and Jijjie's friends. They got uniforms and a free trip to Italy. I suppose the next stop was Africa."

I prayed silently for the misdirected winged youth. Il Duce called them *La Giovanezza*, his name for the young people who would be the future of Italy. I heard of no one who made the return flight to America.

From the height of Balbo's 1933 flight to a 1938 nosedive, it became clear that Mussolini was not a hero but an enemy of America. As if his barbarism in Africa were not enough, he dismissed all Jews in his government and then barred them from much of Italian life. Italy lost a lot of talent, sure, but more importantly, the anti-Jewish laws set off a wave of anti-Semitism in Italy. Calogero described the situation discreetly. His more graphic letters were hidden in cartons of sun-dried tomatoes, and he indicated the letter locations by phone.

Che peccato, what a shame that anti-Semitism flared up in Brooklyn too, and among my fellow Italian Americans! Anti-Semitism had always been there, like a smoking cinder, but we didn't fan it and give it fuel. When times are tough, when work is scarce, when salaries cannot put sufficient bread on the table, it is too easy to look for villains, and Il Duce did not help. At least Generoso Pope, editor of *Il Progresso Italo-Americano*, came out with strong editorials against anti-Semitism. I wondered about his sincerity, but he took a public stand. Il Signor Pope had been a big fan of Mussolini, and maybe he still was. Maybe he was spreading his bets.

Hey, we are Italians, and survivors.

Speaking of Italian-Jewish relations, our mayor, fercryinoutloud, was Fiorello LaGuardia. "The Little Flower" was the product of an Italian-Jewish marriage. Italians and Jews were linked, whether we wanted to accept it or not. My beautiful fair-haired colleen Keira, who was studying Italian in night school, reminded me that *ghetto* came from the Italian. Tante grazie, bella, for bringing up this history.

Myron Pollack, Senior and Junior, were now my good friends, not just my lawyers. They explained yet again how we Italians and Jews were linked in the eyes of our government. The disgusting immigration restriction act of 1924 all but closed America's door to east Europe (Jews) and southern Europe (Italians, Greeks, and other riff-raff) and slammed it shut to Asians.

I thought back to Calogero's 1924 letter that quoted Senator Ellison DuRant Smith's oratory, calling Italians undesirable breeds. Breeds! It wasn't enough that the American door was now closed. I had a frequent nightmare of lower Manhattan being severed from New York and ferried, residents and all, to Europe and parts East.

While Jews in Italy had it tough, this Italian American in Brooklyn was fighting his own battles. The Feds knew I had two strikes against me—the counterfeit olive oil gambit and the Italian American Culture Center. They don't forget, just like Filomena—they never forget. I got the summons one day in the store, a cold March morning, 1939. Again they sent in two Aryan warriors. Their suits might as well have been military uniforms.

I was accustomed to the routine.

"Mr. Ragnuno, I'm FBI agent Michael Schultz, and this is my partner, Terry O'Brien." I actually shook their hands, which interfered with their presenting their badges.

They got right to the point. "We have reason to believe that you are privy to recruitment of Brooklyn youth by Mussolini's agents."

What could I say—that I had no knowledge? Maybe I should have picked up the phone and called the FBI right after I knew something, but I did not want to get young guys like Jimmy in trouble.

"Boh." I quickly reverted to English. "I don't know much. I think a lot of people know what's going on, but it doesn't mean that they're involved or cooperating with Il Duce." I wrinkled my nose on the "Dooochay," but they just looked at me without expression.

"We want to question you downtown about what you know. Just accompany us, and we will make no big thing out of it. You will be back in the store today. We know where to find you."

They let me call Mario to watch the store for a couple of hours.

"Pops? Problems?"

"The same old *camurria* with the Feds. Nun stà anziúso. Don't worry, I'll be back soon," I said, keeping my voice down in the back of the store.

"OK, I'm on my way. Keira can fill in for me in the other store."

I actually felt remorse as I left my beloved aromatic salumeria, with its hanging cheeses and salamis, the showcases of olives, roasted peppers, pickled pigs' feet. OK, it was just an afternoon, but it was such a contrast to the stark, cold, threatening federal office.

During those hours downtown I told the agents everything I knew, which was not much. So, I repeated myself a lot. I did identify a few mug shots of neighborhood toughs. I hoped the Feds came to the realization that I would never work for Mussolini, helping him exploit our precious young people.

In late 1939 I visited with the Pollacks without much warning, except for my phoned greeting to their receptionist. Usually, just a phoned hello was enough, I knew them so well. I chose a warm day in December to walk under the West End el, from the Bay Fiftieth Street stop to Twenty-Third Avenue. Their office was just two stores north of the craziness of Eighty-Sixth Street under the el. I visited the Pollacks so much that shopkeepers on the corner knew me. The lawyers' door on Twenty-Third Avenue bore a weather-beaten sign, "Pollack and Pollack, Attorneys." The door was between a cut-rate clothing outlet on the left, run by Syrian Jews, and a barbershop on the right. Dom the barber knew me, and it would have been unfriendly not to stick my head in to say hello.

"Hey, Dom, *che se dice*, guagliò?"

Dom was standing cutting hair, pontificating as usual. He turned his head, raising an eyebrow, and while looking straight at me kept on cutting and trimming, comb in one hand, scissors in the other. "Hey, paisan, what do I say? I say you're off to see *i giudi* again." I did not take the reference to the Jews as an insult to them. Often *lawyer* and *Jew* meant the same thing in the neighborhood.

But then Dom crooked the index finger of his comb hand and pantomimed the Jewish nose. I hated myself for only smiling and not protesting.

"I giudi have always helped me when I needed them most, and I still need their help." I tried to salve my conscience a little. "They've been honest with me."

Dom refocused his attention on the haircut. "Well, they bought the building, and so far they haven't raised my rent."

"Ahh, you always look at the bad side. Good to see you, paisan. Regards to the signora."

I went back out to the street, then through the middle door to "Pollack and Pollack." A long staircase greeted me with that familiar odor of spice and must. I am sure that the Pollacks were used to the odor, but I wondered how Myron Sr. was able to deal with the daily climb.

At the landing, the left-hand door, over the *schlock* clothing place, had a new sign: "Palm Readings, Tarot Cards." I opened the door on the right without knocking and was in a world so different from all the crazy pazzaria outside. The quiet reception area was small—the door almost banged into the receptionist's desk, which was flanked by two chairs. Receptionist Mamie Falcone greeted me, standing up from her desk. Her wavy hairdo seemed to get more red-orange with each visit.

"Don Giovanni, so good to see you! I warned Mr. Pollack that you might be dropping in."

I gave her a kiss on the cheek. "Ciao Mamie, tutto bene? La famiglia? How's Rocco?"

"Tutto bene, grazie." And then, raising a manicured eyebrow, almost whispered, "Rocco will always be Rocco. Send my regards to Filomena."

"I will."

"Let me see if Myron can chat with you."

After a subdued phone conversation, she nodded to me and looked toward Myron's nondescript door just beyond the right-hand chair. The door buzzed as I turned the knob and found myself in Myron's office. It was lined with thick law books and seemed even more sealed off from the street noises and odors than the reception area. Myron, behind his beautiful dark mahogany desk, stood and came out to shake my hand with both of his. I loved that we both seemed to be shrinking at the same pace, so that we could still look each other straight in the eye.

We exchanged pleasantries, and he directed me to a side table with two chairs. Junior was appearing in court that day, so Myron Sr. was alone in the office.

I got to the reason for my visit. "Mr. Pollack, Myron, the government is still snooping around any connection I might have with Mussolini. You know I have come to hate that man for what he's done to Italy and to your people."

Those last two words echoed back to me; *am I just trying to play him up?* The "your people" reverberated in my head. "Your people" made it sound like "your people and mine" were different animals. *Mannaggia, we are* all *each other's people, though we say yours and mine.*

Myron read no disrespect. "Mr. Ragnuno, first send my regards to Filomena, Mario, and Nunziatina. I'm so pleased to see how Mario has turned out."

The olive oil caper was not mentioned.

"Mr. Ragnuno, I think the Feds have bigger fish to fry than to bother good citizen Giovanni. But I will not let the matter rest. I will not let the matter rest," he repeated, then paused and almost sighed. "We are lucky in this country."

My eyes locked with Myron's, and I waited for the punch line.

"People who escaped Europe escaped the Nazis and the Fascists."

I nodded, but I was still waiting.

"Giovanni, I'm sure you know very well about that infernal 1924 Johnson-Reed Immigration Act?"

I looked at Myron Sr., first, because he had called me by my first name, and second, because I was very much aware that the act all but cut off Italian and Jewish immigration from Europe. I nodded a yes. "The act is always a big topic at the social club. And Calogero is always telling me about it."

Myron repeated himself. "People who escaped Europe escaped the Nazis and the Fascists."

Now came a consequence of that immigration closure that should have been screaming inside my *capo tosto*, this hard head of the Mezzogiorno.

Myron continued, "Do you think any Jew would want to live under Nazism? They would have to be *meshugenah*, real stunad."

"Yeah, Myron, no matta how you say it, they'd be crazy or stupid or both."

Myron went on and emphasized recent events that many Americans did not want to recognize. "This year, yes, 1939. Nazi Germany declared war not so much on Poland as on Poles and Jews. Mark my word, they are aiming for enslavement of tens of millions of human beings, Poles and Polish Jews."

Myron's phone rang. He picked it up and almost hollered into the receiver, "Mamie, I'm having an important conversation. Tell Mr. Applebaum to call later this afternoon. And sorry for raising my voice."

Myron took a deep breath, sat upright, and then said, almost in a sigh, "Ahh, if the worst thing the Nazis did was to make us a little more testy with each other ..."

Well, Il Duce has made me very testy, I thought.

"Giovanni, Germans are very efficient. They started a new world war, and they will need to finance it. Do you think they want to feed and house millions of captive Poles and Polish Jews?"

I was surprised that Myron was not screaming. I got his meaning. I imagined even just one of my grandkids being threatened with murder. "I am not so proud that 1939 will go down as the year that Italy became an Axis power," I said. "What a black mark on our history!"

"My point, Giovanni, is not to deride you for the errors of Il Duce. Yes, he's a tyrant who has mesmerized a nation. I just want to point out the consequences of those infernal immigration acts passed by our own country. How many Nazi and Fascist victims, now and to come, would be living safely in America if they weren't prevented from coming over?"

This hit me in the gut. Here I was, thinking how my mamma and sisters would be prevented from coming to America if they wanted to, but had not fully embraced the reality that having to stay in Europe was a probable death sentence for many Jews, at least those not fleeing across borders to safe countries like France and Holland.

"These are difficult times," he said, "and I am crazy with fear of another major war in Europe." He tugged on his vest, inhaled deeply, and exhaled almost in one breath. "And this new war will have an Asian front against Japan."

Myron saw my discomfort. More calmly, he offered me a glass of Manischewitz. I accepted it gratefully and toasted him and his family. In no way would I say that this overly sweet wine was too sweet.

Walking out of Myron's office, I turned for a more positive goodbye. "Oh, by the way, congratulations, Myron. Dom told me you bought the building."

"Ahh, we were both good tenants of this building, and we always got along. I never got a break on a haircut and shave, so he shouldn't expect a discount on the rent."

"Ha!"

"Yeah, he exchanged one Jewish landlord for another. At least he knows where to find this one. All he's got to do is bang on the pipes." Myron gave me a wizened look and raised an eyebrow. "Like if those furshlugginer sewers back up, like they usually do on Eighty-Sixth Street."

"That's right, a real problem. I know from the club that the sewer and storm systems were put in last century, when I was a scugnizzo in Naples. To modernize it is a big project. You gotta deal with the el and the traffic."

"And with city hall," added Myron.

"We can help each other in our own specialties," I said.

We stood up and embraced spontaneously. *Hey, we ain't so different after all.*

One last kiss for Mamie, regards to her husband Rocco, and I left the building. But I was still hating myself for not protesting Dom's disrespect to Myron Sr. and Jr. I stuck my head in the barbershop. "Dom, Myron Sr. spoke very well of you." I was off before his reply.

Hitler and Mussolini saw to it that I thought a lot about Italian-Jewish relationships. Nunziatina told me more than once that she had both Jewish and Italian American bosses in her Garment District sweatshops, and the Jewish ones tended to treat her better. Vina backed her up. Of course, Vina also put in, "Nonno, when the Italian boss is an SOB, he's an SOB. If a Jewish boss is bad, well, he's a Jew first."

Vina's brother Jijjie's two biggest father figures, after their real father flew off, were guys named Levinson and Liebowitz. If there was any consolation—a very small consolation—it was that most Italians in Italy, including the military, tended to offer a limp hand to the Nazis in moving Jews out of Italy and occupied lands. Filomena agreed that Mussolini was in bed with Hitler, though he was more like Hitler's puttana than a respected consort. Her version was in coarser dialect.

In spite of the news coming out of Europe and Abyssinia, Mussolini still had a big following in America, especially in New York. I think it was because we Americans had not experienced a real war on our territory since our Civil War. World War I—Wilson's "war to end all wars"—was fought in Europe. When war broke out in 1939 with Germany's invasion and conquest of

Czechoslovakia and Poland, America was not home to that war either.

It *was* home to the 1939–40 World's Fair, and in my beloved New York City. The theme of the fair was "The World of Tomorrow," a tomorrow already taking shape in Europe. Italy put a great face on its pavilion, which was a projection of Mussolini's ego. Keira would say something like "ostentatious and self-glorifying" to describe the man and the pavilion. The goddess Roma stood on a two-hundred-foot pedestal, over which flowed a spectacular waterfall. There was a dedication to Guglielmo Marconi at the base. The whole structure smacked of Fascist architecture—straight, bold lines projecting strength and discipline. Of course, inside the structure a grand ballroom displayed Italian luxury items. Il Duce also emphasized industrial products—a land of beauty, fashion, and, of course, modernity.

So, America was seduced into loving an Italy that was becoming our enemy, an enemy of Giovanni Ragnuno. I was a son of Italy, embraced in America's bosom, sometimes too tightly, and I defended my adoptive mother. My birth mother was now scaring me.

Italian hypocrisy continued to grow through 1940. While Mussolini was marching in lockstep with Hitler, he was projecting from the Flushing Meadows Fairgrounds a strong, advanced, and artistic Italian civilization. The fair's location has become bittersweet to me. Flushing Meadows now houses Shea Stadium, the home of my beloved New York Mets, where on October 16, 1969, the Miracle Mets won their first World Series.

In 1940, America was not involved in the war, but danger was all around us. The chances of an attack on our soil were great—we had to guard long northern and southern borders as well as our territories. Who could guard thousands of miles of land borders and seacoasts? We had Japan off our Pacific coast and Germany off the Atlantic.

In spring 1940 the FBI called me into their offices. I knew the way by now.

"Mr. Ragnuno, can I offer you a coffee?"

The same humorless Agent Jackson looked me in the eye across his spacious desk. The distance did not lessen his maloik, though he was no longer the young eagle I had met in 1925.

"No thanks, Agent Jackson. There is no danger of my falling asleep in this chair." Of course, the real reasons were that his coffee was like dishwater, and my accepting it would make my position even more subservient.

"Mr. Ragnuno, what can you tell us of Ruggiero, or Reggie, Bartolomeo?"

"Well, I can tell you a lot, but it would all be lies because I don't know any Reggie Bartolomeo."

Agent Jackson stared at me. I kept a straight face, and then he broke the silence with "What about a Mariano Bartolomeo?"

"Well, my father's middle name was Mariano."

"Aha!" Jackson crowed.

Not understanding his glee, I went back to my stare. Finally Jackson probably decided he would get no more out of me, but before he said anything, a pair of ugly-faces, two *faccia brutta* associates, entered the office and stood on either side of Jackson. Now I had to deal with three pairs of eyes—Jackson's and the pair from each gargoyle. And a longer pause.

"Don Giovanni Ragnuno." Jackson almost sang it in his best baritone. "I inform you that your father did not die on the Neapolitan docks some thirty-five years ago."

Jackson really got my attention then, though my head was spinning. I hoped my face did not transmit too much of my shock. In my dizziness I saw bodies with changing names doing an *abbàllo'e 'a morte*, a dance of death across my mental stage. My best retort was "So, wasn't the body identified?"

"His death was staged. Some poor sap provided the mangled body that carried your father's papers."

The two faccia brutta bookends smirked. I hated the bastards.

Jackson went on. "The victim was a nobody, except that your father took his first name, Bartolomeo, as his last name. And Mariano went from your father's middle to his first name." Jackson was so smug, looking left and right at his gargoyles. "Your father should have used a completely different alias. We were able to track him down because he was vain and lacked imagination."

I did not enjoy being insulted for my father's shortcomings. But Jackson wasn't finished: "Some Neapolitan authorities were happy to help us because Mariano Bartolomeo is a, well, troublesome capo in La Camorra."

Now I hoped the agents read the surprise on my face. I don't remember too much more of that meeting. I left without recalling if I was granted leave, but I knew I would be back. As I exited, Jackson called after me theatrically, "Nunja visit you poppa in Napoli."

I could really learn to hate the guy.

I had to turn back to face my tormentor. "Aren't you, sir, close to your twenty-year retirement?"

"Don't get your impudent hopes up. The FBI needs me for the coming war against your paisans."

My mind was a swirl as I walked through lower Manhattan to the Church Street Station. I didn't remember getting on the train, but the mess in my head did not prevent me from calculating that "Babbo Mariano Bartolomeo" was at least seventy-five years old. Such a ripe old age meant he probably had made it to a "man of respect."

Ha! Respect? What did he ever do for his family? Not a thing. If he had, I would have known. He was probably a wealthy big shot, but he left the care of his family to others—to me, of all people, to Don Toddo, and then to Don

Giuseppe. I would never want to live off the "earnings" of La Camorra. I left the streets of Naples because I could not stomach a life that victimized people.

But have I inherited some of the worst of my father's traits? If I had stayed on those streets, would I have followed Nunzio and the others into the "brotherhood"? Would I have eventually united with my father in a life of crime?

When I arrived at our Bay Fiftieth home after nightfall, Filomena opened the door, worry all over her face. "You go into Manhattan and you don't let me know when you comin' home?"

"Filomena, do you think I inherited some of the worst traits of my father?"

"Well, if you did, you hide them pretty well."

"Sometimes you tell me the most beautiful things."

"Come on inside, I'll warm up a bowl of pasta fazool."

Ahh, pasta fazool, our *pasta con fagioli*, our beans and macaroni. It is one of the greatest medicines to salve a tortured soul.

Later, also out of the blue, came the thunderbolt of the death of General Balbo in Libya in June 1940. *Il Progresso* and the New York papers carried the story. We talked about it over card games at the club. Balbo's plane was shot down by Italian anti-aircraft artillery, yes, his own people. Calogero sent me a June 1940 *Il Mattino* news clipping of Balbo's death. I learned more by phone, Calogero's phone in Villa Valeria.

"It is no secret here, Giovannuzzo, that Balbo was opposed to Mussolini's militarism. That may explain his banishment to North Africa, which is ironic."

"Yes, fràtemo, we Italians are nourished on irony."

"There are whispers among some law professors that Balbo was opposed to Il Duce's official anti-Semitism and his intervention in the Spanish Civil War."

"You have to whisper?" I asked in a subdued voice.

"Ah, in Mussolini's Italy only the bravest or the most foolhardy express such opinions openly. I don't doubt that Balbo was close enough to Il Duce, and brave enough, to express his opinions directly to Caesar's face."

"The brave suffer the consequences" was all I could add, thinking of how cowardly I was keeping news of my father's adventures to myself. "Yes, complicated dirty world we live in." I signed off, extending greetings to my family at the Villa Valeria. Conspiracies could play out from the mean docks of Naples to the highest levels of government.

My father is alive, Balbo is dead, Italy is becoming our enemy, and I'm under suspicion for actions in America and in Italy. My world is coming apart, mannaggia!

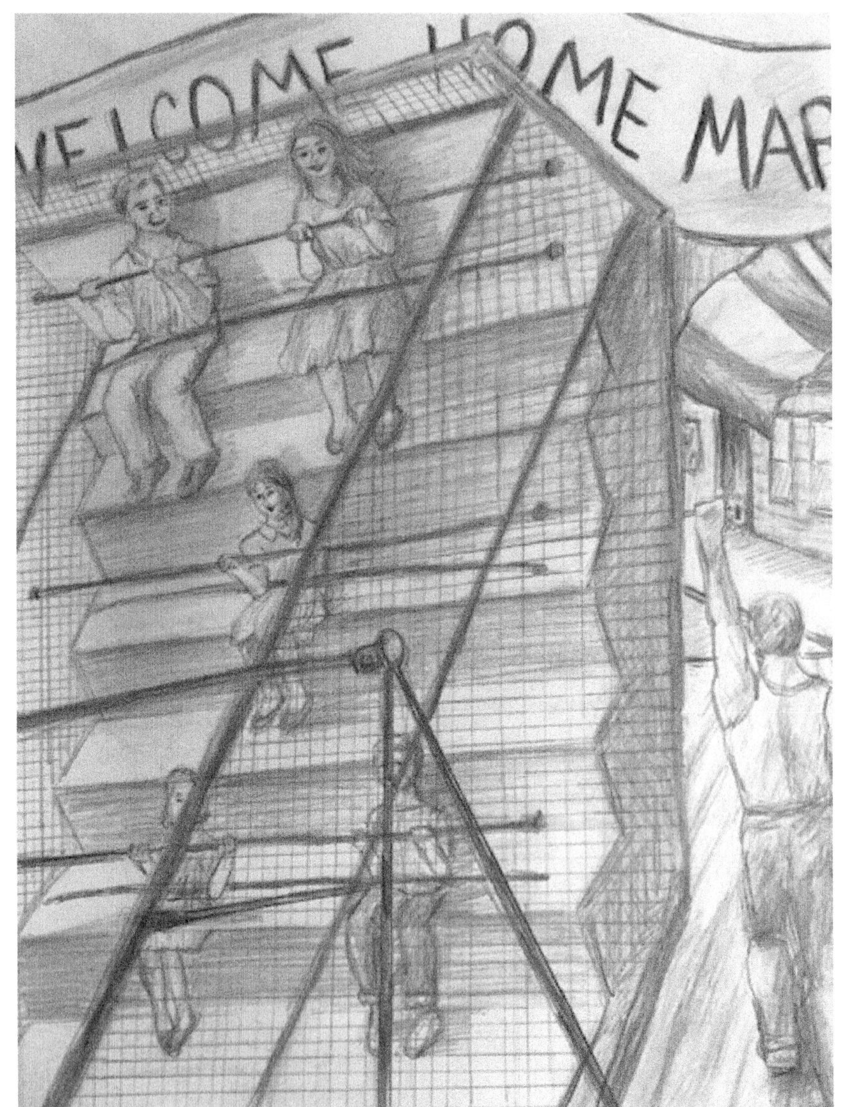
WELCOME HOME MAR

13

ITALY TURNS ON AMERICA, AND AMERICA ON GIOVANNI (1940–1945)

If "what doesn't kill you makes you stronger"
My abandoned fledglings are helpless no longer
With little worry about their plight
They squawk, flap wings, and take eager flight

"Mario!" I was behind the counter of the empty store. Mario was in the back, stuffing sausage skins. He came running out, wiping his hands on his apron.

"What, Pop?"

"Sorry for yelling. You know I visited with our friends again downtown."

"Yeah, I wish they'd leave you alone. All you do is work and worry about family."

"Don't tell anyone in the family, especially your mother."

Mario looked at me as if to say, "My salsiccia's waiting in the back, get on with it."

"My father, your grandfather back in Naples, is alive."

Mario's open hands rose to either side of his face. Palms toward me, he moved them forward and back like bellows, in synchrony with an elongated, undulating "Wha?!" I hated myself for noticing the sausage stuffing on his hands.

"They just told me that he somehow staged his death before Mamma and I got married, and that he was now some kinda capo."

Mario, his hands still raised, stared. His eyes widened.

"He made no effort to contact us ever. And I know he won't."

Mario, a little calmer, dropped his hands and almost whispered, "So, what else is new? He was dead to us from before I was born. He'll stay dead."

I tried to put on a brave face, though my quivering lips betrayed me. "I say we just forget that figlio di puttana. It hurts me to call my father, your grandfather, such a name. And I'm not calling my grandmother a puttana. I think her son was possessed."

Mario actually genuflected, unusual for him. In the process he got salsiccia meat on his shirt, above his apron.

"To me also, Mario, he is dead. He was dead when he abandoned us. I just hope he is not hooked up with Il Duce. That's all I need, giving the Feds even more reason to be on my ass."

"Amen," said Mario as he about-faced and went back to his salsiccia.

Leave it to Il Duce. He'll find a way to make my life miserable.

And then thoughts on my miserable life were interrupted. Mario came running out of the prep room: "Pops, you gotta tell Mamma!" His open hands traced circles on either side of his face. "Better she learns from you if she doesn't already know. She knows everything."

"*Non preoccuparti*, don't worry, figlio, you know I can't keep anything from your mother. If I were ever a bad boy, I'd be dead by now."

That night, we sat around our table, Mario, Keira, and their three kids and Nunziatina and her four, plus Filomena and me. We made an assorted dozen.

Filomena's eggplant parmigiana went just far enough. Only the adults relished the *broccoli di rapa*, or broccoli raab as we say now. Over coffee, fruit, and cannoli, I made the announcement, accompanied by Filomena's nodding *mano cornuto* sign, her index and pinky fingers forming the points of a horn. The horn was to make sure that her father-in-law's maloik did not reach us from Naples, or from hell.

She dropped her hand, breaking her silence. "Who cares? He's an old turd, a *strunz* who never did anything for us. He stayed out of our lives all this time, and when he dies, and I hope it's soon, he'll be out of our lives for good."

Mario explained to the youngsters, as if they needed it, that many a strunz is left on the sidewalks by stray dogs.

This put an end to conversation about Mariano Bartolomeo. *Thank you, Filomena, you have exorcised this sfaccím from our lives, at least for a while.* The kids went to fighting over the last few cannoli, leaving the apples and grapes for the older generations.

The chaotic table scene of chirps and squawks convinced me that my miserable life was really a blessing. But I also knew that I would look on helplessly as our grandchildren set off on their own adventures to set up their own distant nests. Those problems came with being a family head. Troubles with the FBI? A dead father haunting me? Well, those were bonuses. We Neapolitans always understood that happiness brings on taint, like iron attracts rust.

Nunziatina's Jijjie and Ben, without a father, had no choice but to be family breadwinners. By 1941 they were proficient fourteen-year-old carpenters and later were ranked master cabinetmakers. Jijjie bragged he was the youngest in New York at nineteen, though only a few minutes younger than Ben. They were schooled in wood shops but also on the streets. Jijjie further polished his schooling in the boxing ring, where he went undefeated in a few professional fights. He knew, though, that the money boxing provided the family did not justify the damage to his body and brain and to Mamma Nunziatina's peace of mind.

Mario and Keira, meanwhile, were rearing their clutch of Irish-Italian kids in a more stable, less challenged household. Yet I hoped they were not raising cannon fodder for yet another "Great War." *And thank God, they stopped at three, and one is a girl.*

There were threats all around, war in Europe and resentment in America against its own Italians, Germans, Japanese, and Jews. Yet 1941 did not begin as an ominous year. It was one of pride for me, and it had to do with baseball, something that Filomena could neither understand nor stand. In '41 son of Sicily Joe DiMaggio hit safely in fifty-six straight games—in seventy-two out of seventy-three, I liked to remind my goombahs. My beloved Brooklyn Dodgers played against Joe's Yankees in the '41 World Series. The Dodgers lost in five games, but my heart swelled with the feats of Brooklyn's Dolph Camilli, the National League Most Valuable Player. Dolph said of Brooklyn fans: "All they cared about was their family, their job, and the Dodgers. And I don't know which one was the most important."

Hey, Dolph, goombah, I'm family and a fan.

When baseball was over, the "hot stove league" became cold and dismal. The Dodgers lost the series on October 6, and on December 7 came the crippling early morning Japanese air attacks on Pearl Harbor. Ten hours later the Japanese sent air and ground forces to the Philippines, surrounding thousands of helpless American troops.

So started World War II for America, which could no longer avert its gaze from the atrocities of Japan in China, Germany in

Europe, and Mussolini in Africa. It was if my conscience had been wearing a bulletproof Dodgers jersey during the '41 season. America was attacked and we had no choice but to declare war. When "we" declared war on Japan, Axis power Italy was automatically America's enemy as well.

We got a late Christmas present. By early 1942 President Franklin D. Roosevelt was well over his infatuation with Il Duce. On Thursday, February 19, 1942, FDR issued Executive Order 9066, restricting movement and freedom of "domestic enemies" of the US. Enemies were the Japanese, Germans, and Italians living in America, especially those who had not yet become naturalized citizens.

Three days later, Sunday mass was not too comforting on a cold February morning. Instead of going straight home with Filomena, I made a detour to the Benevento Social Club, just around the corner from our house. A few of the guys were sipping espresso at a card table, glum faces all around, with the pages of *Il Progresso* spread out like an uninviting tablecloth.

Bobby DeMaio, who had two boys of military age, pointed to the article on the sinking of the *SS Normandy* in New York Harbor, of all places! America had seized that ocean liner from defeated France, and it was in the process of being made into a troop carrier, the *USS Lafayette*. It caught fire, and a day later capsized into the mud of Pier 88.

"Look at this, Giovanni." Bobby pointed to pictures of the ship lying on its side. "I can see the Japs hitting us with sneak attacks halfway across the Pacific, but how does our enemy sink one of our ships in New York Harbor right under our noses, fercryinoutloud!"

"We'd better get our act together," I said.

"If the government lets us immigrants help." Bobby's worried eyes drew me away from the paper.

Giulio (Julie) DeRamo, a trolley driver, was really worked up. "And how can we help when we're the freakin' enemy?" Julie pounded his fist on the table. "You watch. They're gonna say that the waterfront mob was in cahoots with Mussolini, and they sank the ship.

"And look at this." Julie pointed to the *Daily News* account of Executive Order 9066, his forearm muscles rippling as if he wanted to strangle the paper. "So, what are they gonna do? Round up millions of Japanese, Italians, and Germans? And then what?"

It was time for me to go home and sample Filomena's Sunday sauce. "Bobby, Julie, we're Americans. We all fought in World War I. They're just going after the bad apples."

As I rose, Julie looked daggers at me, as if to say "damn," but he said it better in our native language: "'*A porca miseria!*'" And then, in dialect: "Hope is the refuge of a blind man who is lost."

I couldn't wait to inhale the aroma of Filomena's ragú.

Il Progresso had frequent accounts of Uncle Sam rounding up Japanese Americans on the West Coast and putting them into far-off internment camps. The paper warned of an impending roundup of Italian Americans as well. *As if we were going to escape back to Italy*, I cursed to myself. I knew that Agent Jackson had me in the bulls-eye of the dart board he kept in his office.

I almost went crazy thinking that my beloved Italia, the country of my birth, was now an enemy of America, the country that had adopted me. Even worse, my father in Italy, in his crooked, selfish way, might be helping Mussolini. And his son, this Giovanni Ragnuno, was considered an enemy in the midst of my fellow American citizens. I felt like I was going to be put in a uniform with "POW" on the front. I never shared with Filomena that POW was *wop* spelled backward.

I wasn't the only Italian American who was eyed with suspicion. I suppose it was not much of a leap from *mafiosi* to foreign agents. Movements of many of us were restricted—no kidding. Even Joe DiMaggio's father was barred from fishing in his own boat, the one he moored in San Francisco for over four decades. The Feds seized the boat and with that, his livelihood. As if that were not enough, Il Signore DiMaggio had to comply with a curfew and travel restrictions on land. *Il Progresso* also reported that the elder DiMaggio had to carry photo ID that designated him an enemy alien.

Son Joe played the wartime '42 season for the Yanks, but he missed the '43, '44, and '45 seasons while he was serving in the US Army. Didn't anyone see the mockery of justice?

Closer to Brooklyn, New York Metropolitan Opera star Ezio Pinza was interned, and on Ellis Island! This was *troppo*, too much beyond irony. Millions of Italian immigrants had passed through Ellis Island, the last leg of their successful flight from the old country. But for Pinza and many paisani, Ellis Island belatedly became the Isle of Tears. This time they were not sent back to Italy but were imprisoned on the island after years of contributions to America.

During 1942 I often sang this lament at the social club, in the store, on the bocce court, wherever. "Enough, Giovanni, we know the story" was the usual discordant chorus. In response I would sing my aria: "But for Filomena and me, Ellis Island was a monument, a gateway to this beautiful life in beautiful America."

Why did I throw "beautiful" America in the faces of my paisani? Was it only to instigate a return chorus of Bronx cheers and "*Mannaggia'merica*"? I think it was to test my faith in America.

Then, when I was requested to show up at the FBI for more questioning, I asked myself, *How unshakable is my faith in America? Camurria!* Ancora*! Again! And why is Jackson not retired?*

This time, Myron Pollack Jr. accompanied me to the FBI headquarters near Foley Square.

"Mr. Pollack, isn't that Agent Jackson character close to retiring?"

"Well, he is close. A few colleagues in the know say he's seeking a waiver to work beyond twenty years of service, since we're at war and have enemies all around."

I know the real reason, to continue busting my crocchette.

The federal office was very close to Little Italy. Of course, it was also near Delancey Street, of which I'm sure Myron the younger was aware.

After terse introductions, young Myron and I took our seats before Jackson's huge desk. He immediately brought up my honoring Mussolini in my Italian American Culture Center.

"Mr. Ragnuno, you honor Mussolini here in New York, and your father is probably a capo on the docks of Naples."

Myron Pollack Jr. quickly said, "Agent Jackson, if I may. My client, Mr. John Ragnuno, is a naturalized American citizen, a US Army veteran who served with honor in World War I and who is a respected member of the local community."

Young Myron looked over at me, so I continued. "Agent Jackson, I never honored Mussolini. To me he was a figurehead for Italy, its culture and history." But all the while I was thinking to myself, *Giovanni, you picked* some *beautiful figurehead, you're such a stunad.* "And learning that my father was still alive in Naples was a complete shock. We have had no contact since I arrived in America, and no contact since I heard the news."

Jackson appeared to suppress a smirk, while Myron Jr. added, "My client's loyalty is to America and to his local community, and many of that community are non-Italian, some of whom are now in Mr. Ragnuno's family."

"Yeah, your client has red, white, and blue underwear." Jackson leaned forward, focusing on me. "The bureau has an ABC list, Mr. Ragnuno. You might say an FBI hit parade. You almost made the A-list."

I glanced at Myron as Jackson read from a page in a booklet. "They show the greatest commitment to their nation of birth, by reason of their leadership in ethnic, cultural, or assistance organizations.

"That sounds like you, signore. You showed leadership with your social and Mussolini clubs." Jackson droned on: "To me you were a hit parader, a Glenn Miller, Benny Goodman, well, an Italian version of them."

I woulda preferred Frank Sinatra.

"But I was overruled. You lucked out. You won't be interned, but we're watching your Dago rear end just the same."

What kind of spying device is that?

"Congratulations, you did make the B list. Let me read from the federal hit parade." Jackson laughed at his own sick humor. "Those persons in Category B are under less suspicion but belong to those organizations."

After a few warnings, he let us go with this beautiful sendoff: "Get outta here."

As Myron Jr. and I got up, Jackson had to add, "But stay where I can reach you, Mr. Ragnuno. I don't want no postcard from Naples."

Once we made it to the hallway, young Myron turned to me. "You know who founded the FBI, Mr. Ragnuno?"

Before I could come up with anything, I got his answer: "Joseph Charles Bonaparte."

"Sounds familiar."

"Well, I would say so. He could trace his lineage two generations back to Napoleon Bonaparte, son of Corsica and therefore just about a son of Italy."

"We Americans really are a mixed salad," I said.

Young barrister Pollack gave me a smirk as he playfully punched my shoulder.

We Ragnunos developed more than a marriage link to Keira O'Donnell's family. They became our family in other ways. In 1943, Keira's dear father, Tom O'Donnell, was a stand-in juror. His age of fifty-seven and his injury kept him out of military service. He was available to fill in on jury duty at a time when many men were overseas. Jury duty earned him a few extra bucks.

Tom O'Donnell was tapped to serve in the trial of some big fish, an Italian *pesce grosso*. Tom was shot and killed before the trial. It made the front pages of the *News* and the *Post.* Word on the street was that it was mistaken identity, and it wasn't clear if the big fish had anything to do with it. I was devastated. Tom and I were consuoceri. He was one beautiful guy. Keira's poor mother Maggie was institutionalized, and more than once Vina accompanied her aunt Keira to visit Maggie on Long Island.

I went there once with Keira. The place was state-run, stark, and filled with the stench of johns, stale sheets, hopelessness, and melancholy. The buildings appeared to be built with old bricks. We Italians liked to say "pazzaria" for "madhouse," but that sounded way too spirited for this place. The attendants seemed to go through their rounds almost mechanically but with a curious affection for many of the patients, at least the ones who were not criminally insane, antisocial, or otherwise hopelessly pathological. Mrs. O'Donnell seemed to take a liking to Vina, and I think that made Keira especially fond of her niece. But poor Vina had a difficult time returning to that place, and when Mrs. O'Donnell passed a year later, Vina had strong guilt for not having gone with her aunt Keira more often.

Why are we cursed with consciences?

Keira stored the mass card for her mother's funeral in a designated Velveeta cheese box. The dimensions of the long box were perfect to accommodate the card and at least one hundred others along the length of the box. It resembled a card catalog drawer from the library, but these cards were ordered by date of death. The exception was the adjacent placement of Tom and Maggie O'Donnell, united in life, and in the Velveeta box in death.

After Mrs. O'Donnell's funeral mass, Vina visited our Bay Fiftieth Street home. "Nonno, they were such a cute couple. Being next to each other in a Velveeta cheese box is sorta cute but also creepy. Even a library card catalog drawer would have been more appropriate."

"The important thing is that they loved each other and that their children cherish their memory."

"You sound like a priest." She got up from her seat. Fifteen-year-old Vina had been sitting a long time in mass and at our home, and now she went into one of her routines, almost dancing while talking with her hands. "Nonno, that Velveeta is something else."

I had to interrupt. "Vina, cara, you will never, ever find Velveeta in our Latticini Freschi. Your aunt Keira told me you had it a couple of times at the O'Donnells'."

Vina looked injured. With my index finger across my lips, I signaled her to be silent. "Vina, Velveeta sounds almost like *bella vita*. Beautiful life! I appreciate the American business spirit, and this Velveeta monstrosity is one of the best and one of the worst children of that spirit."

"Well, it is interesting. It isn't really cheese." She was silent for a few seconds and then continued, as if getting permission from herself. "I'm also charmed by their buttered, untoasted white bread."

I raised my eyebrows.

"Nonno, the bread breaks through when you try to butter it, and every other bite is into a piece of butter!"

I tried to suppress the smile encroaching both sides of my mouth. I silently forgave Vina's youthful venial sins, silly little girl. I could see she was growing up into a woman of strength, virtue, good taste, and great cooking skill. Mamma Nunziatina was her paragon.

But I hated myself for talking this way about the O'Donnells.

Who cared how they cooked! They had come to my rescue when I needed them most—like the problems with American government officials. Mario's in-laws had submitted signed affidavits on behalf of family patriarch Giovanni. "You shake the hand that shakes yours," we always said in the neighborhood. My intent was for citizen Giovanni to stay in the neighborhood for the war's duration, to be an American patriot, patron of the local Italian American community, and family to the O'Donnell clan.

At least I was being treated much better than Joe DiMaggio's father.

I knew about the detentions and anti-Italian prejudice, and I did not have to get it from the Pollacks or from *Il Progresso* or the local papers. My paisani who did not bother to read the papers knew it as well—we all lived the daily prejudice. I dramatized our plight while playing bocce at the waterfront park. Bocce to me was as much an operetta as a sport. Caruso may have received many loving shouts of "Encore! Bravo! Bravissimo!" from his adoring audience, but I got lots of venom from my bocce buddies. Their "Ancora!" was more like "Enough already!"

I loved it.

I pointed out to my fellow old *fazools* that many of us were cannon fodder in the Great War or were in internment or under curfew in the second one. I had the stage, and napulitano Caruso was in my blood. With my oscillating right hand, index finger pointed skyward, and cradling a *boccia* ball in my left, I went into an aria on Sicily's son, Frank Sinatra, beloved by all Americans, especially young American girls. For some medical reason Sinatra did not have to serve in the war. He served his country by recording and by playing gigs in New Jersey and at the Paramount in the Manhattan Theater District.

"Frank kept the girls at home happy while the boys were overseas." My comment was intended to have a double meaning and it was not appreciated.

Franco Finnelli, whose two boys were in the Pacific theater, took the cue before tossing his ball. "Mannaggia! Sinatra has the mob and the connections to stay out of combat." Finnelli had gotten our attention. "His father came from the same paese in Sicily as Lucky Luciano."

My mind went to my father working the docks in Naples, and Lucky Luciano and company helping FDR keep the Italian American dockworkers in line.

What is the dividing line between legitimate government and the mob?

Finnelli went on: "We poor wops who don't get jailed on Ellis Island go over to Europe and Asia and get our asses shot."

"Shut up, Franco," said his partner, Pietro Pierangeli, "and concentrate on the *pallino*."

So went another afternoon at the Gravesend waterfront park.

Keira also had a thing for Sinatra. I swear I could read her mind, especially when she was thinking about men: "Could it be I'm fatally attracted to Dagos?"

When seventeen-year-old Anna wanted to catch Sinatra at the Manhattan Paramount, Mamma Keira gave her blessing and even arranged for her fifteen-year-old cousin Vina to join her, much to Nunziatina's great displeasure. Also displeased was the truant officer, and when he reported Anna's absence to Keira, the response was "Didn't you know that Sinatra is in the Paramount? Anna and her cousin went there yesterday."

Of course, Keira was more responsible than just letting two teenaged bobbysoxers brave downtown Manhattan alone. She entrusted the two girls to twenty-year-old Florie Ehrlich, a neighbor farther down Bay Forty-Seventh Street. Florie's mom, Mrs. Rose Ehrlich, also informed the truant officer of her daughter's whereabouts, saying that he should not be such a *yenta*. Even we Italians used *yenta* to describe gossipy busybodies. We were all yentas enough to know every detail of the truant officer–Rose Ehrlich standoff.

I confess. We all became Americans, but in our own ways. While the ladies of the neighborhood followed the exploits of Sinatra, Bing Crosby, and other crooners, I was deeply rooted in baseball (and bocce). In 1943 Camilli showed that there was honor in baseball. He refused to report to the hated New York Giants when the Dodgers tried to trade him to the enemy.

But in that same 1943, my son Mario did go to America's enemy, Italy. He went as an American GI at the ripe age of thirty-seven, and he was stationed in Sicily for the duration of World War II. He saw little fighting but was an important part of organizing food acquisition and provisioning the Allied troops for their move up the Italian peninsula. Keira became even more entangled in the Italian American community around Bay Fiftieth Street. She ran the Salumeria & Latticini Freschi business with help from me, her loving father-in-law, until Mario returned to Brooklyn. He came back in 1945, the year that Mussolini was killed by his own people.

In contrast to Mussolini, Mario was a hero—to his family, neighborhood, and countrymen. Keira and I organized a huge welcome back block party with alternating banners strung across Bay Fiftieth Street: "Benvenuto, Mario!" in red, white, and blue and "Welcome Home, Mario!" in red, white, and green. I emphasized to Keira that the Italian green bar was for Ireland.

For the occasion, Bay Forty-Ninth and Bay Fiftieth Streets resembled the annual summer street festival of the Most Precious Blood Parish on Bay Forty-Sixth. Stalls were set up under strings beaded with hazelnuts and almonds. The nuts alternated with red and green lanterns. Testaverde Pastry offered deep-fried *sfingi* and frozen offerings of *spumoni*, *gelato*, and *limoncello*. There was no escaping the aroma of grilled peppers and sausage—from Salumeria Ragnuno, of course. Fishmonger Peppe Ippolito of Pesci di Sciacca and his sons barely kept pace shucking clams. Games of chance? "Fahgeddaboudit," as my grandkids would say.

Block parties always attracted entrepreneurs like ants to a picnic. Bearishly strong, dark Sicilians showed up with their half-moon ride on the back of a truck. The half-moon was a giant swinging semicircular metal wheel with three or four internal seats running up each side—the top seats eye-level with the axis. The Sicilians swung the half-moon on its axis, almost to a 360-degree full turn, to the delighted and hysterical screams of the children seated inside. The bravest kids sat in the topmost seats, but no one was brave enough to refuse the lap bars. Maybe in my scugnizzo days I would have been one of the riders, maybe even screaming the loudest at the muscular paisans in their tank tops to push harder. But no lap bar? I don't think so.

I took in the festive atmosphere, families reunited, new generations of Italians now melded with our fellow citizen Americans, *cu l'americani.* I was feeling pretty good for an old fazool of sixty. *Could life be any better?*

I answered my own question: *Life would be much better if I knew the fate of my mother. This block party is a little obscene, considering that my mother and her good husband most likely still have to fight for their very lives. Mamma, your well-being is much more important than my being under suspicion by my own American government.*

Ominously, there was no word from Calogero. I could not imagine the confusion and disruption engulfing Naples. Mario did not paint the best picture, and I knew he was going easy on me. My own problems with the American government were so trivial in comparison.

14

POSTWAR, PRESENT TROUBLES (1945–1946)

Victorious survivors gather at our nests
Trumpeting, puffing out proud chests
While we offer hearty congratulations
We must pay homage to late generations

Well after Mario's return, I got the news from Calogero and Don Giuseppe. My almost eighty-year-old mamma did not survive the German occupation and subsequent withdrawal from Naples in September 1943. She had been dead for almost two years, and I had no idea. She was dead when our Brooklyn neighborhood was celebrating the return of its veterans.

Could I be proud of the scugnizzi that had much to do with driving off the Nazis in the heroic Four Days of Naples that September? The Nazi horrors made the scugnizzi into monsters, I'm sure more brutal than I ever knew them to be. Before the war, the scugnizzi were forever scorned, ridiculed, and avoided. They were the schivazzi, the scum of the streets of Naples. But when they became even more violent and bloodthirsty, they became heroes.

This is what war does to us. It puts a premium on barbarism, which then becomes heroism. Heroism or barbarism depend on which side you're on.

The Nazis bombed the harbor and set fire to the National Library and the State Archives of Naples, thereby destroying much Neapolitan and Italian patrimony. In a way, my dear mother was also part of that lost patrimony. Mother Naples and my Neapolitan mother both received the genocidal blows of the Nazis.

How do you kill a people? Is it by genocidal extermination or by destroying their records and cultural accomplishments? It seemed that the Nazis employed a two-pronged strategy in their exodus from Naples.

Calogero gently helped me reconstruct my mother's last days. He hesitated a lot, and not because he was closing up again. The events were truly savage. "Giovannuzzo, we at the villa were at a distance from Naples, and that saved us. The news from refugees who made it to our gates was that the Nazis forced the civilian evacuation of the waterfront."

"And then?"

"I think German bombs and booby traps led to the loss of Donna Nunziata. We never learned all the details, but her remains were recovered eventually, and her personal effects were identified by Babbo and me. Babbo is in deep mourning."

"Oh, dear Mother of God" was all I could utter.

Once this news was out, Calogero pitched in with more news, as if moving the horrible conversation along would prevent me from mourning too deeply along the way. "Her husband went missing in the confusion, and his whereabouts were never determined."

"Ooh, I never got to embrace him, to know him."

"Your sisters survived, as you know."

"Blessed be San Gennaro."

"They provided a few more details about Mamma's last days."

Calogero referred to my mamma as if she were his mother, which was logical, considering that Calogero and I were brothers and he never had known his own mother.

Calogero went on: "Living well beyond Naples's urban limits probably saved your sisters' lives."

Silence reigned again. I knew Calogero had more to say.

"Mamma's ashes are in an urn in Babbo's study, in front of a portrait of the mother I never got to know."

I promised myself to visit Italy before I died, and to pay my respects to my beautiful, strong, loving Mamma, Donna Nunziata.

Calogero interrupted my dark reverie. "Babbo took care of the final arrangements. More important to him, he was able to collect some of Mamma's family records. They are bound in a volume. We will pass copies to your sisters and to you."

Brooklyn life was returning to normal by 1946. People again crowded both stores on Saturday afternoons to prepare for Sunday dinner. We had to control traffic in the Bay Forty-Seventh store. Upon entering, customers were encouraged by arrows, prevailing traffic, and a one-way turnstile to make a left through a passageway of cheeses, then the dried sausage counter, and then a large section of canned goods, including ground espresso blends, and finishing at the "counter of redemption" to atone for a multitude of culinary sins. If the modern Italian housewife could not spend hours in the kitchen, this counter offered prepared, refrigerated items: fresh ravioli, ricotta and salsiccia, rice balls, potato croquettes, eggplant rollatini, seafood salad, orecchiette pasta with broccoli raab and sausage, stuffed peppers and artichokes, and giardiniera—pickled pepperoncini, artichokes, cauliflower, and carrots. All were homemade. After traveling this gauntlet, carrying complimentary "Ragnuno" bags, and passing through the turnstile, customers were offered a small table to rest and catch up on gossip or to wait for husbands and sons-in-law to come by with the car.

I loved this gossiper's table, *'a tavula 'e chiaccharessa* in dialect. I was undaunted by the women. In fact, I loved to gossip with them, including Lucrezia Lucia, the exorcist who had freed Nunziatina from the maluocchio over twenty-five years before. Widow Lucrezia had never remarried but was still an attractive woman in her late fifties—wiry, spry, quick, with dark lively eyes. She did not believe in cosmetics and never frequented the neighborhood beauty parlors.

Where does she pick up her gossip? The possible answers scared me.

"Donna Lucrezia, so good to see you shopping."

"You mean, so good to see me shopping in your store."

I forced an awkward laugh. "How's your family?"

"Eh!" She raised a hand as if throwing salt over her shoulder. Then those dark eyes shone out of a face that in the sunlight showed wrinkles and a few unruly white chin hairs. "Don Giovanni, it's a shame what the *germanesi,* the Nazis, did to Napoli." She made the mano cornuto sign, waving her extended pinky and index fingers in my face. I felt safer.

"Donna Lucrezia, before we get too crazy putting a curse on the Germans, the Allies also bombed Naples without mercy. Some call Naples the most bombed city in the war."

"*Un peccato*," said Donna Lucrezia, snapping her hand so that a loose pinky played a staccato beat with the rest of the hand.

"Yes, a shame, but don't forget that Naples was the enemy of America."

"Don Giovanni, there is much evil in Naples. Vesuvius will punish Naples again, like it did two years ago with the how you say, *fiamme dell'infernno*?"

"Ahh, brimstone—the flames of hell," I proudly translated, and Lucia nodded in satisfied agreement.

I thought of my father somehow getting rich from Italian reconstruction, whether the damage was done by the war or by Vesuvio.

Lucrezia tilted her head to one side, those dark eyes fixed on me. "Is your father part of the evil, *il male napulitano*?"

Mannaggia, Filomena can't keep a secret, and now the whole neighborhood knows that my father is probably alive. "My father, alive or even dead, is probably capable of any kind of evil, but I know nothing about him."

"I see him causing trouble. Be careful, Don Giovanni." She grabbed my right hand with her left and touched her strong nose with her right index finger, telling me to keep quiet. "I can help."

A car horn signaled Donna Lucrezia that daughter Maria was ready to pick her up.

Tante grazie e arrivederci, Donna Lucrezia.

I helped the aging seer, *la chiaroveggente*, and her two bulging "Ragnuno" bags into the passenger seat of the 1939 Plymouth coupe. Kissing Donna goodbye, I told her daughter, "Take care of your mamma, Maria, she's one of my links to the old country."

Maria Lucia, hair in rollers under a kerchief, just winked and sped off down Stillwell Avenue.

At the social club, we discussed, yet again, the heroism of the scugnizzi in ridding Naples of the Nazis, but the Four Days of Naples uprising was a short period of heroism in the horrible living nightmare of mass butchery called World War II.

I could not be cheered that my father did not appear to be a victim, or at least that his body was not recovered. Calogero told me of rumors that Mariano Bartolomeo had cooperated with the Nazis to control the waterfront. True or not, if he was alive, I was sure he would have found a way to cooperate with the victors. His connections were too valuable a commodity. His potential survival just made my dealings with US authorities more difficult. I hated myself for thinking, yes, hoping, that the angel of death would soon take my father, now in his eighties.

Enough! Make peace, not war! World War II over, peace reigned in Brooklyn. Mario and Keira eventually took over the major operation of store number one. They groomed their firstborn, TJ, to run the second Brooklyn branch in Gravesend, next to the Culver Line.

TJ was a natural. His time in the store allowed Mario to take advantage of the GI Bill to get a formal education in business administration. Mario and Keira were able to put something down on a new home, still in the neighborhood but closer to the new store.

What a woman, that Keira! She became Mario's valuable business partner. Keira was even accepted wholeheartedly by le chiacchierone, well, by most of the gossipy old crows.

Colleen Keira, so full of blarney, even learned to speak a passable Italian, but with a proper Tuscan accent. Those limpid green eyes shone beautifully as she enunciated a line from Dante or even the name of a cheese. Keira took night classes in Italian at Brooklyn College. Mario was convinced she was in love with her instructor, a student from Bologna. Il Professore Garfagnana was getting his doctoral degree on the operatic works and life of Claudio Monteverdi. He earned a few bucks teaching evening Italian classes.

I overheard Mario and Keira many times in conversation from my perch in the back of the first store. They didn't seem to mind my presence, even though I too was a chiacchierone.

"Monteverdi was a pioneer of opera, at its dawning, really, and most of his fifteen operas were lost in a fire. *L'incoronazione* is one of only three to survive."

Silence from Mario.

"Mario, Monteverdi's *The Coronation of Poppea* premiered in Venice in 1642," Keira earnestly said.

"*O, che bello*," said Mario, expertly mimicking Keira's fine Tuscan pronunciation. "Oh, how lovely," he repeated in his cultivated Irish brogue. "So, I suppose that because it dwelt on Nero and his royal whore puttana, it was even more of a classic. That Garfagnana is a man of taste."

I could see Mario putting together a rally of punches, but Keira countered with a couple of quick jabs.

"Oh, Mario, you are so jealous. Professor Garfagnana is very dedicated to Italian culture and the Italian language."

"What does he tell you of the peasant dialect we spoke back in Campania?"

Keira, knowing better than to pursue that subject, just mentioned that *L'incoronazione* was performed a second time eight years after its Venice premiere, and in Naples of all places. "It was not performed for another 250 years, right around the time you were born! And such a monumental opera it is."

I could just imagine Mario thinking that his paisani probably saw it for what it was in 1651 and almost killed it. "So, this professor is from Bologna? It's famous for its *mortadella*, and we sell it in the store, though the Americans seem to prefer *bologna*."

"C'mon, Mario. Don't tell me about Professor Garfagnana's load of baloney."

I had to laugh out loud.

"Pops, get busy back there!"

This was a typical Mario-Keira sparring match. Their marriage was strong, the stores were doing well, and they seemed to sell equal amounts of mortadella and baloney. Keira preferred blarney to baloney, and Mario loved to say, "Well, you can almost eat baloney, but blarney?"

Mario often said that Ireland was the Sicily of the North Sea, and Keira agreed, but she did prefer the cuisine of the Mezzogiorno. Mario and Keira's Italian-Irish kids seemed to be driven by a hybrid vigor. Keira explained hybrid vigor to me, or she tried. She used the word *heterosis*, but Filomena did not approve of such language in our home, especially if the word was Irish.

TJ's features were a perfect Mediterranean-Celtic hybrid—dark hair and eyes set in a ruddy red North Sea face. Like his father Mario, TJ married young, to Peggy Mullen, a beautiful Irishwoman. Eighteen months later, in early 1947, Peggy bore him a son, TJ Jr., or just Junior, my favorite great-grandchild. Junior represented the end of the journey from the FBI of his Great-grandfather Giovanni to his own FBI—from full-blooded Italian to full-blooded Irish, at least in appearance. Years later, young man Junior could walk into an Irish pub and not arouse suspicion about his bloodline.

Junior's uncle Padraic did not go into too many bars, not in the neighborhood. His preference was for Manhattan establishments where race and gender identities were more fluid. He was a chameleon, easily going from Pat Ragnuno to PJ O'Runyan, and his Hi-Bar-hardened body could either encourage or discourage male patrons.

To this day, I hurt when talking of Anna, middle child of Keira and Mario. She shared tragedy with her cousin Angelina.

15

MIGRATORY BIRDS, FROM AMERICAN ROOSTS TO AMERICAN ROOTS (1945-1946)

There is little room in this city for us—
For we are immigrants, dark and perfidious
And new migrant flocks passing overhead
Are seen by neighbors to compete for their bread

The war was over. We survived. Our family businesses were doing well. I should have been celebrating my complete baptism as an American. But no, I was in a vise. While looking over my family, I sensed government officials looking down on me, investigating any underworld activities and questioning my loyalty to America.

To me the reality was that loyalty to America and underworld activities could be opposite sides of the same coin. *The government can come up with twisted plots because they do not hesitate to recruit the underworld in the cause of American victory. Me? I chose long ago to give up the immoral life of a scugnizzo.*

My father would have turned eighty-one in 1945. I had no idea if he was still alive or if he was even in Italy—no news from Calogero, none from my friends at Federal Plaza. He had outlived my poor mamma and maybe even Don Giuseppe, who had turned eighty-seven in 1944 and was dying from a malattia he had contracted during the war. Don Calogero was the new 'o donno 'e villa.

My love affair with America was ever challenging, yet always stronger. My greatest loves were here: from my family to Dodgers baseball. I laugh to myself when I say that, but both my American loves made it through the war. The opening of the 1945 baseball season was a celebration of spring and of hope in spite of the April 9 death of FDR.

Baseball's 1945 opening day was April 17, but barbarism was not over. On April 28 Mussolini and his puttana were brutally executed by Italian partisans who found them hiding in the trunk of a car, trying to escape across the Italian border. On May 8 Germany surrendered unconditionally, and the extent of their atrocities was coming to light. Japan surrendered late in the '45 season, on August 15, after atomic bombings of Hiroshima and Nagasaki—our own atrocities committed on large civilian populations.

Roosevelt's death saddened me in spite of his executive order declaring many of my paisani internal enemies. He "won" the war, while he kept baseball going to bolster American morale. The differences in the passing of Mussolini and of FDR were stark. FDR died in office, a leader who had gotten us through that terrible war—a war for which Il Duce shared responsibility. Il Duce died ingloriously at the hands of his own people.

"Filomena, Mussolini's executioners were too savage," I said in our kitchen. She answered with the double fist, the left in the crook of her bent right arm.

I did not mourn for Mussolini, but neither did I find joy in his death, because it emphasized my sense of loss for an Italy that let herself be led by an egomaniacal dictator. Mussolini's downfall in no way fully excised the horrible cancer the Fascists had imposed on Italy. If nothing else, Mussolini achieved a sort of Italian unification. Naples was an abused child of the unified Italy from 1861 on, but

Mussolini made all of Italy suffer for following his imperial and racist folly.

Brooklyn fared a lot better than Italy, and eventually our life returned almost to normal. The 1945 Dodgers, with a depleted roster, finished in third place. The pennant-winning Chicago Cubs were led by National League batting champ Phil Cavaretta.

On a glorious October day I was discussing baseball with some paisani in Peppe Ippolito's fish shop. Cavaretta's name came up. A native of Sicily, Peppe boasted that Cavaretta's parents came from Peppe's hometown of Sciacca—as if I didn't know. He pointed to Sciacca on the map of Sicily mounted on the wall behind his counter.

Peppe was not too tall but built like a fish barrel, stocky up and down. His dark, thick eyebrows met over a large nose proud with flaring nostrils. Dark eyes under overbearing eyebrows were twin roiling Sicilian tar pits. He grabbed a frozen eel like it was a baseball bat, his exposed forearm muscles rippling, a testimony to the schools of fish he had cleaned and scaled.

"Giovanni, you see how Sicily enriches America?"

"Why can't Sicily enrich the Dodgers? With Cavaretta the Dodgers win the pennant and probably the World Series."

"There's a lot of Sicilian talent to go 'round. You let the Yanks grab Joe DiMaggio and this good-looking Berra kid. Joe comes from a family of fishermen." Peppe winked.

"Oh, mannaggia, don't make me sick." I exhaled, slapping my forehead.

"Giovanni, Giovanni, you can also take some credit for Cavaretta. After all, Palermo and Naples were twin capitals in the Kingdom of the Two Sicilies."

Peppe, always the historian, had a point. I was happy to lay partial claim to Cavaretta, but I feared that most Sicilians would not be as generous as Peppe in sharing their native son with Naples. "Peppe, there are some, siciliani and napulitani, who do not look back too fondly on the Two Sicilies. Filomena is one, and I'm sure you know others."

Peppe furrowed his brow, his jutted jaw asking for clarification.

"She would have preferred the Two Naples."

Peppe looked as if he had never harbored such a crazy thought. We did not pursue the subject. Modern-day baseball was much livelier than dead history.

I would never dare ask Filomena her opinion about the equivalent status of Naples and Palermo. Not even the prospect of a quick review of classical Neapolitan curses and obscene gestures was enough of an incentive. Besides, we all knew those *maledizioni* and used them way too much. We children of the South write poetry with our curses, gestures and facial expressions—and sometimes put them to music.

So, with the war over and the Dodgers playing better, and Mario, Keira, and TJ taking care of the salumeria business, bless their hearts, I took advantage of my increasing freedom. I spent more time at home, corresponding with Calogero, reading *Il Progresso*, or playing in the garden. But I was not completely homebound. As a loyal Dodgers fan, I took the West End and Brighton lines to Ebbets Field for day games when the weather was good. Bleacher seats were fifty-five cents. In 1946 I could yell at rookie right-fielder Carl Furillo in dialect. I took grandkids and their buddies to Ebbets. They were instructed to tell their parents that I didn't "feed them no junk-a at the ballpark."

At home, entertaining grandkids was always a joy and usually accompanied by sipping a little wine, properly cut with water. I had a deep bench of grandkids. I could call on Mario and Keira's three—Anna, TJ, and Padraic—or on Nunziatina's four—Jijjie, Ben, Vina, and even fourteen-year-old Angelina—to sample cheese and partake of the diluted vintage of our own grape harvest. But

Filomena never admitted to being charmed by the flush on their cheeks. I felt a little guilty for overspicing Filomena's soppressata, but her response was entertainingly hot. I hoped she enjoyed our verbal tarantella, especially my claim that the young people were only tasting and savoring my wine—"*Solamente assagiando, mio amore.*"

Much of "Mannaggia'merica" disagreed with Filomena. For one, she was blanching from lack of sunshine. "If I was a mushroom, maybe I could be happy here! Italy is sunny and warm." But I think more important was that in Italy she was 'a signora—a lady—from a respected family.

"Here? We live in darkness and Americans don't show us enough respect!" She said this in our garden on a sunny day.

"Filomena, cara mia, come out with me to the Ebbets Field bleachers. You'll get a lot of sun and a lot of respect from your fellow fans, many of them paisani."

Her look scared me, and I still have a sore spot on my skull from the knuckle noogie that comment brought on.

Life was consumed with my love for Filomena and for America—though both often caused me àgita and worse. Of course, many of my problems I brought on myself. I could never imagine my situation if I had not followed Filomena's urgings to fly to America. In Mannaggia'merica, I had all of the old culture I could want—family, respect, bocce on Saturdays, Sunday pinochle, *briscola* anytime at the park or the social club, Old World cuisine, Italian theatre in Little Italy, street festivals, and an occasional opera at the confraternity hall of the neighborhood Most Precious Blood Parish. But Filomena was still complaining. Mannaggia, ancora!

Later that fall of 1946, on a weekday afternoon, Filomena and I were sitting under our grape arbor. Buzzing bees in the overhanging ripe grapes accompanied another of Filomena's angry

"Mannaggia'merica!" arias. Her audience included a row of eggplants, tomatoes, and googootz hanging from their own special trellis boxes.

I had to respond. "But cara, you recall how you hated the poverty, illiteracy, ignorance, and neglect in Naples? You were worried about the secret societies and the government in Rome getting us into stupid wars."

Filomena's face and hand gestures eloquently dispelled those concerns as temporary in the long, glorious history of her homeland. She bunched the fingers of her right hand around her raised thumb and shook this cone near my face, uttering an "Ehhhhh!" and then went on in the flowery country dialect of our forebears. "Wars? Didn't you and Mario go overseas to help America?"

I fell silent.

"And the government is still bothering you about your gangster father, your friend Mussolini, and selling that fake olive oil, over twenty-five years ago now. You should start your own line and call it Camurria Olive Oil because they never leave you alone."

I shrugged. I was surprised that she used the Sicilian word *camurria*—a trouble that never goes away, like gonorrhea. She wasn't finished, continuing in dialect: "This America is so impermanent, always changing. It lacks respect for traditions and for the honor of family. Back home, I was a favored child of a noble family, one with a lineage going back to the kingdom of Naples."

And the Kingdom of the Two Sicilies, with its twin capitals of Naples and Palermo?

I really risked her wrath during one of our after-dinner walks along the waterfront. It was a peaceful night. The kids were playing marbles and shooting baseball cards. I looked at young lovers and then at the moon over Gravesend Bay and blurted out, "Filomena, when I see the moon over the bay, I want to sing 'C'è la luna mezzu mare' … and I'm not even Sicilian!"

Filomena's face dropped, looking genuinely forlorn and at least ten years older. She recovered. "Giovanni, we're proudly napulitani.

And don't forget that it was fine men from fine families who lifted you out of the life of a scugnizzo."

Forget? She'll never *let me forget. I should remind her that this scugnizzo and his children and grandchildren have been good to her.*

"Giovanni, are you listening?"

"Sì, amore."

I reminded myself not to trifle too much with Filomena's feelings, not to make her feel even more out of place in America. Especially since she could not go back to Naples, not after two punishing wars, with Italy finding itself on the wrong side in the second. My blessed father-in-law, the widower Don Benedetto, had passed, and his holdings were disbursed among nieces and nephews. There was nothing for Filomena to return to. Nor for me. My mamma and her new husband had passed during the war. Don Giuseppe had survived the war but passed in 1946, at the age of eighty-nine. Perversely, I resented that my natural father, a capo of the waterfront, could still be alive, robust, and active. A reunion with him in Naples was the stuff of nightmares. In my waking hours I was sickened by thoughts of prosperous half brothers and half sisters greeting me in Naples.

The October 5, 1946 issue of *The Daily News* told how the Brooklyn Dodgers finished in a tie for the National League pennant but lost the playoffs to the Cardinals. *Mannaggia, my team shoulda won it without a playoff—we was robbed in two games with the Cards this season!*

But my Dodgers did not stand pat. During that year and its offseason, my beloved Bums signed Jackie Robinson, and later Don Newcombe and Roy Campanella. The three once played in the Negro Leagues. *Who is this Campanella? He's a Black man with an Italian name, and he looks like he can play. Maybe all three can help us. Could the 1947 National League pennant fly over Ebbets Field?*

Baseball! Whoever even heard of it in Campania? *Sounds like*

Campanella's ancestors came from there, I said to myself, and only to myself because Filomena never saw any use for baseball, not even for paisan right-fielder Carl Furillo. "The Skoonj" had a dynamite 1946 rookie season in Brooklyn. Even the Negro and Jewish fans called him "Skoonj," short for *Scungilli.* I don't know how Carl got that name, maybe because of his nose, like a big conch. I thought that pitcher Vic Lombardi was no slob either, and then there was that good-looking young pitcher, Ralph Branca. All this made me realize that I was *veramente americano.* I was truly American. I cared.

Though the Yankees had Joe DiMaggio, Phil Rizzuto, and their own 1946 rookie, Yogi Berra, they had none of my loyalty. Besides, the Bronx was almost in upstate New York. And even Filomena would agree that two of those Yankees having Sicilian roots didn't help their cause much. The New York Giants were even more hated, though their roster included Mickey Grasso, Ernie Lombardi, and Vince DiMaggio.

Mannaggia, New York baseball is like the Mezzogiorno—full of Italians who are bitter rivals.

16

GRANDCHILDREN IN THE NESTS OF MARIO AND NUNZIATINA (1946–1951)

Young birds repay parents' caring touches
By flying off to start new clutches
Yet alas, some young fail to survive
They fall from the nest in a fatal swan dive

Our brood was growing, and at times it seemed that the roles of grandfather and father and of grandmother and mother had merged. From 1925 to 1927 Mario had three kids, and from 1927 to 1932, Nunziatina had four. *Mannaggia! That's seven grandkids in eight years!* And by 1946, those kids were energetic adolescents and young adults ranging from fourteen to twenty-one years old.

Nunziatina, "widowed" at twenty-five years of age by her deserting figlio di puttana husband in 1932, somehow managed to get through the Depression and the war years. Jijjie and Ben worked hard at their carpentry and building trades, but their support was often generously spiced with àgita for their poor mamma. The teenaged twin brothers reinforced and prodded each other's young bull ambitions and adventures. I wasn't surprised that they took a little longer than most to finish high school. God bless them, they found time and energy for activities beyond school and work.

In 1946, nineteen-year-old Jijjie was making a name for himself in carpentry and boxing. He was undefeated in Golden Gloves amateur boxing, even in a few professional bouts into his early twenties. He trained and did roadwork on the sand of Coney Island Beach, which also gave him the opportunity to become a strong swimmer. Sure, there was sand, surf, and a place to train, but like the neighborhood, Coney also offered attractions, entertainment, and social connections. The beach was divided into "bays." And number fourteen was their own piece of surf and turf—a Brooklyn beach club. The membership list was strongly self-enforced. This Coney paradise, only two West End stops from Most Precious Blood Parish, prepared Jijjie for the Seabees. The Seabee symbol was a mad bee firing a machine gun and holding a monkey wrench and a hammer—Jijjie to a T.

Younger sister Vina became almost a stand-in for Nunziatina, a surrogate mother, as I heard her described by Myron Pollack III, who seemed to take a liking to her. Vina knew her brothers' tricks. She knew the score, and unlike Mamma Nunziatina, she was fluent in English and was not hearing impaired. Jijjie and Ben razzed their sis Vina as "Proper Miss Pratt" because she cramped their style—she could be a real *scocciament*, a pain in the ass, or worse.

On Wednesday evenings, before Nunziatina headed off to movie dish night, she frantically tried to make sure things at home were tied down. Vina told me of one eventful evening, boys nowhere to be found. She dutifully marched her mother to Tonnino's Pool Parlor. The neighborhood knew you could wager on pool in the front and poker in the back room. Miss Pratt and Donna Nunziatina entered the adjacent alley and climbed up the outdoor stairs to the parlor. The "doorman" tried to block their entrance, but Nunziatina, strong as a bull, pushed her way in. She saw her boys and let loose a string of maledictions that included "Ruffiani! Sfaccím!"

"Scoundrels and lowlifes!" was not enough. She was just getting started. "You don't have the decency to be home in time so I can go out for my one night of entertainment, and you spend your time *'ccà*? Here?" Everyone knew this was code for *cacata*—excrement.

The vision of little sis Miss Pratt and their immigrant mother was embarrassment enough. But then Nunziatina went into her aria. The chastened boys headed home, complaining only when they were beyond the earshot of their buddies and goombahs.

I became their "father" but also one of the boys. I once saw Jijjie waiting in line behind police barricades at a downtown Brooklyn burlesque establishment. He saw me leaving the earlier show. I noticed him before he could hide his face, and asked, "Johnnie, are you going in there?"

"Yes, Nonno," he said, looking down.

Jijjie's cheeks flushed, and I could feel his burn. I made sure my English was sufficiently broken. "Well, look-a the blonde on the far right! She's-a gotta some tits!"

By 1946 Vina was a beautiful seventeen-year-old. I looked forward to her visits to our salumeria on Bay Forty-Seventh and Stillwell Avenue, just a short walk from Nunziatina's Avenue T apartment on West Sixth Street. Vina was often her mother's ears and interpreter on her shopping trips to Delancey Street. They would leave very early in the morning, avoiding Saturdays, when the Jewish merchants were closed. Nunziatina believed that the religious haberdashers felt obliged to make a sale to the first visitors to the store, the consequence otherwise being a bad day overall. Nunziatina was a tough bargainer and poverty had hardened her heart. She was a lioness providing for her cubs.

"Nonno, I felt so sorry for the shopkeepers. Mamma would pick up a few socks, look 'em over, open them out, and then just throw them down, and I won't even tell you what she said."

"I can imagine." I didn't want to repeat coarse language to my sweet Vina. Her dark eyes were so radiant, her face like an owl's.

"So, we head for the door, and Mamma is keeping me close to her. She whispers, '*Nun guardà in detro!*' I was too embarrassed even to think of looking back at the poor man."

"Hey, I'm a shopkeeper. I know what it is to see a sale leave my store, especially if he's busted my ... bothered me with questions, complaints, and grouchy looks."

"Nonno, we are walking out and almost at the door and I hear 'Signora' from the shopkeeper. It was pitiful, like he was almost crying."

"Poor man," I said as I cut another wedge of provolone.

"And these guys speak Italian, even dialect! He chats with Mamma about her kids, school, politics, everything! He even gives me a beautiful purple ribbon 'to match my eyes.'"

Vina's owl eyes seemed to shine. I encouraged her to go on, almost waving a piece of provolone like a baton.

"Mamma was charmed, but she didn't want to show it. She was still negotiating. They finally agreed on prices for socks, underwear, and wash towels. The old guy pinched my cheek when we left."

"Vina, figlia mia, we Italians and Jews, and the Chinese too, are people of self-respect, and we learned to respect each other in lower Manhattan. We're all businessmen, and business makes us equals."

Vina did not seem so impressed with my philosophy of equality. "I won't even tell you about picking up *asafoetida* at the Chinese botanicals."

I held up my free hand, begging for peace, then pointed to my piece of cheese. "You know, the strong cheese odor of our store is offensive to many Americans. It probably makes some stay away. Asafoetida would have kept the vampires away."

Vina gave an owl blink of agreement and reached for a piece of provolone.

Jijjie and Ben, fatherless and dealing with a household of females—Nunziatina, Vina, and young Angelina—gravitated to neighborhood "men of respect," men who provided work. Two were family—Uncle Mario and their Nonno Giovanni. But there were others outside the family, businessmen, including those in the gambling business. One was Moishe (Moe) Liebowitz, who befriended Jijjie and contracted him for all manner of renovations in his Brooklyn establishments. Jijjie was a quick study in plumbing, electrical wiring, flooring, and, of course, carpentry.

He also knew how to keep his mouth shut.

Jijjie's boxing success further attracted the attention of Mr. Liebowitz, who was promoting a few professional boxers of his own. I think Moe saw more than just another "palooka" in Jijjie. My grandkid was now in his early twenties. He was an excellent tradesman—we still use the display case he built for the first salumeria. He was also smart and tough, just like Moe. Neither of them was a *domkop*, using Moe's language. Moe saw a leader in Jijjie and did not encourage him to turn pro, at least not in the ring. So, Jijjie had a nonno, yours truly, and a *zaydeh*, Yiddisher Moe.

Uncle Mario, with three kids of his own and a responsibility of running the salumeria, still found time to be a stand-in father figure for his nieces and nephews. As I was mourning my Dodgers' loss to the Cardinals in the 1946 National League playoffs, Mario's own kids were going from fledglings to their nuptial flights. TJ was married and a father at twenty-one and was already helping to plan our second store in a property his father Mario had bought.

Meanwhile Anna, just turned twenty, was seeing an innamorato, Cosimo, a Sicilian as rough as if he were cut crudely from hard wood, or a rock. Cosimo was a stubborn stone head, a capo tosto, and not too finished. My concern about Cosimo had nothing to do with superbia. He just did not seem right for Anna.

Late one afternoon I showed up at Mario and Keira's place with a bottle of anisette.

"Pops! Come in. Let me help you with the bottle. Whaddya doing? You don't have to bring anything!"

"Mario, it's nothing." I winked. "I have friends in the distribution business."

We sat at his dining room table. TJ was in the store. Padraic and Anna were not around.

"So, you didn't come over to impress me with your fine taste in liquors. What's up? Keira and TJ will be home from the store soon."

Mario sensed the reason for my visit. "Scusa, Mario, forgive me, but I don't like what I see in Cosimo."

Mario's expression instantly changed. I had blown off his jovial mask. "Anna really likes the guy," he said earnestly. "He's hardworking, Pops."

I knew my eyes widened, and Mario blurted out, "But he's a real hardhead."

"I can say the same about your mother."

Mario rolled his eyes.

"But your mother has a lot of very good features, Mario."

Mario smiled and then got serious again. "Keira and I have been talking with Anna, but you know how it is with young kids in love." He gave me an exaggerated wink. "I wonder how Professor Garfagnana would have said, 'Love conquers all?'"

"Well, I just hope this Cosimo-Anna thing is not a tragic opera."

"Amen, and health to you, Pops."

"Salute a te, Mario."

We made small talk, no need to write a libretto for Cosimo and Anna. I made sure to leave something in the bottle for Keira.

As I was leaving, I had to ask, "And what about your Padraic, Mario?"

"You know, he's going to be nineteen soon, and he doesn't seem to have a thing for the girls yet. He's still a kid. He's still a kid."

Mario repeated himself too eagerly, and I thought, *Yeah, he's still a kid.* I just said, "What's the rush?"

Anna and Cosimo were in a rush. They eloped soon after my visit with Mario. The newlyweds moved into a converted two-family home just off Harway Avenue. The grandma landlady, Mrs. Talarico, a *calabresa*, lived in the basement, and her daughter and *abruzzese* son-in-law occupied the main floor with their two kids. Anna and Cosimo moved into a three-room apartment on the top floor. Anna told me that the separate front entrance to the top level suited Cosimo because he sensed haughty arrogance in the non-Sicilian family.

It was easy to see that Cosimo felt opposition all around, from his landlady, from his in-laws Mario and Keira, from Filomena and me, and especially from brother-in-law Padraic. Probably because he lacked imagination for other insults, Cosimo usually badgered Padraic, calling him a half-breed, but to Cosimo that same background in Anna was magically appealing. Beautiful dark-red curly locks crowned her freckled face. Her hazel eyes were beacons over high cheekbones. They broadcast both beauty and strength from a face that was a female version of mine, but much more artistically molded, colored in with lighter pastels. She had curves that extended up to her full lips. Anna changed Cosimo's outlook on mixed heritage, at least at first.

I did have to admit that physically, Anna and Cosimo made an attractive couple. Cosimo was a dark and muscular Sicilian. His black hair with an off-center part was combed straight back, accentuating his flat forehead. The aquiline nose, separating his closely set, hard, coal-black eyes, gave the impression of a raptor, and he did constantly peck and bully street acquaintances.

Cosimo worked for a coal delivery company, shoveling coal into chutes that fed basement home furnaces. The truck driver was responsible for first releasing the right amount of coal into a pile on the sidewalk and then writing up the bill while Cosimo shoveled. Cosimo longed to elevate to the driver's position of responsibility. The *baresi* dominated both the coal and ice businesses in Brooklyn—they kept the homes warm and the iceboxes cold. The baresi were from Bari, on the Adriatic coast directly east of Naples on the Italian peninsula. To Cosimo, the baresi were "Northerners," just like the napulitani, and they both looked down on the siciliani.

Cosimo felt exploited, unappreciated, even scorned. A blind person could see that, and by the second winter of his marriage to Anna, his own furnace needed stoking. Cosimo was a man with eyes so wandering that even his male buddies told him to take it easy. After all, not every skirt was a *mala femmina*, a loose woman, and some could even be the wife, sister, or a daughter of a good man, or worse, a man of respect. Cosimo imagined himself as special, a guy sought by women—in his mind, if he could bring a little happiness into their lives, well, so be it. Besides, he always went home to Anna, or at least that's what he told her.

Eventually he came upon a woman who was truly unconnected but who at first appeared uninterested. Teresa was a war widow and one of the very few neighborhood women who was a regular at Tony's Tavern—and usually without an escort. Everyone knew her, and Cosimo wanted to know her much better. Cosimo did not know how to modulate his voice, and he was easily overheard at Tony's, especially when trying to impress a lady.

"Don G, you know I ain't no gossip" was Tony's opener one day when he came by the salumeria to pick up cold cuts, cheeses, olives, and giardiniera for his place. "Barkeeps ain't supposed to blab, but everybody in the neighborhood knows what's goin' on." Tony sampled a couple of olives from my big barrel. His weekly order was still sealed. "First time I see him make his move, he sidles over to her spot at the bar. 'So, how come you're here almost every night?'

"You know Teresa's no dummy. She comes back with something like 'Well, if you didn't come to Tony's almost every night, you wouldn't know that.'

"Now this was a fast comeback for Cosimo, so she goes on while Cosimo's got his mouth open like he's trying to catch flies. 'So, why should I stay home and look at the four walls when there are interesting people right here? You'd be surprised at the stories I've heard.'

"I'm wiping wine glasses as if I hear nothing. He says, 'Like what?'

"She goes on: 'My name is Teresa, but you know that, and nice to meet you too. I know you're Cosimo the Sijjie. I've heard your name here more than once.'

"Cosimo comes up with something like he'd break someone's face who badmouthed him."

I nodded in agreement with Tony—a typical Cosimo comment.

"I keep on polishing wine glasses, and she says, 'Don't be so touchy, Cosimo. I have Sicilian blood too. Buy the next round and we talk nice. I ain't gonna gossip, especially not here. No one would speak to me.'"

All the while I'm picturing Teresa at the bar. Women look prettier or more alluring, or maybe more vulnerable, when they drink in a public place. After all, they could drink at home. Teresa had dark, curly hair adorning a pretty face probably too made up for the tastes of many neighborhood women. She was still trim, and her dark eyes were intelligent, inquisitive, and cunning, but, yes, with a touch of vulnerability.

Cosimo became the hunter.

A predator can at times be surprised, even hurt, by the prey's defense. Someone more discerning than Cosimo might have read these contrasting signals, but he saw only a single, attractive woman who not only appeared to want to talk but carried the conversation.

"So long, Tony. Keep the peace at the tavern, and let me know important gossip."

Tony left with his box of bar treats. I took an unnecessary inventory of my cheeses and salamis to get my mind off the adventures of Cosimo, Teresa, and Anna.

My mind's eye could see Teresa and Cosimo making small talk, for which Cosimo had no talent. Chitchat turned into a pre-mating flourishing of feathers, first at Tony's, when they started sitting at a table for two. They then turned to the more private third-floor apartment Teresa rented in a wood-frame house. I knew of most of his visits to Teresa's because the tenant ladies, the chirping chiacchierone, always knew exactly when Cosimo had alighted. The thin walls of the walk-up helped them follow the progress of the relationship.

I'm sure Cosimo learned of Teresa's ex-husband. It was neighborhood lore. He had run off in 1943 but was drafted soon after. He was a fatality in the Battle of the Bulge at the end of '44 before the divorce was finalized. Most everyone in the neighborhood knew this, but I'm sure Cosimo was hearing it for the first time.

Anna started visiting her mother and me at the salumeria. Anna talked when she could, or I would stroll with her to the Gravesend waterfront when the weather was good, leaving Keira to handle the customers.

"Keira, I'm taking a walk to the bay. I wanna see if they're catching porgies."

Keira, who knew Anna had no interest in fish, yelled out, "Don't let Anna get a chill." We couldn't leave until Keira kissed us both goodbye—Madonna, she was becoming more Italian every day.

As we strolled, Anna filled me in for a while. She imitated Teresa confusing Cosimo at Tony's. 'Luck o' the Irish. My husband and I didn't get around to getting divorced. He gets killed in Europe, and I'm supposed to get something from Uncle Sam. So maybe you can get double lucky with me.'

"Now Grandpa, Cosimo was not too sure of Teresa's meaning. He ain't no poet, as you know. He knew that Teresa was much more Italian than Irish."

Anna was warming up despite the air off the bay getting colder. "I could see Cosimo telling her, 'Hey, I gotta get home. Anna is getting suspicious and I know your perfume is on my clothing.'"

"Nonno, that puttana. Yeah, I could see her saying, 'C'mon, Cosimo, my hot glowing coal, stay for a while longer. It's cold out there and my furnace needs stoking.'"

That was the way Teresa talked, but she had to be even less subtle with Cosimo. I gave Anna a look of sympathy. I felt helpless. If I were really mobbed up, a coupla wise guys would be making a house call on Cosimo.

The chiaccherone neighbors missed few details. Cosimo, coal shoveler from the Land of Etna, no doubt understood Teresa's scream of "*Stromboli!*" at the moments of his frequent eruptions.

Anna told me what she got, not only from Teresa's gossipy neighbors but also from her own imagination. She also let me know how she confronted Cosimo: "I can smell that puttana on you, and I don't mean her perfume!"

I gulped a little as Anna went on.

"And that sfaccím just smirks. Yeah, he took the accusation as a compliment to his virility. His best defense was 'Anna, I always come home to you, and you know that other women mean nothin' to me!'

"Forgive me, Nonno, but I had to tell him, 'You stick that *cazzo* wherever, and it means nothing to you? And what does that say about me?'"

I could only wince at Anna's anger and honesty. She told me that Cosimo was impressed with how much dialect his wife had picked up from her father, Mario, and her Italian immigrant grandparents, especially from her Nonna Filomena, who filled Anna's ears with dirt on neighborhood lowlifes. Since Filomena's English wasn't so strong, words and expressions like puttana, mafioso, and contemptible coward, *vigliacco*, became part of Anna's everyday conversation.

"So Cosimo tries to explain his point of view as a 'man of the world,'" she said. "I couldn't hold it in any longer, and I hit him with *vaffanculo*! I know he understands that, but just in case, I was ready to tell him to introduce his sociable cazzo to his asshole."

"Anna, don't raise your voice. You'll scare the fish, and I'm sure the fisherman can hear you."

"Sorry, Nonno." She looked straight into my face but did not seem contrite.

That same look had to have an effect on Cosimo. I could just see newfound respect breaking through Cosimo's face of stone, but I could also picture his frustration because he could not reason with this Irish-Italian she-beast.

"So," she went on, "his response was to slam the door on his way back to Teresa's apartment. Of course, our landlady and her family were again on the alert. TJ, Padraic, Mom, and Pop know all the sorry details, and now you know, as if you didn't already."

The months dragged on. We could not make Cosimo see the light, the consequences of his actions. Neither fatherly advice nor threats seemed to work. Filomena said it best, in our dialect: "There is none so deaf as he who will not hear, *'o peggio surdo è chillo ca nu' bbo sentí.*"

Then came that snowy night in early spring. Cosimo returned

home after dark and found landlady Mrs. Talarico and her son-in-law's family on the front stoop. Cosimo's front entrance door was open and the odor of gas wafted out. Neighbors from next door joined the family. I could imagine their looks of grief, loathing, and fear. The police and Brooklyn Union Gas had already been notified.

Later they told me Cosimo flew up the stairs and through the open door to his apartment. He closed the door to any eyes peering behind him, but the family downstairs had already seen sweet twenty-two-year-old Anna on her knees, her head resting sideways on a towel inside the open oven. There were no signs of life.

Cosimo pulled Anna's limp body away from the oven. All the windows were already opened. He dragged her to a windowsill, but Anna was long gone. Did he think of the irony of Anna killing herself in her gas oven in a building that still had a coal furnace? Filomena told me that if Cosimo could read the last inscribed mental notes of the dead, he would have learned that just before she lost consciousness, the gas chambers of the Third Reich were on Anna's mind. I don't know why Filomena said this, but I do know she could all too often read my mind.

Dealing with police and the coroner was a nightmare, made all the worse because Cosimo became very scarce. Anna's funeral was at our place. It was packed, and some young kids had to sleep in the main parlor with Anna's open casket. They giggled all night. "I think she moved!" "I think she likes you!" Those were shows of bravado. The showing of the body, *la veglia funebre*—sounds more poetic in Italian—was only a day. Anna had taken a precious life, a holy gift from God. This was a mortal sin, and she could not have a funeral mass at the church. A very nice Protestant minister, Reverend Tom Moorehouse, came by and gave a eulogy. I offered him an envelope, but he refused and said, "Pay me by praying for Anna's soul." I did not want him to see my tears.

The burial was in nondenominational Greenwood Cemetery, where there was a lovely place for precious Anna. I could not get the thought out of my mind that Anna could not divorce, another mortal sin. She was squeezed between the Church and the devil and eventually did the impulsive thing, the thing that did not require lawyers and planning. She turned on the oven, and that night, she followed through.

Cosimo did not attend the *veglia* or the burial. Neither did his people, and they never came into the salumeria. If Mario and Keira were capable of a maluocchio, it would have been cast on the House of Cosimo. Later in 1948 Cosimo left town for the baresi community of Metuchen, New Jersey. He knew he could be of use to the coal and ice vendors there. With his natural physical strength, he had little problem shoveling coal and lugging large blocks of ice up four-story walk-ups. I refrained from saying anything good or bad about him to his new employers.

Teresa decided not to join him in Jersey. She also made herself rare at Tony's. A new haunt for her, at least on Thursdays, was the Most Precious Blood confessional. She wore a kerchief over her locks, dressed modestly, and tended to look downward, avoiding people's stares.

Padraic took Anna's death very hard. I feel like an idiot saying that —she was his sister fercryinoutloud. But even for siblings they were especially close. Padraic had opened up to Anna as to no other, not even to me, his nonno. Anna understood that he felt different, and she did not care that he wasn't interested in girls. They both took the brunt of Cosimo's abuse, which probably only strengthened their bond.

After Anna passed, Padraic and I talked much more, and I hoped my receptive ear was as much of a comfort to him as it was to me.

Less than a year after attending Anna's *veglia* in his nonno's front parlor, Padraic enrolled in Brooklyn College as an accounting major. He told me on the phone, "I start in the fall semester, 1949."

"If you don't make a fortune," I said, "you can at least count other people's dollars and maybe even be of use to your Papà Mario, your Mamma Keira, and your Nonno Giovanni, especially around tax time."

I was thinking of that earlier conversation when the phone rang in the salumeria. "Pops, it's Padraic," yelled Mario.

I grabbed the receiver. "Ciao, bello, comme staje?"

"Ciao *unonn*. I was thinking, you should see more of the world."

And I was thinking. *My Irish-Italian grandson calls me grandpa in napulitano. The kid is turning out all right.*

"Well, Padraic. I've seen Naples, France, and Brooklyn and the FBI headquarters, what else is there?"

"Come on, let me show you a Brooklyn you don't know. Can you meet me at Brooklyn College? Lots of pretty young ladies here."

"Padraic, you're enough of an attraction for me, and never talk like that around your Nonna Filomena."

"Hey, I have some free time before my next class. Can you take the B6 bus to the college?"

"I took a boat from Naples to Little Italy. I think I can find Brooklyn College."

"OK, see you in an hour? I'll be in front of Boylan Hall. Just ask anybody when you get off. Or ask the driver."

I took the West End two stops from Bay Fiftieth Street to Bay Parkway, where I caught the B6 to the college. The bus driver appeared to be my age and had a napulitano accent. I sat almost across from him on the other side of the aisle, next to the entrance. We spoke in dialect, mostly about raising kids in this America. He liked that I was visiting a grandson student at the college. I was let off near the hall in the beautiful Midwood neighborhood of one-family homes and well-kept gardens. "Gràzie, paisano."

"At your service," and he followed with dialect, just in case I mistook his meaning: "*A ggrazia vosta.*"

I saw beautiful Padraic straight off. He gave me a hug and then a recommendation for a coffee place, Il Nascondiglio, just across the street. "You know it means 'the hideout,' but I tell the Jewish students it's Yiddish for something like 'nosch finger.'"

I laughed, not really knowing why.

"Whatever, Nonno, we can have a demi-tasse and real sfogliatelle or, if you prefer, a bagel or knish with Cel-Ray soda." Padraic emphasized "prefer" with that Irish wink of his late grandfather, Tom O'Donnell.

I had to laugh, this time for real. "Padraic, you look great. Bread and water would make me happy if I shared it with you."

Over espressos and sfogliatelle we talked, and of course Anna came up.

"Anna was always open with me," he said. "She'd say, 'Padraic, you're my brother. Who cares about your private life? Some people never get married. Nonno's got enough grandkids and great-grandkids.'"

"Well, you might think you have enough, but try losing one," I said, and immediately felt like a dumb jackass chooch, 'cause my loss was Padraic's even greater loss.

Not even blinking, he added, "It was so great that I could talk with Anna."

"I'm so sorry you don't have Anna anymore, Padraic."

He actually laughed, telling me what Anna once told him: 'Hey, take it from your sis, having a boyfriend is not always heaven like the love songs sing. Frank Sinatra, shut your Dago mouth!'"

We both let out a laugh, and I said it, I really said it, "Well, I hope for you a boyfriend is a blessing." I felt honored that Padraic could open up with me.

"Nonno, I can walk into a pub in Brooklyn Heights and be

picked out as queer bait. I should have no trouble finding a boyfriend. They know I'm material before they suspect I have Italian blood."

"Well, me fine broth o' a lad," and here I was doing a poor imitation of Padraic's Irish grandparents, "go for it. Someday the whole family will know, and you know something, I bet no one will give a flying fuck."

My outburst surprised me. I was glad Filomena was not in earshot, but she probably could read the blasphemy in my mind. I admitted to myself, *English is a great language for blasphemy, but I can very fluently genuflect in Italian.*

Padraic smiled. "Yeah, I guess it's better I tell the whole family. If they learned from someone else, like the gavoons at Tony's, it would hurt everybody. One of Myron Pollack Jr's boys is queer, and he's the best lawyer in the family. Damn it, the Jews always seem to be a step ahead of the Micks and the greaseballs."

I could only smile and wiped a tear I blamed on the cigarette smoke.

"You know what Anna used to tell me? 'Hey, my brother, whatever I can do, just let me know when you make the big announcement, and I'll make sure that my gorilla of a husband stays off your case.'

"Nonno, I called her Anna-Banana, but you know that, and I'd tell her, 'You're the best sis a guy could have.'"

I had no answer, so he went on. "She was a feisty one. 'First, I ain't a banana, and in the real first place, I'm your only sister.'" Padraic chuckled. "Oh, by the way, I'm staying away from courses in interior decorating, hair styling, and fashion design," he said in a fake falsetto.

I was thinking *Fake falsetto? How false can you get?*

"Those occupations do nothing for me. But, sonuvabitch, I wish I coulda told all this to Anna."

"Paddie-boy, you just told *me*, and I'm sure Anna hears you."

By 1950, I was much more concerned with the misfortunes of my Dodgers than by the revelation of Padraic's sexual tendencies. It was said that Leonardo da Vinci, and maybe even Michelangelo, had the same inclinations, and don't tell me that sixteen major league teams—four hundred players plus coaches—had no homosexual men. "Straight and virile" men were not always the best examples of sexual behavior—just look at Cosimo. Besides, Padraic was not *un effeminato*, so no one would mess with him after seeing his Hi-Bar routine with his shirt off.

Mario and Keira passionately cherished their surviving offspring. The hope was that TJ and his Peggy would be prolific.

In the late forties, Moe Liebowitz took off for Las Vegas, where gambling was legal and where there was no shortage of players, including Hollywood celebrities and wannabes. Among the visitors from LA was one Angelo Piccolini. Going on Jijjie's information and playing his own contacts, Moe was able to locate this wayward dad.

Moe sent me a letter about his encounter with Angelo, the escaped uccello.

Las Vegas, NevadaJanuary 20, 1950

Dear Mr. Ragnuno (Giovanni): I don't often write personal letters. Business letters I dictate to my stenographer. This one I write in my own hand. I hope my penmanship is legible. To think that my father told me more than once that our family were scribes, going back thousands of years.

Enough already. I want to inform you that I have made contact with your fugitive son-in-law, Angelo, father of the twins Jijjie and Ben and of beautiful Vina and Angelina.

You have fine grandchildren. Their mother Nunziatina deserves a medal for raising them so well, alone and through tough times. But you know that. You and Filomena deserve some of the credit for overseeing Nunziatina's family. I don't write to be a yenta, as my own wife likes to say. Your expression *chiacchierone* sounds so much more like a gossiper.

So, back to brass tacks. I was able to track down Angelo and got word to him to visit my Vegas office when business pulled him from LA to Vegas.

I was surprised to see this Angelo, this worldly, creative gentleman. He was timid as he entered the office of my small downtown casino. The gambling business has made me a good judge of human nature—I can watch my pit bosses all night through my one-way mirror as they watch the games on the floor. You get to be able to read people.

So, this Angelo. I saw a nervous, well-dressed man, hat in hand. His stooped shoulders were just one sign of his insecurity. Another was that he held his hat over the fly of his pants.

He starts off with "Mr. Liebowitz, it's very nice to meet you. I am in Vegas to meet with some potential clients, and I learned that you wanted to talk about my family in Brooklyn."

I told him I appreciated his agreeing to meet with me, and on short notice. So, I got to the point, and I'm writing this from the notes of the steno. She's a woman I can trust. I want to send you accurate information.

I told Angelo, "Your family in Brooklyn is doing well. Your wife and children are talented, hardworking, and tough people, but it has not been easy for them. It would be a personal favor to me if you helped them in their struggles."

As I said, I'm a good judge of people, especially people under pressure. Gambling will do that to you. When I mentioned helping his family, Angelo dropped his head and studied his hatband. Then he said in a voice so low I had trouble hearing him: "Well, Mr. Liebowitz, business has been slow out here. I hope that with the war over, people go back to buying hats. You never can tell if hats will go out of style."

So, I try to comfort him. "We can only hope that they don't, but whatever the situation, family never goes out of style, and a man's responsibility is to his family."

He started to say something, but I shut him up. "I have the greatest respect for your son John and for his twin brother, Ben, and their two younger sisters. Their mother is a fighter just like Jijjie. The whole family is fighters and they stick together. I would consider it a favor to me if you could somehow see to send some support their way."

He got the message. You know I don't look like a hit man, but I do have friends. Angelo knows that, of course, so I hammed it up by giving him my unblinking stare, our version of the "eye."

He recovered enough to tell me, "I appreciate your concern, Mr. Liebowitz. I know you have contacts in Brooklyn [pause], and I am sure they will send you news that Angelo is helping his family."

I thanked him for understanding and held out the teaser that we might do business in the future. This is from the steno's notes: "I can use creative people to help outfit casino entertainers."

He offered me a limp hand and got up to leave. I told him that my secretary would show him out. I "phoned" Jinx the steno as if she were well out of earshot. She's a retired show girl with a great sense of timing. She eventually got up from her cubby next door and showed Angelo out.

By the way, Giovanni, Vegas is full of characters. I thought Brooklyn had them by the dozen, but Vegas has Brooklyn beat. So, Jinx, all six feet of her, after showing Angelo out, returns to my office, and she tells me, "That is one tormented man."

Yours truly,

Moe

Whatever happened between Angelo and Moe, a check periodically arrived at Nunziatina's place starting in early 1950. There was no note with the check that was signed by one Angelo Piccolini. It was elegantly folded in fine linen stationery. Each check helped, of course, but Nunziatina always made the sign of the cross before redeeming the payment from Angelo, that scum-of-the-earth sfaccím. Nunziatina also genuflected when asking for the blessing of one Moishe Liebowitz at the Most Precious Blood Sunday mass.

The last check arrived in 1956.

17

THE BIRDS, THE BEES, THE WORMS, AND THE VIRUS (1950–54)

Stowaways on ships between coasts
Or creatures hitching on flying hosts
Can spread much good to the coveted zion
But also pestilence—the good overriding

The Feds must like Jackson. Every time I see him, his desk is bigger. But he shrinks in comparison. Is this how he saw himself when the FBI waived his mandatory retirement?

Jackson sat back in his swivel chair—an aging fifty-something behind a majestic dark mahogany desk. Twenty-five years after our first encounter, he had developed a double chin and permanent shadows under tired eyes. His mouth was framed by wrinkles, witnesses to constant scowling. He locked his hands behind his head, jutting out his elbows like useless wings.

"Have you heard of the Marshall Plan, Don Giovanni?"

I hated the way he pronounced "Don," like the first name of

Don Newcombe or Don Ameche. I also hated his tone, like he was my history teacher.

"Yes, Mr. Jackson. It's very generous of our government, and wise, to help the non-communist countries of Europe."

"And I suppose it's no surprise to you that Italy is one of those countries. A country that declared war on us is now receiving our aid."

"Yes, very wise, Mr. Jackson. Italy suffered greatly, and I believe America's help will make it a strong ally of America."

"Yeah, they should be so good to us if we lost the war. I didn't call you in to make small talk, Don. Your father is missing." He drew out "missing" for effect. "Mariano Bartolomeo was seen after the war and as late as 1948, but now, two years later, he is nowhere to be found. He's an old Dago, about eighty-five years old, but some people just stay spry longer than others."

"Mr. Jackson, I do not insult you. I do not like being called a Dago, *not by you, anyway.*"

"Don't look so distressed. You're the son of Dago Mariano Bartolomeo. I don't know what that makes you." Jackson gave me a leer that made him look even older. "St. John, I'm sure you people use words like Mick, Limey, and worse—like what do call Neee-gros?"

Jackson sang out the "Neee" like a soprano. And then he answered his own question.

"Oh yeah, mool-inyonna. That's really good. My niece got a Mr. Potato Head, but an eggplant, a mool-inyonna, would be even better." I could only stare, and snarl inside. *What a disgusting person, a real* schivazzo*!* Maybe he was trying to incite me to spit something out. He became only slightly more civil.

"Mr. Gee-o-vanni, lots of ships make the round trip to Italy under this Marshall Plan, and they're doing it for almost two years now. Mariano Bartolomeo was recognized as a labor organizer of the docks—if you want work, you pay the union bosses. No doubt he has customs agents on his payroll." I got an all-knowing smirk.

"You know he's going back and forth like a first-class stowaway and dealing with his goombahs here. It's probably easy to shake a few dollars loose from the billions Uncle Sap is spending on the waifs of Europe."

"Mr. Jackson, thinking you know something doesn't make it the truth."

"OK, John Ron-yoo-know-who, here's the truth I do know. You sell imported Italian stuff in your store. And what's not imported you fake, like that olive oil caper. You import those canned tomatoes from your old stomping grounds and export grape rootstocks to the old country. By the way, I can just see you stomping grapes back when."

"So?"

"So, with ships going back and forth, and your father and his goombahs controlling the docks, maybe, just maybe, they pay off a merchant marine captain, and Uncle Sam is importing some bad cargo from your old country, cargo like … "

He waited for me to finish the sentence. He waited some more.

"Get outta my office. We'll get to the truth. Keep those Pollack mouthpieces on your payroll. You'll need them."

I walked out as fast as I could. Even running I could not outrace my thoughts.

My father still alive? And my mamma, Don Giuseppe, Zia Bettina all gone? Do the meek inherit the earth? Yes, Giovanni, time kills the good and the evil. Births, baseball seasons, and harvests mark the passage of time—endlessly, sènza fine, *at least until my end. I'm sixty-five! But I don't plan this year to be the end for me, not yet. I'm not giving Jackson the satisfaction of seeing me go first, certainly not before the FBI pulls the plug on this old buzzard.*

A couple of weeks later, Keira and Mario were working in the store while I was trying to chat.

"Ahh, *figliulanza*, 1950 has been a big year."

Keira raised an eyebrow, alerted by my dialect for "children." She had learned my style—a disarming opener and then a surprise jab with bad news or a comment on the Irish. She put down the big cheese knife, wiped her hands on her apron, and prepared for hand-to-hand combat.

"Yes," I said, "a big year, but big doesn't always mean good." I paused on the last word, letting my line out.

"How so, Pops?" Mario took the bait.

"Well, besides my being eligible for FDR's Social Security, it's now fifty years since I was let into Don Giuseppe's villa, where I met your mother, Mario."

"Well, all of that is good."

"Yeah, but we're halfway through a very bloody century. The bleeding of America *non finisce mai*, it never stops."

Keira's greenish eyes glowed at me. "Don't I know we're fighting in Korea. You were in World War I and Mario in World War II, and now we have two boys of military age and so does Nunziatina!"

"Sorry for bringing it up, Keira. Maybe the boys will stay out of Korea by the time it's all over."

"Don't bet on it, Pops," Mario said. He grabbed Keira's arm as if seeking reinforcement to end this conflict. He also changed the subject. "Hey, we finally got the second store going. And I like that area around McDonald Avenue."

"I like the way your TJ is taking it over," I offered.

Keira sighed. "Maybe he'll stay in the store instead of going to Korea."

I tried to raise her spirits. "I think TJ is going to do a beautiful job running the place. He has a head for business, that lad."

But I couldn't leave well enough alone. Agent Jackson was a permanent itch I could not scratch. I let out some dialect: "*'O pesce fetta d'a capa.* The fish starts to stink first from the head. We said that back in Naples, and I bet the Irish say something similar."

I had hit Keira right between the eyes, and those emerald lanterns were fixed on me.

"Been a big year in New York City," I went on.

Mario shot Keira a quick glance. "Oh, come on, Pops, we all know about our crooked Mayor O' Dwyer."

"Mario, I get so much grief from people, and not just from Agent Jackson—those knowing looks, the smirks, as if every paisan has a Black Hand tattooed on his heart."

Keira piped up. "Let me give you a shortcut to where you're heading."

"A shortcut? To where? You gonna tell me something I don't know?"

We all knew and had loved our Irish-born Mayor O'Dwyer. He was a war hero and ex-seminary student. As Brooklyn district attorney he sent Murder Incorporated hit man Lepke Buchalter to the chair. He easily won the mayoralty in 1945, backed by the Tammany Hall Irish political machine. His 1949 reelection was a snap, and then just like that, he resigned in mid-August 1950, just as the Dodgers began their slide. Truman got O'Dwyer out of the country by the end of August—named him ambassador to Mexico. Turned out he was covered with filth.

Keira snapped me out of my recollections. "Nonno, O'Dwyer was filthy for sure, but he had Italian and Jewish allies, not just Irish ones, like his deputy fire commissioner Moran. That bastard ran betting rings right out of O'Dwyer's office! He had to grease a lotta blue. Coupla cops in my family took early retirement all of a sudden."

"Keira, *bella mia*, beautiful mother of my TJ and Padraic and dear, departed Anna, we need to glorify our heroes and not the filthy among us."

Brooklyn DA Miles McDonald was the hero of that episode, putting the heat on O'Dwyer and the police. I said, "Bet you don't know McDonald Avenue is named after Miles McDonald's father."

"Oh, I know it, Nonno. And I'm making sure that your Mario stays one of the good guys."

A tear streamed down my smiling sixty-five-year-old face.

For the Dodgers, the end of the '50 season really was an end. My Dodgers lost the pennant on the last day. To me, Jackie Robinson was the only Dodger fighting to keep the team alive. I was beginning to feel that Naples and Brooklyn shared a curse, a maledizione.

New seasons, new demons. The Korean War started in the middle of the '50 season and was still going strong in '51. Near the end of spring training, on March 25, 1951, we had Mario and Keira's "clan" over for Easter Sunday dinner. TJ and Peggy came with their two kids, five-year-old Junior and four-year-old Therese. Padraic brought his friend Kevin, but I did not know if he was a "steady." Jijjie and Ben went to their girlfriends' homes. Nunziatina took a blessed day off.

A big hit was the ricotta-filled ravioli with a light, creamy white sauce infused with diced ham. The ravioli came from store number two. TJ's idea was to make the second branch, "his" branch, known for ravioli, if only to get people into the store and to associate it with Easter. Customers waited in lines going around the corner to pick up their orders. But the pall of war was hanging over us. My four grandsons were of draft age—not only TJ and Padraic but also Jijjie and Ben, who were a source of support for single mom Nunziatina. There was a draft, and we expected the hammer to drop anytime.

Filomena served dessert, sfingi, and zeppole, the famous St. Joseph's Day pastries, while Keira helped me out in the kitchen. I read the worry on her face. She again became the poetic Irish sage.

"Nonno, each assault on our civilization makes us all less civilized."

I could only add, "Italians and Irish—we both know tragedy. We're great at being victims."

"We don't learn the lessons of war. We just learn that new wars are necessary to 'clean up' the messes of the last one." As Keira voiced those words, her intense eyes, now unusually green with dew, showed me what drew Mario in from the day of their first encounter.

Early in the '51 regular season, Jijjie and Ben enlisted in the Navy, over Nunziatina's strong objections. Jijjie was eager to be a Seabee underwater construction expert. A little while later, TJ and Padraic enlisted, over Keira's objections. Padraic kept his sexual preferences to himself. I had lost a granddaughter, and now my four grandsons, my only grandsons, were fighting a nasty war half a world away! I knew better how Filomena had felt when I signed up as a doughboy during World War I over thirty years before.

I prayed that fate would be good to our family. But I was convinced of a curse over all of Brooklyn when the Dodgers lost a huge lead and faded in the stretch of the '51 season. They finished tied with the hated Giants and then split the first two games of the three-game playoff. It looked like the Dodgers would not go meekly this year.

Mario and I watched that third game on Channel Four, the NBC broadcast from the Polo Grounds. I couldn't stand the Giants' announcers. We had the lead, bottom of the ninth. Ralph Branca relieved Don Newcombe. I wished grandson Ben, a crazy Giants fan, was in the room with us as Branca shut down the Giants.

Filomena peeked into the living room. "I don't understand why you get so excited over a stupid game only Americans play."

She was ignored, and then Branca gave up Bobby Thompson's clinching miracle homerun "shot heard round the world." A stab in the heart. Mario and I stared at the TV. I was almost happy Ben wasn't there. Filomena gently retreated.

Ralph Branca was a nice Italian boy, well, half Italian. He was one of seventeen children, the son of immigrants—Italian father and Jewish mother. How much more Brooklyn can you get? How much more American? Ralph was truly a good boy—college educated, he was also Jackie Robinson's best friend on the team. He lined up with Robinson on opening day 1947, when other Dodgers refused.

I mentioned this later to Filomena. She was not enthralled.

"Filomena, baseball is not an escape from life, it is life."

Filomena couldn't believe how worked up I got over baseball when our four grandsons were fighting a nasty war in Korea. Neither could I, for that matter.

If something were to happen to them, would Jackson send me a sympathy card?

The hot stove league always made me look back. Especially now, with four grandsons in Korea, I realized time was flying like an uccello. The ageless bird of time flew over troubled landscapes, from Naples to beloved Brooklyn and beyond to Korea, an open, festering wound since World War II. Daily I was reminded that I was no longer a kid, not a guagliò, but an old fazool turkey flapping my wings toward seventy. Even the Irish said "guagliò" for an adolescent and "fazool" for an old man.

The initial direction of that young uccello from Naples to Brooklyn had set the rest of my life in motion. I recognized that every action had a consequence. If I hadn't befriended young Calogero, I'd probably have wound up dead in the streets of Naples or the Campania countryside, or a corpse in an Italian uniform in some forsaken battlefield.

Calogero, who stayed in Italy, was the real survivor of the two wars whose battles took place in his beloved country. The second was especially devastating because Naples and Campania were war victims, as was my mamma. The German occupation of 1943 induced unrelenting American bombing around Naples's beautiful bay. I was thankful that the Four Days of Naples uprising was a relatively short extirpation of the Nazis. But the retreating Nazis detonated as much materiel as possible, as if a pogrom against Naples's millennia of cultural *patrimonio*.

I was sick thinking of the cultural and human carnage done to Naples. Yes, there were monumental reconstruction projects planned or underway—in Naples, Montecassino, Pisa, and elsewhere—but mannaggia, new bricks and mortar do not erase human tragedy nor bring back lost writings and masterpieces.

The family learned that Cosimo had enlisted as well. I was not proud of my thoughts. *Who cares about that sfaccím? Maybe he'll go over and die in the place of one of my grandkids. He already killed one of them.* I made the sign of the cross and promised myself to attend confession the very next Thursday.

I dared not express such sentiments to Filomena, who would have preached mightily against harboring such hate in my heart. We both knew what such preaching really meant: she feared an evil eye born of hate being directed back at our family.

What an opera it could be—a faraway Asian peninsula "hosting" my four grandsons, TJ, Padraic, Ben, and Jijjie. They formed a lineage initiated in Italy and Ireland, bred, reared, and molded in Brooklyn, and now to be "fire-burnished" in Korea. I was too fearful to imagine the message of the coda.

The Most Precious Blood Parish was a meeting place where Filomena, Nunziatina, Mario, Keira, and I joined friends and family for Sunday mass and for lighting candles for our boys in far-off Korea. Novenas were said for the neighborhood children and grandchildren.

Early in 1952 Agent Jackson lit a cigarette, though there was a "No Smoking" sign in the office. He took a couple of deep drags and blew smoke in my direction. I wished I had a pungent De Nobili cigar on me. I would have won that arms race, but I probably would have been fined.

"How old are you Mr. Gee-ovanni?

"Sixty-seven."

"Do you love your wife?"

"What kind of question is that? Is that why I'm here?"

"Well, yes. If you're sixty-seven, that makes your father an old codger in his mid-eighties, no?"

"So?"

"So, he won't get a day older. The Neapolitan police found him in a hotel bed, plugged with twenty-three bullets."

My head was spinning. *My father was alive, but no longer. Shot over twenty times? By whom? I hate this sonuvabitch Jackson. I'm not giving him the satisfaction of my showing emotion.*

"So, your response?"

"You have some way of breaking news. Does this give you pleasure? My father abandoned me when I was a child. I lived on my own and tried to help my mother raise our family, including my two younger sisters."

"So, this is news to you?"

"News, yes. Not bad news, not good news. He was never part of my life. The shame is that he outlived my poor mother."

"He checked into the room under an alias, and then he had a rendezvous with a sweet little thing of nineteen."

Jackson looked over to read my face, my posture. Neither showed him anything.

"Since he was naked, the young lady must have been there for a while."

"Mr. Jackson, I find no pleasure or grief in my father's death. He abandoned us in Italy when we were poor and starving."

"Well, he made some decisions in his life that got him ahead." Jackson raised both eyebrows at the last word, and I had no desire to know his meaning. "But his last move was a bad one. He was playing with the granddaughter of a rival capo. Can't always mix business and pleasure. You gotta admire his spunk, though, randy old goat."

I could not wait for him to finish. My father had been dead to me for many years, and making it official was like closing the coffin on this evil Vesuvian spirit who had haunted me all my life.

"My condolences," Jackson said with little sincerity. "I don't think this necessarily lets you off the hook, Mr. Ragnuno. La Camorra is a rat warren, and you guys are always backstabbing each other. Maybe you changed associates?"

"Mr. Jackson, my associates are my family and my friends in Brooklyn. Good day."

I did not wait to be excused. I just walked out. But though my father was finally gone, I did not feel as if a weight were lifted. *Jackson's going to try to link me to mob dealings in Vegas, I know it. I hope Moe Liebowitz is behaving himself out there.*

Glory to Jesus! And *Grolia Giesú*! By the end of the Korean War in 1953, my four *nipoti americani*, my American grandkids, returned home. We drank too many toasts with Keira's O'Donnell clan. Having all the boys home was a real blessing, especially since Ben had been MIA for months. Ben showed no outward signs of being shell-shocked. When prodded he talked of his ordeal, but only in humorous terms.

Ben visited Brooklyn shortly after settling in LA. We had a get-together in Ben's former home, Nunziatina's small apartment on Avenue T: Mario and Keira; Vina and her two boys, Joseph and Michael; Ben and his Mexican Italian wife, Kay; and Junior and his dad, TJ. Filomena and I made eleven in all. Peggy was off shopping with Junior's sister, Therese. I loved the noise, not to mention the smell arising from the kitchen.

"Uncle Ben, tell us about the war!" begged Joseph.

When pushed for details, Ben flipped into his comedy routine. "Well, you see, I was lost from my platoon, walking through a jungle on some island off Korea. I had only one bullet in my rifle."

Vina looked at Joseph and Michael and then at TJ's Junior and finally over at her brother. He was now fully into his routine. But she had gotten his attention.

"Vi, let me finish my story. Then I'll help you with the *zuppa di pesce*."

"Your story takes longer than the fish sauce," she said. "It's almost done. I just added the clams, and I'm draining the linguine in the *scolapasta*."

Vina's kitchen lure almost worked. Ben got up, grabbed an open clam from the zuppa, and tasted the nascent juices.

He moaned, "Hmm, o che bello!" his face the picture of ecstasy, only slightly hammed up.

The elongated *bello* was a signal to the children, who clamored for his attention. Vina and Nunziatina pushed Ben out of the kitchen and back to the living room, where he got on with his story. Mamma Nunziatina, peering into the living room, wasn't too keen on interpreting Ben's pantomiming, which was the way she followed most spoken English. She stayed in the cramped kitchen helping Vina. Ben's diminutive wife, Kay, joined them but knew not to get in the way.

Beyond the piercing eyes of the women, Ben went on. "So, I'm walking along, and what do I see? A half-dozen enemy soldiers. They were very disciplined. They marched through the jungle in a straight line, one in front of the other. The first ugly guy saw me."

"What did you do, Unca Ben?" asked Joseph, completely rapt.

"I had only one bullet. So, I aimed for the first one, and the bullet went right through his heart and continued to the second and then the third, and finally the sixth. All of them were shot in the heart with the same bullet!"

"C'mon!" Joseph groaned.

"But," continued Ben, "I was lucky they had thin, cold hearts;

they were not like us napulitani and Irish, with big, fat hearts." Ben, directing his voice to the kitchen, added, "Or the warm-hearted Mexicans."

"And then what?" shouted Junior.

"Well, when the local natives learned what I did, they rescued me from the jungle and brought me to their chief. He rewarded me with his greatest possession, a beautiful porcelain toilet bowl!"

"Where is it?" was the enthusiastic chorus.

Kay stuck her head out of the kitchen. "It's back in California. We are trying to decide whether to use it or keep it as a trophy in the living room."

That night the only thing better than Ben's story was the festa—the food and family around the table.

Not all neighbors were so blessed. Many lost loved ones in Korea, and many who stayed behind in America were fighting another scourge—polio. Great-grandson Junior faced this personally.

Junior spent a lot of time with me in the garden. I know we were a hilarious pair, a spritely little leprechaun and his dark, leathery napulitano great-grandfather. He didn't call me Great-Grandpa, but Nonno Giovanni. And Grandpa John was also fine.

One midsummer day in 1954, the '52 and '53 National League pennant champion Dodgers were chasing the New York Giants, of all people. But my beautiful eight-year-old Junior was walking up and down the rows of my garden, smelling the tomato leaves, catching asparagus beetles, and just enjoying our little piece of Brooklyn nature. I loved his wonderment as I gazed from under the grape arbor that sheltered our driveway.

Filomena interrupted my appreciation of this specimen of *giovinezza* in the garden. "Here, you and Junior try some of this lemonade."

"Grazie, bella. It's like summer in Naples out here."

"This heat is not good for that piccirìllo. And he's not dark like us, so he shouldn't spend so much time under the sun."

"He always loses his hat. I should get him a Dodgers cap."

"Eh, sure, and then he's got that little nose stuck in the business of bugs and plants."

"He's learning a lot."

"You mean he's-a learning about allergies."

I gave her a look, raised both eyebrows, and then winked through the smoke of the De Nobili cigar lodged in my mouth.

"If your cigar doesn't kill him, his resistance goes down, and then who knows what he's gonna catch-a?"

"Ma quando? Mai, Filomena! You know I love-a that little boy. He loves his Nonno Giovanni, and we both love-a the garden."

But there were storm clouds everywhere, even in Brooklyn. In 1952, while TJ, Padraic, Jijjie, and Ben were still in Korea, the polio epidemic in the US claimed a record number of victims, and it showed no sign of slowing down. Most of its victims were young, and about half ended up with a crippling paralysis.

By 1954 it looked like Filomena could be right: my eight-year-old Junior could be one of the young victims.

Thank you, San Gennaro! Thank you, because Filomena did not make the situation worse—she did not blame the maloik, as if this were brought upon us by the senior TJ's absence. I could read her mind: *Junior is like a golden child, with his red hair and blue eyes, in our family of Mediterraneans. But why think the worst—that some evil-thinking* malepenzante *neighbor would focus hideous jealousy on Junior?* She even told me that the Irish and the Italians were in the same boat, and there was no way any one "of us" would wish bad luck, *'na desgràzia*, on Junior or our family.

My wife was becoming more American, even though she would never admit it.

At first it appeared Junior had a bad cold or flu with a sore throat, headache, and fever. He had trouble holding down his food, and the symptoms did not abate even after a few weeks. Filomena administered much chamomile tea, emphasizing the "Roman" variety, but it was to no avail, and when Junior exhibited back and neck pain and difficulty getting out of bed, Peggy, Filomena, and I saw our worst fears materialize—a polio diagnosis by the neighborhood doctor, "Please call me Joe" Seminara. It was too late for a vaccine, even if it were available. Certainly, there was no treatment.

Junior was bedridden for several weeks. Since Filomena and I could provide Junior with around-the-clock attention, Peggy and TJ deferred to us. And praise Giesú, Junior gradually improved. He avoided the paralysis that many other victims suffered. Filomena's novenas were answered, and thanks were given both to *Santa Filomena* and to *San Gennaro*. Best to spread the thanks from Filomena's namesake to the patron saint of Naples. St. Patrick was also thanked—no need to arouse Irish ire, especially of the holy hell kind. After all, Junior's uncle Padraic's namesake saint was St. Patrick.

Junior's illness put me into a deep depression, although his recovery made me feel alive. I wanted Junior to feel the same way about life—his life and the life around him. I made sure that Junior, while sipping Filomena's chamomile, could concentrate on something other than his malattia. I presented him with two handbooks I picked up from the Brooklyn Botanic Garden—tough reading for an eight-year-old, for sure, but full of photos of flowers and insects of North America, and advice on how to make an insect collection.

Junior loved thumbing through the books but took his major therapy in our garden when he was strong enough to move about. His gait improved when walking among the "gravid *googootz*," green squash stalactites of nature's bounty. Yes, I described our heavy calabash in the poetry of Junior's Irish forebears. Peggy loved the description, and we explained to Junior that "gravid" meant that a baby was about to be born, maybe another Junior from an unusually heavy googootz.

I set up a trellis from which the growing fruit was suspended. Every neighborhood gardener said *googootz*, dialect for *cucuzza*, squash, or calabash if you must. I was so very proud of my googootz: "I have the longest on Bay Fiftieth!" However, I was not motivated by masculine pride in the garden. It was about family and the connection to Campania, even to Kerry County in Ireland.

Junior was my little green googootz. I threatened to steal his pug nose and replace it with a googootz. Between my fore and middle fingers wiggled my "green" thumb, his nose protesting for its return to Junior's face. I always gave in, and Junior always laughed.

Junior and I cultivated a butterfly garden. We learned which flowers attracted which butterflies. We cherished and cared for the eggs and caterpillars left by each species. Fennel and parsley were attractants for beautiful swallowtails. Of course, these herbs did double duty. Fennel seed was great in sausage, and fennel leaves, stalks, and bulbs went into that wickedly good Sicilian dish *finocchio e sarde*—fennel and sardines. Parsley? Well, I'd never ask Filomena to make a marinara sauce or a white clam sauce without it. But I kept quiet about the parsley-poaching caterpillars.

We even rescued tomato hornworms to observe their pupation to sphinx moths. Yes, this meant we had to feed tomato leaves to the fat caterpillars. We pruned the leaves from tomato plants in the dark of night, away from Filomena's hawk eyes. Junior loved raising the hornworms, but I think he especially loved doing so with me as an accomplice. And how those worms could eat! "Junior, these-a worms are like-a Italian insects at a festa!"

We were both amazed when, at times, the succulent green caterpillars stopped feeding and turned into paralyzed pincushions, and from each cottony pin eventually emerged a tiny black wasp. We learned that these were parasitic wasps, so Junior understood biological control before the vast majority of his generation. I advised Junior to release the wasps in the tomato patch. "Everybody gets a cut, guagliò!" We Italians and Irish understood that basic rule of nature and commerce.

Wonders were unending in the garden. We cherished colorful asparagus beetles. Huge orb weaver spiders feasted on eggplant beetles. Filomena saw no use in all of this, especially in the husbandry of insect pests, but Junior was entranced and loved my response to his nonna, in which I emphasized the usefulness of bees and fig wasps. "If you don't have bugs, cara Filomena, you don't have plants."

Both sides of Junior's family knew of their connection to plants. Junior understood the importance of the potato to Ireland and how the blight had forced his mother's side to America. I regaled Junior with tales of Campania's San Marzano tomato—the essential ingredient of marinara sauce. Junior loved the fritelle di fiori di zucca just as Calogero and I had delighted in them fifty years before in Donna Bettina's kitchen. Peggy insisted on calling them zucchini flower fritters, but she ate them with an Irish poet's passion.

One early evening in late summer, while we were partaking of the fritelle in the garden, I asked, "Junior, how does the pollen from the male flowers get to the female flowers, the ones that grow the zucchine?"

My English was never very good, and I pronounced "pollen" as if it were a shortened version of *polenta.* To Junior, this was the correct pronunciation.

"I know, you told me," he said. "The bees visit the male flower and then pass the po-LEN to the females."

"And then what do the flowers do for the bees?"

"The flowers give the bees nectar. Then the bees make nectar into honey in your hives. Nonna Filomena uses the honey to make honey balls for Christmas."

"You are such a good-a student, Junior! Whassa the name-a the honeyballs?"

I let him struggle awhile, but finally Junior shouted out, "*Struffoli!*"

I was about to ask him, "And what's the name of the cooked *fritelle*?" I challenged him by asking in Italian" "*E, come si chiama 'o piatto delle fritelle?*"

"*Ciurillo!*" was the shouted answer, and his accent was perfect.

My soul was singing. *This Irish guagliò is a gift from heaven.*

For a Brooklyn kid, Junior was well versed in horticulture, and he learned it from both the Irish and Italian sides. I was his Don Giuseppe, and our house on Bay Fiftieth was my Villa Valeria. If challenged, Junior might have asserted that his Nonno Giovanni might come up with a cure for the Irish potato blight. Junior was fully absorbed in all my lectures, like about how the beautiful domesticated cheese fly had become another useful insect servant. I expressed to Junior my love of the Sardinians for letting those flies and their "young" take part in the maturing of their goat cheese.

Before turning off the lights one night, Filomena gave me grief for filling Junior's head with nonsense and the "disgusting" things of nature.

"Filomena, cara, you can't just appreciate nature for the pretty flowers and songbirds. All of it is nature, and it gives us valuable lessons." She sat up, and her gesture—open left hand delicately placed in the crook of her bent right elbow, told me what to do with my own "nature."

I could not resist. "Not just me, Filomena, but spiders also love insects, and they help us by eating them. Our last name, Ragnuno, I bet comes from *ragno*, the spider." This was too much, even for me. I never brought it up again, could be grounds for divorce.

That evening I did not get my goodnight kiss.

Filomena found me depressed looking at my bee hives. She thought she had discovered my foil when I learned that wax worms were eating the honey. They ate through the wax to get to the honey, on which they feasted.

Yes, she chided me, her long-suffering husband: "Ehh! So now you don't like-a de worms so motch-a!"

Though crestfallen, I could not concede the battle. "Bahh. Filomena, God gave Adam and Eve a garden so they could learn." I went on about how, if those worms could eat through wax, maybe we could use them or train them to eat garbage or old wax paper. "And then we feed-a the worms to chickens, or we use them for bait in Sheepshead Bay."

"Giovanni, but you are crazy, really crazy!" was Filomena's wide-eyed response. Just to make sure I understood her, she repeated herself with "*Ma tu sî pazzo, 'o vero!*" I confess that I took an almost perverse pleasure in seeing Filomena so exasperated.

I was going to tell her that crazy Galileo was almost executed by the Church for maintaining that the earth moved, but humility stopped me from making a comparison to the great Renaissance scientist. Besides, the Church had been very good to the Ragnuno family lately, if I did not think of poor Anna. Well, I was not sure I could give the Church 100 percent credit for the health of my surviving grandkids, but I would never say that to Filomena.

Ahh, the Church. I think about fate, faith, and luck a lot. When Junior recovered from polio, I wanted to thank all of the saints. But what about the parents of paralyzed and crippled children? And what of Mario and Keira's loss of Anna? Why did the saints not spare Anna and the paralyzed kids? For sure, not all parents were less devout than Filomena, and certainly than Giovanni, for I often had doubts about the Church, saints, and popes. Was my joy at Junior being spared insensitive to the bad luck of others? Was it only luck? Or did the more intense prayer always win? And if so, did the losers deserve to lose? We had "good fortune" when all four grandsons survived the Korean conflict. Was this a result of our praying more than others? Or would we pay in some other way for this good turn of events?

And what of the Jewish soldiers? How did their prayers measure against ours, or the prayers of the Korean soldiers on the other side? Who sorted all this out? I trembled when I asked myself, *Is God an accountant, a scorekeeper*?

18

BENEVENTO SOCIAL CLUB (1955)

No longer the fight to win a young mate
Nor brood eggs to guard and incubate
Old birds just squawk the daily complaint:
Grown nestlings must heed the patron saint

I was proud of grandkids Jijjie and Ben, fledglings who flew to the West Coast from the cluttered old Brooklyn nest. This old bird was on the brink of seventy in 1955, and in no way was I willing or able to join them in another migratory flight. Flapping my wings would raise only dust in the Brooklyn nest. I dared not mention a West Coast migration to Filomena, who was still trying to cope with Brooklyn, America. Those were good reasons for staying in Brooklyn. Staying close to Federal Jackson was not one of them.

My two Brooklyn grandsons were also independent and living well. Padraic was well into his accounting career. TJ, barely twenty-nine years old, had taken over management of the second salumeria store in Gravesend. A real businessman, TJ put his mark on it, making sure it wasn't a duplicate of the first store. For one, it became the neighborhood *di rigore* place for Easter ravioli. And for Christmas it had Brooklyn's best selection of dried figs and sweet *panettone* bread. Year-round it offered daily hero sandwiches made to order. Construction workers feasted on the sidewalk or in their trucks, and high school kids on neighborhood stoops. Peggy became the Irish cop on the beat, keeping after the kids to clean up after themselves—bad business for all if they did not comply.

TJ and his Peggy bestowed upon me beloved great-grandson Junior, grandson of Mario and Keira. One of the greatest blessings of my life was learning that Junior did not have the paralytic form of polio. Still, I wondered if maybe a *residuo*, a memory of polio, kept Junior from being a star in athletics—just imagine, a New York Met in the family!

TJ had to be very busy, because he never looked overjoyed when I dropped in. He was usually behind the counter as if on stage, flanked by curtains of hanging salamis and torpedoes of cheeses. In his white button-down shirt and tie, he projected military formality among the aromatic treasures of the old country. His hands were usually spread over the display case of roasted peppers, fresh mozzarella and ricotta, olives, pickled giardiniera, seafood salad, potato croquettes, and other wonders. He seemed much more a businessman than cultural ambassador.

"Hello, Grandpa" was his unchanging greeting. *Mannaggia, would be nice to be called Nonno once in a while, and how about a kiss for the old man?*

"How's business? How are Mamma and Papà?"

"Fine, Grandpa." I usually did not know if he was talking about his parents or the business, but business seemed to be doing OK, if the number of complimentary "Ragnuno" shopping bags circulating on the street was an indication. TJ had wanted them to bear the name "Rag-Bag," but I was able to nix that idea. Hey, I had fought against changing our name to Runyon when we arrived from Italy forty-three years before. No way was I going to trivialize our proud family name now. *We Italians are the butt of enough jokes. Why give our detractors ammunition?*

"Looks like you're busy, TJ. I was on my way to the club, and I just wanted to drop in and say hello. Say hello for me to that beautiful Junior boy of yours."

"S'long, Grandpa. Say hello to the men at the club and a hello to Grandma for me." He tugged at his tie as if yanking a pulley cord to drop the curtain on my stage exit. *At least the tie ain't red, white, and green.*

The thought of my twenty-one-year-old bride Filomena as the grandma of a thirty-one-year-old American businessman hastened my exit. I hoped that TJ did not notice that "his" store branch off McDonald Avenue was way out of the way from the club. Ha!

The Benevento Social Club was really a mutual aid society, Società di Mutuo Soccorso di Benevento. We helped each other in Brooklyn and our paisani back in Campania. Back there, back then, we fought like cats and dogs for any advantage. The Italian Northerners were much better than we napulitani in coming to each other's aid and connecting in unions, guilds, football clubs, even birdwatching societies. In the South I recalled my father saying, even in the best of times, "When the neighbors are sick, make sure you have enough food and water and then lock your doors." But just to show that we were unpredictable, we Southerners did have these mutual aid societies, and the tradition continued in America.

The club, under the el just around the corner from our Bay Fiftieth Street home, was always a simple affair. It presented a plain storefront bearing its name in the red and yellow colors of the province of Benevento, regione di Campania. Curtains in the show windows blocked street views to the interior white walls. We usually sat in front to gossip, complain, and sometimes look at the passing ladies. We preferred this "street seating" even though the overhead West End interrupted our conversation.

Inside, when there were more than three of us dealing with club business, we usually sat at a roundtable that seated about half a dozen on folding chairs. There were eight permanent stools at the bar, which featured an espresso machine at one end and offered jars of taralli and biscotti at the other. The mirror behind the bar was framed with scenes of Benevento's beautiful bluff, on which the ancient town was built. Other posters showed the Bay of Naples, Vesuvius, and the Italian national football selection, Gli Azzurri. Glasses were arranged in front of the mirror, along with bottles of amaretto, strega, anisette, sambuca, and red wines.

I was a founding member of the club, which was aging, like me. We were losing old-timers over the years. The front windows were eventually covered with a cataract layer of brick. But inside there was life. The club family helped me stay connected with the one in Campania—Calogero and my sisters, Giorgietta and Elena. Each sister had become a grandmother. I loved telling family stories to my goombahs, and I listened attentively to theirs. It was as if the families on either side of the Atlantic were knitted together. But I did feel pangs of longing for my sisters and two generations of nieces and nephews. At least my father was out of the picture.

On this early summer day there was important club business—planning the annual celebration of the Festa di San Gennaro on September 19, 1955. I was on the planning committee, but whenever we old fazools got together, gossip usually trumped serious planning, at least at first. Joining me were ancient Mr. Armando, the mason; Rocky Falcone, the schoolteacher; and bullish Sam, founding owner of the prosperous Bottiglia and Sons, Excavation. There was the usual anise-tinged cloud over the table, at which members dunked biscotti or hard taralli in anisette or in anisette-spiked espresso. A couple of De Nobili cigars, "guinea stinkers" Keira called them, enriched the bouquet of the cloud.

The Festa di San Gennaro is named after Naples's patron saint, and festa is right! Filomena liked to say, both hands lifting on her pancia, "Enough is enough-a, but too much is-a BEDDA." The big feast was in the streets of Little Italy, but there were observances in other Italian American neighborhoods—*enclaves* is the fancy word Keira used. For our mini-festa the club hosted a dance in the Knights of Columbus hall with live music and a sumptuous supper, a true feast.

Looking back at previous festas, there was n'abbunnànza, an abundance of food, and live music to dance it off. Each year the music told me how times were changing from the old days. A few old-timers still played the mandolin, tambourine, and Neapolitan zampogna bagpipe. But the young birds played drums and electric guitars, and other young kids flapped all over the dance floor. Mario and Keira joined in, I'm afraid to say. I thought how much the giovani were missing out by not touching each other while dancing. Then again, they probably were doing a lot more touching overall than we did back in Campania.

On this early summer day inside the club, before serious planning for the festa, my commentary on San Gennaro got me into trouble with the planning committee. I should not drink before I talk.

We all knew that Roman Emperor Diocletian ordered San Gennaro beheaded at the turn of the fourth century. Over the ensuing sixteen centuries, especially on September 19, coagulated samples of our patron saint's blood were reported to liquefy inside their ampoules. I looked around the table and said, "To me, Gennaro is truly a sainted Italian Catholic. But come on, my friends, how can blood liquefy every year for sixteen centuries? I know we wanna believe, but the Vatican should put it to the test."

Ancient Mr. Armando's look was as bitter as broccoli raab. I was in for it.

My mind was racing—if the Most Precious Blood Parish priests could read what was in there, I'd surely be excommunicated. Calogero had filled my mind with stories, and Keira loved to confirm them. *People forget that the apostles were Jews and that the early Church had little resemblance to the Church of the Vatican. The Vatican became the site of St. Peter's Rock years after the martyrdom of San Gennaro. Some of the popes who ruled from the Vatican could be just as cunning, pleasure seeking, and militaristic as Naples's many conquering rulers.*

Signor Armando woke me from my reverie. "You commit a mortal sin." Armando, who always went by his first name, was ancient and tiny with leathery, sunbaked skin. His ears and huge, bumpy nose resisted the shrinking of the rest of his body. He was a lifelong mason—specialty concrete—a man of amazing strength and endurance and of unshakable faith. He embodied Roman concrete and would tell the naysayers that Roman concrete got stronger with age, not like the impermanent American kind. "Just-a looka de *Colosseo Romano* anna de temples in Napoli—still-a dere." Armando owned a huge sledgehammer and was always ready to use it in a neighborhood project. Breaking up old concrete seemed to rejuvenate him, while everyone in the neighborhood thought each project would be his death.

"Mr. Armando, I have-a learned that it is easy to be fooled, especially when you really want to believe in a miracle, but I have faith inna da Church. I pray almost every day. I go to confession, and I wanna my grandchildren to be educated in da Church." *Armando is making me speak with an accent.*

Mr. Armando gave me a look of disgust. The fleshy wattle, that *canniccio* under his chin, truly waddled as he retorted, "Agh, *nunja* tell-a me about faith anna dedication, Giovanni!" His accent seemed to grow heavier as he assailed me with increasing vitriol. "I know you love-a you family, and you say you respect-a da Church, but you might have false idols like-a dis American baze-a-ball."

My ears pricked up. I could be no prouder of my beloved Brooklyn Dodgers—Jackie Robinson, Pee Wee Reese, Snider, Erskine. Hey, Gil Hodges even married an Italian girl, Joan Lombardi, and settled in Brooklyn. I loved them all, not just the adopted Hodges, but certainly also Lavagetto, Furillo, Camilli, and Branca.

Armando had hit me with a pointed feeling of guilt that somehow I held my Dodgers in almost idolatrous awe. *Brooklyn is in first place. '55 could be our year!*

Armando made me recall the first time I had visited Ebbets Field. Its manicured infield and the greenest grass I ever saw made me feel like I was in a cathedral. Could his comments on baseball go unanswered? I'd been married too long to Filomena to face a challenge without defending myself. And what would barrister Calogero say about my being so submissive?

"What's so bad about being a fan? At least we do not march in goosestep to the preaching and posing of Il Duce," I said, with more passion than I wanted to show. I felt hot. Perhaps guilt drove my passion. The choices open to the *giovinezza*, the youth of America, were in rich and lavish contrast to those of prewar Italian youth.

"Mr. Armando, you know that the Fascist anthem was 'Giovinezza,' no? How many young people did Il Duce Mussolini kill for his selfish vanity, his stupid visions?" With a wrinkled nose and my lips forming an obscene puckered kiss, I spat out the "Duce" as DOOO-chay in my best—or worst—derisive baritone.

Armando responded with "*Nun c' pensá*," don't even think about his supporting Mussolini, waving his left hand over one large ear. He shook the hand a few times before dropping it. I'm surprised he resisted the Bronx cheer, the famous *pernacchia*, the raspberries you don't get at the fruit stand. *Well, sometimes when you try to lift an apple…*

I, Don Giovanni, was a man of noble values and sensitivity when it came to American youth—especially Italian American youth. Yes, I was riding a prideful wave, perhaps fueled by the anisette. My thoughts went to exploitation of young people in the evil boxing game.

Why are such beautiful Italian boys allowing themselves to be butchered to make a few dollars? Why would any *boy choose this life? Mannaggia, they won't have any brains by the time they're my age—if they live that long.*

"You know something, Mr. Armando, I can't stand-a watchin' the fights, and now they're on-a the televizh. Eh, sure, champs Paddy DeMarco and Rocky Graziano are from Brooklyn, but how many punches did these guaglioni have to take to be called champs! This Joey Giardello is gonna be another champ and then another stunad. I crossed my eyes for effect.

Drilling an index finger into my right cheek I continued. "The Black Hand is probably makin' the big money arranging fights. We have-a the small-time Mussolinis right here in Brooklyn leading our young men to ruin."

I could see the workings of Armando's mind—he was about to bring up Willie Pep. Yes, Guglielmo Papaleo was a magician in the ring. He almost never got hit and had all his marbles at the end. But I was on a roll. I could deal with Armando in English or in dialect.

Armando was no jackass chooch—no *ciuccio*. That mummified head of his still held an agile brain. He probably wondered how I could distance myself from the fight game and yet make a confident prediction of Giardello becoming champ.

I still had the floor. Mr. Armando would have his day, but today was mine. "We came from Campania to build a better life here. So, why are *nuoste guaglioni stúpeti* willing to have their young brains beat out for a few bucks in the ring?"

I looked around. I was getting polite attention—at least there were no shut eyes. "If our kids were not stupid when they went in, the racket will make them stupid before they get out. Haven't we learned that there is no future in being a gladiator? And …"

Rocco "Rocky" Falcone, facing me from the opposite side of the table, interrupted. I was definitely hogging the conversation and repeating myself. Rocky was short and thin and usually wore a tie and long-sleeved shirt—he looked not at all like a boxer, more like the schoolteacher he was, especially with his horn-rimmed glasses over his button nose.

"But Giovanni, remember how the Irish used to gang up on us? We had to take on Irish names just to get into the ring. Now we proudly represent our heritage, and all of America is behind us."

"So, let-a the Irish drink themselves stunad and finish the job in the ring," I said, sipping my anisette-laced espresso. "We can be better than that." I could see a black and green hand descend, because I knew that my Irish in-laws and Irish-Italian descendants would not appreciate my assertions, to put it mildly.

Yes, guilt was freezing my tongue, and I experienced more as I looked across at Rocco. Biting his open hand between the index finger and thumb and raising the other three fingers, he glared at me through the slits of his eyes. The other hand flapped close to his chest, as if putting out a fire of àgita. He was giving me the hand gestures of silence.

Sam Bottiglia, on my right, got my attention with a term of respect. "But Don Giovanni, we all have come a long way—Italians, Jews, the Micks, even the moolinjana."

"Italians, Jews, the Micks" went through my head. *The Irish call each other Micks. We Italians call each other Dagos, and not always in a flattering way. And I learned from the Pollacks that Jews have not-so-loving distinctions, like* Litvak *versus* Galitzianer.

But what really got to me was "moolinjana," our street dialect for eggplant—*melenzana* in high Italian. So, we not only owned it, we sold it. Even "true white" people like Federal Jackson bought it—what a contribution we made to America! I thought back fifty years to the boat that brought us from Italy, and how a little over fifty years before that, other boats were bringing in the last waves of Black slaves. What right did we have to join the racist mob, or to complain about our own treatment?

Historian Calogero would have pointed out the unspoken truth about great boxers, because we all knew that the best boxer of the fifties was Sugar Ray Robinson—a Black artist-warrior. Sugar Ray's title fights against paisan Jake LaMotta were classics, and I was proud that LaMotta was able to give Robinson his first loss in one of them, and maybe LaMotta should have won one of the other four. I loved that LaMotta said the three toughest fighters he ever faced were Sugar Ray Robinson, Sugar Ray Robinson, and Sugar Ray Robinson.

Bottiglia blunted my musings by grabbing my right forearm. The grip of his meaty hand was like a vise. "Giovanni, you are a man of business, a man who commands respect. You did not have to box or join with the Black Hand. You had a valuable sponsor back in Campania."

Bottiglia was a bull of a man with flaring nostrils and slits for eyes. His thick white mane contrasted with his eternally flushed complexion. He never said much, so his first gravelly comments at the table commanded attention. I almost resented his implication that I had had it easier than most of my paisani, but I said nothing in my defense. My success spoke for itself, and it hurt no one.

Sam had a very profitable construction and excavation company in Bensonhurst and Gravesend. He probably had to break a few heads in the early days. His rambunctious sons—John, Sally, Anthony, Ignazio, Joe, Peter, and Ronnie—were known to engage in boxing matches on the streets for absolutely no prize money, only for respect, the best prize of all.

I wished I could keep all my grandchildren close to me at home in Brooklyn, even if it meant that they or their kids would have an occasional street fight. But in this America our best strategy was to form alliances with our fellow migratory birds, and not just birds from the same paese. We allied with birds of a different feather, like Keira's people or the Pollack lawyers. These alliances helped fend off predatory birds, and street fights were usually not necessary.

We actually got around to planning for the Festa di San Gennaro. That business finished, I made my way to visit Mario in the first store, just a couple of blocks away.

"Ciao, Pops," he said from behind the counter as a customer walked out. The place was empty for a while.

"Mario, do you ever think about being alone in the store?"

"Well, we have mirrors to keep an eye on customers …"

"No, I mean, just you, no customers. What if trouble walks in?"

"Keira was tending the store the other day, and here come two wise guys."

"Mannaggia! Is it safe to leave her alone?"

"Safe for who?"

I lifted both hands, palms toward the heavens, as if feeling the heft of Mario's response.

"Listen up, Pops, I was right here in the back. I could hear them, and I caught glimpses of them through the one-way window."

"Mannaggia" was all I could say.

"One guy was short and beefy in a leather jacket, and the other guy, taller, dark, with a fedora and a long black overcoat."

"I don't care how they dressed!"

"The tall one takes his hat off, as if out of respect for a lady, and shows a head of shiny black hair combed straight back. Then he turns his eagle nose toward Keira: 'Ciao, signora,' he says, and then he hits Keira with 'I don't suppose you speak Italian.' She looks him right in the eye and says, '*È p'che dice cchisto?* Like why do you say that people with red hair and freckles can't speak your dialect?'

"You know better than me, Mario. Keira fears no one, so don't ever rouse her Irish ire."

Mario nodded in agreement. "The tall guy gives a bow, and in his broken English he starts to explain that the neighborhood is changing, lots of non-Italians—she really loved that comment—and it helps to seek the protection of the Brotherhood. 'You never know when you will need the help of friends.'

"Keira looks him up and down, and while making sideways

looks at the short wop, she says, 'I got lots of protection. My family is full of cops, and I have friends in city hall. I can have a squad car here in five minutes. How do you know that my husband in the back hasn't already called one?'

"The short guy is sweating in his leather jacket, but he doesn't want to open it 'cause I am sure he's packing a rod. The tall guy just bows again. Then he says, 'OK, signora, we will return at a better time and maybe speak with your husband or the owner.'

"Keira shows no fear. 'Come whenever you want, and for your information, I happen to be part-owner. I can get you a deal catering a wedding, baptism, or funeral wake.' She raised her voice on the last word, and her eyes got big. They made a beeline for the exit."

"Mannaggia" was now my standard response.

"They haven't come back."

"Ahh, maybe they never will," I said, more hopeful than certain. I suppressed the thought *How would Keira's TJ have handled this situation?*

"They spoke our dialect, so they were probably some small-time La Camorra. If they were Sicilians, who knows?"

"Mario, my son, figliemo. I am-a so tired of this fighting. Micks, wops, Jews, moolinjana. Who cares!" I found myself imitating Filomena. Fingers at my Adam's apple moved to a kiss-off at my raised chin with "cares." "We napulitani fight siciliani, and Irish Catholics don't like-a the Protestants, and the Jews are not always one happy family. Why do we waste energy growing hate? Let's be proud-a what we built in America."

Mario raised his right hand, signifying "peace." He was about to say something.

"You know, Mario, I'm not that fond-a Frank Sinatra, but Jijjie told me that son of Sicily pushed for Nat King Cole to play at the Sands."

Mario nodded in agreement. "You know something, Pops? Keira told me he was 4F 'cause he was born with a punctured eardrum. Imagine, singing with only one ear. And Keira let me know that Frankie Boy won a special Academy Award for coming out against anti-Semitism after the war."

"And that Tony Bennett is a true gentleman," I said. "He saw action and he stood up for all of his fellow soldiers."

This time Mario just said it: "Peace."

As if on cue, the front door opened and in came Reggie, the colored truck driver for the Reliable distributor that supplied us canned goods and olives. Such a nice guy, and he always asked about the family.

"*Ciao, Reggie, come stai, guagliò?*" I had taught Reggie a few expressions. He was a quick learner. I used to kid him about being named for Reggio Calabria, a city on the big toe of the Italian boot. We both understood the unspoken connection to dark-skinned Italians.

The first time he visited me on his new route, Reggie met my great-grandkids Joseph and Michael, who happened to be in the store. On later visits Reggie showed me pictures of his family in Bushwick, Brooklyn.

I became Don Giovanni to him. He pronounced "Don" the way he pronounced Don Newcombe's first name. This did not bother me at all, since Newcombe was an important Black Dodger, and all we Dodgers fans went by the American pronunciation of Newcombe's first name. Reggie and I were both Brooklyn Dodgers fans, and Negro players like Don Newcombe, Jackie Robinson, and Jim Gilliam were a special connection for us. We were all Dodger Blue.

Some of my friends, when they came into the store and spotted Reggie, gave him extra space. If I noticed them doing that, I'm sure Reggie always did. I didn't know how a guy could go through life like that and not be bitter. But Reggie was such a sweet, beautiful guy. My family had no problems with Reggie, and I feel like a stunad for saying that. Why should they have a problem?

Mr. Pietro Sviluppo was another regular. It seemed like ever since I knew "Pete the Tweet," he was at least ninety years old. Very thin and frail looking, he always had a song to sing. The purchase of a pound of locatelli was his ticket to the stage. He was very entertaining, and he could really belt out the lyrics of the old ballads, in dialect, even. Keira loved him. He spread his gift to other food stores—Peppe's fish, Testaverde's pastry—all were his stage.

So, on this day when Reggie was making a delivery, Pete the Tweet came into the store. He started to sing and invited Reggie to join him. Sonuvagun, Reggie knew the words to "O Marie!" and sang right along.

That day was extra-special for Reggie: "Hey, Don Giovanni! You know, I'm a grandfather!"

Before he could take out his pictures I was thinking, *He's a much better grandfather than my son-in-law, Angelo.*

19

YOUNG BIRDS FLUSH OUT AN OLD VULTURE (1953–1959)

Young Angelo, winged Angel, held court
With many a nubile fine-plumed consort
But the years flew by faster than he
And left him a frail ghost of his apogee

By late 1953, with Korea behind them, Jijjie and Ben went west to greener pastures—the desert towns of Las Vegas and Los Angeles. Nunziatina was having an espresso in our kitchen as snow fell on my hibernating fig tree outside. She picked at the pile of Filomena's Christmas season struffoli honey balls. And she moaned, "How much can I take? First, they go off to war, and then they come back in time to leave me alone at Christmas! And they go to *n'altro cchianeta*!"

"Another planet! Nunziatina, cara, they're still in America. They're young, adventurous birds. We can't stop them, and we shouldn't try."

She kicked back the espresso. Before I could make the offer, she asked for another. This one got anisette.

"Nunziatina, what you gonna do to make Brooklyn more attractive for the twins? What can I do?"

I got her hard look.

"Niente. Nothing!" I answered my own question.

Filomena echoed my answer from the bedroom. "Nunziatina, cara, your boys inherited the traits of uccelli di passo from both grandfather Giovanni and father Angelo."

This prompted another obscene curse in husband Angelo's direction. I knew she held me in higher esteem.

Jijjie's connections with Moe Liebowitz were a lure in Vegas. Brother Ben settled in LA as a cabinet-maker. He was propelled by his wife, Kay. She was born in Brooklyn, but her widower dad, Pedro Sosa, had moved back to LA. Just as my mamma was left with Elena and Giorgietta when I flew west, stationary bird Nunziatina was left behind with daughters Vina and Angelina when her twins flew west.

As true birds of passage, Ben and Jijjie made frequent transcontinental flights. One day Ben alighted in the store, in March 1954, *mannaggia, just before St. Joseph's Day and the Easter season*. He found me explaining the difference between scamorza and mozzarella to a sweet American lady married to a paisan. I excused myself, passing *l'americana* on to Keira. Ben and I found two chairs at the table by the exit and tried to chat in hushed tones.

"Hey, get this, Nonno. I have to move to the City of Angels to get in touch with the Angelo that flew away from our family." Ben was always more of a poet than Jijjie. I'm glad he chose the store to break the news, smart boy. Filomena would have invoked the maluocchio yet again if she heard Angelo's name uttered in our home.

The runaway fathers in our family find a way to come back from the dead. I knew Angelo was alive, but I preferred that he let us know by the checks he sent to Nunziatina.

Moe Liebowitz, with contacts that extended from Vegas to LA, had arranged the reunion of Angelo with his twin boys. They met in an East LA *taquería*, in the back room used for poker games. *La familia* "screened" the players, and Moe, in turn, provided protection, paid the right people, and got a cut of the proceeds. Moe was trusted by the Mexican family.

Ben (Mr. Gossip Exchange) arrived at the taquería without Kay. She would have disapproved. "So, Nonno, I greet the owner. '*Muy buenas tardes, soy Benjamin, y vengo para la reunión con el Señor Angelo Piccolini.*'"

I looked at Ben and was about to praise his accent, but he continued.

"Good afternoon, I'm Ben, and I am here for the meeting with Mr. Angelo Piccolini," Ben translated for me, as if I needed it. I think just saying "Angelo Piccolini" would have been enough. Terse, Ben is not.

"Then?"

"So, I'm escorted to the back room, and there's Jijjie."

I could just picture brother Jijjie—fidgeting and steaming in his folding chair.

"Nonno"—Ben raised his voice and started speaking fast—"Jijjie was flown in from Vegas in a Piper Cub belonging to his new uranium prospecting company."

That boy works fast.

"You know Jijjie. He's irritated and his jaw is clenched. But of course, he never stops being a businessman."

"Thassa my boy. He'll never starve."

"So, he's sitting at a square card table facing the single door. Just behind him is this beer cooler with the name 'Pilsener' under the label of El Maestro."

I looked at Ben. "So, get on with the story."

"Jijjie doesn't let grass grow under his feet. He told me later this beer was not available in Vegas, but in East LA the proprietors found a way to get it across the Mexican border from the *Cervecería* El Maestro. I bet it will be available soon in Vegas."

"Ben, get on with the story."

"When I opened the door, Jijjie stared at me so hard, I thought he was looking at something behind me. So, I greet him with 'Hey, Little Johnnie, Johnuzza, che se dice, guagliò?'

"He comes back with 'Whaddya SAY? I say I can't believe we're going to meet with the sonuvabitch who left us flat over twenty years ago!'

"'Nice to see you too, little bro' was all I could say, Nonno."

Jijjie always reminded Ben that the only reason he looked up to his brother was birth rank. Ben was larger than Jijjie, but Jijjie had more vinegar and vitriol—his disposition made him seem even darker compared with Ben's fairer complexion and lighter eyes. No one ever mistook them for identical twins.

"So I tell Jijjie, 'Hey, c'mon, little brother, let bygones be bygones. Pop left years ago. It is done.' All I got was poison out of the crevices of his eyes. I expected to see a forked tongue snake out through his clenched teeth."

"I can just picture it. If looks could kill, we would be visiting Jijjie in prison."

Ben seemed annoyed that I'd interrupted him. "Jijjie isn't talking, so I say, 'Vina tells me and Kay that the checks have been arriving at Mamma's place in Brooklyn for some four years now. But you know that.'

"So he says, 'Big fuckin' deal.' That coming from Jijjie was like him opening up."

I had to smile.

"I tell Jijjie, 'They aren't big checks, they're getting smaller, and they don't come that often anymore. But they help Mamma, and I'm sure she gives him the maluocchio every time she opens one of his envelopes.'"

"I can imagine Jijjie's response."

"He hits me with 'Fuck the checks! He's a *shidroo*!' And he makes that mean smirk that looks almost like a smile. Nonno, what the heck does *shidroo* mean?"

I laughed at that. "I don't know. Jijjie saves it for the scum of the earth. Maybe he picked it up on the street, at a pinochle game, or at Tonnino's pool hall. Maybe it's Sicilian. At the social club we say figlio di puttana a lot, but calling him that would insult your other grandmother, may she rest in peace."

"Nonno, you and Jijjie have a lot in common, and not just your first names."

"Is that a compliment to me or to Jijjie?"

"To both of you, I guess. You're both scrappers."

"I'll take that as a compliment, even though it rhymes with *crappers*." Ben laughed, and I got more serious. "Your other grandfather was another Giovanni. So, two Giovannis pioneered family moves from Naples to New York. And your brother Jijjie/Giovanni drove the second move from Brooklyn to the West Coast."

"No way he was just following our deadbeat dad to the Golden West," Ben reassured me, and possibly himself.

"It wasn't so golden for your father, Ben. Grandma Filomena always said, 'Che peccato, what a shame, Angelo's not doin' so good,' pointing straight down with both index fingers—as if to say, 'Maybe he'll have better luck in hell.'" I was lost in my thoughts. *Angelo's lovely New York consort flew the coop shortly after alighting in LA. Gossip travels faster than a cross-country Pan Am.*

Ben interrupted my musing. "So, the back door of the taquería opens, and there, alone, is Angelo. Oh boy, did he look apprehensive, though he had to be afraid to show any shame. Then Jijjie opens with 'Well, look what the cat drug in!' I was surprised at how bent over and aged Angelo looked. After our meeting I mentioned this to Jijjie, and just like I knew he would, he says, 'Fuck him, he deserves everything he had coming.'"

"So, tell me about the meeting, Ben."

"Poppa Angelo tried to keep his composure facing Jijjie's blast furnace. He gave each of us a dignified hello—no handshakes offered. He sits so that I'm between him and Jijjie, leaving only one empty chair, the one to Jijjie's right."

I pictured the four-place poker table. Angelo was buffered from Jijjie by Ben to his right and an empty chair to his left. The problem was that Angelo was right across from Jijjie, making direct eye contact hard to avoid. Angelo had to be startled at how mature and virile his boys appeared to be. Every time I saw the boys, I felt older myself. *Nunziatina did an amazing job, and no thanks to Angelo*. "How did Angelo come across to you?"

"Well, he looked a lot older than I expected. And I think he knew that his face and posture gave away his shame."

"Get on with the story, Ben."

"So, Jijjie wastes no time: 'OK, Pops.' He exploded the 'Pops.' And then he hits him with his prepared speech: 'You just had to take off for Hollywood, the glitz and the babes.' His nostrils were really flaring. 'You made a career decision, and the babes were a bonus, but when you were with your bimbos, did you ever think of your wife, our mother, and how she struggled?'

"Between you and me, Nonno, Jijjie had trouble finding a stable relationship as well. He left a wife and two kids in Brooklyn and is now cavorting with that Pennsylvania Dutch Hannah woman."

"*Aspetta*, wait a minute. Jijjie's breakup was a legal divorce, and he's paying child support. Sure, guagliò, we all get our heads turned around a few times, even here in the neighborhood."

"Sorry, Nonno. Did not mean to get on a high horse. Anyway, Jijjie wasn't finished: 'Bennie, Vina, and I did what we had to do. Vina is sharp as a tack, but Grandpa Giovanni couldn't keep her in St. Edmund's High School. Hey, he has six other grandkids, and he didn't run out on them. And then Vina had to work to help pay the bills. You know she doesn't even have a high school diploma? Your namesake, Angelina, might be the smartest of all of us. Is she going to be a waitress or secretary the rest of her freakin' life?'"

I felt a pang for both Vina and Angelina.

"Angelo was prepared for the onslaught. But all he could say was 'I know you and Ben are not identical twins. You captured most of your mother's fire, Johnootza.'

"This really set Jijjie off. 'Enough with the Johnootza crap. Jijjie will do just fine. Pops, how the fuck could you do it?'"

Ben looked at me, his eyes glistening. I kept quiet, and he went on. "So, Poppa Angelo gives us the 'two sides to every story' line and then admits he was wrong and that he just wants to be a good father from here on and to help our mother as much as he can. He reminds us that he has been sending checks, though business has not been good."

I nodded but thought, *For this he wants a medal?*

"The last comment about the checks got a rise out of Jijjie. 'Yeah, you just try sending nuthin' and Moe Liebowitz arranges for you to walk around with two crooked legs!'"

"Ahh, my grandson, you know that Jijjie and your Nonna Filomena don't take any crap."

"Nonno, I got a little emotional when our father said something like his biggest driver was the guilt he felt leaving our family in such a terrible situation."

I blinked a little, drawing on pent-up anger to stay in control. "Well, if he doesn't feel guilt, he is not human."

"We thanked him for showing up. That couldn't have been easy for him. Then Jijjie throttles him with 'Don't get tired of sending those checks.' But we did shake hands all around."

Angelo's professional drive had definitely mellowed from those heady days as a milliner-designer in the New York Garment

District. He was refocused. Ben's calls and letters said that Angelo's most precious and sentimental moments were spent with his boys. Angelo actually told them so, and I think they believed him. The meetings were progressing from uncomfortable almost to the stage of real father-son interaction. Angelo even had more spring in his step, according to Ben.

Then, on February 8, 1956, Angelo Piccolini hit a hard Los Angeles sidewalk. He was felled by a coronary and expired in the ambulance on the way to the UCLA Medical Center. The damage to his heart may have started the day he left his Nunziatina in Brooklyn.

Before he was pronounced dead, was he seeing the same scenes of his family that my mind's eye was now witnessing?

The Ragnuno flock soon saw the loss of another nestmate. Shortly after her father's passing, Angelina, kid sister of Ben, Jijjie, and Vina, established herself and her son, "Little Ben," in Vegas, joining her brothers on the West Coast. She was trying to raise a child, go to school, and support herself. The father of her child had walked out, just like her own father.

Angelina found work with the Las Vegas Police Department, assisting in the booking of suspects, taking mugshots, and doing more than just clerical work. She was adjusting very well to life in the desert. She was smart and smart-alecky and was perfect for aiding in questioning those brought in and for filling out their rap sheets.

I visited Vina in her Quentin Road apartment, where she showed me one of Angelina's letters. It was typed on the back of a booking form from the Las Vegas Police Department. I should not have grabbed it so fast, but I compounded my sin by blocking Vina from retrieving it:

One day a week I work in the I. D. Bureau—Identification

Bureau to you—where they fingerprint them and mug them. I sure love to work in there; it sure is fun. I meet some characters in there, and believe it or not, quite a few from New York. You see, one fellow takes the prints and mugs them, and I have to get all their past history—their physical descriptions, whether they have any tattoos or scars, and I'm telling you, I sure have seen some dillies. Oh, Vi, I wish you could have been here when I had to shake down my first woman prisoner. You see, when the matron is not on duty, one of the girls in the outer office has to shake down the women. I'm telling you, I was scared silly—some of those women are worse than men; you'd be surprised at the things I have found, and heard. Oh, *man*.

Vina said I would not be interested in page two, but I was. I was on the first line when she pulled the letter out of my hands. I never saw that second page. According to Vina it was full of girly stuff—losing weight, characters of the gambling world, the Vegas dating scene, and finding proper day care for Little Ben.

A few weeks after she sent that letter, Angelina left for a weekend office outing—a relaxing stay in the area around Mount Charleston, snow-covered and full of hiking and ski trails. She was even looking forward to getting in a little exercise. Mount Charleston was a beautiful contrast to Vegas, and not just weather-wise. Right before she left, Angelina wrote to Vina that she wanted to take Little Ben up there when he was older. Little Ben stayed with his uncle Jijjie that weekend while Angelina enjoyed the change of scenery.

Halfway back from Mount Charleston, still about twenty miles from Vegas, Angelina was involved in a one-car accident. She was one of four fatalities. There were no survivors; in 1958, hardly anyone used seat belts. She had just turned twenty-six. She never knew her father.

I knew that Mount Charleston was not responsible for Angelina's death, but I looked at it looming near Vegas like a white-capped angel of death. And yet, that black-capped Vesuvius had spared my mother and sisters and the large household of Don Giuseppe. By sparing me, Mount Vesuvio also spared the living members of the growing family of Giovanni and Filomena.

Angelo and Angelina of Giovanni and Filomena's flock of uccelli ended their migration on America's West Coast. We prayed that both had earned their wings and that Angelina would at last meet her father—at least, Nonno Giovanni prayed they would meet.

There was the matter of great-grandchildren. Vina's sons Joseph and Michael, aged eleven and nine, stayed in Brooklyn while their mom attended Angelina's funeral and discussed the fate of orphaned Little Ben. Filomena got me smart real fast—we were no match for another rambunctious great-grandson. Hey, I was having trouble bending over to pluck the plump, low-hanging San Marzano in my garden. Raising a four-year-old was a lot harder than lifting a tomato. But there was a perfect match for Little Ben with his uncle Ben and auntie Kay. The pair adopted more kids later, and I became a great-grandfather to two beautiful children of the Yaqui of northern Mexico. Blessings come in joyful variety.

Ben settled down, but Jijjie? He had divorced just before going off to Korea, so there was no one to reel him in when he returned. Jijjie was hooked by more than one fisherwoman with a line in the Vegas waters: Pennsylvania Dutch Hannah, a leggy Southern lady with a strong accent, a local desert gal, and a singer in a touring Japanese act. Her troupe went back to Japan, but Yoko did not. At least those were the ladies I met in Brooklyn on their separate visits. Jijjie was too good-hearted at first, then too explosive at the end of each relationship—hypnotic like a quiet Vesuvius and then raining brimstone down on the relationship.

While women were Jijjie's own problem, he got his nonno in hot water again with the Feds. When he arrived in Vegas, Jijjie did some carpentry and renovation work for his old Brooklyn boss, Moe Liebowitz. Moe, in turn, alerted old pal Ed Levinson to one tough, driven Dago, a guy who could be trusted to work hard, stay loyal, and not ask a lot of questions. Levinson had a history going back to illegal casinos in Kentucky, just across the Ohio River from Cincinnati. Before Vegas he had managed one of Meyer Lansky's casinos in Cuba.

Levinson preferred to work in legal casinos, and in America. He became an owner of downtown Vegas's Fremont Hotel, which had opened in 1956. Jijjie handled much of the nuts and bolts of the Fremont, an enterprise that catered to all kinds of nuts. A money-making venture is always prone to corruption. This is especially true in the gambling industry, where money is both the raw material and its product.

But Jijjie kept his hard nose clean, with no inclination for wise-guy activities. He worked like he boxed, relentlessly, with good footwork and effective combinations—a uranium prospecting company and a layout company that designed and produced surfaces of roulette and craps tables. Father Angelo had passed along genes for working with felt and an eye for a seductive tabletop. Patrons left many cigarette burns in the felt, and Jijjie was selling new layouts like it was a fire sale.

To me Jijjie was too busy and too smart to be crooked.

Nunziatina visited Ben and Jijjie in 1958. She was thankful they were well and appeared to be happy, but she had trouble with impermanent relationships in LA and Vegas. Impermanent? How long could a desert support such large and growing towns? Napoli was four thousand years old. Back in Brooklyn, Nunziatina told me that Vegas had been a desert forty years before.

"Papà, will it be around forty years from now?"

As I was trying to come up with an answer, the home phone rang.

"Signor-ee Gee-o-vonnie, I see your grandsons are in Vegas and LA. Remember, this is a big country. The same laws apply in Nevada and California."

"Hello, Jackson." I did not mean to leave out *Agent*. "Congratulations on your retirement."

"Don't be a wise-ass. I did not die on the job, and I sure as hell ain't gonna let you hasten my departure from this earth."

The line went silent for a while, but I knew there was a hook at the end of it.

Nunziatina saw that it was time to leave, and genuflected in my direction after a kiss on the cheek.

"I see that your nephew John Piccolini is dealing with some unsavory characters in Vegas, guys like Levinson. Remember, that same tribe includes the Rosenberg rat traitors. They got the chair five years ago, 1953 to be exact, the same year your ex-Brooklyn Dodgers blew another series."

Thanks for the history lesson, Jackson.

"My old and new buddies at the bureau are watching, Gee-o-vonnie."

The line went dead. *Mannaggia, will I always be a gangster?*

20

BROTHERS OF THE MEDITERRANEAN AND THE NORTH SEA (1959)

My adolescente *yearns to spread his wings*
To soar, to escape the pecks and slings
Of his rancorous, nosy, clucking friends
While fueled by vision through a holy lens

As our family blossomed and expanded, '*a vecchiaia*, cursed old age, took its increasing toll on me. But my heart beat with purer love for each new generation, especially for my two favorite great-grandkids—Junior, the cream-colored Irishman, blue eyes and flaming red hair, and Joseph, his brown-eyed, olive-skinned second cuz. They were photographic negatives of each other, but they had so much in common, connecting under the skin. Junior spoke my dialect much better than swarthy Joseph, who did not have enough exposure to his Nonna Filomena and Nonno Giovanni to gain real fluency. Junior was under my thumb so much, he had to speak dialect for self-defense. Yes, I had a green thumb, but it was also very napulitano. I looked for opportunities to interact with those adolescents, especially when I could bring them together.

Joseph was by Vina's side when she visited salumeria number one in late June 1959 to greet me and her aunt Keira. He was a strapping young man of thirteen going on fourteen, at that crazy age, a boy facing the challenge of living up to the expectations of manhood. Joseph's face did not light up like it usually did when I gave him a kiss on each cheek and a hug.

"Hey, guagliò, whassa matter?"

Joseph looked away. Vina bent her head toward me, almost whispering, "Nonno, you know what's going on with Carmine DeSapio and Tammany Hall, no?"

"Hey, I read the papers. That Carmine DeSapio faccia is all over *Il Progresso*. Finally, an Italian leads an Irish political machine, and what happens?" I asked with my index finger spiraling skyward.

Vina gave a knowing nod, and bitterness crept into her beautiful smile. "A paisan makes it, and the system gets after him."

I chimed in: "Yeah, and those dark glasses don't help."

Vina's eyes sparkled, two question marks.

My voice rose more than I wanted it to. "Mannaggia! Carmine's got more problems than his sensitive eyes."

Vina gave a quick glance at Joseph, then re-fixed her owl eyes on me. "You know, the kids in the schoolyard found out Joseph's middle name is Carmine. Now they won't leave him alone, like, 'Carmine, how many elections did you fix today? Can you fix my bicycle?' Oh, how cute."

"Santissimo San Gennaro! We paisani have to be on our best behavior. Then some guy named Carmine makes it, and we suffer all over again."

"Wha, Nonno?"

"Well, hey, c'mon, mia nipotina Vina. You know your grandfather was a scugnizzo. There's scugnizzo in all of us, especially the politicians." I winked.

"Oh, don't I know it!" Vina winked back, rotating her index

finger into her cheek. Each turn of the finger ratcheted up her wry smile as those beautiful dimples deepened. But there was concern in her eyes.

I thought about the oppressive blanket the law was keeping me under—I was suspect because of my father's activities in Naples. *Now the association of Jijjie with casino operators in Vegas! And today's special, Tammany Hall.*

Joseph wandered off and ran his fingers down a huge hanging imported provolone. I could see him trying to read a label. I put my back toward him.

"Cara Vina, Mr. DeSapio has done a great job leading Tammany Hall. He had to fight the Micks and he finally made it. He ran a clean shop, for a machine shop, I mean."

I winked at Vina again. I didn't care that Joseph's great-aunt Keira was in hearing range. We Micks and Dagos understood each other, especially when we were family.

Keira waved to Vina, then turned to Joseph. In her Irish-Neapolitan brogue she asked how he was: "Comme staje, guagliò?" Joseph shrugged as he gave the provolone a gentle push.

Vina moved to my side, waved back to her aunt Keira, and confided in me. "But Nonno, why do we always have to be under this freakin' suspicion? Gimme a break. If we make it, it's because of some wise guy behind the scenes, pulling the right strings, paying someone off, even stickin' a gun in some schlemiel's face."

For Vina this was a long, and strong, speech. She usually knew to keep her mouth shut. She wasn't finished, though I was able to squeeze in "Vina, Carmine is a beautiful name, a holy name."

Vina changed directions on a dime: "You know what your daughter did the day Joseph was born?"

"Ahh, I can just see your Mamma Nunziatina."

"So, I'm in the Bensonhurst Maternity Home on Bay Parkway. Beautiful Joseph is in my arms, and I can hear Mamma's heels tapping on the hallway terrazzo, in a hurry. No hesitation—she walks right into my room and says, 'You have to name him Carmine! He was born on Our Lady of Mount Carmel Day!'

"I can just see her now," I said for the second time. No matter, Vina was into her story.

"Nonno, I was ready. I already told the home his name was Joseph Carmine. So, I tell Mamma. She's not that happy, but she smiles 'cause at least I knew the day of Our Lady of Mount Carmel."

We were both silent for a while. Joseph was talking baseball with Keira, probably about the Dodgers' second year in LA and how their young players were winning. *Players they pulled out of the Brooklyn Dodgers farm system*, I told myself.

"Vina, I got an idea. Joseph's birthday's coming up. I'll take him and cousin Junior to the Giglio festival. It'll make him proud to be named after Our Lady of Mount Carmel."

"*Ué Mari!* That would be wonderful. I saw the Giglio once. I was afraid that huge steeple would fall over and turn a lot of Italians into martyrs."

I gave a quick glance at Vina, then loudly got Joseph's attention. "Joseph, *viene ccà*. Come over here!"

He pulled himself away from Great-Aunt Keira, slumping over to me.

"Your birthday's in less than three weeks. Whaddya say we celebrate it right, with a parade, music, dancing, food—a real festa, on a weekend?"

"Nonno, I play ball in a Saturday league at the Parade Grounds…"

"Mannaggia, you can take a Sunday off, no? The Dodgers are in LA, they don't care about Brooklyn baseball no more." I added, for Keira's benefit, "And they didn't take the Giglio with them!"

Joseph gave me that look, between a smile and a question. His thick eyebrows almost closed the gap over his proud nose, his eyes narrowed, and the ends of his mouth didn't know whether to move up or down. Vina smiled at him, giving him encouraging nods.

"What if I get Junior to join us?" I said. Junior, though six months younger than Joseph, played on the same team with him.

"OK, Nonno, if Junior goes too."

Just what I wanted to hear.

With no customers in the store, Keira was capturing the whole conversation with Joseph. "Sure, my grandson loves Joseph, and he's never seen the Giglio. I'll get him to go along, nicely." She closed with a wink, one that probably still scared Mario.

Sunday, July 19, three days after Joseph's birthday, we took the Culver Line from Coney Island to the Church Avenue station, then asked directions. I mean, Joseph and Junior asked directions, 'cause they got more respect from Americans than an old fazool with an accent. We got on the GG and rode into the wilds of Williamsburg. It was worth it. We asked directions while walking through groups of Hasidic Jews. They kept pointing north. Eventually we found Havemeyer and Eighth Streets, just as the Giglio started dancing.

Oh, Madonna mia, what can I say about the Giglio—a huge, seven-story spire, a lily stem, with Our Lady of Mount Carmel and San Paolino di Nola the flower on top. That I knew, but it was more ornate than I recalled. The spire was adorned with all kinds of plastic and papier-mâché scenes, saints, streamers, and smaller lilies —i gigli. Its platform also contained a boat, a singer, and his eight-piece band.

Guy next to me saw my admiration. He jabbed my rib cage. "The whole thing has to weigh more than three tons."

"Che bellezza" was all I could say.

The platform was lifted by a bunch of very strong guaglioni, who took their duty seriously, training for four months. By tradition, training started on March 19, Joseph's name saint day—*Il Giorno di San Giuseppe*. The guaglioni danced to the band's music, carefully, following the directions of the Capo del Giglio, who faced them as he marched backward, marking the rhythm and direction with his staff. The boys were so synchronized, the Rockefeller Center Rockettes would be envious.

As I talked about the loving preparation, it wasn't lost on Joseph that "Joseph Carmine" had the Giglio covered, from St. Joseph to Our Lady of Mount Carmel.

Joseph took all this in. He looked over at Junior as if to say, "Don't you wish you looked more like a Dago?"

They didn't say a word to each other, but I swear I could read Junior's mind: *Sure, but I wouldn't want to be called Carmine.*

I'll say this about Junior, he eats like a full-blooded Italian. I love that boy, my combined gift from San Gennaro and St. Patrick.

Hotel
Fremont
LUCKY
FREMONT
Trader
BILLS

21

RED WORMS AND THE RED WAVE (1962–1967)

The nest is refuge after long flight
But it can also attract a red parasite
So, we uccelli must be ever on guard
Lest red worms leave our family scarred

"Hey, Nonno, how's everything in Brooklyn? Give my love to Nonna, Vina, and Mamma."

"Benedetto, so good to hear you voice! We all fine, except I'm-a freezing my motz."

Ben had called me in the store—the conversation was not for Nonna Filomena's ears. The place was empty on a very cold early December day, 1962. It was too cold, too Monday, and too far from Christmas to attract a lot of customers. I was in the back, looking at the front door through our one-way mirror. Snow was starting to fall.

I shut up 'cause I knew that Ben wanted to talk about more than my cold rear end. But for him, he was quiet.

"I supposa the weather is beautiful in LA, no?"

"Just beautiful. Like always."

"We have to go through another miserable winter for my New York Mets to open their second season. Can't come fast enough, and '63 can't be the disaster that '62 was."

"Nonno, I didn't call to talk baseball, but since you mention it, the '62 Mets will go down in history as baseball's worst team."

"At least they're my team. The Yankees give me àgita. They won another World Series two months ago, Madonna mia."

"And my San Francisco Giants shoulda beat the Yankees in that series."

"Abbastanza, enough with baseball! When you lived in Brooklyn, you rooted for the Giants, and now you live in LA and you root for the Giants. Ancora! Still!"

"I'm true to my team, Nonno. And they followed me to the West Coast."

"So, why you call? Comme staje, guagliò?"

Everyone was fine, and Ben got into his story about Jijjie, Vegas—and the FBI.

Jijjie's boss, Ed Levinson, was comfortable as executive director of the Fremont Hotel in Vegas. Who wouldn't like the title and the respect? But a few months before Ben called me from three thousand miles away, Levinson couldn't make a phone call across the street in downtown Vegas. So, he paged John Piccolini, Head of Engineering.

Ben narrated the story that came from Jijjie, from the horse's mouth. I sat back in my swivel chair, engrossed, though apprehensive about the outcome, and with one eye on the front door of the store.

Ben was my playwright.

Ed appeals to Jijjie as he enters Ed's office.

ED: John, my phone is giving me fits. Sometimes the line goes dead, and other times I hear shadows of other conversations. Straighten it out before I call the phone company flunkies, but who knows if the call will go through?

JIJJIE: Sure, Ed. Lemme give it a look-see.

Jijjie rapidly kneels under the desk, occasioning Mr. Levinson to move faster than he wants.

JIJJIE: What's this stupid red wire?

Ed knows gambling and gambling odds—electrical wiring, not so much. So, Jijjie does not expect an answer, but he gets another question.

ED: Where do you think it goes?

JIJJIE: Good question. That's how we learn.

Jijjie shows comfort at being a little smart-alecky with Levinson. They understand and respect each other.

JIJJIE: Ed, lemme follow this wire and talk to the engineers of a few other places.

Ben didn't keep me in suspense for long. "So, Jijjie follows the wire through the guts of the Fremont, and guess what? His buddies also found them in their joints. There was a bunch of red wires, and they all came together at the Henderson Novelty Company on Eleventh Street in downtown Vegas."

"Why? And what kinda bizhiness is that?" My heart was racing because I thought I knew the answer.

"That 'business,' as you say, has about forty employees, and it turns out that all are FBI agents." He whispered the full name, the Federal Bureau of Investigation, nice and slow, as if I didn't know. "They were listening in for who knows how long?"

I shouted at Ben through the phone, "Mannaggia! We Ragnuno are still fighting our own government!" *I've been fighting the Feds in New York ever since World War I. I don't need to open another front on the West Coast.*

"Not just mannaggia, Nonno, but Mannaggia'merica, as Nonna Filomena always says. I don't think they're listening now. Just kidding."

I had heard enough. "Ciao bello, when do you visit Brooklyn?"

"Soon, I hope. Kay wants to visit her family."

You can't say you want to visit your *family?*

"OK, soon." I hung up, closed the store, and got back on the phone, this time with Jijjie. The Fremont Hotel operator recognized me and put me through. I caught Jijjie between maintenance emergencies. I was afraid to say anything, but Jijjie didn't care. I think he wanted the Feds to know what he thought of them.

"The damned government is its own mob," Jijjie growled.

I could just see Jijjie saying the same thing to Ed Levinson in Ed's office, which I'm sure was already scoured for bugs. I know Jijjie scoured his own office.

"You heard me, Nonno, the government is its own mob. The difference between them and the mob is that they can work the law against us."

"I know my federal friends in Manhattan will call me in," I said. "They're gonna try to pin something on me. You sure you clean?"

I wished I could have pulled those last words back.

Jijjie exploded. "I'm as clean as anybody in this filthy town! You think the big boys would clue me in on how they share their earnings? I do my job, all legit, and I keep my mouth shut."

"Good boy, guagliò."

Jijjie had told me more than once that Ed Levinson was as close to a father as anyone he ever knew, but there were things a father did not tell his son, to protect him. Besides, Jijjie knew that Giovanni Ragnuno was his real grandfather.

"Nonno, Mr. Levinson told me that he worked under some not-so-nice characters, but he was always straight with them. He's always been straight with me, the staff, and the patrons. He told me more than once, 'My casinos are clean—no patron is a patsy.'"

Wow, what a great guy, Levinson. He didn't make the odds impossible for the patron to win, as if the house needed help. I did not share those thoughts with Jijjie.

I walked the three cold blocks home. Filomena gave me that all-seeing witch look.

"Why such a *fàccia di misèria*?"

I tried to smile-wipe the misery from my face. "It's nothing, just a short, dark, and cold day and very few customers."

I poured myself a small glass of strega, witch's brew, in honor of my wife, Filomena, the witch of Benevento who knew all.

"You talked with our *nipoti*?"

"Just a little baseball with Ben, then business with Jijjie." *Do I have that nipoti expression on my face?*

I got that look, that raised right eyebrow and the nod. She knew enough not to press. And she would soon know all. I found my easy chair in the dining room—just me, my strega, and my thoughts, with Filomena the strega eavesdropping.

I'm a little jealous that Jijjie and Ed Levinson are almost like father and son, especially since Papà Angelo dropped dead on that LA street half a dozen years ago. Jijjie opened up to me *today, that's something to cheer about. I'll be in Jijjie's corner as much as I can. My own tormentor, Jackson, will be biting my rear end real soon. I'm one of his retirement hobbies. Maybe I can bite back a little.*

Filomena shook me awake. I must have nodded off. "*Viene a mangiare*, come to eat something. You shouldn't drink on an empty stomach."

Especially if I dream about Jackson.

Months later, juicy transcripts of "skimming" were leaked. The Fremont was the distribution point for undeclared loot pooled from the take of several Vegas casinos, including the Fremont itself. The cash then went out in suitcases to Midwest mob operators—in Kansas City, Cleveland, Chicago, and other cities. This was definitely not right. That was untaxed money. It was an investment in the mobsters instead of America. I prayed that Jijjie was not involved.

Jackson must have loved the news, and he probably knew more than what came out in the papers. For sure, he was going to drop something on me. He had been quiet so far. So had Jijjie. Then I learned that Jijjie and Levinson were preparing a case against the FBI for illegal wiretapping. I still thought that Jijjie was the brave, innocent shield and a loyal employee.

Casino owners counted cash. I counted my blessings—my five surviving grandkids. Cash comes and goes, but lost blessings hurt to the core. Anna and Angelina had drifted off to heaven. TJ, one of my blessings on earth, became capo of store number two, more interested in gorgonzola and grana padano than in his Grandpa Giovanni, or so it seemed. Blessed Padraic entered my life occasionally from his own circles in Manhattan and downtown Brooklyn. Jijjie and Ben were very close to me, but they had nested on the West Coast a dozen years before. Only Vina stayed close, both in proximity and affection. And her Joseph was a blessing to me, as was TJ's Junior.

Years after the Ben-Jijjie twins left for the West Coast, I feared that Junior and Joseph, my Irish-Italian twins, would take their turn to leave Brooklyn. Leaving for college was the first step, and Joseph would be the first—he was a year ahead of Junior. Joseph graduated in June 1965 from his Manhattan science high school. I comforted myself in that I at least had the summer with him, but then I lost most of that when Vina and Jijjie arranged for Joseph to spend summer '65 in Vegas.

Jijjie and nephew Joseph really hit it off. Tight-lipped Jijjie opened up to me about some of Joseph's adventures. We were on the phone a lot that summer.

"Nonno, Joseph came in on a late flight from JFK/Idlewild. Between me and the plane he was bending down to pick up bugs attracted to the floodlights. The next morning he's standing in front of our patio glass door, looking at the desert. I wish him a good morning and he just tells me, 'I feel like I'm in the Twilight Zone.'

"So, I told him, 'Joseph, there's more to the world than Brooklyn.'"

I laughed, and so did Jijjie.

"Sheesh, Nonno, did I have that thick of a Brooklyn accent at his age?"

"What do I know about accents?"

Joseph had little interest in the Vegas glitz and the casinos. Just being out of Brooklyn was enough of a radical change—he went out from those three rooms behind his stepfather's store on Eighty-Sixth Street to a wide-open gambling town sprawled out in a desert, with mountains on the horizon.

But Uncle Jijjie's outlook also changed, like on the youth sports scene. "I was Joseph's transportation to baseball games in Vegas, Henderson, and Boulder City. Every Vegas kid his age has a driver's license, but not Joseph."

"Vina would not approve of him driving so young."

"Whatever. I really didn't mind, and he liked seeing me at his games. He even attracted a girl or two. One of 'em had a girlfriend leave a goofy note at our door."

Then there was a call near the end of the summer. "Nonno, I'm gonna miss that pistol. Know what he's doing now? After a day of hauling beer kegs and crates of melons, he works out with the Bishop Gorman football team—he wants to toughen up for freshman football at college."

"Well, I hope his mind is also being developed."

"Don't worry, even though a lot of his mind is on girls. Last night I just wanted to lay out and watch TV, and he comes downstairs into my hideaway. 'Hey, Unca Johnny, let's go bowling!'"

"Ahh, bocce is an Italian sport."

"And he loves that the championship tournaments are televised from the Showboat Lanes."

Joseph, back from Vegas and before going off to his upstate college, shared stories with Junior and me. My Bay Fiftieth home became our clubhouse. Such funny kids, I should have written a book. In Vegas Joseph came across Nick Kelly, an old Brooklyn acquaintance of Jijjie and me. Nick was always large, in size, spirit, and ego. He had "Kelly" customized on his license plate. Nick Kelly was an alias. His real first name was Nicola. Nick longingly told Joseph about the old days in Brooklyn and the Manhattan Garment District.

Joseph was sitting under my grape arbor, sipping on a Yoo-hoo chocolate soda. "So, one night, I'm leaving Fremont restaurant supply, and I bump into Nick going out to the parking garage. He gives me that look, you know, like we share a secret. He wrinkles his forehead, and then almost butts mine with it. 'You're Nunziatina's grandson,' he tells me."

"Go on, guagliò."

"I nodded back, and he says, 'She's one tough lady. I saw her slap a fresh guy right across the kisser at the dress shop, and then she tells the creep in dialect, "May your eyes turn to wax and your blood to sawdust."' I told Nick that was news to me, and he says, 'But here's the punch line. She points the two cornuto fingers in his eyes and tells him she'll pray that his patron saint urinates on his tombstone.'"

"Joseph, your Nonna Nunziatina had to be tough. She was a good-looking single mother of four during the Depression." *Do kids ever imagine their grandparents young and beautiful?*

"I never heard that story about Grandma."

"There are more, guagliò. You were too young for a lot of them."

Later, on the phone, Jijjie confirmed the Joseph-Nick conversation, complete with accents, and I almost lost my prosciutto.

Junior joined Joseph on most visits to our Bay Fiftieth Street home. Joseph bragged that the Fremont cocktail waitresses were friendly, especially toward John Piccolini's nephew. On workdays, Joseph and Jijjie had breakfast in the Fremont's low-key twenty-four-hour cafeteria, just off the main lobby. It catered to patrons who pulled frustrating all-nighters at the tables and the slots. The cafeteria waitresses were motherly and more understanding than the cocktail waitresses on the casino floor. Then came the morning when three lovely young casino workers, their graveyard shift over, sidled up to Jijjie on his side of the booth. One of them, hand on Jijjie's shoulder, fluttered her eyelashes at Joseph. She told him, smiling through perfect white teeth, "John is our uncle."

"So, Nonno, I said, 'That makes us cousins!' Then Uncle Jijjie smiles and tells them, 'Pretty quick, no?'"

I nodded proudly.

"When the ladies left, Uncle Jijjie was ready to go to work. He looks at my second plate of pancakes and tells me I eat like I have two assholes." Joseph looked to see if Nonna Filomena was in earshot.

"Joseph, don't let praise go to your head," Nonna Filomena yelled from the kitchen in amazingly good English.

Joseph and Junior took advantage of the remains of the summer before going their separate ways in the fall—Joseph heading north to college, and Junior to his senior year at St. John's Prep, a fine Catholic high school in a decaying Brooklyn neighborhood. After an early September Monday dinner at our place, Joseph and Junior were fighting over the last sfogliatella, and as usual, one divided and the other got first choice of the better half.

Junior's Irish blarney came through a mouth full of Italian pastry. "St. John reminds me of my Great-grandfather Giovanni."

"I feel more like old St. Nick," I said, "and that's the role of a great-grandfather."

"But Nonno, we learned at school that St. John was a lot of things, including the patron saint of hospitals, nurses, and the sick. You and Nonna Filomena were my hospital when I was sick, and you nursed me back to health."

"OK, who am I to argue? I'll carry your recommendation to St. Peter when I see him. And I'll put in a good word for Nonna Filomena."

Joseph and Junior had more to discuss than the ecclesiastical, like Mitchell's Drive-In in the hoity-toity section of Fort Hamilton, near Brooklyn Poly Prep. The music was doo-wop. The place was full of hot-rodders and cute mini-skirted waitresses on roller skates. Everyone's favorite was vivacious Frenchie.

"Joseph was full of stories about the Vegas hot-rodders."

"I'm sure he told you only the good parts. His uncle Jijjie had to drive him around, unless, Joseph, you learned how to drive on those desert highways…"

Joseph said nothing.

"So, Nonno, day before yesterday we went to the confraternity welcoming dance at St. John's. I knew that Vegas gave Joseph more confidence with the girls, but I didn't expect Joseph the Dancing Fool." Junior tapped into that Irish gift of storytelling. He had me in stitches, and Joseph knew to keep his mouth shut. "Grandpa, we walked into the St. John's Confraternity Hall and there were girls on one side and guys on the other. We were checking each other out—we guys were talking baseball, and I have no idea what the girls were talking about."

"Ahh, things never change," I said. "The first time I saw your great-grandmother Filomena, I knew I loved her and I wanted to marry her, but it took me a long time to feel comfortable around her."

"Nonno, you really felt that way? From the first day?" Junior almost jumped at me.

"Well, there were not that many girls around, but I can still picture my Filomena in that white blouse with her long braid going down her back, her beautiful face with those flashing eyes …"

"Really, Nonno?" asked wide-eyed Joseph.

"Yes, Junior, and Joseph, and I'm not kidding you. If another girl told me she loved me, I wouldn't have felt any interest."

"But if Nonna Filomena was one of many girls in the confraternity hall…"

"Bahh, that is history, Junior. Tell me about Joseph." *You know the kids are getting older when they don't accept everything you say, hook, line, and sinker.*

"OK, we were in the hall, and the band was warming up and Father Varriale was giving the welcoming speech, and all of a sudden, some of the girls started screaming."

"At Father Varriale?"

"Nooo, Nonno! This huge spider was walking along the wall on the girls' side—well, it wasn't really their side, but that's where they were. I mean, that spider was huge, Madonna mia!"

"Junior, you know that Nonna Filomena doesn't like you to use our Holy Mother's name in vain."

"But you shoulda seen it! It was bigger than my thumb, and it could jump!"

"Madonna." I quickly made the sign of the cross.

Joseph had to interrupt. "It wasn't that big."

"It was HUGE, Joseph. So, Nonno, one of the girls took off a high-heeled shoe and was going to squash the monster."

"Brave girl."

"But Joseph ran over and put himself on one knee between the girl and the spider. He stared up at her and said, 'The spider won't hurt you. It's been eating bugs in the hall all summer!'

"She looked at him like he was completely crazy. Look at him now— sun-browned from playing baseball and football in Vegas. Maybe she thought Joseph was some crazy Sicilian."

Joseph couldn't contain himself anymore. "I told her to control herself and wait. I grabbed a cup and napkin from the refreshment table, put the cup over the spider, slid the napkin under, and turned the cup over real fast, keeping the napkin on top."

"Brave guagliò."

"Nah, spiders don't want to mess with us. I went out to the school garden and let the spider go."

I was thinking, *sî cumplèto pazzo, ma cu core d'angiulo*, and so told Joseph, "You're completely crazy, but with the heart of an angel."

Junior chimed in, as if Joseph needed a lawyer. "You're right, Nonno, Joseph is crazy, but guess what? The girl, Anna-Paola, you know her, no? She's from the neighborhood."

"Oy, yeah, she's-a very pretty, and smart."

"Well, Joseph and I both noticed that she's pretty. She's going to Marquette this fall."

"I cannot-a believe her father will let her go all the way to Milwaukee, and it has boys."

"Ahh, you were talking with her father. So, you know it's a good Jesuit school," said good Catholic Junior.

"Go on with the story, 'cause I see your pancia is busting."

Junior reflexively put a hand on his stomach. "When Joseph finished his rescue act, he realized there was a crowd following him back into the hall. All of a sudden, he was embarrassed, and you could tell he was blushing—even through his tanned face."

I looked at this blessing of a great-grandson, talking to me about my other great-grandson, sitting right next to him. *America, you have been good to me, after all the heartbreak and àgita.*

"The ice was broken." Junior burst into my thoughts. "Anna-Paola just had to know more about this crazy guy, and I did my best to introduce them. No way she believed I'm Joseph's cousin, but she went along 'cause we both seemed harmless."

I could picture the scene crystal clear, but from above, as if I were a great-grandfather uccello—an old owl, a *gufo* flying around the hall.

"Joseph and Anna-Paola start gabbing. You know how Joseph

talks real fast when he's excited, and then he stutters a little? Sorry, Joseph." Joseph looked down a little, and Junior carried on. "Well, he was doing all that, but Anna-Paola didn't care. She was hanging on his every word. He went from spiders to the Dodgers to Vegas to his new Ivy League school up north."

"Yeah, and I bet that Anna-Paola got in a few words of her own. She's a sharp young lady." *Dark eyes, wavy, jet-black hair, long legs, and a body that curves like a beautiful climbing vine.* I did not share these last thoughts with the young men.

"Sure is, Grandpa. The band was warming up the whole time. Father Varriale finished his welcome speech, and he made sure to thank Joseph for making the hall safe. He finished, and the music started, and loud."

"Mannaggia, Junior."

"Anna-Paola didn't wait to be invited. She grabbed Joseph by the elbow, and they were dancing, I mean really dancing."

I looked over at Joseph, who was blushing but proud.

Junior went on. "Cousin Joseph can play baseball and football, and I learned that he has great footwork and moves on the dance floor too."

I was transported to my own wedding party in Campania and to weddings since then. I got to know Junior's great-grandfather Tom O'Donnell at Mario and Keira's wedding. The music was always changing, but the tarantella and the stuff they danced to now were not that different. Filomena and I always danced, but to the slow numbers, waltzes, and Caruso love songs. While looking at Junior, as my mind circled over the confraternity hall, I was thinking, *The bite of the tarantula made people dance the tarantella, and it was a spider that introduced Anna-Paola and Joseph. Spiders and insects are always a part of my life and the life of my family.*

Filomena was busy in the kitchen, but I'm sure she couldn't wait to get on the phone with Anna-Paola Palumbo's parents.

Just before Joseph trekked north to college, he and I discussed Mitchell's Drive-In, drag racing on the Belt Parkway, and the finer points of contemporary Brooklyn music.

"Nonno, what a scene! I didn't know there were places like Mitchell's in the neighborhood. And the music was all oldies."

"Oldies? Whaddya talking about, guagliò? I'm more than sixty years older than you. You tellin' me, of all people, about oldies?" My smile belied any consternation.

"Yeah, and they specialize in Brooklyn groups like the Chimes and the Mystics. And the Passions are from Bensonhurst, even."

"Fercryinoutloud!" Those groups were almost all nice Italian boys—at least they weren't boxing. Maybe they would have a real career someday, maybe even like Dion DiMucci and his Belmonts from the Bronx.

Joseph must have read my mind. "Of course, they play Dion and the Belmonts but never Beach Boys music."

"You know something, Joseph? There are a lot of good Black groups. I remember the Ink Spots. Now the Platters are a throwback to the good old days. Why can't we get together with Black kids and make great music?"

"But there are mixed groups. The Del-Vikings and the Crests are great. And so are Booker T and the MG's."

"Well, I'm-a glad to hear that. I hate to see Italian boys alone identified with doo-wop. Where did that name come from?"

"I don't know, but no one seems to mind. Maybe we can say that the paisans invented it."

What a wise-ass, my great-grandson. I knew he would do well in college.

So, Joseph related Brooklyn tales to the well-bred coeds at his fancy university. How could they resist? He regaled the ladies with stories, from spiders to Vegas to Brooklyn drag racing and, of course, the

Giglio procession of Williamsburg. But on dates the gals drove because Joseph did not have his license.

Cousin Junior visited campus a few times. Joseph fixed him up with blind dates, and Junior in turn was under oath not to question the veracity of Joseph's tales.

Joseph told me that he played freshman football with a young Pinza. Pete Pinza was Ezio's son. I bet Joe and Pete never talked much of the immigrant experience, if they ever talked about it at all. Their biggest concerns were making the team, getting good grades, and finding a date for the weekend, and maybe not in that order.

For us birds who passaged from the old country, how many generations to be completely beyond suspicion? Have Joseph and Pete made those first steps into true Americanhood, to being americani davvero? Will they escape the red worm that infiltrated the lives of Joseph's uncle Jijjie and Pete's father, Ezio?

While Joseph and Junior were in college, Ed Levinson decided to retire. Embroiled in lawsuits and charges by the FBI and the IRS, he sold his interest in the Fremont and moved to Beverly Hills in 1967. Jijjie told me Ed was enjoying his retirement. And then in 1968, Richard Nixon became our new president. His enemies, and probably a few allies, called him Tricky Dick, and I could just see him using wiretapping and espionage to get at his own political enemies. His FBI director, J. Edgar Hoover, was in office way too long—since 1924! That was three years before Nunziatina married Angelo. Sheesh, Hoover was his own dynasty—but Calogero confirmed that the original Bureau of Investigation was founded in 1908 by a son of Corsica. So, the history of government agencies can resemble Neapolitan history. If strongman Hoover OK'd wiretapping in Vegas, who knows what else he would do to get dirt on his enemies or even eliminate them? My inner scugnizzo saw these things clearly. One thing I had trouble seeing was these politicians surviving one week in the bassi of Naples.

Jijjie went on with his life as a Vegas functionary. Joseph confirmed that his uncle had told him more than once during the summer of '65, "It ain't the good guys versus the bad guys. There are no white hats against the black hats. Everyone plays an advantage and some people with the law and religion on their side can be the biggest crooks of all."

I learned in Naples and Brooklyn that everyone has scugnizzo tendencies. Joseph was also learning this valuable lesson. Cynical? Maybe. But people who trust with no reservations are victims, martyrs, or saints, or all three.

Speaking of saints, I got a phone call from Mr. Federal Jackson in '67. He called me at home, the SOB, and after dinner! He could not resist telling me that my grandson Jijjie was involved in casino skimming.

"Don Giovanni, you can't seem to get the filth of the Naples harbor off your family skin, no matter how much you bathe in our American waters."

"Why don't you look into poetry as a second career? You can work from your retirement home."

"Watch your Dago ass, gutter rat, and pray your nephew doesn't step in it."

I'd had it. I lost it, as my kids would say. "'Filth of the Naples harbor?' Oh, is our precious America as white as an angel's feathers?"

"Don't get smart with me."

"'Filth of the Naples harbor?' Treat me with respect and I will answer you respectfully. Remember the sinking of the *SS Normandie* right under your federal nose in New York Harbor? We were at war for two months!"

Silence from Jackson.

"Everyone knows that FDR then made a deal with Lucky Luciano to keep the waters of our American harbors uncontaminated during World War II. And you didn't have to read the Italian of *Il Progresso* to learn it."

"Watch what you say! It may come back to bite you."

"Oh, is this such a great secret? This is the same Luciano who worked with Alberto Anastasio, Al Anastasia to you. Yes, Anastasia, the head of Murder Incorporated, such a nice American business name. Albert and Lucky became Yankee war heroes."

"You better watch it, Ragnuno. My FBI friends find any skimmed Vegas money passing through your greasy palm, and you're in federal pen so fast your head will spin."

"That is a great opera, Jackson: the American government hires the devil and his angels to guard the portals of heaven."

The line went dead. I hoped he hurt his fingers slamming the receiver down.

I knew there would be hell to pay.

I also hoped that Jijjie was clean.

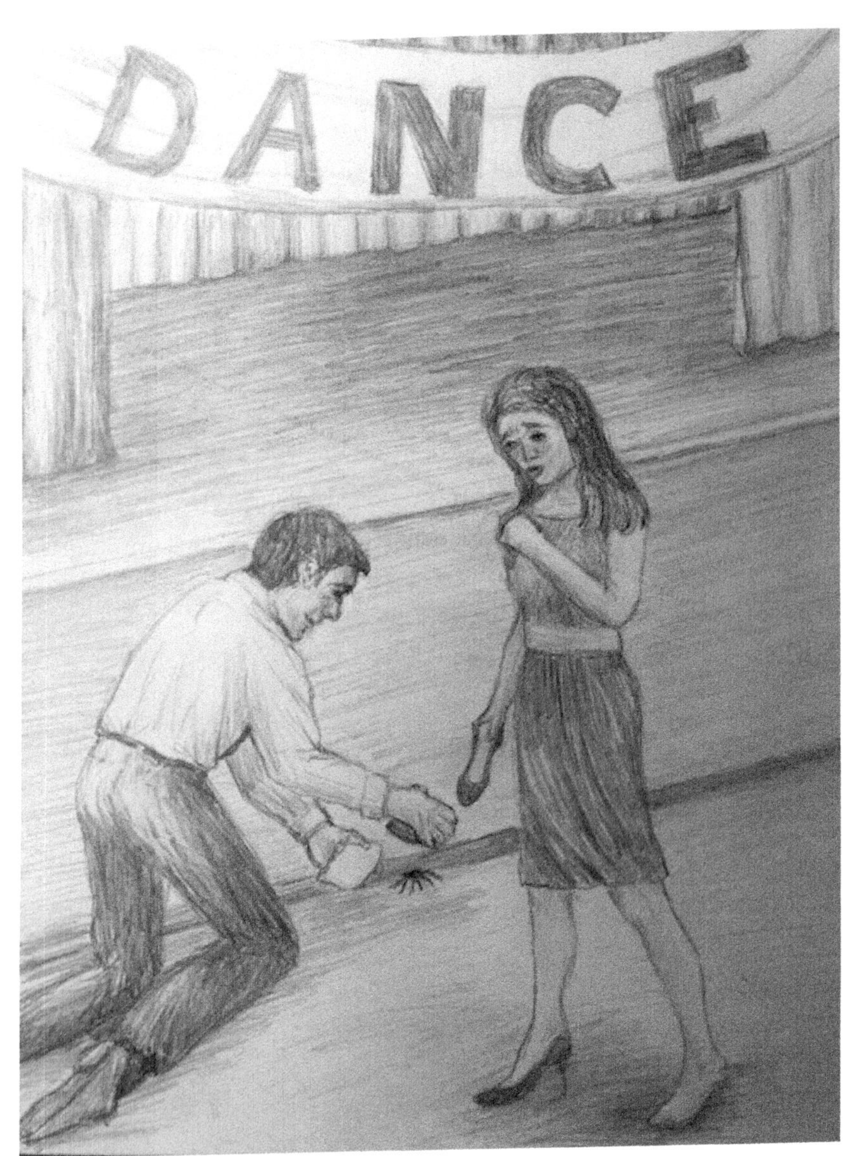
DANCE

22

MY NESTS IN THE EAST (1958–1969)

Feisty young birds do many a crazy thing
Rejoicing the escape from under Mom's wing
We watch from afar, we wonder and fret
If our young are ready to meet each threat

Dinner over, I escaped to my easy chair in the living room. It was easy to read that Filomena did not want me in the kitchen, but neither very welcoming was the June 30, 1958 issue of the *New York Post.* The front page reported that the Soviet *Sputnik 3* was orbiting the earth. America was challenged. But finally America had a space agency—some comfort, I supposed. The back page followed the disastrous first year of the LA Dodgers. *Well, they deserved it. Let's see how faithful the LA fans are now.*

I tried to sweeten the news with a bitter, an after-dinner amaro. I raised my voice so Filomena could hear me over the racket of her washing dishes. "Amore mio, forty years ago they dragged me into court for mixing a few oils with olive oil and calling it olive oil. But who controls what goes into this witch's mix of amaro—herbs, bark, flowers, spices, wild berries, roots, orange peel. Who knows what else? A poisonous mushroom? And it's called *Amaro Bisnonno*, great-grandpa's amaro. I hope I smell better."

Filomena appeared in the doorway to the living room. She shrugged and wiped her brow with her forearm. "Would be nice to have an automatic dishwasher. We send rockets into space, why not?"

My amaro digestivo and 'a vecchiaia, my old age, were a daily one-two punch. Filomena always foresaw what was coming next: "Filomena, cara, did we do all we could to prepare our children, our grandchildren, our great-grandchildren for this crazy world?"

The burnt sienna amaro dark-colored my outlook—interlacing rivulets of umber, ochre, and sepia draining the low-tide delta of my unease. *Will my life ride out on the next low tide? And what of the family I leave behind?*

Filomena knocked off my wizard's cap with four words as she waved her dish towel near my head: "Tu sî pazzo, Giovanni." She was right. I was crazy, and the amaro just brought it out. Her eyes told me, before she even asked the question, "Who knows how much-a is enough to keep you kids safe and happy?"

Those Moorish arches still cast a spell, but her words were more like a hammer blow. "Put that amaro down and worry about maybe what you canna control. Call you lawyer friends. Get all-a that crap off you record. You no-good father still torments you from de grave. And that so-called Papà of Johnny in Vegas, who knows?"

Filomena, with a fly swat, killed the conversation but not the buzzing of my haunted thoughts. *We faced risk and danger. Was there an easier way to achieve the wisdom to pass on to our children? Could we—should we—have completely sheltered our fledglings? If so, could we expect them to act with wisdom and bravery as they reared their own clutches?*

Is my life a numbers game? Like the game on the streets or the games in Vegas—sometimes you win, usually you lose. "Multiplying and becoming many" improved the odds of a tragic fall. Anna and Angelina were always in my prayers, but could prayer have prevented *their tragedies?*

I did not express these doubts to Filomena, and never to Father del Giudice, not even in confession. God working in mysterious ways was never fully comforting to me.

"Don't wake me when you get to bed, Giovanni 'O Pazzo." Filomena headed back to the kitchen.

On a nice spring day almost ten years later, TJ and Peggy called to invite me to visit the second store. Only important business would pull TJ away from tending "his" salumeria. I made sure to arrive no later than midmorning to avoid the lunch hero rush. There were two helpers behind the counters—a nice Puerto Rican kid, Danilo, and a young Italian gal, Maddalena (Maddie), both from Gravesend. Funny, they looked like brother and sister—short, dark, and curly haired, and both with Brooklyn accents. Ahh, what a country, even though it gives me àgita.

TJ signaled me to the back.

I was settling into my seat when he opened with "Grandpa, you know that Vina and Mike split about sixteen years ago."

Hey, I can do math. "Well, of course guagliò, such a sensible kid had to fall in love with a gambler almost ten years older." No, I didn't say that eighteen was too young to marry, since we Ragnuno made a habit of marrying young.

"Vina was doing piecework at home on Aunt Nunziatina's motorized old Singer. She had dropped out of school, and I guess she had time to fall for Mike Popo."

"OK, get to the point, TJ. We all know that Mike was a charmer, life of the party, poet, storyteller, bullshit artist, and compulsive gambler. He was—"

Peggy, who always liked Mike, interrupted. "Mike lost both of his immigrant parents to the Spanish flu when he was a one-year-old. He was passed around by relatives who hardly spoke English—not a stable upbringing. I'm sure it led to his gambling addiction."

"Ahh, always the same story, *sempe a stessa storia*. The same malarky. Yeah, the gambling debts, the loan sharks with the vig, the con artistry, the federal penitentiary. He gets out, and Vina still marries him!"

"Grandpa," TJ said, "please don't go over sad history."

Hey, you brought it up.

"At least Vina had two beautiful boys with Mike. And her husband, Lou, treats Joseph and Michael as if they're his own. The family has adjusted to life in back of the store on Eighty-Sixth Street."

"So, you called me here to tell me that?" *Old guys have a right to be cranky.*

TJ got to the point, finally. "Michael's not going to college. He's a talented guitarist and songwriter—been playing at a few local restaurants and societies. He got a Manhattan demolition job with Lou's people and was discovered there, right on Park Avenue. This guy kept coming around, and Michael was trying to avoid him. Then he learns the guy's Leon Silverman, a semi-retired Broadway impresario. Michael played for Mr. Silverman, who was impressed. He even wrote him up as a 'New Face' in *Cue* magazine!"

I could not help raising my eyebrows.

"OK, but there's a punch line."

Finally.

Just then, Danilo stuck his head in the back office/storeroom. "Mr. Ragnuno, we're almost out of capocollo."

"OK, Danilo, go get some from the other store."

The other store? This is the other store. I tried not to let my thoughts make it to my face.

TJ went on. "Silverman noticed Vina's creations on Michael and his girlfriend, Theo. He's impressed and wants to make an investment in a Manhattan boutique, Creations by Vina. He's got a rich Midtown Manhattan friend, a woman, who's willing to go in with him."

"Why does it take Jewish people to recognize our talent? Ed Levinson and Moe Liebowitz with Jijjie, and now this Leon Silverman with Vina and her Michael? Why can't we help ourselves?"

"Grandpa, I don't know the answer, but this is a great opportunity for Vina to get ahead. God knows she deserves a break."

"OK, I'll talk with her."

I got out before the lunch hero rush.

Vina was a great seamstress, and more than that, a creative designer. Like her father, she could imagine a finished piece and had the talent to sew it into reality.

I looked at Vina across the lovely Formica top of our Bay Fiftieth kitchen table. She usually visited on her way home from an operators shop near Coney Island.

"Vina, you are so talented and so good. You deserve the reward of being recognized and making a few bucks off your talent."

"Thanks, but first of all, I'm not so sure of my talent. I was never trained, and the Manhattan fashion business is a jungle. I might get eaten alive."

"Well, cara mia, the Brooklyn sweatshops and your International Ladies' Garment Workers Union are eating you alive. You get niente in return except for àgita."

"But the real reason, the real first place—I want to stay close to the boys and help Lou in the store." Vina had her head down, with her voice trailing off.

"I know you help Lou, you're there for the boys, but they won't need you forever. They're growing up."

"The boys need me now, Nonno. We had to pull Michael away from the bad element Rampers on the waterfront."

"Sure, all kids need their mamma, and I know you help out with church charities. Michael told me how you invite some of the disgràziati street people to the back of the store for a bowl of hot soup. He even wrote a song about it ..."

Vina raised a hand as she raised her head. Those owl eyes became almost predatory. "Stop it, Nonno! You just told me what I have to do. My family, my flesh and blood, they need me to stay in Bensonhurst!" Those eyes, now glistening, bored into mine.

"I know that Keira would not agree," I offered meekly.

I was assailed by a strong gale off the Bay of Naples: "Keira has her own life!" Vina seemed surprised at her own outburst. She went on, but more subdued. "Keira has her relatives, and she and Mario are business partners. She's college educated. I love and admire her, but I do not have to copy her!"

Tears streamed out of those lovely dark hazel eyes.

"Vina," I mumbled helplessly. "I am so sorry for putting this pressure on you."

Vina stood up and gave me a long hug. "I love you, Nonno, you know that. And I love how you care for every one of your children, grandchildren, and great-grandchildren. My Joseph loves you more than you could know."

She headed out for Bay Fiftieth Street, going out the side door and around the house, probably to avoid Filomena. I thought of how much Vina's morale must have sunk every time she sat down to sew someone else's uninspired designs back in a neighborhood sweatshop.

TJ and Peggy had been a great comfort to Vina in her dealings with Mike Popo, and that was the start of the special relationship between Vina's Joseph and TJ and Peggy's Junior. Now, the two college kids explained that each had 12.5 percent of my genes, or one out of eight, and also 12.5 percent of Filomena's genes. So, the rest of them, or three quarters of Junior's genes, were Irish genes, and those three quarters of Joseph's were Italian. But they did not stop there. The genes they got from Filomena and me were not necessarily the same ones.

To me, the genes that counted were the ones that instilled in Joseph and Junior love for their bisnonno, Great-grandfather Giovanni. I tended to think this way when it was just we three together, like on a Sheepshead Bay fishing boat in the "Bite," a couple of miles down toward Sandy Hook off Jersey.

TJ and Peggy's Padraic did not establish a nest, at least not with an innamorata. He had his own roost in Greenwich Village. His heft and height got him work as a bouncer at gay clubs such as the Stonewall Inn. The place was run by the wise guys, or so I was told. In June 1969, when the Mets were finally getting some respect, so were Padraic's paisani at the Stonewall, but the police had other ideas and a riot broke out. The Stonewall riots were the incident that won some respect for the gay community, the ones who openly declared themselves gay. I always wished they would find a better word—we all deserved to be gay in our own ways.

Padraic set me straight. The wise guys who ran the Stonewall Inn were just looking for a good income, not to take part in a social movement. I couldn't believe that I was using modern words like *movement*, *gay*, *community*. They meant different things in days not so long gone by. The police seemed much less likely to tolerate the atmosphere at the Stonewall and at other places in the Village. I liked to think that Padraic played a role in the uprising. His bouncer jobs earned him respect from all, though I knew he felt terrible if he thought he hurt someone.

Of course, Padraic was much more than a hard body who knew martial arts. He became a successful accountant. In fact, he was my accountant and his brother TJ's as well. His business partner became his life partner, nice Jewish-Italian boy—Renni (Renato) Gutman.

On a lovely day Padraic and I visited Anna's grave at Greenwood Cemetery. "Padraic, I think of my family as migratory birds setting up nests in America. Anna and Angelina's nests are now in heaven."

"I hope they are looking down at us with love, the same love we cast up to them," said Padraic.

I ready myself to fly up to you, Anna and Angelina, I thought as I lifted my head to the sky. Padraic gave me a pained look. Did my face give away my thoughts?

I am comforted that this uccellino escapee from Naples will have few worries about Joseph, Junior, and the rest of the family of Giovanni and Filomena. Call them what you want. Genes? Well, OK. Our genes will always be with Junior, Joseph, and all our other great-grandchildren. They will treat their inheritance well.

There are genes, and then there is honor. Before I take off, I need to clear my family's name with the country that adopted me, the country that suspects me of being more devil than angel and of raising a coven of devils.

23

STREETS OF BROOKLYN (1969)

We look beyond our primal nest,
And see friends and kin—truly we're blest
While raptors may have oft assailed us
Our family and allies ever did shield us

"Happy New Year, Nonno."

"Jijjie! So good to hear you voice! What's new, besides 1970?"

I was at the phone extension in my study. *Jijjie, of all people, calling me on New Year's Eve morning. He must have good news.*

"I wanted to be the first to tell you and Nonna. My application to the Nevada State Gaming Commission was approved for my new place in Laughlin on the Colorado River."

"*Maravigliuso*! Wonderful!" I yelled into the phone. But still I wondered what he had to do to get approval.

"Ever since that weird Howard Hughes character bought up

most of Vegas, most of the mob left, and the town cleaned up its act, mostly."

"That's great news. I don't want to know how clean is clean, and you keep saying 'most' and 'mostly.'"

"If I got past the Commission, it means I'm as clean as anybody here—cleaner than most, even. Funny how religious money chases away dirty money…but you know, Nonno, the holy ones ain't so holy either."

Jijjie sounded a little annoyed.

"Jijjie, that is great news. I'll tell Filomena, guaglione. Now, you call your Mamma Nunziatina." I realized he would have to holler into the phone, but they'd manage.

"I will, Nonno. Happy New Year."

I heard the click, and I did not want to hear more. It was great news to end the year on.

Ahh, the years. Since arriving in America in 1911, our family celebrated every New Year's Eve with a fish feast. And the tradition was alive and well in 1969, my eighty-fourth year. Jijjie put more spring in my step as I ambled off to Peppe Ippolito's fish store. One advantage of being old is that no one laughed at me for pulling a two-wheeled shopping cart. Hey, those shellfish got heavier every year, and the cart always had room for a bag of ice and a bottle of anisette. My concern was not my image but to return the cart to Filomena in the best possible condition.

On the way to Peppe's, I thought about who the real napulitani were, and did it really matter? No one cared anymore whether we said Neapolitans, napulitani, or napoletani. Favorite great-grandson Junior Ragnuno looked like he kissed the Blarney Stone, but he started off speaking my dialect. Did his looks make him more American? Did my napulitano looks make me less so? What was an

American supposed to look like? If Junior looked American, what did that make the moolinjana?

Peppe Ippolito, founder and owner of Pesci di Sciacca, like most fish store proprietors in South Brooklyn, was a son of Sciacca, a fishing village in southwest Sicily. Some people in Brooklyn and back in Napoli did not consider Sicilians real Italians. To me, Sicilians were concentrated Italians, the tomato paste of the peninsula—darker, more stubborn, and stronger family men than the rest of Italy. I never told Filomena that Sicilian Peppe made me a prouder Italian American.

Well, I did, once. It wasn't pretty.

Peppe, about ten years younger than me, still worked very hard. Scaling and cleaning fish and hauling bags of clams kept him hale. His forearms always rippled. He sold fish to help support his grandchildren's college educations, but he was educated in his own right. His penetrating, deep-set eyes under bushy salt-and-pepper eyebrows in a strong, dark face always captured my attention.

College education for our grandkids and great-grandkids? But what kinds of outrageous things they were learning! Lately, Joseph loved to tell me that we humans descended from a fishlike creature that crawled out of the water to muddy land many, many years ago. Joseph knew better than to make this assertion to Filomena. Being a great-grandson, educated or not, would not spare him from the hard dope slap to his college-enhanced head.

Even before the door closed behind me at Peppe's place, I was wonderfully captured by the smell of the sea and the sea's bounty. Peppe and I were alone, except for the fish. Some of them were alive, like the eels undulating in their open low tank near the entrance. As youngsters, Junior and Joseph tried to grab the eels with their bare hands when they thought I wasn't looking. The eels reminded me again of Joseph and his crazy proposition that we were all related to fish. If so, why the concern over who was better, who was the real Italian, who was the genuine American? We have all been very far removed from those eels, and for a long time.

Don Peppe gave me that look, as if sharing a secret, wiping his hands on his apron. I knew we would discuss more than fish. He wished me a happy New Year, 1970: "Buon Capodanno, Don Giovanni. Good wishes to you."

I answered with a benediction in my best Sicilian dialect: "*S'a benediggu,* Don Peppe." I asked about his family but quickly got to the first objective of my mission: "And the *baccalà*?"

"My family has been in America for almost sixty years"—Peppe turned to his walk-in refrigerator—"and back then if you said 'codfish' to most of the old-timers, they wouldn't know you meant baccalà."

Peppe had a way of sneaking up on his punch lines. I saw a lecture coming, and there was no extra charge! He came back with the desalted codfish and the opener "Each of us carries a piece of each conqueror."

"What are you talking about, Peppe?"

"Ah, Don Giovanni, when you buy baccalà, you pay for da fish, but you also pay respect to your Norwegian blood."

At least we resemble Norwegians more than we resemble that primitive fish flopping around on that muddy beach. "What? Peppe *che cosa*?"

"Did you ever wonder why baccalà is so popular with us Italians? Why we have to have it for the holidays? Where did we get the custom? Baccalà swims in cold waters, like off the coasts of Canada and Norway. If a Sicilian fisherman fell overboard, he couldn't last five minutes in that ice water."

My answer was a shiver.

"Giovanni, have you heard of the Normans?"

I resisted responding, "Like Reverend Norman Vincent Peale or the cereal box artist Norman Rockwell?"

I could see that Peppe was bursting to tell his story, and my wise-ass response would have unleashed a string of Sciacchitano curses. He fixed me with his dark stare, the one that claimed rapt attention and also scared grandchildren. I was glad he couldn't read my mind.

"The Normans were Norsemen originally from Scandinavia, the

land of baccalà." He went back to his stare to let the comment sink in for a while. "They went to France, and from there they eventually invaded Sicily and Naples, and they controlled it—for a long time. It was the same land that much later became the Kingdom of the Two Sicilies."

I told Peppe I had a tough time reconciling the fair Vikings and us dark-skinned children of the Mezzogiorno.

He looked like he had a big baccalà on the line. "Giovanni, when you add ricotta to tomato sauce, does it get less red?"

"Well, a little, depends on how much you add and how much you mix."

Peppe raised both eyebrows and gave a little nod. "So, we mixed a little, and we started eating baccalà centuries ago thanks to the Normans, even after our Viking guests left or just stayed and enjoyed life in Naples and Sicily."

Just as Mrs. DiRienzo came into the shop, I asked Peppe how many of us have blond-haired, blue-eyed relatives back in the old country. He gave me a quick look, and smirked. "How about Ol' Blue Eyes Sinatra?"

Ah yes, Frankie Boy, Exhibit A.

I lost no time putting in the rest of my order: scungilli conch, mussels, clams, octopus, and squid. Peppe rapidly wrapped them up—my order was almost always the same. He threw the *frutti di mare* in my cart along with a free bag of ice. So off I went, with fish in my wake and a lot more than fish on my mind.

Peppe always had a roundabout way of making a point. I took home the lesson that we were such a mixture—we Italians, Normans, Europeans, human beings—that we should not get worked up over small differences. I told myself that the next time in Peppe's, I would assert that we are certainly identical compared to the fish that Joseph said we came from.

I presented my marine haul to Filomena for the dinner to welcome 1970. Yes, our family was a little bigger than it was when Filomena and I had to worry only about feeding ourselves and little Mario and Nunziatina on the edge of Don Giuseppe's villa. Back then, our food was the product of the villa's groves and gardens and the farm animals that gave us cheeses and salted meats. Of course, Calogero was always welcome at our table, and Don Giuseppe usually invited us to the villa house to welcome in the New Year, joined by Zia Bettina. We learned always to remember our humble roots by downing portions of lentils, as we still do in Brooklyn.

Now Filomena and I were the villa, or at least the Brooklyn family headquarters. We were in a land of plenty, though we had survived much to arrive in this state of abbunnànza. We could offer our guests not only the bounty of this American land but also the harvest from its fertile waters—the frutti di mare. We had the sumptuous feast of the fishes for Christmas Eve, but we repeated it a week later, this very night, to welcome in the New Year. Such was the blessing that America brought into our lives—feasts that only the very rich could enjoy back in Naples.

Filomena brought my musings down to earth.

"Well, took you long enough!" was her expression of gratitude when I presented the fruit of the sea from Peppe's place. "Have the *cozze* and *vongole* given up the ghost?"

"Filomena, I don't see the mussels and clams gasping with their tongues hanging out." I beseeched forbearance, shaking both hands in front of my face, Neapolitan for "Gimme a break!"

"Hmmph," she said while unwrapping the fish, "Looks like the baccalà was desalted just in time for you and Peppe to give the poor fish a headache."

I paid no attention to her, and Filomena repaired to the kitchen, aided by Vina, Nunziatina, Keira, Peggy, and Mrs. Di Domenico, the widow from next door.

I was always comfortable around women, maybe because I was the only male in a family of four. I learned to put this trait to use during my scugnizzo days, gaining the confidence of potential female clients. On this New Year's Eve, I sat down to sample my wine, joining the ladies in the kitchen, maybe even join in the gossip. But no, Filomena gave me the bum's rush outta dere.

"Eh, you spend lotta time with the old men *vicchiaconi* at the social club. Anything you pick up in the kitchen is gonna be passed around there. You men are worse than women. Who knows what lies you shared with 'O sciacchitan Peppe? *Lassà stà le fëmmene!*"

I let the ladies be, exaggerating my slow, bent-over gait to find another warm spot. I sampled my wine in front of my basement fireplace, constructed with the help of Mr. Armando's mason son, Pietro: "Mr. Ragnuno, Papà always told me of the fireplaces of the old days in Campania."

"Sì, Pietro, the fireplace was the hearth—the family center and center of food preparation."

Warmed by the fire in my easy chair, I was still dwelling on history and my Norwegian ancestors. History turned my thoughts to Calogero, who was now a retired magistrate living and writing on the estate of his late father. Could it be that we two young brother-friends were now two old men, *due ommi viecchi*? The old people in Campania would say, *A vecchiaia è na carogna!* but I was glad to have made it to foul-smelling old age. It was much better than the pitiable alternative of not arriving at all: *Ma per chi non ci arriva è na vergogna*, such a shame.

As though a firebird, I saw my sleepy self in that easy chair through the fireplace embers. *May the sparks signal heavenly light and not be a harbinger of hell fires.*

Visions of old age, Calogero's history lessons, and Norman baccalà made me think about dynasties. If the Chinese and Egyptians marked their prodigious histories by their own imperial dynasties, we Neapolitans marked our four thousand years plus by usually being under the heels of serial conquerors. I knew broadly of the Etruscans, Samnites, Greeks, Romans, Germanic tribes, Byzantines, Saracens, and European royal houses, including Peppe's peripatetic Normans.

The phone brought me back to Brooklyn.

Myron Pollack Jr.'s unmistakable high-pitched voice came through. "Giovanni, happy New Year! Sorry to bother you on a holiday, Mr. John, but I just learned from my connections that Agent Aloysius Jackson was, er, advised in the strongest terms by his ex-bosses to stop harassing former 'clients.' You just tell him that next time he calls."

"Couldn't have happened to a nicer guy."

"Instead of taking his medicine like a good boy, he flew off the handle, and now he's fighting to keep his retirement. Between you and me, he was losing it at the end."

"Oh, Myron, I hope this is the end of my problems."

"Well, let's hope it's the beginning of changes at the bureau."

"Let's hope so," I said as I genuflected. Since Myron Jr. couldn't see me, I supposed my actions were kosher.

I waited for a second punch line, and then Myron Jr. broke the silence. "I see a revered old man calling on you tonight—bearing late Chanukah presents."

"Bless you Myron. Happy New Year!" was all I could blurt out in my confusion.

"*Mazel tov.*"

As I placed the phone on the receiver, I realized that of all the dynasties, I had forgotten those of the Pollacks' people. *Oy vey.*

Could it be that the FBI is now off my rear end? Giovanni, you are too napulitano to believe that. Jackson may have turned into a real strunz, but there were still suspicions about Giovanni 'O Scugnizzo. And the FBI had a deep bench.

I was under suspicion by a government that had no problem making deals with the sfaccím of the mob or with crooked governments overseas, for the greater good of America. Like when the

Dodgers tried to trade Jackie Robinson and Dolph Camilli to the Giants. And hey, even I learned to love ex-Giant Sal "the Barber" Maglie when he became a valuable Dodger in '56.

If that were my biggest sin.

New Year's Eve visitation by a Jewish Santa Claus bearing presents? Could a present be Jackson's head on a platter? What if the new "capo" is even worse? Well, some things are getting better, like my wine. The latest vintage from my cherished backyard vines, 1968, was a good *vendemmia*. In wine, family, and baseball 1969 was a very good year, and 1970 could be even better. But an *if* sailed through my mind.

If Nixon doesn't follow up the mistakes that LBJ was making in Vietnam. The politicians make the mistakes, and we pay for them. Just let their *boys go over, and then we'd see the patriotism of our leaders. If politicians could read minds, it would all be over for me.*

Wines have good and bad years, and so do dynasties. Back in 1955, our beloved Brooklyn Dodgers, "dem Bums," finally won a World Series. They did it the hard way, the Neapolitan way. They were down three games to two against the Yanks, and they won the last two games, in Yankee Stadium, even!

That was a crazy night in the neighborhood, with the Dodger Sym-phony in the streets, serenading Yankees fans, who were wheeling Dodgers fans in shopping carts and soapboxes up and down Bay Fiftieth Street. How could I not love my Dodgers? For fifty-five cents I could imagine I was under the Mediterranean sun in the bleachers while enjoying the Sym-phony's classical music.

Dem Bums were the scugnizzi of baseball, and baseball was loved by America. Love? Take Leon Cadore. In 1920, he pitched all twenty-six innings against the Braves in Boston. He never got a win —the game was called because of darkness, a 1–1 tie. Now, that was a Neapolitan tragedy. Love? Cadore married Maie Ebbets, daughter of the Dodgers' owner, and he once roomed with Dodger Casey

Stengel. Yes, that same Stengel who managed the Yankees to a seven-game World Series win over the Dodgers the year *after* 1955. So, instead of "Wait 'til next year!" 1956 became "Wait 'til *last* year." Did I say tragedy? The Brooklyn Dodgers were a freakin' opera!

These events were ominous. In 1889, when I was four and the Dodgers five, Brooklyn lost its first World Series appearance—against the hated New York Giants. The 1956 series, in my seventy-first year, was Brooklyn's last. They won *one* series in their total glorious seventy-four-year Brooklyn history.

In 1957, the aging Brooklyn Dodgers finished third, and in 1958 they were playing as the bumbling LA Dodgers in front of Hollywood's beautiful people. Benedetto 'O Pazzo, my crazy grandson, went out to the LA Coliseum to root for the San Francisco Giants, just like he used to embarrass me in Ebbets Field rooting for the New York Giants.

Why didn't the Dodgers change their name? I often thought as I tried to focus on a pinochle hand or measure a boccia toss. Yes, there was some kind of maluocchio on the *Brooklyn* Dodgers but not on the *Los Angeles* Dodgers, who went from a laughingstock in 1958 to World Series champs in 1959.

After four years in baseball wilderness, forsaken Dodgers fans could switch their National League allegiance to the brand-new New York Mets. From 1962 through 1968 the Mets were beloved, though with six straight last place finishes in the National League. Then, just like Giovanni 'O Scugnizzo, they went from abject poverty to world champs in one year, 1969, the year of the Miracle Mets. The start of a new dynasty?

Something was hitting the back of my head. No, not Filomena's hand, but a real feeling of loss, much more than the loss of the

Brooklyn Dodgers or the many losses of the early Mets. Were we Americans, all of us, losing something?

Were we losing our soul? Vietnam haunted me, and I was so thankful that Joseph and Junior did not get drafted. They certainly did not want to go, and I did not ask how they avoided the draft. At home America had lost two champions, champions of *all* Americans. Over two months in the spring of 1968, we lost Martin Luther King and then Bobby Kennedy. Yes, I blamed RFK for the tapping of my grandson's phones in Vegas back in '61, but in '68 RFK represented hope for America in the midst of racial injustice at home and horrible experiences in Vietnam. Then came the assassination of Dr. King.

MLK, what a man! So dignified, a fighter for peace and justice for his people, for all people, really. He saw two possible Americas, one in which we are victims and perpetrators of racism, or a much better one in which we all fight for a victimless society. He made the choices so noble and logical, and then he was gone. RFK picked up the gauntlet, and I think he really meant it, and then he was gone too—fate dealt us a twin killing, an evil double play.

Make that a triple play. Before MLK and RFK, the first one out was JFK, in '64. My scorecard, the Warren Report, is full of American mob figures and many have names ending in vowels. America sounds more like Italy every day.

Filomena shook me awake. "Hey, stop dreaming of beautiful ladies."

It was time for our New Year's Eve dinner.

The older I got, the more boring were my tales of the old country to my grandchildren and their children. Our 1969 New Year's Eve seafood feast was no exception. How could anyone stay awake after antipasto, linguine alle vongole, mussels steamed in white wine, baccalà baked with tomatoes, pine nuts, and onions, Filomena's exquisite seafood salad, baked artichokes, a bunch of vegetable dishes, and Testaverde's *semolina* bread to wipe our plates clean? So, over coffee, fruit, and pastries, I left Naples for news items of more recent vintage.

I toasted our miraculous landing on the moon. "Here's to science! Thank you, Galileo and other giants."

Joseph was bursting with his own news of science. "Nonno, I'm studying genetics in grad school, and I always wondered about Guido Pontecorvo. He's an amazing geneticist, and he works in Edinburgh, Scotland. I asked myself, why is this Italian working in Scotland?"

People looked at each other. Some even appeared to be curious.

"So, why?" asked Joseph's kid brother, Michael.

"He was there thanks to Benito Mussolini." Joseph looked around the table as if the gathering were hanging on his every word. Then, realizing he was losing his audience, he spoke faster to get to the punch line. "Before World War II, Dr. Pontecorvo was visiting Scotland as part of a collaboration between Italy and Scotland in animal breeding."

Another quick, furtive look around the table.

"There he learned that Mussolini had dismissed him and other Italian Jews from their government positions, so *il dottore* did not go back to his Tuscan post. He stayed in Scotland, where he has been having a beautiful career ever since. He's famous worldwide."

"Oh yeah?" piped up Michael. "Who ever heard of this guy?"

Junior gave his cousin Michael a scowl from across the table.

Joseph started to stutter and finally yelled out, "Your loss, Benito, was Scotland's gain!"

If Michael was not impressed, Padraic's partner, Renni, very much loved this story. Renni understood the plight of outcasts. He, the product of an Italian-Jewish marriage, often felt excluded by both sides of his own family. Having unorthodox sexual inclinations did not help, and one side of the family was only too willing to blame the other for those inclinations.

"Joseph, this is just another example of the stupidity of prejudice. I am so glad that Dr. Guido found a productive and accepting place to do his research."

Joseph looked over at Renni, teared up a little, and was about to say something, but I cut him off. "Ahh, but Joseph and family, we are here, united and happy." I held up a glass of wine. "To the moon over the Bay of Naples, the same moon America landed on this year!"

I was about to break into the "Meet the Mets!" song. Had I already had too much wine? Ma quando, mai! Never, indeed! Besides, this was New Year's Eve, and I was with my family. I could see Filomena giving me that look, loving and chiding at the same time. A smile stole across her face, her plump lips now baring beautiful, strong teeth.

With English theatrically accented for the benefit of younger generations, I wished happiness, health, and peace for my beautiful family, and then, as I was about to repeat it in my best polished high Italian, came a knock on the door. Who could have such a poor sense of timing and drama, and on New Year's Eve, with me in the middle of my toasts? *I wonder if the FBI and the NYPD waited 'til this moment to pull me away from the hearth of my American home. If so, their timing is perfect, perfectly evil.*

I signaled to Filomena to stay seated, and ambled to the door, very much slowed down by the effects of 'a vecchiaia and *vino*—and worry. "Aspetta!" I pleaded, and opened the door to find standing abreast three men, one of them a stranger.

In the middle was old friend Myron Pollack, in his eighties now and still spry, though retired. His completely bald head was adorned with a black Russian fur hat. It accentuated a well-trimmed snow-white goatee of the same texture as his brown woolen coat. His button nose somehow supported wireless glasses, which seemed to amplify the sparkle of his eyes.

I was so pleased to see Myron and took his hand with great enthusiasm before I had the presence of mind to invite him in.

"Myron, *comme staje, amico mio*?" Myron shed his overcoat and hat, thanked me for my question, and waved hello to the folks at the table. "Happy New Year! Don't get up, Filomena, this is just a short visit."

He then turned back to me. "Giovanni, I want to introduce Mario MacAuley, chairman of the Bensonhurst Democratic Club, and I think you know Dario D'Agostino, president of the Benevento Social Club."

"Buonasera, Dario, my longtime bocce partner!" I grabbed his hand, kissing him on each cheek. "Buon Capodanno," I whispered. His look, as if harboring a pleasant surprise, calmed me down.

I took the hand of Mario MacAuley and resisted the urge to look over at Padraic at the table. Except for age, Mario and Padraic uncannily resembled each other—Irish complexions, mixed Italian-Irish features, and dark eyes.

Vina carried off overcoats, hats, and scarves to the bedroom, as Myron went on: "Giovanni, I know you have been haunted by run-ins with federal authorities. Let me tell you, when it comes to run-ins, you choose major league enemies."

I couldn't help thinking that for a Yankees fan, Myron was still a very nice man.

Myron looked left and right at his companions and mentioned the counterfeit olive oil, the Italian (Fascist) American Culture Center, and the accusations of recruitment of Italian American youth to serve Mussolini's cause in Italy and Africa. "I have been talking to people in the community—no, not to worry, you will not be billed," said Myron, and I laughed out loud. The wine had loosened my restraints.

Myron continued. "I made phone calls to Dario and Mario, and they made more phone calls and then personal visits. It helps to have friends."

Sheesh, Myron talks like one of us.

Dario interrupted. "Don Giovanni, you have been a model American citizen. You served in World War I and became the head of a large family, one that productively contributes to our America, overseas, and at home."

"Grazie" was all I could say.

"And you were a giant in the Benevento Social Club, a founding member," Dario went on.

He looked over at my son, Mario, who took the cue. "My pop helped set up collections for World War I widows in the neighborhood. Our government was a little slow. Mr. Pollack was part of the effort. We put up collection urns in neighborhood businesses and social clubs." Now, Mario got a little choked up. "I wasn't the best citizen during World War I, but Pop straightened me out with the help of Mr. Pollack."

There was an awkward lull, into which Dario jumped. "Mario, you performed important service in World War II, and you are a model of the family man." Holding the floor, Dario went on. "Our club has helped many in our community achieve public office. We know who the good citizens are, and you, Giovanni, are one of them, one of the best of them. Your good deeds with customers in need and your participation in important events in both Italian and American history have not gone unnoticed."

I was rapidly becoming more sober, or maybe too much wine put me into this delirium.

Dario was still speaking. "We don't want to take away from precious time with your family, or from ours, for that matter, so we leave you with a replica of a plaque of thanks that will be posted in the Benevento Social Club. Mr. MacAuley assures me that a duplicate will be mounted in the Democratic Club."

"And the wording on the plaque will be proposed as a bill of appreciation in the New York State legislature by your local representative, a good Democrat, I might add."

"It looks like it might snow, and we do have to be getting back to our families," Myron interjected.

"Please, Giovanni, a wonderful Capodanno, and *prosperità e molta felicità nel nuovo anno.*" Dario embraced me and actually kissed me on the lips in front of the others. Vina retrieved their coats from the bedroom, and off they went.

Silence embraced the table as all eyes were on me. I could not hold back my tears. Filomena got me back to reality: "*Tante mòse!* Such a fuss! It's about time they recognized you after making your life miserable."

I looked at this long-suffering woman who meant so much to me and who truly loved me, poor thing. "Filomena, cara, I think Myron left his gloves." I guided Filomena down the short hallway to our bedroom.

Out of view, I embraced her. "Cara mia, you are the love of my life. Filomena, mio tesoro, please join me in a dance." Her eyes acquiesced. We left the bedroom, our arms around each other's waist.

"Mario, can you put my favorite Caruso album on the stereo?"

We danced to "Core 'ngrato," our beautiful Caruso song of lost love. But we were as those songbirds back in Villa Valeria. Our love was not lost. The family was silent, almost reverent. I peeked at the mirror at the end of the hallway to the bedroom. Just as I thought—and felt—Giovanni 'O Scugnizzo, in his finest, was dancing with the beautiful Filomena, newly bloomed, fragrant flower of Campania.

We bowed to applause.

Renni and Padraic proposed yet another toast,

as if we might run out of them.

ACKNOWLEDGMENTS

Family was the primary source of Giovanni's story. Thanks Mamma Vina for telling me how Giovanni parlayed friendship with young squire Calogero into an education. If I did not write that fifth grade essay, I may have never written this book. Thanks for your encouragement, Georgette Seminara Adams, now looking down on me alongside Vina. Melody Kroll, my literary muse, encouraged me along the way, but never hesitated when I needed a course correction. Mary Barile, writer, playwright, a child of Bensonhurst and the old culture, provided great literary advice, and the impetus to forge on, obliging me to face the message and form of Giovanni's story. Janice Loveland-Grandi continues to be a wonderful source on the early days of Vegas. Ellen Nitka, of LA but indelibly Brooklynese, I thank you for imparting that old flavor. Thanks to you, and to Florie Ehrlich (and to Chairman Frank). I benefited from interacting with a slew of editors—Katherine Pickett and Christina Frey are heroines. Barbara Peck is not only an artist but a mind reader. She abided my instructions and corrections on the chapter sketches which agree amazingly well with my sketchy mental images and even more diffuse instructions.

Members of the Columbia Chapter of the Missouri Writers Guild give frank advice—yo, I'm from Brooklyn, I can take it. So, thanks my CCMWG colleagues, especially Frank Montagnino who knows his way around a story, the West End Line and homemade *struffoli* and *cannoli. Mille grazie e buon appetito.*

This retired Biochemistry Prof had to learn history. I seined paper clippings, NY Times obituaries, family papers and more. Important books stand out: *The Guarded Gate* (Daniel Okrent [Scribner 2019]), *Making Democracy Work* (Robert T Putnam [Princeton 1993]), *97 Orchard* (Jane Ziegelman [Harper 2010]), *Modern Naples, A Documentary History, 1799-1999* (John Santore [Italica Press 2001]), *Naples Declared* (Benjamin Taylor [Penguin 2012]). A Smithsonian Magazine article on NYC Mayor Tom O'Dwyer and Brooklyn DA Miles McDonald (David Kinsella III [Oct 2019 pp 66-75]) was invaluable. Thanks MU Professor Mike Cook for your suggestions.

Neapolitan Dialect? My Tuscan is bad enough. Three sources very much helped: *Dictionary: English-Neapolitan; Neapolitan-English* and *241 Neapolitan Verbs* (Dale Erwin and Maria Teresa Fedele [2013 and 2014, respectively]), and the generously illustrated *Na Juornata 'e Sole, Proverbs of Naples* (Antonio and Leonardo [2008]). My dialect was enriched by interactions with Pietrantonio (Tony) Lombardi, author of *Nonno, Tell Us a Story* [2017], and with cousins Rosalie and Jim Mangano (our own Italian dialectical).

Nancy Malugani-Polacco, my long-suffering life partner, "thank you's" are not enough. But, here goes: Thank you for your forbearance and tough love and advice. My gratitude is not gratuitous. Translation: I love you, and I am amazed that you love me.

ABOUT THE AUTHOR

Joe Polacco is a native of the Bensonhurst neighborhood of Brooklyn, New York, where he attended PS 200, PS 101 and JHS 128 (Bensonhurst Junior High). He attended Stuyvesant High School of Science in Manhattan. He earned a bachelor's degree in biochemistry from Cornell University in 1966, and a doctorate in biochemistry and genetics from Duke University in 1971. Polacco is a professor emeritus of biochemistry at the University of Missouri.

He did important research on nitrogen metabolism in plants and on plant interactions with bacteria. He was twice named a Senior Fulbright Fellow, which allowed him to conduct research and teach at institutions throughout Latin America and Europe.

Polacco combined his love of science, writing, and Latinx culture and has published several bilingual poems. He published his first full-length book, *Vina, A Brooklyn Memoir*, in 2016—a memoir of his mother and his Brooklyn motherland. *Giovanni* is his first novel.

https://josephpolacco.me

Made in the USA
Monee, IL
11 October 2020

44720018R00203